His Secret
Family

BOOKS BY ALI MERCER

Lost Daughter

His Secret Family

Ali Mercer

Bookouture

Published by Bookouture in 2019

An imprint of StoryFire Ltd.

Carmelite House
50 Victoria Embankment
London EC4Y 0DZ

www.bookouture.com

ISBN: 978-1-83888-104-7
eBook ISBN: 978-1-83888-103-0

This book is a work of fiction. Names, characters, businesses,
organizations, places and events other than those clearly in the
public domain, are either the product of the author's imagination
or are used fictitiously. Any resemblance to actual persons, living or
dead, events or locales is entirely coincidental.

For my mum

Prologue

Paula

When I was a child I had a book that told the myth of the Furies, the three terrifying goddesses of vengeance who pursued people who had done wrong. Once they were on your case, there was nothing you could do to placate them. They would haunt you and torment you without pity, because that was their job: they were there to inflict justice. To make sure that even hidden wrongdoing came at a cost. You could keep secrets from other people, or defend yourself against them. But there was no defence against the Furies.

I never would have imagined that one day I'd play the Fury myself.

But times change, don't they? People change. And motherhood changes you. The Furies weren't mothers. If they had been, they really would have been too horrifying to contemplate. Because if there's one thing more insatiable than a goddess bent on vengeance, it's a mother who is driven by the wrong that has been done to her child.

Anyway, I didn't just decide to hunt him down out of the blue. I was provoked.

I'd done my best to leave him in peace. To move on. To forget, if not to forgive. I didn't even think about him all that much. I was always busy, and anyway, he'd asked me to stay away and I'd chosen to honour that request. After what he and his wife and family had been through, it seemed the least I could do.

But then I found out – quite by chance – that his daughter was getting married.

It had to be the older one. The first one. By now, she'd be the right sort of age for all that. Mid-twenties. Heading into the baby-making years. Young-ish to settle down with the four-slice toaster and the his 'n' hers TV trays, but not too young.

Marriage wasn't something I saw in my own daughter's future, but I was well past being bitter about that. Still, it struck me as odd that they'd chosen to stage the big day in my town, right under my nose.

It made me wonder how much they knew. The family he'd chosen. The wife. The girls.

Had they forgotten? Or had they decided it didn't matter?

Maybe they had just assumed I wouldn't find out. But I had. I had a friend who did bookings for the abbey hall where they were holding the reception, and she mentioned it to me. She recognised his name on the seating plan. And she knew he'd lived with us, once. A long time ago. Small-town memories are long – longer than the internet – and there's no right to be forgotten.

She warned me so that I could stay away.

But I didn't.

When it came to it, I couldn't.

I didn't make a conscious decision to do what I did. It was as much of a shock to me as everyone else. But we were in town that morning anyway, and the abbey hall drew me like a magnet.

It was a beautiful day for a wedding. Even a wedding you weren't invited to, that you most definitely wouldn't be welcome at. Daisy came with me quite willingly, and the sun beat down on us as we skirted the car park and turned down the narrow path that led to the abbey hall.

We went up the steps to the double glass doors. The reception was already in full swing; I could hear the hum of conversation. I pushed on through and held the door open for Daisy. She didn't hesitate. We went through the lobby, past the sign displaying the seating plan, and came to rest in the dim space under the arch that led to the long medieval hall, the only surviving building of the abbey that had once dominated the town.

It was beautiful. There were flowers all along the middles of the long narrow tables. White roses. The air smelled sweet and heady and the thick old glass in the ancient windows dimmed the light streaming in from outside and made everything watery, as if the hall was at the bottom of a lake.

A spoon chimed against a champagne flute and the room fell silent.

Silent for him. There he was, at the head table, standing to give his speech.

Twelve years since I'd last seen him, ten since our divorce. He was older, yes – greyer, a bit more tired-looking, and he'd put glasses on to read the notes on the cue cards he was holding. But in spite of everything he looked fit and well.

He was handsome still. Dignified. Tailor-made to wear black tie. His wife was next to him, looking up at him adoringly, oblivious to us.

I didn't care any more what he had suffered. I took Daisy by the hand and stepped forward out of the shadows.

He saw us. He opened his mouth to speak. Nothing came out. The champagne glass fell from his hand and smashed. But nobody looked at the shattered crystal. They were all staring at us.

He pressed his hand to his heart as if he'd been poisoned, then to his head. He sagged forward; his hands scrabbled for purchase among the shards of glass. He made a strange and terrible sound, the scream of someone who can't breathe.

We all looked on in horror as he crashed down onto the ancient wooden floor, and it occurred to me that I might just have killed him.

Chapter One

Ellie

After everything she'd been though with Dad, Mum was in no mood to get involved with anybody. What she said was, 'Men are terrible to live with – always leaving toenail clippings in the bath.' I knew that when she said this she was thinking of Dad, and that the toenail clippings were a stand-in for other failings that were worse and made her reluctant to let him into our flat at all.

I couldn't actually remember what it had been like when he lived with us, as he'd left when I was a baby. It seemed very odd that there had been a time when we'd shared a living space with him, toenail clippings and all, and though part of me was secretly very sad that he had gone, another part of me shared Mum's relief.

Mum only joked about men and their annoying personal habits when she was in a good mood. At other times, she made it clear that what was wrong with men was serious. And every now and then she'd open up a little bit and I'd get a glimpse of what she was sheltering me from. One of those times was when she told me about her old schoolfriend Karen, a story which explained even better than the toenail clippings why we lived as we did.

Karen had two daughters who were about the same age as my big sister Ava and me, and like Mum, she was divorced. So far, so much like us. Except that Karen had got herself a boyfriend. And then, after a while, Karen found out that the boyfriend had been coming on to her older daughter, the one who was Ava's age.

When Mum let this slip, her expression of disgust told me everything I needed to know: she wasn't going to start seeing someone anytime soon. She resented it bitterly when people asked her about her love life. It annoyed her that they seemed to think she either ought to have a man in her life, or want one. Sometimes she imitated them to us as if their presumptions were totally ridiculous: '*Do you have a boyfriend? Are you seeing anybody yet?* As if I'd have the time for *that*!'

And I was glad. I hated the idea of some weirdo coming into our lives who might make a pass at Ava, or even at me. Anyway, Mum really didn't have the time. She worked long hours, she looked after the flat and she had us. A man would have been an intrusion, and would have taken up time and energy she didn't have to spare.

A man would change things, and toenail clippings in the bath would be the least of it. He might not mean to, he might even not be a weirdo, but a man would take over.

Luckily, Mum was reliable. She wasn't like Dad, who'd turn up three hours late if at all. When she said something, she meant it.

I thought we were safe. I took her at her word when she said there was no way, no way on Earth, that she'd ever get herself a boyfriend. She was on the shelf, and that was where she was planning to stay – for her own sake as much as for ours.

And then a huge bunch of red roses arrived for her. And after that, everything was different.

When the roses turned up, I was reading in the kitchen – Ava always turfed me out of our bedroom after school, so she could do her homework. Everything was always a big deal with Ava and her homework. This was because Ava was a swot, which was something I had decided not to be.

I read all the time, and grown-ups sometimes said that I talked like I'd swallowed a dictionary – I knew plenty of words, though I didn't always know how to say them, which they always seemed to find funny. I was better at reading than talking, and unfortunately, my love of stories didn't help me all that much in school. I wasn't very good at following instructions or writing the kind of sentences my teachers wanted me to write. My reports always said I was easily distracted. I certainly wasn't top of the class like Ava, and there didn't seem to be much point in trying to be when she had got there long before me, and never showed any signs of slipping up.

She was going to be doing her GCSEs that summer and I was never allowed to forget it. I had tests coming up too, the standard tests everyone sat before leaving primary school, but they didn't count for much as far as Ava was concerned. I got in masses of trouble if I woke her up when she was trying to have a lie-in, or did anything else that might run counter to her becoming a well-rested, fine-tuned exam-taking machine.

The doorbell rang, which was a pain because our buzzer wasn't working and Mrs Elliott, the landlady, was being rubbish about getting it fixed. Ava came out of our bedroom into the hallway and yelled at me through the open kitchen door, 'Can't you go and get it?'

She couldn't even be bothered to come and ask nicely. That was typical of Ava: her homework was so important that the extra seconds it would have taken to come right up to me and ask in a normal voice, or the extra minute it would have taken to go down to the front door herself, were out of the question.

'Suppose so,' I said.

Ava didn't even say thank you; she just disappeared back into our room and slammed the door shut. I stuck my tongue out at her, grabbed my door key from the hook and set off downstairs, shutting the front door of the flat behind me. Mum was as paranoid about security as she was down on men, and it was fair to say that we'd had one or two dodgy neighbours in our time. I had been trained to do my bit to make sure it wasn't easy for someone to walk in and rob us.

All I could see through the glass panes of the main entrance onto the street was the red of the roses. I opened up and the delivery man said, 'Flowers for Mrs Harris, 25b?'

'That's my mum,' I said.

Mum had kept her married name: she said she'd earned it, having survived her time with Dad. (He was usually 'your father', as if acknowledging his connection to us was the only way she could bear to talk about him.) Ava thought Mum should be Ms, but Mum said that sounded like a single woman who didn't want people to know she was on her own. Ava said that wasn't very feminist and she was always going to be a Ms and she was never going to change her name, and Mum said it was the world that wasn't very feminist and Ava was too young to understand that but she would find out one day.

Both of these were arguments that were hard for Ava to beat. Mum always said that Ava was way cleverer than she was, but she wasn't above reminding Ava that she was ahead when it came to worldly wisdom, and especially when it came to knowing about men.

'It's your mum's lucky day, then,' the man said, and held the bouquet out to me.

I took it. Those roses were amazing. They were just perfect: velvety and crimson. And there were so many of them! As far as I knew, nobody had ever sent my mother flowers before.

'Someone's keen,' the man said.

He went off whistling to his van, and I went upstairs with Mum's flowers. I felt like I was carrying something very serious and important, like a bride's train or the corner of a coffin, as if people were watching me. I was so flummoxed by the whole thing I nearly forgot to shut the main entrance behind me... which could have meant that everybody in the whole building ended up getting robbed, not just us.

Ava came into the hallway at the same time I did. She said, 'What the—' and reached out to take the flowers from me.

'I think I'd better take care of these,' she said.

'Yeah, well, if you're so keen to take over, maybe you should have opened the door in the first place.'

I let her have them, though, and followed her into the kitchen. I'd learned that it was usually best to let Ava get what she wanted: a token protest was about as much as I could manage.

She laid the flowers down on the draining-board and got up on a chair to start looking in the top shelf of the big cupboard, where we kept things we didn't need very often, for a vase.

Our cupboards didn't have all that much in them, but they still weren't very tidy. Once in a while, when she came round to do the three-monthly inspection, Mrs Elliott would have a moan at Mum about it. This kind of thing worried Ava – she was paranoid that we'd get booted out and then wouldn't be able to find another flat we could afford near her school. But Mum said she kept the place clean and paid the rent on time, so Mrs Elliott could do a lot worse, and anyway, people like Mrs Elliott didn't know what to do with themselves if they couldn't find something to criticise.

There was a card attached to the flowers. I flipped it over: Ava still had her head in the cupboard. The message was brief and printed, so at first glance it looked impersonal. It said, *To Jenny. Here's to the future. Love, Mark.*

Future? Love? Mark?

Ava turned and said, 'You are a little snoop, aren't you?' and I dropped the card as if I'd been stung.

I said, 'Well, don't you want to know who they're from? It's not like this is something that happens every day.'

Ava brought down a vase and a jug from the cupboard and put them on the kitchen table.

'Sometimes her clients send her things.'

'No way,' I said. 'They're definitely from an *admirer.*'

Over the years, Mum had brought back an odd assortment of gifts from grateful people whose hair she had cut. As well as the bottles of wine and boxes of chocolate, there had been more unusual offerings: a framed picture of children in a forest created by snipping holes in folded black paper, a miniature chest of drawers formed of matchboxes glued together, and, once, a full set of old encyclopaedias, which someone had given to us because Mum had told them how brainy Ava was. Ava hadn't been in the least grateful and had pointed out that they were out of date and it was all online now and we didn't have space for them anyway, and the encyclopaedias had ended up going to the charity shop.

Once someone had given Mum a primrose in a pot that had died the following week. But no one had ever, ever sent her red roses.

Ava had a quick look at the card too.

'I think someone's fallen in love with her,' I said.

She turned and shot me a look that fell somewhere between *You don't know what you're talking about* and *You might be right*, and just at that moment she looked sly and lovely, with her big eyes and smooth cheeks and slightly unruly blonde hair. Like a girl who would be the main character in a film, while the other girls who didn't quite match up had to be her friends or rivals or comic light relief.

Ava was really pretty, but when you lived with her all the time, you tended to forget about this and just notice whether she looked tired or whether her hair looked good that day or if she had a spot on her nose. But sometimes other people commented on it and then you remembered. And sometimes you just looked at her and the light hit her face in a certain way and you just had to admit it – it was a fact of life, like bananas growing on trees or the North Pole being cold.

In one way it wasn't great for me, because I wasn't especially pretty myself – my eyes were too small and my nose was too big and everything else about me was middling and nondescript. On the plus side, though, I saw an awful lot of her, and you might as well have someone good-looking around the place as not.

Ava said, 'Someone's definitely *interested* in her. That doesn't mean it's love. It could just be some creepy old guy with a fetish for hairdressers. Ellie, one of these days you're going to wake up and realise the real world isn't as sweet and innocent as you think it is.' She started running water into the sink. 'I'm going to put them in here for now. Mum can split them later. She might as well get the full effect first.'

She left the bouquet in an inch of water and went off to our bedroom and shut the door, and I settled back down at the kitchen table and carried on reading *Harry Potter*. I was distracted by the red roses, though. They looked like something that ought not to be in our kitchen, or in our lives – as if they'd been beamed down by an alien spaceship.

I couldn't wait for Mum to get home. I wanted to see how she'd react – that was what was going to tell me if Mark was some creepy old guy who'd had a trim and developed a fixation, like Ava had said, or if he was a genuine, proper romance. Someone who might sweep Mum off her feet.

When she did come in, she was talking – she was always talking, even after a whole day on her feet hearing about people's kids and their difficult old parents and their health problems. She had an inexhaustible supply of chat, but she knew when to listen, too. She always said that what people really paid her for was the chance to offload, not the haircuts, and if she could only charge them what a psychotherapist would, all our money worries would be over.

'Ugh, it is so cold out there, and my feet are killing me.'

Then she saw the flowers.

She'd taken her shoes off at the door and put her slippers on, but she still had her coat on; it made her look eccentric, like someone on the way to being a bag lady. She approached the sink as if drawn towards some kind of miracle. Her shoulders hunched and one hand went up to her mouth. She didn't say anything.

'Mum? Mum, are you all right? Are you crying?'

'No, no, I'm fine. It's just a bit of a surprise, that's all.'

'There's a card. Don't you want to see who they're from?'

I got the feeling she already knew. Hopefully that meant it wasn't some completely random oddball or stalker. Though maybe it made the stalker thing more likely, not less.

She found the card, turned it over, read it.

'I'm guessing you've had your sticky little fingers on this,' she said.

'Well.' There didn't seem much point in denying it. 'I just sort of happened to see it. Who's Mark?'

Mum let go of the card and sighed and stretched – cutting people's hair all day gave her terrible backache. It was obvious how pleased she was about the flowers. She was blushing slightly, and she suddenly looked about ten years younger.

She wasn't the Ava kind of pretty – she was more friendly-looking, and also, she tended to look a little bit frayed at the edges, like a school shirt that had been worn and washed and ironed so often there was no hiding the fact it was plain worn out. People didn't always notice her. But when she was happy like this, she would have made an impression on anyone.

'Mark's a friend,' she said.

Ava said, 'Is he your boyfriend?'

I nearly jumped out of my skin. Ava was standing in the doorway: she'd slunk out of the bedroom without me realising. Ava could be stealthy, and she had a knack for turning up when you didn't expect her.

'I think I'm a bit old for having a boyfriend,' Mum said.

'You're not that old,' Ava said. 'You're not even forty yet.'

Ava was sixteen, old enough to have a boyfriend herself, but she didn't have one, had never had one, and said she didn't want one. She poured scorn on all the boys she knew at school; they were stupid, they had BO or bad breath or bad hair, etc., etc. I could see why nobody ever asked her out; they were probably scared of her. I wasn't an ice queen like Ava but I was too shy to be chatty like Mum, and as I wasn't pretty either, I couldn't see that there was much hope for me.

Mum said, 'Thank you for reminding me how old I am,' and rolled her eyes to show she didn't really mind. 'Let's just say Mark's a special friend.'

Ava didn't look too thrilled about this. She folded her arms and raised her eyebrows, as if Mum had done something suspect. 'Oh, really? Is he going to be sending you more presents?'

'I think I'm going to be seeing a bit more of him, if that's all right with you.'

That hint of sarcasm was about as close as Mum ever got to telling Ava off. I was the child of the household and the only one who got bossed around, and she treated Ava more like another adult. Usually she consulted Ava about things and took note of her opinions and praised her for her good judgement, which I always found annoying. Especially because she never asked me.

Ava said, 'So how did you meet? Have you been online dating or something?'

'No way. If you want to meet idiots you don't have to go online to do it. Plenty of them out there in real life, just walking down the street.'

'So how, then? Did you cut his hair?'

'Actually, I did. Then he got in touch and asked me out for lunch, and so… well, here we are.'

I thought, *She's hiding something.*

This piece of knowledge arrived out of nowhere, or rather, it didn't seem to come from me.

Ava said, 'So you just really hit it off?'

'Yes, we did,' Mum said, as if that was a stupid question, as if the flowers had already answered it.

She turned her back to us and lifted the bouquet out of the sink and laid it down on the worktop and let the water out.

'When are you going to see him again?' Ava wanted to know.

'I don't know. Soon, I expect.'

Mum carefully detached the note from the flowers and tucked it in her pocket. She was going to keep it somewhere, long after the flowers had wilted and been thrown out. A memento. A marker of something significant. How long was it since somebody other than us had sent her love?

Had Dad ever given her flowers? If he had, would there have been so many? I could picture him showing up late with a bunch of wilting carnations from the service station. But this… this kind of grand gesture… He would never have done it.

Mum fished a pair of scissors out of the drawer and started snipping the ends off the stems of the roses. Then she said, 'Someday I think Mark might want to meet you. Both of you. He's already heard a lot about you.'

Ava said, 'You've been talking to him about us?'

'Of course. You're a pretty big part of my life.'

'Well, that's fast,' Ava said flatly. 'You cut this guy's hair, and then you went out for lunch and now he's sending you roses and he wants to meet your kids?'

Mum dropped the rose she'd just cut down onto the draining-board, a bit more vigorously than necessary.

'I know it seems fast,' she said. 'But I think you'll feel different about it when you meet him.'

Ava persisted. 'When you cut his hair, did you go to his house?'

Mum hesitated. 'No,' she said.

Almost all of her clients were women and their children; she had a rule that she didn't take on men as clients unless she knew them, or had a personal introduction. And she would never go to the house of a man she didn't know.

'Then where *did* you cut it?' Ava persisted.

'There's no need to interrogate me,' Mum said stiffly. 'If you must know, it was some time ago. When I was still working at a salon.'

Ava and I looked at each other. Mum carried on trimming the roses. Ava said, 'But Mum, you haven't worked in a salon since Ellie was born.'

Mum ran a couple of inches of water into the vase, tore open the sachet of flower feed that had come with the roses and poured half of it in.

'No,' she said.

'And Ellie is eleven.'

Mum picked up a handful of roses and stuffed them into the vase. 'Yes.'

'So you must have cut this guy's hair at least eleven years ago.'

'Uh-huh.'

Mum filled the jug with water. 'Well,' Ava said sceptically, 'that must have been quite a haircut.'

Mum shrugged. 'We hit it off. Sometimes people open up when you're cutting their hair. You might be surprised by the things they come out with when you're standing over them with a pair of scissors.'

Ava shuddered. 'Most people are just dying to talk about themselves. Any excuse. You're a captive audience. Are you sure he isn't married?'

'He's definitely not married. Any more questions?'

'Is he rich?'

Mum took her time answering this. She stripped a couple of leaves of one of the rose stems and said, 'Yes. Compared to us, anyway. He's not got a yacht or anything, but he's comfortably off. He's a good man, Ava. You just need to give him a chance.'

'You seem to have decided that already,' Ava said and went off and shut our bedroom door loudly behind her. Not quite a slam, but near enough to show that she wasn't at all happy.

I could see why she was worried; I was, too. Everything Mum had told us, not to mention the way things were between us and our dad, had led us to believe that to have dealings with men was to dice with disaster. And Mum was all we had, all that stood between us and chaos. We both needed her so much that if you stopped to think about it, it was terrifying. We needed her like we needed a place to sleep and breakfast in the mornings, because she was the person who provided both those things and without her absolutely none of the ordinary, everyday things we took for granted, like having a home and food on the table, were guaranteed.

Mum said, 'Maybe it's just because we're so used to nice things not happening that she doesn't know what to do with herself when they do.' She put both the vase and the jug on the kitchen table in front of me. 'They're beautiful, aren't they?'

'Beautiful,' I agreed.

The roses were so red it hurt to look at them. I closed my eyes and gave my head a little shake to clear it but the red was still too bright, almost viscous-looking, like blood. I could make out a buzzing or rumbling somewhere that was somehow related to them, a kind of vibration almost like thunder, but too distant to recognise. And once again, a thought dropped into my mind fully formed, as if someone else had put it there.

It isn't just about her. He wants something else, too.

Mum said, 'Are you all right?'

I looked up at her – my worn-out mother with the aching shoulders and the sore feet, and the inch of dark in her dyed blonde hair.

'I'm fine,' I said. I wrinkled my nose. 'I think maybe the flowers are giving me hay fever, a little bit. Is there anywhere else you could put them?'

'In this tiny pill-box of a flat? Not really,' Mum said, but she moved them to the windowsill.

With the flowers out of my line of sight I felt a bit better. Mum put a readymade pie in the oven and got some potatoes on to boil, and then she sat down with me and asked me about school and told me about some of the people whose hair she'd cut that day.

I didn't have her to myself that often, so it felt good to be sitting together in our snug little kitchen with the supper cooking and Ava shut away somewhere else. It felt good, but at the same time it felt awful because I could tell she was happy, really happy, too happy even to worry about Ava being in one of her funny moods. And I knew for a certainty – much as I knew that she'd lied to us about how she'd met Mark, and that Mark wanted more than just her, and that the roses spelt danger – that her happiness wasn't going to last.

Chapter Two

Ava

At the end of the day I came out of school and walked round to the side road we'd agreed on earlier and there he was, waiting for us. Mum's new man, the comfortably-off sender of red roses who'd fallen for her after a haircut and wanted to meet her kids. The potential weirdo/con artist/stalker/paedophile/axe murderer.

Well. We'd see. If he messed with me or my little sister, he might not live to regret it.

And after all, it really could just be love.

I knew which car was his because Mum hopped out and waved at me, like this was all great fun, like we were about to go off somewhere thrilling instead of to a hotel in Kingston for tea. She had a nice new dress on, a blue one that she must have picked out to match her eyes.

She got back into the car and I made a point of not hurrying to join them.

He drove a Jag. My mum was dating a man who drove a black Jag, and one that looked like it had been lovingly cleaned and polished. And probably not by him.

Was he for real? A middle-aged businessman who drove a Jag, dating my mother? It just didn't add up. You'd expect someone like that to have the kind of wife who did lots of Pilates to stay in shape and wore frilly aprons to bake cupcakes. Or the ex-wife might be like that, and he'd have moved on to someone younger and showier in leopard-print.

But would he really have fallen for a single mother-of-two, who cut people's hair for up to twelve hours a day to pay rent on a too-small flat? Not likely. Cupid was pretty selective when it came to shooting those arrows. OK, I'd never fallen in love myself, but I knew *that* much.

Mum wasn't exactly past it, and I didn't begrudge her the chance of happiness… after all, she'd been married to Dad, she deserved a break. But this? There had to be a catch.

What was really infuriating was that normally Mum would have agreed with me. But since Mark had come on the scene she'd turned into someone I couldn't quite reach. She kept saying things like, 'Let's just wait and see how it all turns out, shall we?' But I'd seen her forgiving Dad, taking him back, fighting him, being sad when he left again. As I might have said to her if we'd actually talked about it, she didn't have the greatest track record.

And would Mark *really* have looked her up just because she'd given him a trim years ago? That story didn't seem any more likely now than it had done when Mum first came out with it. There *had* to be more to it. None of it added up.

I got into the back of the car next to Ellie, who gave me a tight little smile. She was giving off a weird, intense vibe – a mixture of excitement and nerves, but too much of both. That was Ellie for you. My mum always said she was *sensitive*. Other people had been known to say *she's not all there*.

Mark turned round and looked at me. Was he handsome? If you were into older men (which I wasn't) then the answer had to be, yes he was. He had good skin and a well-made face and a slightly nervous smile.

I didn't smile back. I knew I probably should, since he was obviously making an effort, but I just didn't feel like it. I wasn't the sort of person who went round smiling at people just because they smiled at me.

He glanced briefly at Ellie, who was gazing at him like a slightly anxious puppy, and turned back to me. Maybe he figured that

Mum would listen to my opinion. But if he really wanted to get in with us, shouldn't he have figured out that the three of us came as a package – that he needed to make a good impression on *all* of us?

'Good to meet you,' he said, and reached out with his hand and waited for me to shake it.

At least his hand wasn't too gross: it wasn't hairy, and he wasn't wearing a signet ring. Actually, it looked pretty much like a woman's hand – soft and slim, with tapering, sensitive fingers. A piano-playing kind of hand.

Dad's hands weren't like that at all. They were broad and practical, as if they were made for fixing things. But they shook from too much booze, and it wasn't easy for him to fix things any more.

My own hand was a bit hot and sticky and embarrassing, but there was no way out of it, so I took Mark's and pressed it quickly and let it go.

He looked at me as if there was something he really wanted to say, but couldn't. Something he felt bad about. Then he moved across to Ellie and held out his hand to her. She took it and clasped it and dropped it as if it had burned her, staring at him unblinkingly all the while.

Maybe Mum had warned him about how strange she was sometimes. Her reaction didn't seem to faze him. He turned away and started the car, and off we went.

It was a pretty smooth ride. Mum drove an old banger, and I'd never been in a car as expensive as that. It smelled good, too. Mum never cleaned our car, and it smelled of old farts and feet; Mark's car smelled of air freshener and manly aftershave. I didn't want to like it. But I did.

Mark probably liked showing off his fancy car, and who could blame him?

I'd told Mum there was no need for him to pick us up. I could have taken Ellie into town to meet them. No big deal. But Mum had been keen for us to all go together. No doubt she loved being chauffeured around, for a change. She'd spent years driving Dad home from places back when they were still married, before Ellie was born. I could remember feeling worried for him when he'd thrown up out of the window, and cross with her for being angry with him about it. I hadn't understood why he was being sick. I thought he was ill, which in a way he was.

Dad actually wasn't a bad driver, though I wasn't crazy about getting into cars with him because I knew how much he drank; I was always really nervous that he was going to get pulled over and breathalysed. (I worried about that more than about him having an accident.) Mum was always nervous on the road; she let other people bully her and stress her out. But Mark was a good, confident driver. He was scientific about it, like a pilot in the cockpit of a plane.

I thought, *one day I want to be able to drive like that.* And that was the first thing about Mark that I liked. When it came down to it, even though I had been suspicious of him to start with, I felt safe with him in a way that I had never done with Dad.

The hotel Mark had chosen to take us to was a Victorian manor house set in manicured grounds. He parked and we went inside and the maître d' smiled at Mark like he knew him, which maybe he did. Then he smiled at us like he didn't know us, but would really like it if we went there all the time, and showed us to a table.

The dining room was all done up like the set of a BBC period drama, with oak panelling and a chandelier and china that would probably be expensive to replace if you broke it. There weren't all that many people there and they were mainly either old or really old. Probably the place had to charge a fortune for a cup of tea just to break even. It was grand and it was intimidating, but it wasn't at all cool. That was the one thing that made me feel entitled to sneer at it a little, which I felt obliged to do because I hated the idea that the kind of people who usually hung out somewhere like that might feel entitled to sneer at *me*.

We sat down and looked at menus. Mum was nervous too: she was holding her menu in a weird way, as if she was trying to be ladylike. In a minute she'd be taking tiny little sips of tea, so as not to slurp, and picking like a bird at a few crumbs of cake, because when it came down to it there was something inelegant about eating, too.

It struck me as a drawback of going to that kind of place – you were never going to be relaxed enough to really enjoy it. But then I caught Mark's eye and he looked anxious, as if this was a treat that he really wanted us to like and he was worried that we wouldn't, and that made me feel bad and resolve to make the most of it.

In the end we decided to order afternoon tea for four and Mark said, not to any one of us in particular, 'Well, I hope you're hungry.'

'Starving,' Ellie said. I could see that she was going to get over the awkwardness of all this pretty quickly once something nice to eat was put in front of her.

Actually, I was starting to feel peckish too. It'll sound like boasting to say I could eat more or less what I liked without it making much difference to my figure, but it was true. Mum sometimes made melancholy little comments about it. Every now and then she'd go on diets that made her very bad-tempered; she wasn't fat, but she wasn't exactly trim either. She was mum-shaped, basically: she'd softened up and fleshed out after having us, and didn't have the time or energy to go to the gym and turn the clock back.

Mark cleared his throat and asked what our days at school had been like. I didn't say much because it didn't seem likely that he was seriously interested in my History test, and I wasn't exactly about to start telling him about spotty Toby Andrews having a crush on me, or my friend Jasmine being caught smoking outside school. But Ellie took the question and tried to run with it. Then she lost her thread halfway through, broke off and gazed into the middle distance as if waiting for inspiration to return to her.

Mum and I were used to Ellie's long-windedness: Mark wasn't. He didn't show any signs of impatience, though. He definitely didn't seem to be a total bastard, though that might just have been a cunning pretence.

'… and then we're going to have to do it all over again next week,' Ellie said, finishing her complaint about being made to go cross-country running that morning.

'Cross-country's no big deal,' I said. 'You can usually get away with walking most of it if you run at the start.'

Mark frowned. 'I'm not sure that's the right attitude. Out in the real world, you have to compete if you want to win.'

I shrugged. 'Yeah, well, at my school, nobody takes that stuff very seriously. Anyway, I'd rather hang out with my friends at the back than get all sweaty.'

My friend Jasmine was worse than me at absolutely everything, including PE, and couldn't run ten metres without getting out of breath. But people liked her, which meant I got the reflected glow of her popularity and she got to copy my homework. It was a calculating friendship, but then, relationships at school *were* calculating, if you had any sense. It was like the Serengeti with a herd of impala crossing it; you didn't want to be one of the unlucky ones who ended up isolated and got picked off. Heaven only knew how Ellie was going to cope when she moved up from the little primary school where she was now.

'The other thing that happened was, Bella Montie went round telling everyone there's a ghost in the girls' toilets,' Ellie went on. 'She got them all worked up about it. Girls were coming out of there and crying and Jessica Thomas nearly fainted. But I know for a fact that there isn't anything to be afraid of.'

'Well, no, because there's no such thing as ghosts,' Mark said.

Ellie gave him a slightly pitying look. 'Definitely not in the girls' toilets at my school,' she said.

Mark said, 'Or anywhere.'

Mum gave him a slightly panicked look, as if to say *Don't go there.* Mark frowned. He said, 'You're not seriously telling me you've seen a ghost somewhere else, are you, Ellie?'

'You don't *see* ghosts. You *feel* them,' Ellie said, blushing slightly but clearly delighted to have the chance to explain. That was Ellie all over. She had no idea when to hold back. 'Bella doesn't really know anything about ghosts. They were all just scaring each other. You don't need an actual ghost to do that. Most people scare pretty easily. All you need is one thing they don't understand and they're spooked.'

'You sound very sure of yourself,' Mark said. 'How do you know Bella didn't *feel* something?'

She looked at me blankly. 'Because there was nothing there.'

'How do *you* know?'

Ellie shrugged. Mum cleared her throat. 'I don't think now's the time to get into all of that. Have we all decided what we're having?'

Ellie hunched her shoulders and pulled a face. 'I wasn't getting into anything.'

Mark said, 'Do you think there's anything to *feel* here?'

Ellie relaxed her shoulders and looked around and sniffed the air, the way somebody might do if they'd picked up a faint smell of burning.

'Not much,' she admitted. 'Right now, it just all seems a bit closed off.'

'I *think* that's reassuring,' Mark said. 'Do you *feel* ghosts too, Ava?'

'I don't feel anything if I can help it,' I told him, and then the waiter arrived to take our order.

I'd wanted to warn Mark off. *Don't think you can get to know me just like that.* But it didn't work. He looked as if he felt sorry for me. As if it was a shame that I'd become someone who could say, *I don't feel anything if I can help it.*

Usually the idea of anyone being sympathetic like that – especially a stranger, especially someone who was dating my mother! – would have driven me mad. But with Mark it didn't. Even though I would have thought that was the last thing I wanted, it turned out to be another thing I liked about him.

I didn't particularly *want* to like him. I didn't feel like I *needed* to like him. Maybe like isn't even quite the right word. There was something about him I recognised because it was how I secretly wanted to be myself: in control, with the money and the car and everybody's respect. I admired him. I was very relieved, and not a little amazed, that this time round Mum had managed to fall for someone who wasn't a total loser.

Not that Dad *was* a loser, exactly. He just didn't help himself. Or us. And he was *very* different to Mark.

Tea arrived, and it was just as fancy as you'd expect: a three-tiered silver cake stand loaded up with mouthful-size treats, tiny eclairs and choux buns and a selection of patisserie adorned with swirls of piped cream, slivers of strawberry, chocolate curls and fondant icing in shades of pastel pink.

Mum got out her phone and took photos, which bothered me – nobody else was doing it. And who was she going to say she was with? Was she going to tag Mark? However much her friends might hit the like button… what would they really think? Take her friend Karen, the divorcee with the dodgy ex-boyfriend who'd made a pass at her teenage daughter. Wouldn't it be rubbing Karen's nose in it?

Then I thought, *Oh, who cares* and got my phone out, too.

It wasn't like I was going to put the pictures anywhere – I was a lurker, not a sharer. I never posted anything. I didn't want people at school knowing things about me, not even something quite harmless like my mum dating someone new who'd taken us to a posh hotel for tea.

Mum was much less guarded than I was, but even so, she hadn't yet put anything on Facebook about her hot new romance. I knew, because I kept an eye on her. These days she was forbidden to mention me unless I'd agreed, which I never did. But I liked to be sure.

Maybe she was worried about jinxing her new romance. Or maybe she and Mark had talked about this, and he wasn't keen on being electronically introduced to a bunch of people he didn't know.

Once I'd got his surname out of her – it was Walsh – I'd found his Facebook profile, which gave away the bare minimum and had a profile picture of a pair of feet in flippers. It was about as impersonal as you could get, a bit like mine, which was a picture of some rhubarb that I'd taken ages ago after Mum randomly brought it home one day. Apart from that, Mark barely seemed to exist online. All I'd found, buried among the stuff about all the other Mark Walshes, was a boring LinkedIn profile that wasn't even public.

I put my phone away and Ellie and I tucked in. Mum didn't eat all that much. Probably watching her figure. I wondered if she'd had sex with him yet. Almost certainly – why would you meet someone's daughters unless you'd established that you had at least some kind of basic physical compatibility?

The thought was almost enough to put me off the patisserie. Sex was either embarrassing or disgusting, or both: it was putting condoms on dildos in personal, social and health education class, or the really dirty stuff you found out about as soon as you moved up into secondary school, the stuff it was hard to believe anybody would actually want to do. Sex was what the popular girls got up to – girls like Tasha Evans and Janette Crosby, sullen-faced and heavily made-up and awash with likes on social media. I couldn't be bothered with all that. I couldn't begin to see what might be in it for me.

I could see what might be in it for Mum, though, with Mark with the Jag and the bank balance, who could spend on an afternoon tea what we would have paid for food for a fortnight.

And anyway, why shouldn't she like him? He was almost too good to be true.

After she'd eaten Ellie started prattling away about what she was reading. Mark listened politely but his eyes began to glaze over. Then he said to me, 'So what do you like to read, Ava?'

'I don't read,' I said. 'It takes too long.'

Mum looked concerned. 'But Ava, your English marks are so good—'

'English is pointless,' I said.

'I'm afraid I can't agree with you there,' Mark said.

'Mark studied English,' Mum said. 'At university.'

'Oh yeah?' I couldn't help myself; I was curious. How had he made all his money – if he *had* made it, rather than just coming from a rich family? 'What do you do now?'

'I work for a big IT company,' Mark said. 'Probably the best way to explain what I do is to say I'm in customer relations. I help people work out what they want and then check they're happy when they've bought it.'

'Your English degree turned out useful, then,' I said.

Mark looked stung, and Mum frowned at me. I could feel her willing me to behave. Mark said, 'You're doing your GCSEs, aren't you? What are you studying?'

'*Macbeth, An Inspector Calls, Jane Eyre,* a bunch of poems.'

'What do you think of them?'

I shrugged. 'What is this, some kind of exam?'

'Just making conversation,' Mark said.

'We're reading *War Horse*,' Ellie piped up.

'Your mum tells me you're very ambitious,' Mark said to me, ignoring Ellie completely. 'If you want to get ahead, don't you think you'll need to be able to express yourself?'

'I can talk fine, thank you,' I said. 'And you shouldn't just ignore Ellie like that. Maybe you need to learn to listen.'

I tried to swallow a mouthful of tea and nearly choked. Then I pushed back my chair and walked off, and it seemed like everyone in the restaurant was watching me as I went.

Mum was waiting in the ladies' when I came out of the stall. She said, 'What was that all about?'

'What was what all about?'

I started washing my hands. I could have done with running a comb through my hair, but I didn't look too bad, even in my school uniform, which wasn't the most flattering get-up: bottle-green V-neck jumper, white shirt, green and black tie, black skirt. We were meant to wear skirts down to our knees, but literally no one did. I had to be careful about bending over in mine, and plenty of other girls wore them even shorter.

Mum sighed. 'You know what I mean. You biting Mark's head off like that. In public. He may not be handling this absolutely perfectly, but he's trying. He's not particularly used to kids. And right now, he's absolutely mortified. You need to cut him a bit of slack, OK? You don't have to be quite so hostile. Or defensive.'

'I'm not.'

'Look, I know you haven't got any particular reason to trust him. Or to trust any man, after what we've been through. And I blame myself for that. I should have protected you both better.'

'It's not your fault that Dad is the way he is. You tried to stop him.'

She shrugged. Her face was bleak and I knew she was remembering the rows she'd tried to shelter me from before he'd left. Then she gave herself a little shake. 'What's done can't be undone,' she said. 'But I promise you, Mark has only the best intentions. He may not get everything right, but he's willing to learn. Just give him a chance.'

That was when I realised how serious she was. That it wasn't going to be a case of 'If you don't like him, I'll get shot of him'. It was like he was already part of our lives whether Ellie and I wanted him there or not. Like he was suddenly just as important as we were.

'Look, I didn't particularly want to meet him,' I said. 'But I'm here, aren't I? Are we going to go soon?'

She looked at my reflection in the mirror like there was something she wanted to explain but couldn't. Then she said, 'Please, Ava, for once in your life, just try to be nice,' and banged the door on her way out.

I checked my phone. Sure enough, she'd posted an update with a picture of the spread we'd just tucked into, and a slightly cryptic caption: *A nice cup of tea… and the rest.* Poor old Karen had already liked it. I only hesitated for an instant before liking it too. A guilt like. Dad wasn't on Facebook, didn't believe in it, so he'd never see it.

How was *he* going to feel about this? He could probably have coped with Mum dating someone who ticked all of the boxes, who was well-off and had a good job and so on. He could have just been cynical about it. But if Mum was properly serious about it… and if we didn't think Mark was all bad, apart from the situation taking some getting used to… how would he deal with it then?

Back at our table I made a bit more of an effort, but it didn't come naturally. I felt exhausted by the whole thing. It was a relief when Mark paid the bill and we left. I wondered how much it had all come to, but didn't get the chance to see.

He took us all the way back to our flat. You didn't see many Jags on our road – even our landlady only drove a Ford – so we were pretty conspicuous. It felt good, and at the same time I felt uneasy about it.

It reminded me of when we'd lived in a part of south London that was notorious for kerb-crawling, and one evening, not even that late – I'd been walking home from the supermarket or something – I'd seen a young woman, scantily dressed despite the cold, getting into a car. I had felt awful about it, about what was going to happen between that girl and the driver next, and furious: not with her, but with him. It was frightening how vulnerable she was, and maddening how easy it was for him to exploit her.

It wasn't like Mark was exploiting *us*, and we weren't in any danger from him as far as I could see. But mixed in with everything else, I still felt a bit of the same kind of resentment towards *him*. It wasn't even really a personal thing. It was because he was a man and he had money and that gave him power, and I couldn't hide from that and I didn't know how else to deal with it.

Should I be grateful? It was all right for Mum – she was clearly smitten, and that let her off the hook. She could accept all of this almost as if she'd earned it. But what about me and Ellie?

He pulled up outside our flat and leaned across to kiss Mum goodbye on the cheek as if they were an old married couple or even brother and sister, not a hot young-ish couple in the first flush of romance. It could hardly have been a more a demure sort of farewell, and I guessed he was trying not to make us uncomfortable. Another point in his favour. Then we said our final thank-yous and got out of the car and Mark drove away.

Mum rummaged in her handbag for her keys and let us in. She looked more flushed and brighter in the eyes than usual.

'So that was all right, wasn't it?' she said as we went into the downstairs lobby.

Neither Ellie nor I said anything. Mum closed the door to the block behind us. 'Don't fall over yourselves rushing to tell me what you think of him.'

'He's nice,' Ellie said. 'Also, he really likes you.'

'Why do I hear a "but" underlying that sentence?' Mum said. She looked on the verge of being upset.

'No buts,' Ellie said diplomatically. 'The only problem is what he thinks of us.'

'Not so much of a problem,' Mum said. 'He thinks you're both great. What did *you* think of him, Ava?'

'Why does it matter what we think? He's *your* boyfriend.'

'Ava, of course it matters.'

We made our way up the stairs to our flat. Mum unlocked our front door and we went in. I said, 'Does Dad know about him?'

Mum stepped out of her shoes. She'd put on her best high heels for the occasion. 'It's nothing to do with him.'

'So I shouldn't mention it?'

'When are you going to get the chance? We haven't heard from him for months.'

'Which means we're probably about due,' I said. 'If you're really sure about this, if you think Mark's going a big part of our lives, sooner or later one of us is going to have to tell him.'

'Let's worry about that when the time comes, all right? It's still early days,' Mum said.

'Yeah, except you've known him since before Ellie was a baby, and you were pretty keen for us to make a good impression. You know what, Mum, it's either serious or it isn't. You can't have it both ways,' I said.

And then I couldn't take it any more – the confusion on Ellie's face, and the way Mum was looking at me, almost pleadingly, wanting something from me that I didn't understand and wasn't sure I could give. So I did what I always did when the emotional temperature of our little family of three got too hot for me to handle: I went into the bedroom I shared with Ellie and closed the door.

*

That night I couldn't sleep. I lay there listening to Ellie's quiet breathing and thinking about Mum and Mark, and about what might happen if they really were serious about each other.

Mum being with someone would change things. However nice he was.

I'd always assumed that *I* would be the one who who'd rescue us. I had it all planned out. I would go to university and get a decent job and make some money, give Mum some security in her old age and help Ellie to get by in an adult world that wasn't always kind to daydreamy, nightmare-prone girls. And now it seemed like Mark was going to be the one to do the rescuing.

After a while I went into the kitchen, so as not to wake Ellie, and started reading *Macbeth* again. I hadn't said so to Mark, but I thought it was brilliant, probably the best thing I'd ever read. People always went on about marriage like it was something good, but *Macbeth* told you something different. It showed you that being together could bring out the worst in people, as well as the best.

I just hoped Mark wasn't going to have that effect on Mum. She'd survived Dad, but it had been a struggle. Mark might look a whole lot better on paper, but if he turned out to be awful in some way that wasn't currently obvious, I wasn't at all sure that she'd be able to survive him.

Chapter Three

Jenny

Ava thought I was angry with her after the tea at that hotel in Kingston, but I wasn't – I was upset. Upset for myself, a little, but mainly for Mark. He'd hadn't expected all that much, to be fair, but he'd tried his best, and it meant so much for him. I'd tried to warn him… I'd told him that Ellie would be sweet and Ava might be all right but could be, well, unpredictable. But he hadn't listened. He didn't want to believe me; he'd hoped for so much more.

And Ava had a point. She could have made it more sensitively… but Mark hadn't been paying Ellie proper attention. He couldn't start off with them by playing favourites, even unintentionally. But how was he to know about the delicate balancing act of having two children – how you had to find it in yourself to give as much as you could to each of them, even if you felt like you were running on empty? Because otherwise, it wasn't you they'd end up hating. It was each other.

Problem was, I couldn't get Ava to go easy on him just by telling her to change her behaviour. She'd never been one for just doing what she was told. She had to understand why, or she'd resist all the way.

I'd always been in awe of my oldest daughter: she was so smart, so strong-willed. So unlike me. I had learned long ago to avoid confrontations with her. It just didn't help. I shouldn't have spoken sharply with her in the ladies' after she'd snapped at Mark; she was as stubborn as anything, and I'd only got her back up.

It was just so frustrating, and it only made it worse that I understood how she felt. Because as far as she was concerned, why *should* she welcome this new man who'd suddenly walked into my life, and hers and Ellie's by extension? And she'd always been protective of Ellie: yes, she was prickly with her, but the moment she thought someone else was doing Ellie down, that was it.

I had to speak to her. I'd have to watch what I said… but there had to be some way to make this easier for her.

But I was busy the next day – six appointments, scattered all around our part of the outskirts of London, with the usual mix of clients: kids, older ladies, new mums, working mums. And as usual, being with other people, talking, working, keeping busy, helped put it all out of my mind.

One thing no woman ever has enough of is time. So I'd always been in demand, right from when I started freelancing, back when Ava had just started school and Ellie was a baby, and I used to cart her round to the appointments with me. People knew they could slot me in for a cut and colour between one thing they had to do and the next.

Also, they trusted me – they knew they'd come out looking pretty much the same as before, just a bit neater and possibly less grey. And I had a reputation for being good with kids. I enjoyed the work, always had – it was really satisfying, all of it, the combing and cutting and drying, painting the colour onto the foils, the chatting, and afterwards, seeing them look pleased with what I'd done.

Just lately, though, it was giving me a few more aches and pains, which was an occupational hazard: all that stooping and twisting. I'd started to wonder what it would be like to still be doing this when I was fifty. Or sixty. And it had occurred to me that there might come a day when I might not be able to do it any more, and I had no idea what I would do then.

But then Mark had turned up, and suddenly figuring out a plan B didn't seem quite so urgent any more.

Because there he was, so different to Sean, so keen, and so *perfect*.

No dating algorithm would have matched us – he ticked all kinds of boxes I didn't tick, being well-educated, professional, a homeowner, and a higher-rate taxpayer, something I'd never managed to become however many hours I worked. But we had something even more important than all that in common. We both wanted a second chance, and we both had exactly the same ideas about what that might involve.

I was only thirty-six, not too old to have a different life. If he'd found me five or ten years later… then it might have been different. But as it was, I knew I could give him everything he wanted.

Both of us understood that. We'd talked about it, but we actually hadn't needed to discuss it at any great length. It was all astoundingly clear, compared to how dating usually seemed to be, compared to the stories of hope and betrayal and confusion I heard as I cut people's hair all day long.

But I couldn't explain all that to Ava, or Ellie. Not yet anyway. He wouldn't let me. That was one thing he was absolutely clear about.

I had to stay calm, to behave as if I was just letting things unfold rather than pushing them forward as quickly as possible. I had to carry on as if it wasn't yet a done deal, as if I might opt out at any time if I decided I didn't like him after all. As if it was casual. No commitment.

But nothing's casual when you have children, in my opinion.

My last appointment of the day – a full head of highlights at half past four – got cancelled, and when I got back to the flat I bumped into Peter, my downstairs neighbour, coming into the lobby. Peter lived in the garden flat, which he owned; he lived alone, was in his fifties, and grew the most beautiful roses. My gaydar was pretty unreliable, but in one of our first conversations he'd made a passing reference to his husband having passed away. This had two immediate consequences for our relationship. Firstly, obviously, I was sorry for him – how rotten to find someone you could actually be happy with, only to have death snatch them from you. And secondly, I felt safe with him. I knew I could be friendly to him without being accused of leading him on.

Peter had the most beautiful silver hair, which he'd never let me anywhere near. He always had it done at an upmarket barber's in the West End, and smelled of their pomade. He had a part-time job at one of the museums in London, and always dressed immaculately for work – wool suits in winter, linen in summer. From the outside his life looked calm and orderly and peaceful, but the snatches of heartrending opera that sometimes drifted upstairs to our flat suggested that from the inside, it sometimes felt very different.

Peter insisted on carrying my case of hair colours up the stairs for me. I didn't try very hard to stop him, as it was pretty heavy.

'That was rather a swish ride you came home in the other day,' he said.

'Oh. It was, wasn't it? You saw it?'

'I certainly did. And I want to hear all about it. I've made some cake with courgettes from the allotment – pop down later and try some, if you want. It's almost healthy. Bring the girls if they'd like some, though then we might not be able to talk quite so frankly. But of course, if you don't want to tell me about the man with the Jag, we don't have to speak frankly at all.'

He went off whistling down the stairs, and I wondered how he'd react if I told him everything about my history with Mark. Not that I was about to do that. A little bit of the truth would be quite enough, at least at this stage. It would be more than I'd told my daughters, anyway.

But the prospect of even a cautious chat with a sympathetic outsider was a huge relief. Suddenly I realised how anxious I was about the whole thing, however happy and hopeful I was about Mark. It was because I was happy and hopeful that I was anxious – I wanted so much for it to work. We both did.

We *needed* it to work. There wouldn't be another chance.

The chance to offload even a little bit was too good to pass up. Peter wasn't involved, he didn't know Mark and he had no axe to grind. I had thought that I needed to talk to Ava… but actually, maybe what I really needed was to let off steam to someone else.

Ava was doing homework in the girls' bedroom and Ellie was reading in the kitchen. We didn't have all that many books in the house – I didn't have a lot of time for reading – but I'd always taken the girls to the library when they were little, and Ava still took Ellie most Saturdays, while I was working. It was scary how quickly one phase succeeded another, without you realising it at the time. For years on end it had seemed as if Ellie read nothing but books about fairies, and now it was *Harry Potter* – great big books, but she chewed through them like nobody's business. When she'd finished the series we'd need to find something else.

Neither of them liked the sound of courgette cake – either that, or they realised I wanted a chat with Peter on my own. Or maybe they were just happy doing what they were doing and didn't fancy being dragged away from it and into social contact, particularly not with their mother and a neighbour who was getting on in years.

My girls weren't ill-mannered, but they also didn't go out of their way to find company. They were very different to me like that: I dreaded being alone – both of them seemed to quite like it. I sometimes wondered whether it was my fault, and if perhaps they would have been keener to go to people's houses or have people round if we'd always lived somewhere that you'd feel comfortable inviting visitors to. Our current flat was fine – we'd been in grottier places – but the girls still didn't have their own rooms, and when Ellie was a baby, after I'd broken up with Sean, we'd had just one bedroom for all three of us, with me and Ava sharing a double bed and Ellie in a cot to the side. Ava in particular seemed to have got into the mindset that home was out of bounds, and it was inevitable that Ellie would follow her example.

I told them I'd be back in half an hour and went downstairs to Peter's. I liked being in his flat; it was so obviously a home, rather than somewhere that was rented – the furniture was old and solid, pieces that Peter had picked up at auctions down the years, there were carpets that weren't the cheapest you could get, and there were lots of framed prints and pictures hanging on nails he'd put in the walls. Also, the place had an atmosphere of calm that must have been something to do with Peter living alone there.

When I was working I listened to people as much as they wanted me to, but when I was with Peter, I was the talker. We sat in his dining room and had tea the old-fashioned way, from a teapot, and ate the courgette cake – which didn't taste all that much of courgettes, a good thing in my view – and looked at the daffodils coming up in the garden. Then I told the story of how I'd cut Mark's hair years ago and then our paths had crossed again and we'd started seeing each other, and explained that I'd recently decided to take the big step of introducing him to the girls.

Peter showed no obvious sign of smelling a rat. He said, 'So what did they make of him?'

I shrugged. I couldn't bring myself to pretend it had been an out-and-out success and anyway, when you're lying, you're meant to stick to the truth as far as possible.

'Ava was frosty and Ellie overcompensated,' I said. 'And then Mark tried to draw Ava out and she accused him of ignoring Ellie.'

'Oh dear. Was he?'

'Not really. I mean, not consciously. He's just feeling his way, you know? It's a big thing for him.'

'He doesn't have kids, then?'

'No. And before you ask, he's divorced.'

'I would have assumed that he was single and that you're serious about each other,' Peter said. 'Given that you've introduced him to the girls. I hope he appreciates what a token of faith that is.'

'Oh, I think he does,' I said. 'Anyway, I'm sure they'll like him once they've had the chance to get to know him a bit better.'

'So they don't like him now?'

He said this with one eyebrow raised, as if to suggest that the whole situation was absurd and faintly comical. As if there wasn't really that much at stake, and everything would sooner or later magically resolve itself.

'They don't like the *idea* of him,' I said. 'They're not used to me having a man in my life. They're used to Sean, basically. They think what men do is go away for longer and longer periods until they just show up once in a blue moon to take you out for dinner, and then promptly disappear again. But this is completely different. This is someone who wants to get closer. So naturally, the girls find it a bit strange. Also, you know, Mark's very different to Sean. Solvent and sober, for a start.'

I usually sounded bitter when I talked about Sean, which I resented – there was something demeaning about being the critical ex-wife. Also, it made the girls feel sorry for him, which was sympathy he didn't deserve. It sounded so much better when I had Mark to compare him to. Not so much as if I was down on Sean because things hadn't worked out, but more as if I was being matter-of-fact.

That was one of the amazing things about having been found by someone who actually wanted me. All the stuff that had happened before, during the years of my failed marriage, seemed less my fault: the rows and the humiliation, the lack of money, the being left to manage alone. The rejection. You might have expected it to be the other way round, but Sean was the one who had finally called time on our marriage.

Peter said, 'Does Sean know?'

'Last I heard he was working in a bar in Cologne, but that was a while ago. Right now, I don't even know what continent he's on.'

'How do you think he'd feel about it?'

I sighed. 'Why should I care? He has no right to know, and no right to object, either.'

Peter raised his eyebrows and waited for me to respond to the question. Sometimes there was something rather schoolteacherish about him.

'I think he probably won't like it at all,' I admitted.

'I suppose no one likes to feel that they can be replaced,' Peter said. 'Especially if the replacement is such an obvious improvement.'

'That's true,' I said. 'He's bound to take it as a slap in the face.' That really was true. Truer than Peter had any way of knowing. 'I mean, they're so different. Like chalk and cheese. Sean's chaotic. No impulse control. If he goes past somewhere that looks like a good place to eat, or wants a drink or sees a woman he likes... or gets an idea about where he wants to take off to next... off he goes. Mark has a plan for everything. He's always thinking ahead, whereas Sean carries on like the nuclear bomb's going to land the next day. Like there's almost no future at all.'

'But Mark's been rather impulsive where you're concerned, hasn't he?'

'Impulsive?'

'I mean, it's all moved rather fast.'

'I think you get to a stage in life where you don't feel the need to mess around. He's a bit older than me, so that's even more true for him.'

Then – before Peter could ask anything about Mark's ex-wife, and what had gone wrong, and if he was still on friendly terms with her and all of that – I said I had to be getting back.

Peter kissed me drily on the cheek and showed me out. I could tell he wanted to say more and was biting his tongue, and I was glad that he'd kept his thoughts to himself.

That's one of the things about being a single woman in your mid-thirties, whether you have children already or not. People tend to assume that what you really want is a baby, and any new romance is a means to an end... or that, even if it's not on the cards just yet, you're at least mulling over the possibility.

If Peter had asked me whether I wanted another child, I might even have told him the truth. Because I did. It was driving me crazy how much I wanted it. And this made me very different with Mark to the woman I had become in the dying days of my marriage to

Sean. It had turned me into a sex demon, to be frank. I'd never been like that before.

And Mark wanted it, too. Not just the sex. If it had only been sex for the sake of it, it wouldn't have been like that. There wouldn't have been as much need in it.

We hadn't discussed it, as such. We hadn't needed to. Our bodies had done the talking for us, much more explicitly than we could ever have managed with words. In the first of the hotel rooms we'd shared, with daylight seeping round the edges of the curtains, we'd made love with most of our clothes still on – it had been fast and desperate, as if the other person might vanish at any moment, as if this was a chance that had to be seized.

We hadn't used contraception. I'd told him not to worry about it, and he hadn't. Afterwards, when I was lying in his arms, he'd said, 'What if something happens?'

I'd said, 'Something tells me you wouldn't mind.'

'You're right,' he'd said, nuzzling my neck. 'I wouldn't mind at all. It would be amazing. I can't think of anything that would make me happier… except maybe for us to do what we just did all over again.'

And that settled it. We were in perfect agreement.

He wanted a baby, too. *My* baby. The baby he knew I could give him.

Chapter Four
Paula

Back in the days when I still thought of myself as happily married, I was never a particularly angry person. Or a bitter one. Live and let live, was my philosophy. I was easy-going; Mark wasn't. I used to say (probably too often) that it was just as well I wasn't fussy about details the way he was, that it would have been tricky for him to be married to someone who was equally particular. It was our little joke. It wasn't especially funny, but it suggested that we were ideally suited – compatible – made for each other, and I found it comforting to repeat it.

What neither of us realised was that I was capable of a slow burn. Glacial, in fact. I guess we're the ones you really have to watch out for: the ones who are most unpredictable when we finally blow.

All the years I was with Mark, I probably seemed like a bit of a pushover. A doormat. Not always, though. Even when I still thought myself in love with him, and imagined that we had a good marriage and a successful one, I had a mind of my own. I didn't make all that much use of it, but it was there. And eventually, there came a time when I was ready to fight for something that I wanted.

Soon after the new millennium, our friends started dropping like flies. It wasn't just the people we knew from university, but the people we worked with, too – the ones who were categorised as my friends or his, colleagues from our past or current jobs. It was like a thirtysomething plague, except they weren't coming down with fevers and boils and coughs: they were coming down with babies.

We'd see them perhaps once or twice, notice the symptoms, get a breathless email with the news, be given a brief opportunity to greet the newborn… then nothing. They'd disappear.

That was when I started to think about it. Might I be able to persuade Mark to change his mind?

Did I really want to?

We'd met as students and married relatively young, and we'd had to grow up together. We'd survived a wobble, an awful time when I'd developed a painful crush on someone at work. I still felt guilty about that, not because I'd done anything about it – I hadn't – but because I'd felt it, and I'd told Mark and I'd hurt him and he'd asked me to move out, and then he'd had that funeral to go to, the one we never spoke about, and I hadn't been there for him.

But we'd got through it.

We'd always agreed that we weren't bothered about having kids, that the really important thing was each other. So what if I wanted change and he didn't? What then?

Things came to a head the day our new dining chairs were delivered. They were Mark's choice: expensive designer things shaped like something from an aristocrat's chateau in the years before the French Revolution, but made of moulded transparent plastic. I'd have been quite happy with regular wooden chairs that didn't cost a small fortune, but I hadn't said so. Mark chose most of our furniture, and this was one of the areas of our marriage where I'd long since learned that it was best to let him have his way.

Isn't that what it takes, to keep a marriage going? You have to pick your battles. Let go of the things you don't care about, save your energy for the things that are really worth fighting for. And what could be more worth fighting for than a child?

I was the one who waited in for the chairs to be delivered. Neither of us would have said so directly, or accused the other of thinking it, but when push came to shove, Mark was paid more and that meant his career was more important than mine. Besides, it was easier for me to arrange to work from home.

After the chairs arrived I checked them all over carefully before signing for them – it wouldn't have done to let some flaw or scratch slip past unnoticed. I knew Mark would be pleased with them, and he was, which made for a good start to the evening. I cooked us a couple of steaks and we shared a bottle of good French red, and over coffee, which I'd made on the hob in the Continental-style pot just the way he liked it, I suggested that we should throw a dinner party. That way we could make use of all six of the new chairs, not just the two we were sitting on.

At first he liked the idea. Then we ran into difficulties with the guest list.

'This is hopeless,' Mark said eventually. 'They'll want to bring their babies with them. Or they'll get a call from the babysitter before dessert and have to rush off. And the women either won't be drinking or they'll be off their faces after a couple of glasses, and all they'll want to talk about is mastitis and nappies and stretch marks and…' He pulled a face. 'You know what I mean.'

And I did.

I looked at Mark, at the good shirt he was wearing and the glossy black top of the dining table he was leaning on and the outline of the transparent chair behind him, and suddenly I knew for certain that he wasn't enough for me and never would be.

There was someone missing. I could almost see her, sitting in the chair next to me: a small child with the big presence that all small children have, soft-skinned and plump-cheeked and slippery-haired.

I said, 'How would you feel if I stopped taking the Pill?'

He froze as if I'd just threatened him and he was working out how to hit back. But I wasn't about to backtrack. That little girl, the child at the table, was too real for that. And this was the only way to conjure her into existence.

He said, 'Have you stopped taking it?'

'No. I would never do that without telling you.'

'Do you want to?'

If he was to believe that we could do this and it could all turn out all right, I had to stay calm. I couldn't allow it to turn into an argument. The minute you start arguing with your husband about having children, you've already lost.

I looked into his eyes. He was frightened, that was all. He needed reassurance. If I showed him I could cope with this, he'd relax and it would all be fine.

'OK, I admit it,' I said. 'I want your babies.' And then I lied: 'But not if you don't want them too.' Then I reached for the coffee pot and said, 'Would you like any more?'

He shook his head. I poured myself another half-cup, added milk, stirred. I didn't look at him. I could sense him wavering between reluctance and resignation, about to come down on one side or the other.

Then he exhaled. 'You're not suddenly going to make me start wearing baggy boxers and eating oysters to improve my sperm count, are you?'

He was smiling. I smiled back. I'd done it! And it had been so easy. Why had I even been so worried about it? In the end, all I'd had to do was come out and say it.

'I thought you like oysters,' I said.

'I do,' he conceded. Then, almost plaintively: 'I do love you, you know. I can't think of anybody I would want to do this with, other than you.'

It occurred to me to say, *I hope not – I'm your wife*. But it was no time to be snide, and anyway, I knew what he was trying to say.

He was scared. I knew that. But he trusted me enough to do it anyway.

'I love you too,' I said.

A huge wave of relief washed over me. Relief and triumph. In the end I'd barely needed to persuade him. There'd certainly been no need to even think about the kind of trickery some women seemed to resort to, quietly stopping using contraception and then presenting their men with a fait accompli.

It was as if, through nothing more than force of will – through wanting her so badly – I'd rewritten our story already, and conjured that ghostly little girl at the table into the reality of our lives.

Chapter Five

Ellie

Mum's phone rang while she was washing up after dinner and she rushed to check who it was. That in itself was a dead giveaway: she really, really wanted it to be Mark.

She got calls and messages all the time from people wanting haircuts, and she'd got her phone set up so that calls from my school or Ava's had a special ringtone, in case there was an emergency. But Ava and I were both safely home, and there was nobody else she'd hurry for. Especially not Dad.

Still, at least she hadn't got to the stage of giving Mark his own special ringtone, too.

She took the phone into her bedroom and shut the door.

I tiptoed into the hallway so that I could listen. Ava was in the room we shared, as usual, doing whatever it was she did in there – homework, or so she claimed. I didn't think it very likely that she'd come out and find me eavesdropping, but it was possible. Anyway, I decided to take the risk.

Mum said, 'That's what I told them.'

Them? She must mean me and Ava. But told us what?

'Exactly. All in good time,' Mum said. 'I know.'

Then she dropped her voice so it was hard to make out the words. 'Maybe, but I don't think so, to be honest. She's always been like that. It's just the way she is.'

Was it Ava they were talking about? Or me?

Then Mum said, 'No, she does have friends at school, but she's never had a boyfriend. She's pretty wary, to be honest. She tends to keep people at a bit of a distance. Even me and Ellie, sometimes. You really mustn't take it personally. I did try talking to her about it, and she pretty much brushed me off. I think you're right, actually. We need to give her time.'

Of course they weren't talking about me. I was just the little one, the one it was easy to forget, and Mark wasn't interested in me and Dad didn't care either.

Tears came to my eyes, and I began to sniff. Maybe I should run away. But they probably wouldn't even notice.

'Ellie.' It was Ava. She'd come out and caught me red-handed. 'What are you doing?'

'I was just going to ask Mum something,' I said, blinking very fast to make the tears go away.

'Oh yeah? Like what?'

Mum wrenched her bedroom door open. She still had the phone in her hand. She said, 'What's going on? Were you listening to my private phone conversation?'

'I just wanted to ask you to test me on my spellings,' I said. 'I didn't dare ask *you*,' I said to Ava, 'because you're always so grumpy.'

'Well, you could have waited until after I'd finished,' Mum said. 'Come on then, let's give these spellings a go.'

Ava gave me a look as if to say, *A likely story*, and went back into our bedroom and closed the door.

I got the spellings all right but Mum was so distracted she hardly remembered to praise me. Thinking about Ava, no doubt, and whatever Mark had said about her.

I hated Ava sometimes. Hated her more than I could ever have brought myself to hate anyone else.

It was just so unfair. No matter how hard I tried, and no matter how little she tried, people always noticed her. And they always would, even when she was an old, old woman, and well past being pretty any more. Even if it was only because she was cantankerous and disagreeable, she'd always be the one who came first.

And at the same time I loved her. After all, she was the one who'd had a go at Mark for not listening to me. She always looked out for me, and I knew she always would.

That was part of the problem. I owed her too much, and there was no way I could make it up to her. She was a great big walking reminder of just how small I was, and of all the ways in which I could never catch up.

A few days later Mark showed up at the flat when Mum wasn't there.

She was out at work and Ava and I were both home, in our usual places – she was in our bedroom, which was somehow more hers than mine, and I was in the kitchen, writing a story about a future world that was dark all the time and filled with wolves. The story was going to end with the most dramatic thing I could think of, which was for the narrator to die an unpleasant death. I had a big A4 notepad to write in, which Mum had got me, and a specially nice pen. I would have preferred to type my stories up on the laptop, but Ava hogged that most of the time and Mum never gave a proper answer if I asked when I could have a laptop of my own.

I'd done about a page of the story, which was about as long as it usually took before I got bored and started moving things on so I could bump the narrator off and finish. Then the doorbell rang and I looked out of the window and there was Mark's Jag, parked a little way down the street because the space directly in front of our building was taken. And there was Mark, walking from the car to our building with a great big pile of red hardback books in his arms.

He pressed the bell again. Impatient. But the books did look heavy. And they had to be a present for us. Why else would he have brought them?

Our buzzer still wasn't working, so I grabbed my keys and ran downstairs and opened the door to the block. When he saw who it was he smiled as if I wasn't quite the person he was looking for and said, 'Hi, Ellie. Is your mum home?'

'She's working, but she shouldn't be too much longer. Would you like to come in?'

Mark checked his watch. 'I thought she was always home by five,' he said. It was already quarter past.

I wondered what she'd been telling him. She was often back later than this, and it wasn't unusual for Ava to emerge from our bedroom at some point in the evening and make us something to eat, leaving a plateful for Mum when she finally got home.

Maybe Mum wanted Mark to think that she was always here to cook dinner and look after us. Which would have been nice, if only because Ava did her best to ignore me most of the time. But we managed fine the way things were.

'She'll be home soon,' I said. 'Do you want to come on up? Those look heavy.'

'Sure, if that's OK,' Mark said. 'Is Ava in?'

'Yeah, she's in,' I said.

How *typical* that he wanted to know if Ava was there. What a disappointment it would have been if it'd just been boring little me.

I showed him up to the flat, and he put the books down on the kitchen table with a sigh of relief.

There were perhaps six of them, beautifully bound, with gold on the edges of the pages and the titles printed on the covers in gold script. The one on the top was *The Mayor of Casterbridge*, which didn't exactly sound exciting, but it looked so fancy it could have been the most boring book in the world and I'd still have wanted to try and read it. I don't know why people say you shouldn't judge a book by its cover. Everyone does.

Ava came in. She was wearing an old hoodie and skinny jeans and she didn't have any make-up on and she probably hadn't brushed her hair since the morning, but she still looked good.

'Hello, Mark.' She didn't exactly sound pleased to see him. 'Mum's not here.'

'So I gather. It's OK, I won't wait for her. I don't want to intrude. I just wanted to drop these off for you.'

For *Ava*?

But *I* was the one who loved reading. He knew that.

Ava cast an eye over the books. The corners of her mouth turned down. She said, 'Why?'

'Because they're classics,' Mark explained patiently, 'and if you haven't read them, you should. As part of your general education.' He glanced at me as if only just remembering I was there. 'And you should too, Ellie. When you're a bit older.'

I was speechless. What made him think I couldn't read them right now if I chose? Any words I didn't understand I could just look up in the dictionary. Did he think I was too stupid? Or did he think that I was too naïve, that there would be things in those books that were too adult and shocking for me? I didn't need him to protect me, and the sooner he realised that the better. The world was the world, and nobody could shield you from seeing at least a little bit of how awful it could be. Not even Mum.

Ava reached out and brushed her fingertips across the cover of *The Mayor of Casterbridge*. I could tell she wanted to pick it up and have a good look at it, but she withdrew her hand as if it was too hot to touch and said, 'These must have been expensive. I don't think I should accept them.'

Mark looked just as wounded as I'd felt when he'd said at first that the books were for Ava. *Give them to me*, I screamed at him in my head. *I'll take them. She's just proud and stiff-necked and ungrateful. But I'm not. I don't care. I just want those beautiful books, and I would have told Mum you're the best thing ever if only they had been for me.*

He tried to make light of it. 'You'd be doing me a favour. They were rather heavy, and I really don't fancy carrying them back down those stairs.'

'Then you should have thought of that before you brought them here,' Ava said. 'Did Mum know you were doing this?'

'Probably I should have checked with her first. But I can't see that she would object.'

Ava picked up the books. She had a strange expression on her face, like this was hurting her and was satisfying at the same time. 'I'll take them downstairs for you. Ellie, get the door.'

'Put them back,' I said.

Both of them turned to stare at me. They looked so shocked, you'd have thought I'd have suddenly spoken up in the voice of a demon. '*I* want them,' I said. 'You did say they were for me, too, Mark. And anyway, I'm much keener on reading than Ava is.'

'That seems fair enough,' Mark said to Ava. 'Maybe Ellie will let you borrow them if you change your mind.'

Ava shot me an angry glance – *how could you?* – but she put the books back down on the table.

'Whatever,' she said. Then, to me: 'You're going to have to find space for them on your side of the room.'

'I'll manage,' I said. 'Mark, would you like a coffee or something?'

This was what you were meant to say to visitors; Ava had been neglectful in not offering. Mum might tell her off later, and I could come out of this pretty well, with both the books *and* the victory of having been a good hostess.

But Mark shook his head. He brushed his hands against each other as if to say, *job well done.*

'No, I'd best be off,' he said. 'Enjoy the books. Take care, Ava.'

'I'll show you out,' I said.

I followed Mark downstairs to the lobby and let him out of the building, and then, on impulse, trotted along behind him all the way to his car.

I knew Ava would feel I'd let the side down, and I felt bad about it but not enough to change tack. If Ava was going to be mean to Mark, that was up to her. *I* was going to be extremely nice to him. After all... why shouldn't I be? Who was I being disloyal to? Not Dad, who we hadn't seen for ages. Not Mum, who was in love with Mark and wanted us to get on with him. Only Ava, who seemed to have decided to make things difficult. Like she was testing him. Why did she have to be so weird about it?

And yet...

There *was* something about it I didn't really understand. Something about *him*.

Something he'd done, perhaps, a long time ago? Or something he ought to have done, and hadn't?

Whatever it was, it bothered him, and it wasn't going to go away. I'd felt it that first time we met him, when he took Ava's hand in the car. And I could feel it now.

He didn't seem to have noticed that I'd followed him. He pressed his key fob to unlock the car door and I said, 'The books are really nice. I think Mum will like them, too. It was very kind of you.'

He started, and for a moment he looked almost as if I repelled him. Then he smoothed his face into a more appropriate adult-to-child expression – friendly, and slightly patronising – and said, 'Sorry, Ellie, lost in thought.'

I shrugged. 'It's OK. People often forget I'm there.' *Especially when Ava's there too. And even when she isn't.* 'I'd probably make a brilliant spy.'

'I'm sure you would,' Mark said. Then: 'Ellie, I hope you don't mind me asking, but how much do you see of your dad?'

'It depends,' I said. 'It's been a while.'

'When you do see him, do you get along with him?'

I hesitated. How to sum up our relationship with Dad in a sentence or two? You couldn't just say it was awkward and leave it at that. You could say that of any relative you didn't see very often, and with Dad it was different. It always felt like something big was still unfinished, and maybe always would be.

It was like the picture that I'd got started on in school last summer, which was going to be of the most beautiful garden in the world. I had a big piece of sugar paper to work on, and I was planning to make it perfect. But I'd only got as far as the beginning of the path and the outline of the borders, and then there'd been no more time and the picture had somehow got lost.

I shrugged. 'Yeah, we get along.'

'And Ava? How is she with him?'

Suddenly I didn't like this any more. Ava wouldn't be at all happy that I was even having this conversation. I'd gone against her once already today. I wasn't about to do it again.

'She's fine with him, actually. Thanks for the books,' I said, and turned and walked back towards the flat.

He's just going to get in the way. Still, nothing to be done about it. Not yet, anyway.

Had I imagined it? The words were so clear it was as if he'd just spoken them. He looked startled when I turned back and stared at him, then attempted to smile and wave and got into the car and drove away.

Upstairs in the kitchen, Ava was looking at one of the books. They seemed somehow ominous – too big, too red, radiating a faint sense of *not-quite-right*. I remembered the roses Mark had bought Mum, the colour of them, dark and bright like blood.

'Don't do that,' she said.

'Don't do what?'

'Play his game. Whatever it is.'

She put down the book. It was *Great Expectations*, which I had heard of, maybe. It seemed like a good idea to have quite a long word in a book's title, so that people knew to take it seriously.

'You just don't want to like him,' I said.

'You want to like him too much,' she said. 'You should remember this isn't that big a deal. He gave us something he could easily afford to give. That doesn't mean we owe him anything.'

And she went off to the bedroom and closed the door, leaving me alone with the books.

Chapter Six

Ava

After Mark gave us the books, any time he came near our place, Ellie would start ostentatiously reading. He couldn't help but notice, and seemed pleased, though I got the impression Ellie's approval wasn't crucial to him.

Maybe that was because it was so easy to get. If he was the kind of guy who liked a challenge, I was currently the only one out of the three of us who was giving him one. I wasn't hostile, exactly, but I wasn't falling over myself to make him welcome. He'd have to earn that, and he couldn't do it just by buying us expensive presents.

Every now and then it was obvious that Mum wished I'd be a little warmer towards him, but weeks went by without us really talking about it. The only person who seemed to realise that I was out of sorts was Toby Andrews at school, who got up the nerve to approach me and actually asked if I was OK. I wasn't about to admit how I was feeling to Toby, though. I wasn't mean to him, I just gave him a discouraging look and told him I was fine. After all, what could he have done about it? I half hoped that Mark would lose interest. But what really bothered me was that part of me really didn't want him to abandon us.

Mum went off every now and then for dinner dates: the Jag would pull up outside the flat and off she'd go, smelling of the new perfume Mark had bought her. He bought some for me, too, but it stayed in its packaging. Ellie got some bubble bath and a pencil case, which she was delighted with and carried round as if it was treasure.

He treated Mum like she was precious and slightly incompetent: opened doors for her, helped her with her coat, all that kind of thing. Mum loved it. She was always looking at him adoringly, and he would look back at her with smug relief, as if she was the one he'd been searching for all these years and had finally found.

They weren't all over each other all the time, which was something, but instead they were romantic, which was quite bad enough. The handholding, the pecks on the cheek – it was all vaguely nauseating. Mark in the abstract I could tolerate, even admire, though I wouldn't have admitted that to anyone. But Mark and Mum being lovey-dovey? There was just something really unsettling about it.

He took us all to the theatre, to see *Romeo and Juliet* in the West End. 'It'll be good for your studies,' Mum said. The tickets cost a fortune – I made sure to check out the prices, but didn't make a big deal of thanking him. Ellie was entranced by the performance; I was begrudging, and didn't enthuse.

'You're a hard woman to please,' Mark told me afterwards, when he was driving us back to the flat. 'That's supposed to be one of the best productions in recent years.'

'I just don't like it when actors declaim their lines like they're doing you a favour,' I said. 'Besides, I'm not all that keen on romance.'

'Well, *I* thought it was beautiful,' Mum said brightly.

She was wearing yet another new dress, pink with a pattern of little white blossoms. It was the kind of thing you'd expect someone to dress up in if she lived in the country and cooked on an Aga. Was that the kind of person Mark wanted her to become? I didn't know whether he'd got her the dress; she might have chosen it herself. It was getting to the point where it was hard to tell whether her things were gifts from him or attempts to please him.

'Ava's just heartless,' Ellie said.

'I'm sure that's not true,' Mark said.

'It is, actually,' I said. 'I'm never going to fall in love. Or get married, or have children. I'm going to live on my own my whole life.'

'Surely you're a little young to decide that,' Mark said.

'Then I'm too young to decide I want to be a wife and mother, aren't I?'

'You're too young to decide anything,' Mum said. 'You just never know how things are going to turn out. Life is full of surprises.'

And she gave Mark a special smile, and he reached out and squeezed her hand and I felt like throwing up.

It was all so *fast*. A whirlwind romance was probably great if you were in it, but if you were on the sidelines, being spun round and round without the power to stop everything and step off – well, you were much more likely to feel queasy than to enjoy the ride.

Soon after the trip to see *Romeo and Juliet*, something that was both inevitable and unpredictable happened: Dad got in touch.

There were other people at school who had parents who were separated or divorced, and they all seemed to have these set-ups where they saw the parent they didn't live with every weekend. When I'd first realised that was usually how it worked, I had been absolutely astonished. Then I'd felt cheated. Then I'd figured out that spending more time with Dad wouldn't actually have made anything any better. Anyway, if he didn't want to see us, I didn't want to see him.

There was a small chance that seeing Dad more often would have changed our relationship with him – made it more regular, part of the routine world of cornflakes in the morning and homework in the evening and a fixed, sensible bedtime. But Dad wasn't fixed or regular or routine or sensible. He lived for the moment and the moment blew him around all over the place, and when he came to see us our lives became unpredictable too.

I resented him for that and secretly loved him for it too, because what child doesn't want to see the usual order of things undermined? He was dangerous, though. He couldn't be trusted; he was unreliable. He'd say he'd come at six and rock up at nine; he'd forget birthdays and compensate by sending huge, extravagant gifts that weren't quite right – dolls for Ellie that might have been suitable for a much younger child, clothes for me that were expensive but not the kind of thing I'd ever wear. He was dangerous because if you just let yourself love him, if you ever forgot to brace yourself for disappointment, you'd be crushed.

Compared to Mark, though, he was a known quantity. So when Mum rapped on our bedroom door and said he'd been in touch, I was pleased. More than that, I was relieved.

I don't know what I was hoping for, really. Maybe I had some vague idea that Dad was going to help me get my bearings on Mark. Like he might be able to reassure me: *Oh, don't worry, it's bound to fizzle out.* Or *well, I always knew this was going to happen, Ava, but don't worry, I'll always be a part of your lives, and I'm going to be a changed man from now on and come see you both every weekend, like all those other divorced fathers.*

Maybe what I really wanted was some push-back. *Who is this creep? I don't like the sound of him at all. Don't you worry, Ava, I'm going to see him off.*

Fat chance.

Still, I did get something out of it his visit. Consistency. Dad behaved exactly as I would have anticipated, if I hadn't allowed myself to hope for something more. In the end, the wild card was Mark. It was the first time I saw how ruthless he could be, and how much he liked to win.

The evening with Dad started badly. Surprise, surprise, he was late. The worst thing about that was how patiently and uncomplainingly

Ellie waited for him, sitting right by the kitchen window where she could keep an eye on the street and getting paler and sadder as time went by. I sat it out in our bedroom, where at least she wasn't right under my nose. It wound me up too much to see her like that, all the more so because it was just something else I couldn't do anything about.

When it got to half-seven I couldn't wait any longer. I went into the kitchen, where Mum was washing up her dinner for one and slapping plates in the drainer as if she didn't care if they broke. Ellie was still sitting by the window with one of the red-backed books open in her lap, looking as forlorn and starved as an orphan.

I put a couple of pieces of bread in the toaster. 'Have a bit of this, if you want, Ellie. You look as if you're about to pass out.'

'You'll spoil your appetite,' she said primly.

And then we all heard a car outside.

Ellie got up straight away and dashed over to the window and looked down, and said – as if this was a triumph – 'It's him!'

Mum and I exchanged glances. Mum grimaced. I rolled my eyes. Ellie had already gone, hurrying down to get into the taxi – Dad never drove us any more, Mum had put a stop to that.

'Some toast there if you want it,' I said to Mum.

'Take care,' she said. 'Remember what we talked about.'

'He won't make any trouble,' I said. 'Or at least no more than usual.' And then I hurried downstairs too.

We went to a Portuguese place in Kingston. It wasn't as posh as the hotel Mark had taken us to, but it was nice – probably nicer than Dad could really afford. He always tried to take us somewhere different; Thai, Chinese, Indian, whatever. This place specialised in steak, which Dad liked. He was a red-meat, red-wine kind of guy. Actually, he was a beer and whisky kind of guy, too. He didn't discriminate.

'I'm thinking of going vegan,' I told Dad as we studied the menus.

Dad raised an eyebrow and looked at me pretty much the way the snake might have looked at Eve in the garden of Eden if the snake was a middle-aged alcoholic and Eve was his teenage daughter. Like, *Who are you trying to kid, coming over all virtuous? Who do you think you are?*

'What does your mother think of that?'

'She says it's OK as long as she doesn't have to fiddle around with pulses and I cook for myself.'

'Fair enough. What's it going to be today? A nice bit of T-bone?'

Again, that look. *You think you're above temptation now, do you?* He was steaming drunk – you could tell just by looking at him: his eyes were too bright, his face was too red, and his hands had stopped shaking. But also, he was at the manageable stage, where he was still perfectly capable of holding a conversation. The conversation might get a bit more obsessive or repetitive as the evening wore on, but we were a long way away from the ranty/obsessive stage, which didn't usually set in till two or three in the morning. Now Dad didn't live with us I never really saw that side of him any more, and Ellie had pretty much never seen it, which made it nice and easy for her to pretend it didn't exist.

'I'll have the rump steak and chips,' I conceded, and Dad grinned at me.

'That's my girl,' he said.

'I'm going to have the same,' Ellie said.

'Good for you,' Dad said, not really paying her that much attention.

The waiter arrived with the wine – Dad had ordered a bottle of red as soon as we'd sat down. Dad tasted it – he loved that little ritual, though I'd never seen him send wine back. Then he poured a bit into my glass. He always preferred to drink in company. I'd learned quickly to watch it with him; his hand would slip a bit, the wine would splash in and the look of temptation would come out. Before I knew it I'd be feeling all the emotions I never usually let myself feel and talking about all the things I never usually let myself talk about, and Dad would be looking at me in delight.

Well, it wasn't going to happen this time. Mum trusted me to keep an eye on Ellie and come home sober, and that was what I was going to do.

I sipped my water. Suddenly I felt really nervous, which was stupid because nothing bad was going to happen to us here, in public, and Dad wasn't *that* drunk, anyway.

Dad raised his glass and proposed a toast. 'To being together,' he said, and we all chinked glasses.

Then he swigged some wine and gave me that wicked look, the look that meant he was about to attempt to induce me to do something I maybe shouldn't do, or might be reluctant to go along with.

'What's all this I hear about your mum having a new boyfriend?'

Totally predictable: he wanted me to dish the dirt on Mark. Mum had warned me he'd do this, and I'd promised her I'd steer as far clear of the subject as possible.

'She mentioned she'd told you about him,' I said, playing for time.

'What I wondered was, what do you think of him?'

'I think he's quite nice,' Ellie piped up.

We both stared at her. 'He gave us some books,' Ellie explained defiantly.

'I wasn't going to accept them. I thought it was too much,' I said. 'But Ellie was keen.'

'They're lovely books. All classics. But I would still think he was nice, even if he didn't give us anything,' Ellie said.

I kicked her under the table, and she reddened and quickly changed tack.

'Not as nice as you, Daddy, obviously. But I think he's making Mummy happy and it's only fair, isn't it? I mean, she should have her chance to be happy.'

Dad's bonhomie vanished – it was remarkable how quickly that could happen – and he glared at her.

'*Fair* has got nothing to do with it. He's just come crawling out of the woodwork because he's free.'

I said, 'What do you mean, *free*? Was he married?'

Dad narrowed his eyes. This was the next stage on from the Face of Temptation: the Face of Compulsion, which said, *I really need you to do what I want you to do next or I won't be answerable for the consequences.*

'Ask your mother,' he said. 'What do *you* think of him?'

I hesitated. I could tell this really mattered to him, and that made it impossible to know what to say.

I could have said, *He treats Mum well and he's making an effort, so what's not to like?*

I could have said, *At least he turns up on time.*

I could have said, *I've kind of got used to him being around.* Because I had, in spite of myself. And yet I, of all people, knew exactly how easy it was for a man to disappear. The way Dad would, after this visit. The way he'd done for years.

So instead I just shrugged. 'Seriously, what did you mean about him coming out of the woodwork?'

'Oh, they'll tell you all about that, by and by,' Dad said. 'I guess they're waiting for their moment.'

Suddenly he looked completely crushed. This was the next stage after the Face of Compulsion: the Face of Defeat.

'I'm going out for a smoke,' he muttered, and grabbed his jacket and hurried out of the restaurant without looking at either of us.

'He's jealous, isn't he?' Ellie said.

'Well, obviously it's going to freak him out.' What was I doing defending Dad? This never normally happened. 'What was that all about, anyway? All that "Mark's really nice, he gave me a big expensive present" stuff?'

'But it's true,' Ellie protested.

'Just because something's true doesn't mean you have to say it.'

Her eyes shone a bit: any minute now she'd cry, and everybody in the restaurant would stare at us and it would be embarrassing – even more embarrassing than Dad stumbling as he weaved round the tables – and I'd feel like a total bitch. Even though none of this was my fault. Her lower lip was trembling, and when she spoke it was in her most plaintive voice.

'But isn't it better for Dad to think that Mark's OK than to think he's horrible and we hate him? He'll only worry about us.'

'He's not going to worry. He never does. I mean, he might, for five minutes, and then he'll just go and have another drink. If you big up Mark, all you're going to do is make tonight more awkward than it needs to be. Just play it down, OK? Chances are we won't see Dad again till Christmas and by then Mark might have disappeared back where he came from, who knows?'

She looked at me, all wide-eyed and innocent. 'But he *isn't* going to disappear.'

'How do you know?'

And that was it, like a switch being flipped. Suddenly she was looking at me as if she was about a million years old and had seen everything. Her eyes had gone very dark, almost all pupil, and her face was as still as a mask. There was a kind of power coming off her like when something radiates heat and it distorts the air. Like invisible lightning. She was *scorching*. I don't know how else to describe it. She was my sweet little sister and about the least scary person in the world, but at that moment she was terrifying.

I'd never seen Ellie change like that. I'd never seen *anyone* change like that.

Then she looked down at the tablecloth and put her hand up to her forehead, and when she faced me again whatever it was had passed.

'I just know,' she said.

Dad came back, weaving, but only slightly. He sat down and said, 'So I suppose Mark's taken you all out, has he? Given you some special times to remember him by?'

He was smiling as if to imply that it was all fine with him, he didn't care that much either way. Except it was obvious that he *did* care. Not enough to turn up on time to see us, but enough to mind when Mum seemed to be auditioning his replacement.

'Please, let's not talk about Mark any more,' Ellie said.

She had gone so pale it was as if there was no blood left in her at all. She stood up and pushed her chair back and hurried out of the restaurant, as if an alarm had gone off and she was only reacting as any sensible person would do – except no one else, me included, had heard it.

Ellie felt faint, as it turned out. She wasn't well. She wanted to go home. Dad sighed and grumbled and rang Mum, and said he'd bring us back.

'We could still spend some time together,' I said diffidently, but he pretended he hadn't heard me.

It took a while for us to get a taxi, but once we were on the way, we seemed to get home in minutes. When we got to our street Dad paid off the taxi driver and said, 'I'll come in with you.'

I said, 'Are you sure? I mean, you don't usually.'

'Your mother said to bring Ellie home. She didn't say to drop her off,' Dad said.

'Maybe you should ask the taxi driver to wait,' I said. 'You don't want to be hanging round outside waiting for another one. It looks like it's going to rain.'

'Ava, stop fussing,' Dad said. 'I promise you, this is going to be fine. Your mother will be perfectly happy to invite me in, under the circumstances. After all, she's happy with somebody else now, isn't she? So what has she got to be bitter about?'

No way. That's just what you want to think. You're kidding yourself.

I didn't say it – how could I? I thought he probably had it wrong. But maybe, just maybe, *I* was the one who had got it wrong. Maybe Mum *would* want to see him. Who knew?

It was beginning to spit with rain as we went up the steps to our building and the taxi driver drove off. The door to the downstairs lobby opened and there was Mark, arms folded, looking like he wasn't about to put up with any nonsense.

Mark said, 'Hello, Sean. I'm afraid Jenny really doesn't want you coming in.'

I didn't often wish that Dad was different: I'd resigned myself long ago to him being the way he was. But just then a huge wave of longing rose up in me for that other version of Dad, the might-have-been sober version. He would have been terrific. Unbeatable. Mark would never have had a look-in.

As it was, Dad swayed as he attempted to square up to Mark. He was slightly taller, an advantage taken away by the fact that he was standing on a lower step. He looked Mark up and down, and all of a sudden the fight seemed to ebb out of him.

'Mark. I suppose I ought to say welcome back.'

Mark stared at Dad and a muscle worked away somewhere in his jaw: I'd never seen someone's face do that unless it was on TV. Then he turned to me and Ellie and said, 'You two should go inside.'

'Dad was thinking he could come up,' I said.

'Then he's got another think coming. Ava, take Ellie up.'

'Don't tell me what to do.'

He didn't like that. Not one bit. 'Your mother's been worried. You should go and speak to her. Put her mind at rest.'

Mark stepped aside to let Ellie through and she went past him into the hallway. I reluctantly followed, and Mark shifted so that he was blocking the entrance again.

'Go home, Sean,' Mark said. 'And when you've sobered up, here's something to think about. If you can't behave yourself when you see the girls, you're not going to see them at all.'

'You don't get to decide that,' Dad said.

'No,' Mark said. 'Jenny decides. And I will respect her decision. As should you.'

'You go,' I told Ellie, and ushered her up the stairs to the flat.

'Don't talk to me like that,' Dad said. 'Where were you when she needed you? I'll tell you where. Nowhere. I may not have been perfect, but I was a lot better than nothing.'

I turned back just in time to see him give Mark a little shove.

'Stop it, both of you,' I yelled, but I already was too late and neither of them was paying me any attention.

It happened so fast there was no chance to put myself between them. One minute they were both standing there eyeballing each other and the next minute Mark was still standing and Dad was bellowing like a gored bull and reeling back down the steps, clutching his nose, and there was blood on his face and all down his shirt, as if he'd been caught in an explosion.

'You bastard!' I shouted at Mark, and shoved him aside so I could get to Dad. 'Dad, are you all right? Your nose isn't broken, is it?'

'Don't think so,' Dad mumbled. It was hard to hear him; his hand was still covering his nose. 'Bloody hurts, though.'

I hated him for the way he looked up at Mark – resentful, beaten – almost as much as I hated Mark for looking down at us with such disdain.

'You should come in so we can clean that up and give you some ice to put on it or something,' I said to Dad.

Mark relaxed his fist and shook it out.

'He's not coming into your mother's flat,' he said. 'Not tonight. Not any night.'

'You are not the one who gets to decide that,' I told him.

'Neither are you. Your mother is. But it looks like Sean agrees with her. Look, he's already gone.'

He was right. Dad was hurrying away down the street, one hand still pressed to his bleeding nose.

I ran after him. 'Dad, come back! You don't have to go like this.'

'Ava, go home,' he muttered.

'Well, where are you going?'

'To get a drink. Leave me be, Ava. It's no good. I can't do this any more. Why kid ourselves? I was never any good at it. The whole Dad thing. And now it's over.'

I stopped in my tracks. 'Of all the pitiful, pathetic things to say…'

'There's no point being angry with me,' he said. 'I'm done.'

He kept on walking and I stayed where I was. Then he turned the corner of the street and disappeared and I turned and trudged back towards Mark. He was waiting in the doorway and looking on in satisfaction, as if he'd just seen off an interloper.

As I approached he made a slight move as if to lay a hand on my shoulder to soothe or placate me, and I flinched away.

'You're very loyal to him, aren't you?' he said. 'In spite of everything.'

'He may be a drunk. But you're a bully,' I said. 'Mum may not be able to see it. But I do. Dad said you'd come crawling out of the woodwork because you were free. Free from what? Where have you been?'

I'd never seen him angry before. It wasn't pretty. He was cold angry, not hot angry, and it made his face look as hard as a skull. But he made a real effort to control it, and when he spoke he sounded almost as charming and reasonable as usual.

'I was married when I first met your mother years ago, and now I'm not.'

'You never said.'

'You never asked. It's not a secret. It was a clean break and it's all over and done with, and it's none of Sean's business. He's jealous and he's trying to stir up trouble, and that's all there is to it.'

'*You're* the one who's jealous. You just hit him, and he barely even provoked you.'

He didn't like that. Not one little bit. But what was he going to do, thump me the way he'd just thumped Dad? That was one thing Mum would never have forgiven him.

'I'm sorry you had to see that,' he said.

'I'm sorry you felt you had to drive him away. Anyway, it didn't take much. He's already given up.'

I went upstairs into the flat. Mum and Ellie were in the kitchen, and Mum was making tea: whenever either of us was unwell, that was Mum's first line of defence.

Ellie still looked pale, and she started guiltily as I stuck my head round the door.

'I'll be in the bedroom,' I said.

Mum said, 'Where's Mark?'

'I expect he'll be up in a minute. He just punched Dad. You might want to ask him about that.'

I withdrew and shut the bedroom door. I could hear the sound of conversation going on in the kitchen – it was Mark and Mum talking – but not what they were saying.

Maybe that would be the end of it. Maybe Mum would dump Mark now she knew he was capable of lashing out like that.

I had a feeling she wouldn't, though. That was one of the problems with having been married to someone like Dad; you got used to making allowances.

Chapter Seven

Jenny

I had never been the kind of woman who goes to hotels in the afternoon to have sex, whatever kind of woman that is. A rich and busy woman having an affair, or one whose lover is rich and busy, I suppose. Not me, the divorced single mother-of-two who was always working and never had any money, who hadn't got involved with anyone since her marriage fell apart.

But what were the alternatives? Mark travelled constantly for his work as an IT consultant, but his home – which I'd never seen – was in the Oxfordshire countryside, and my flat wasn't much of a love nest. Even when it was empty, the girls' presence lingered: the smell of Ava's shampoo, Ellie's books and notebooks. It wasn't nearly anonymous or private enough. We had neighbours all around; they didn't have to be nosy to notice a sudden new visitor – sound travelled, the entrance to the building was shared, and it was difficult to avoid picking up details about each other's lives.

I couldn't begin to see how Mark and I could recreate, in my single bed, the kind of freedom we found in rooms that we paid for so we could use them for an hour or two, and never see them again.

We paid for? *He* paid for. That was another attraction. He *always* settled the bill.

I knew it didn't reflect very well on me to enjoy that as much as I did. But I'd spent so long scrimping and saving and watching the pennies, and making small, practical, dispiriting decisions so as to be able to cover the weekly food shop: bananas or apples that week?

Tinned chicken or fresh? It was just so nice to be taken care of. I'd spent years fantasising (now and then, when I had the energy) about looking pretty in lingerie for a rich and masterful man who would find me irresistible. Well, now I had him, and it wasn't a fantasy.

It was a miracle that I still managed to cut people's hair, cook the dinner, clean the flat and settle the bills. I was so distracted I was like an amnesiac. It was as if I'd had a knock on the head that had displaced all the usual, sensible, day-to-day stuff, leaving me with erotic obsession and not much else.

But that day I wasn't just thinking about sex with Mark. I was thinking about the future. The glorious future. My head told me it wouldn't be plain sailing, but my heart didn't care. My heart had decided to believe in happiness.

I went back to the flat after the last appointment of the day to get changed, and put Otis Redding on to get me in the mood – that was our music: 'Dock of the Bay' was our jukebox song. I had it on quiet, though – one of the nurses upstairs might be sleeping off a nightshift. Quiet worked fine, anyway.

I had new lingerie, new lipstick, I was in love, I was beloved, I was almost certainly about to have sex, it was spring and the sun was shining and a whole new life was opening up in front of me. What more could any woman want?

Even Ava didn't strike me as being that much of a problem.

We just needed to talk to her – to both the girls – and explain what was really going on. This was the only bone of contention between me and him: I thought we should do it sooner rather than later, and he was holding back. He was nervous. Terrified. Well, that was only natural. I was doing my very best not to pressurise him: pressure from me was the last thing he needed.

Mark wanted it all to be perfect; he didn't want to risk any of it slipping through his fingers. He wanted to control it. But keeping control of anything was impossible with Sean around. You were always up against the power of his appetite for booze, which was pretty much boundless.

I'd talked everything over with Sean before he took the girls out for dinner, and he'd promised me – *promised* me – he'd keep his mouth shut and behave himself. I should have known better. I should have known that his promises were worthless.

Mark had warned me, but I hadn't wanted to believe it – I'd wanted to give Sean the benefit of the doubt. I'd said to Sean, *If you want this all to work out, don't rock the boat.* Naturally he hadn't been too happy about it, but that was Sean all over – always thinking about himself.

Mark had just said, *Are you sure we can trust him?* And I'd said, *Yes. He's kept quiet for years. He just has to keep quiet for a bit longer.*

And then, after all that, Sean had got stupidly drunk. Mark had told me he'd let something slip. Some throwaway comment about Mark having come to find me once he'd got his freedom.

Sean had told Ava that Mark hadn't been there when I needed him. Which was true. But she needed to know why, and that was what I was afraid to tell her. Because what if she couldn't forgive me?

Anyway, I couldn't think about all that now.

I examined my reflection in the mirror, turned sideways, struck a pose. Sex was all about confidence. That was the conclusion I'd come to since my long drought had ended. You couldn't just tell yourself someone wanted you, or at least, I couldn't. You had to *feel* that they wanted you. You had to *believe* it. So much of everything to do with love and sex was about having faith.

Time had been kinder to Mark than it had to me, at least in terms of appearance. I was in my thirties and I'd had two children, and I could hardly claim to look good from all angles. But he loved my stretch marks, my episiotomy scar. He really did.

And Sean never had. Given the choice between the old, unscarred, taut-bellied, smooth-skinned me – the one who'd never been pregnant – and the woman I was now, Sean would have chosen my younger self in a heartbeat.

Which I could understand, in a way. But that was the thing about youth – nobody got to keep it, not even the richest, best-preserved Hollywood stars. And when you *did* have it, you didn't quite realise what you'd got – or I hadn't, anyway. I hadn't understood that it was a kind of power. I'd never tried to use it the way other women did, to get things that they might want later. Things they could keep.

Sharing a house with Ava, I was presented with a vision of youth and beauty day in, day out. Even if she was tired and fed up and had pimples in her hairline, Ava looked lit up. She was astonishing, really. Even when I'd been young, I'd never had that kind of beauty – the kind that stops people in the street.

I didn't resent her. I've never understood mothers like that, who are envious of their own daughters. After all, it wasn't her fault that I was getting older. Though in a way it was. Having kids does wear you out. Especially if you're doing it pretty much on your own. But anyway, the point was that I didn't feel old on the inside, at least not yet. My body still worked in the exact same way. If anything, it was even more responsive. It might not look the same, but Mark worshipped it.

It had been a long time, since Sean. And actually, in all the years when Ava had been little, sex with Sean had never really been that satisfactory. I don't mean to say it had been terrible. But I'd always secretly felt a bit like Sean felt he was doing me a favour, overlooking my post-baby flaws and fancying me anyway.

With Mark, everything was different. He wanted all the things Sean had never really wanted. Things I could give him. Myself included.

I put on my dress and a light coat, and hurried out of the flat.

We wouldn't have long. I'd have to leave the hotel at five to get home in time to put the supper on. Ava could have done it, but I didn't particularly want to give her the opportunity. I didn't want the day to be spoiled by her looking at me accusingly to let me know she'd guessed what I'd been up to.

This was my time – mine and Mark's, at last. It definitely wasn't the time to be worrying about whether we'd run out of frozen peas or not.

I was due to meet Mark at three, and when I got to the hotel bar at five to he was already waiting for me.

He was well dressed as usual in a suit and tie – he was always dressed in formal work clothes when we met. Because he was fairly senior and spent so much time away from his office, he had almost as much freedom to manage his schedule and sneak off during the day as I did.

Usually when I arrived he was all smiles, but that day he seemed preoccupied and distracted. My heart sank. This might be just a bad day at work. Or it might be something more.

Then I remembered the news I had to give him, news that would turn his day around for sure, and I kept the spring in my step and my head held high as I crossed the bar to join him.

When I reached his table he stood up and pecked me on the cheek, and then sat down again as I settled opposite him. There was an empty bottle of beer and a glass with about an inch left in it on the table in front of him. He never usually drank before our daytime trysts. There wasn't time. I'd never seen him have beer before, either.

'We need to talk,' he said. 'Do you want a drink?'

'I'll have an apple juice,' I said. I wasn't much of a drinker at the best of times; Sean had cured me of that.

Mark gestured to the waiter – he was always confident with waiting staff – and asked for my juice. Then he sipped his beer and gazed into space as if trying to work out where to start.

Part of me wanted to tell him my news straight away. Then this frozen nothingness would be impossible and everything would be out in the open and this scene would be over. But I forced myself to wait.

Hold on. Don't show your hand just yet. Let him go first.

He sipped his drink. I loved the way he drank – how he could have just the one, and then stop. I loved it, but it was also slightly scary – that ability not to get sucked in, to say no, to keep a clear head and retain his dignity.

With Sean, nothing was ever cut and dried. He was the one who'd called time on our marriage, but even after we'd started the divorce proceedings he'd still talked about us getting back together, and me giving him a second chance.

But someone like Mark could just decide that it was time to cut you loose, and that would be it: over and out.

The waiter delivered my apple juice. When he'd gone Mark drew a deep breath. 'We need to tell them, Jenny.'

My mouth was dry: I drank some juice. I said, 'Are you sure?'

'I am,' he said. 'We should do it soon. I was thinking that I could take the three of you away somewhere. Maybe to France. They've never been abroad, have they? Make a treat of it. A special occasion.'

'But Ava's got exams.'

'A break would do her good though, wouldn't it? And her half-term holiday's coming up. We could do it then. South of France, long weekend. What do you say?'

He'd looked up Ava's half-term holiday dates. He knew she *had* such a thing as a half-term holiday. Sean had never got his head round that concept. It seemed to baffle him, and it wouldn't have occurred to him to look it up. He probably wouldn't even have been able to remember the name of the school she was at.

Under other circumstances, I might have tried to persuade Mark that we should wait. Let Ava get her exams out of the way. She'd worked so hard, been so conscientious. Last thing she needed was a bombshell family revelation right in the middle of it all.

But then, there were also some very good reasons why it shouldn't wait any longer than it already had. And also… it wasn't just about Ava.

'Ellie has some tests coming up, too. But those will be out of the way by then,' I said. 'Anyway, we'll have to ask them.'

He raised an eyebrow. 'Ava will want to come, Jenny,' he said. 'You know she will. She's so desperate to live a different kind of life.'

And even though I was slightly wounded by this, I had to admit that he was right.

'And she's doing French, isn't she? For her GCSEs? And she's never been to France? Well, better late than never.'

I said, 'There would be passports and things to sort out.'

'Oh, don't worry about all that. You can actually do it pretty quickly if you need to.'

'I suppose.'

'I'd like to tell Ava first. I think I'll know when it's the right moment. And then you could explain it all to Ellie.'

'Don't you think we should sit down with both of them, all four of us together?'

He pulled a face. 'Really? I can't say that's how I've imagined it.'

'But we don't want either of them to feel left out of anything,' I pointed out. 'And they both need to know. We have to face this as a family, together. We have to start as we mean to go on.'

'You'll be inviting Sean along next,' he said, with a cold look that was almost a rebuke. Then he held up his hands. 'OK, I'm sorry, I shouldn't have said that. I'm just nervous about it. That's all.'

'I know. So am I. More than nervous. Terrified. But we have to tell them, and we have to do it right.'

'OK. If that's how you want to do it, that's how we'll do it. We'll sit them down and tell them together.' He interlocked his fingers and pushed his hands away from him, stretched out his arms and shoulders and exhaled. 'We'll go away in May, and when we come back, it'll be sorted. And there'll be nothing that Sean or anyone else can do about it.'

'Mark,' I said. 'Does *she* know?'

He finished his beer and put the empty glass back down. 'You mean Paula? You really don't need to worry about her. She doesn't want to have anything to do with me, remember? She was very clear about that. Anyway, how would she find out? Unless someone tells her, she's got no way of knowing. And I'm not about to fill her in. Apart from anything else, it's really nothing to do with her.'

'I suppose so. I guess… I just wondered how she would feel about it.'

'About what? About us being together?'

I sipped a little bit more apple juice.

Really, why hadn't he guessed? He was the one with the degree, the top-drawer education, the fancy job. How could anyone so intelligent and successful be so blind?

But then, he thought the biggest possible deal was what Ava and Ellie would think once they knew the truth. He'd forgotten that there might be something else to think about. Something that would change things for all of us just as fundamentally as the news we had just agreed to share with the girls. Maybe even more so.

I put my glass down carefully on the coaster on the glass-topped table. Whatever he said later, his first reaction wouldn't be a lie. I'd know straight away whether this was really what he wanted.

'I'm pregnant,' I told him.

His jaw dropped. He gazed at me in pure astonishment, and then in awe, and then he shot up out of his chair and rushed towards me, and I stood too and we embraced so tightly it was as if nothing and nobody would ever be able to come between us.

Right then, I felt myself turning into someone else: not the vamp in black silk underwear, but the carrier of children. The mother. The worker of Mark's little miracle: the woman he'd never, ever want to let go.

Chapter Eight

Paula

Months, seasons, then a whole year went by. Still nothing.

I didn't tell anybody we were trying. When I met my remaining childfree friends, we talked warily, each eyeing up what the other was drinking or not drinking. You couldn't make assumptions about anybody. We'd talk about jobs, holiday plans, moving house, other people we knew. If the friend was still single we talked about who she was dating. If the friend was in a settled relationship we talked about other things, apart from minor gripes about our other halves that could be used for comedy value. That was the real difference between being married (or equivalent) or not: the married did not discuss their private lives.

But it was a strain.

I didn't talk about it with Mark. I was waiting for the right time. I knew I had to choose carefully. Otherwise he'd just go into full-on defensive mode. He might even say he didn't want to carry on trying. I knew how afraid he was of having something wrong with him. It wasn't entirely surprising that he should feel that way. If there was one lesson his family history might have taught him, it was how vulnerable you were in the hands of doctors.

Understanding didn't make it easy. But like I said, I'm a slow-burn kind of person. Patient. Made for distances, not for sprinting. I'm the tortoise who gets there in the end, long after the hares have even forgotten there's a race going on.

It's petty of me, I know, but there's some satisfaction in that. Vindication. Showing the lot of them. *My goodness, it's her! She's still going!* Such terrific surprise. What did they expect? Didn't they realise that absolutely nothing was going to stop me from getting what I wanted? The right moment always presents itself eventually, whatever it is you're waiting for.

Mark always organised our holidays, and usually he booked places that were sleek and modern and sexy, but for our eleventh wedding anniversary he took me to a country house hotel near Oxford that was about as traditional and romantic as you could get.

We had an enormous four-poster bed in an oak-beamed room with mullioned windows and a view over an Elizabethan knot garden. I was very taken with it, and struck by the concession he'd made to my taste, which he usually disparaged. And that got me thinking: *Maybe here... maybe tonight could be my chance.*

The atmosphere of the place was dense and solemn with history – all creaky stairs and heavy drapes and shadowy corners – but it didn't have a dampening effect. We reacted to it by turning as skittish as a pair of teenagers. It was one of those nights when there's a kind of wildness in the air and you don't feel at all like yourself, the sensible, professional you who knows the last three debits that went out from your bank account and remembers your colleagues' birthdays and cleans out all your cupboards once a year.

After dinner we didn't even make it to the four-poster bed; we ended up making love on the floor in front of the fire.

That was the thing about Mark. The only time he ever really loosened up was when we were having sex. All that pent-up energy, that frustration, that uptightness: he let it all go. And I was the beneficiary. It was the one way we could always connect. It was like magic: it seemed to bring us back into focus, and made the minor irritations and fault-finding, the slow grind of compromises that made up day-to-day life, not matter.

If you want a satisfying lover, look no further than someone who has something to lose. Or who is afraid of what he might lose, which comes out as the same thing in the end. That's who Mark was: he went through life as if it would all go to pieces if he stopped concentrating for a minute, but every once in a while he let himself off the leash. And that was when you realised how much he was holding back.

He was the only lover I'd ever had. I'd never wanted anybody else. I couldn't imagine that anybody else could begin to match up. He'd had a few other girls, before we got together: 'Practice runs before I met you' was how he'd always described them. No one who mattered. We were both quite clear that there was nobody out there, nobody at all, who could hold a candle to the other.

But as we lay side by side on the hearth rug in our oh-so-romantic room in that country house hotel, I wasn't really thinking about him at all.

I was thinking about the baby I wanted. More than wanted: *had to have*. If I couldn't... If I didn't... That was an unbearable prospect. Truly unbearable. I knew it would drive me out of my mind.

He was naked, and I still had my dress on, unbuttoned to the waist and rolled up to my hips; there was a candle burning above the blocked-up fireplace and I knew I'd look good in the light. I propped myself up on one elbow and said, 'You know, once we've been trying for two years we could think about IVF.'

It was as if I'd broken a spell. He sat up straight away and gave me that look of his, the one I always dreaded: that cold, glassy, uncompromising look that was almost as if he wasn't really seeing me, as if I'd become someone it was necessary to keep his distance from. It was the kind of look you might see on the face of a judge about to pass sentence. It wasn't the way you want your husband to look at you ever, let alone just after sex when you're desperate to have his baby.

'I didn't realise you were keeping track of time like that. Or that you thought of making love as *trying*,' he said.

I sat up too. Suddenly I felt ridiculous. Not a sex goddess. Not a beloved wife. Barely even a woman.

I was a failure. *We* were a failure. And he couldn't even bring himself to talk about it.

'I just wonder whether it might be time to look into things,' I said. 'To rule out any potential problems. And it's easier to start with you than me.'

'I'm not getting into all of that. It either works or it doesn't. And you either want me or you don't. If you think you'll have better luck with someone else then go ahead and find him. But I won't be waiting for you, and I think you'll regret it.'

He stood up and went off to the bathroom, and I got up and lay down on the bed and cried.

I knew I'd have to pull myself together quickly. When he was like this, tears didn't move him: they just made him cold. After a while I forced myself to stop, and sat up and blew my nose and buttoned my dress. The shower was still running. I checked my reflection in the mirror on the old-fashioned dresser by the bed, wiped off my smudged eye make-up and brushed my hair, and lay down on the bed again.

When he came back he was wearing one of the hotel dressing-gowns and smelled of lemon-scented shower gel. He sat down next to me and put an awkward, consoling hand on my shoulder.

'I'm sorry,' he said. 'I just can't. I can't do it. I love you, Paula, and I don't want to lose you. But if it's going to be all that... test tubes and injections and God knows what... I don't think I can bear it.'

I could have tried to reason with him, to point out that it might be something that could be easily fixed, that it was foolish not to at least try and find out. But I didn't. Instead I straightened up and gave him my brightest smile.

'Let's just enjoy this weekend, shall we? Because right here, right now, I'm really happy to be with you.'

He put his arms round me and embraced me, and I felt him sighing in relief.

'It's going to be all right,' I told him, remembering the little girl I'd once imagined so vividly, who had seemed so real.

In a way, it didn't matter what I felt... If I wanted her, I had to keep Mark happy, had to keep him on board. I had to push all the bitterness down and stay sweet. I needed him to want me, because how else was I going to make it happen?

I suppose you could say that in a way I was deceiving him too. But I did it for love. For the future. For the child I wanted. And everything he did, right from the start, was for himself.

The next day we went to the Pitt Rivers Museum in Oxford and I touched an old black clay bottle, shaped like a little vase, that women two centuries before had sought out for good luck when they wanted to have children. Mark didn't see me; he was looking at something else.

I thought of the man I'd been in love with once, the colleague from my first job in publishing. The affair we'd never had. Not because I hadn't wanted to. At the time, I'd wanted him more than I'd ever wanted anything.

That man was now happily married with twins, and last time I'd seen him – in the street, by chance – I'd felt nothing for him. Next to nothing. A flicker. It had been the twins that caught my eye, side by side in the double buggy.

And then I thought of that little girl – my little girl – with such longing that it seemed impossible my wish wouldn't be granted.

Chapter Nine

Ellie

Mum never took us on holiday. She said that if all she could afford was a weekend in a soggy tent, what was the point? Might as well stay at home where at least it was dry. And so we were forever stuck in Kingston, which wasn't even proper London, just a suburban town with a shopping centre and too much traffic.

One time I'd started talking about how Bella Montie was going to Spain with her family and it wasn't fair that we never went anywhere, and Ava had given me such a look I'd shut up straight away. Later that night, in our room, she'd taken me to task: 'Don't you realise if Mum stops working she doesn't get paid? If she takes us somewhere to keep you happy, she'd spend the whole time worrying about how she couldn't really afford it. Is that what you want?' I had never mentioned the subject again.

Back in the days before Mum met Mark, she had been fond of telling us that she had *champagne tastes and beer money*. 'Your grandma used to say that,' she'd remind us. 'That line is your inheritance. And the way things are going, that'll probably be *all* you inherit.' Then Ava would give her that sly look that meant, *it doesn't matter because I'm going to make my fortune anyway.*

But since she'd started seeing Mark Mum's life was full of fancy things, and she didn't talk about champagne tastes and beer money any more. Luckily, I had a much better way of remembering Grandma than a few jokey words. Sometimes – and it was always a comfort – I could *feel* her.

Grandma had lived long enough to hold Ava but not long enough to see me. Still, I could pick up a strong but hazy sense of who she was. She lived on as a kind of golden glow, like the sun on a misty morning: heartening, but uncomfortable and possibly even dangerous to look at too directly.

We had a few photos of her, but they didn't seem to conjure her up anything like as powerfully as the sense of her I had in my own mind. Mum always said I had an overactive imagination, but this wasn't something I was making up: she was just *there*, and from time to time I knew it.

When I was younger I'd assumed that Mum could feel the golden glow that was Grandma in just the same way that I could, and that Ava could as well, but was too haughty to talk about it. But then, in the months since Mum had started seeing Mark and everything had started shifting in ways I didn't fully understand, it had occurred to me that maybe Mum felt more cut off from Grandma than I did. That maybe her Grandma was more like photos, a mixture of pictures of the past that were sometimes faded or black and white. This made me feel very sorry for her, because there was something so warm about Grandma and I liked to turn to her when I felt sad. Not in a having-a-conversation kind of way, or even a huggy way – you can't hug or chat to a golden glow, you just have to bask in it.

So I carried on not saying anything about Grandma to Mum. If she didn't have the same thing, it would have sounded weird and she might not have believed me. And if she *had* believed me it might have sounded like boasting, like I was making out I had some kind of special access. Or it could have scared her, as if I was some kind of spooky little kid out of a horror film.

I didn't say anything about the bad stuff I picked up from time to time because the bad stuff was too frightening to talk about and anyway, I couldn't be sure whether it had happened already, or was maybe going to happen, or even who it had happened to or would happen to.

Most of the time, the way the bad stuff came in was just a vague, ominous feeling – like the way the light changes when it's about to rain, and the air smells different. A waiting sort of feeling. I'd had those bad-weather feelings a few times that year. I didn't know if that was because I was getting older or because more of the kind of events that prompted them were happening around me. They didn't always come to anything – or maybe it was just that I didn't always get to find out whether they were right or not. I didn't ignore them, exactly, but also, there never seemed to be a lot I could do about them.

One of the nurses who lived upstairs had gone out one evening wearing a bright red shirt, and something about that red shirt had freaked me out and I'd known something bad was coming and then I'd found out a few weeks later that she'd been stabbed on her way home, and had left nursing and London and gone back to her family in Derbyshire.

Then there was Annie Waters, who I'd heard talking about her new horse at school. I'd felt a sudden, heavy sense of dread, followed by an equally sudden, raging headache that took hours to fade. Later on, we'd been told that she'd been thrown off that horse and hit her head, and they weren't sure whether she'd be able to walk again. She didn't come back to school, and I never found out what happened to her after that.

But honestly… what could I have said that would have stopped Annie, or the nurse upstairs?

Nothing. Nothing at all.

So what was the point of having these inklings of disaster? Maybe there *was* no point. In which case… it seemed like the best thing was to keep quiet and pretend they didn't exist.

After all, what about Mum and Ava? If I told them about the bad-weather feelings and they didn't believe me, it would hurt *me*… and if they did believe me, wouldn't it hurt *them*?

For me to be *living in a dreamworld* or *always with my nose in a book* or the other, slightly less kind things Ava sometimes said about me, was fine – not fine exactly, annoying or irritating, but not scary. But if I knew things I couldn't possibly know – well, that would be much harder for everybody to accept. Me included.

I decided not to say anything about Mark.

As time went on, I gradually became aware, on and off, of the cloud he seemed to trail around behind him. One day, out of the blue, it occurred to me what it might be. Guilt. A guilt he couldn't escape. But what on earth could he have done that he felt so bad about?

I watched and waited in case there would be something clearer, a sign it would actually be possible to act on. I kept on reading the books he'd given me, as if touching the leather covers he himself had handled might bring me closer to understanding what he might be capable of.

But nothing happened. When Mum said he was going to be taking all three of us to France I felt only excitement. Perfectly ordinary, common-or-garden excitement.

I preoccupied myself with the question of the clothes I might need. Ava was the same as me, maybe even worse. After a token show of fretting about revision for the GCSE exams she'd have to take when we came back, she seemed to see the trip as an opportunity to get a whole new wardrobe. Luckily, Mark seemed to be more than willing to pay for everything. It was a dream, really – so much money, so much shopping.

I stopped noticing the shadow Mark sometimes seemed to have; I even asked myself if it had ever really been there. Maybe it had faded. Or maybe I just couldn't see it any more.

The big day came closer: my first time on a plane, my first trip to France, my first journey overseas. Ava's too, though she was obviously embarrassed to have got to her age without ever flying, and wouldn't admit what a big deal it was.

The day before, when we were both in our bedroom packing, she accused me of going on about the holiday too much and stomped off in a huff. Totally unreasonable, because what else were you going to talk about when you were remembering your swimming costume and checking you had the right number of pairs of underpants? What else were you going to talk about when you were going to stay at the four-star Grand Hotel?

I managed to sleep all right, and then it was morning and our three new suitcases were waiting by the front door. Mum was checking all the plugs were unplugged and the windows were locked, and Ava was taking forever in the bathroom, like she thought she was about to get scouted to be a model or something.

Then the buzzer rang – it was Mark who'd got that fixed, having made sure he was in the flat for one of Mrs Elliott's inspections. She'd been rather more receptive to him saying it should be sorted than she'd ever been to Mum.

Mark came hurrying upstairs to help us bring the cases down and joked about what we must have packed to make them so heavy. Mum looked as if she couldn't quite believe her luck, to be jetting off on holiday with this man who loved her enough to take all of us away with him. And even Ava looked quite pleased with how life was treating her, for once.

She had clearly chosen her travelling outfit with care. She was wearing a strappy coral-coloured sundress that left most of her back and upper arms and chest exposed, and she looked very pretty in it and a lot older than sixteen. No, not just pretty, *sexy*, though that was a gross thing to have to think when you were looking at your sister. She certainly didn't look like a schoolgirl who lived in a tiny flat in a boring London suburb.

Mum was wearing a yellow shirt and pale blue trousers and she looked summery and fresh, and I looked as cute as I was ever going to in a flowery blue-and-purple top and skirt, but there was no doubt that out of the three of us, all decked out in our new outfits, Ava was the most attention-grabbing.

Mark looked different too, in a blue polo shirt and white trousers. Impractical clothes, but if you couldn't be impractical on holiday, when could you? He kissed Mum on the cheek and asked me if I was looking forward to flying for the first time. Then, without paying much attention to my reply, he turned to Ava and said, 'Have you got a cardigan or something you can put on? It might get quite cool on the plane.'

'Obviously I have,' Ava said. 'I'm not stupid.'

Mark didn't look annoyed with her for being rude. He seemed hurt, but resigned. Like he was prepared to put up with pretty much anything from her. Almost as if he deserved to be rebuffed.

And there it was, that slight uneasiness I'd picked up about him before, that might or might not be guilt. Something he carried round with him that he was far from comfortable with.

'Just thought I'd mention it, especially as you haven't flown before,' he said.

He picked up Mum's case and reached for the next biggest, which was Ava's, but she beat him to it.

'I'll take it,' she said.

Mark let her, but turned to Mum and said warningly, 'Don't lift a finger. I'll be back in a sec.'

Ava and Mark went off down the stairs to the taxi. Mum suddenly went over to the kitchen sink and leaned over it as if she was about to be sick. I said, 'Are you all right, Mum?' but she ignored me.

When she straightened up she was very pale, almost greenish, and her skin was beaded with tiny drops of sweat.

'I'm not feeling too good,' she said.

'Are you going to be all right on the journey?'

'I don't know.'

'Have you told Mark?'

'Oh, yeah. He knows. Don't worry, Ellie, I'm sure it'll pass. It's not going to stop me going.'

I was so relieved by this I didn't question it. At that stage, the very worst thing I could imagine was us not being able to go on that holiday because Mum was ill. It didn't occur to me to wonder what was wrong with her, or what it might mean for the rest of us if it was something she couldn't shake off.

On the plane I read about a ghost.

Mark had offered to buy us all magazines, a luxury that Mum wouldn't normally have considered. Ava had said no, typical Ava being awkward. It seemed like she was still being weird about accepting gifts from Mark, even though he'd paid for everything she was wearing. Mum had picked out a glossy fashion magazine with an amazing picture on the front of a very tall, very elegant model in a turban and a short silver chain-mail dress, walking barefoot on a beach with a tiger on a leash. But she wasn't reading it. She was sound asleep. I couldn't see her – she was sitting in front of me – but I could hear her: soon after take-off she'd started snoring.

Ava was in the windowseat on my right, staring sullenly out at the view of clouds over the English Channel. I didn't know why she didn't just plug herself into her earphones and listen to her music, which was what she usually did if she wanted to shut everyone out. It was like she was determined to be bored.

I had just started *Wuthering Heights* – one of Mark's red books. It was sort of hard going, but I loved it even if I didn't understand it all, and I was so proud of myself for reading it that there was no way I was going to give up. Besides, I wanted everyone to notice it. Maybe eventually they'd take me seriously, for a change.

I was just at the part of the story where Lockwood settles down in his room at Wuthering Heights for the night, and a little hand comes in at the window and a voice pleads to be let in.

Lockwood was terrified, and desperate to shut out whatever it was, and he brought the window down so hard on that little hand that he drew blood. It was exactly as if it wasn't a ghost at all, but a real girl, begging to be allowed to come out of the cold.

If it had been a traditional ghostly hand, a wisp of white that wasn't really there, it wouldn't have bothered me nearly so much. As it was, it made me feel sick.

I looked away from the book, past Ava to the window. No ghosts up here, and the windows couldn't be opened anyway. Planes were never haunted, were they? Much too modern. You wanted an old house for that kind of thing. A place that was warped and crooked and badly maintained, with windows that didn't shut easily and gaps where things could get in.

For a moment I saw it – just as you see the landscape below you when you're flying and the clouds part.

There *was* something. Someone. Someone Mark didn't *want* anything to do with, but couldn't or hadn't got rid of. Did he want to? Or did he want to hang on? I couldn't tell.

And then the moment passed. Ava wasn't about to talk to me and we had at least an hour left to go.

I went back to *Wuthering Heights*. There was a load of other stuff going on with Hareton and Heathcliff and all sorts of people who were nasty to each other and hard to keep track of, but that little ghost girl scratching at the glass didn't turn up again, and for that I was grateful.

Predictably, the French official who checked our passports eyed Ava up – he tried not to be obvious about it, but I noticed it all the same. Honestly, *men* – they were like animals. Dogs with their tongues hanging out. When Ava was around, anyway, though she did her usual frosty thing of behaving like it was all beneath her.

I didn't realise how warm it was till we stepped out of the airport. Then – whoosh! It was like being drenched. The air was so still and heavy, we might as well have been walking through hot water.

Ava slipped off her cardigan and walked on looking proud and indifferent, as if she was determined not to notice any attention people might pay her. It occurred to me that in some ways it would be a disadvantage to be so conspicuous. There was something to be said for being comparatively invisible, even though I often wished I wasn't.

A series of wonderful surprises followed, which Ava pretended to take in her stride and Mum and I were thrilled by.

First there was the hire car, a long flashy sporty white thing and air-conditioned, so Ava got goosebumps and had to put her cardigan on again. Then there were the glimpses of the sea from the road – so blue, it was obviously far from home. And finally there was the Grand Hotel itself, with its name spelt out in gold above the glass revolving door, and pillars to either side and an attendant with a cap and braid on his uniform.

I had spent a lot of time poring over the brochure Mark had given us, and the place didn't disappoint. Inside the lobby there was a vast reception desk, polished to a glasslike sheen, with clocks telling the time all around the world mounted on the wall behind it, and uniformed staff standing round just waiting to help us.

We went up to the room Mum and Mark were going to be sharing – Ava and I were next door – and it had a balcony with a sea view and the thickest carpet in the world and the biggest bed. Which was a strange and intimidating sight. It was just enormous, and so official, somehow. It announced that Mum and Mark were together the same way that thrones and crowns announce a king and queen.

I knew all about sex – they'd told us about it in school, but I'd already known, anyway – and I had assumed that Mum and Mark were doing it, and had decided that the best thing to do with this knowledge was to ignore it. Hard to ignore a bed that size, though. It wasn't the kind of thing you could turn a blind eye to.

When I was a bit younger, I'd written several stories that sounded rather racy, because the heroines kept going down the corridors at night into the rooms of the men they liked and sleeping with them. That was before I knew the facts of life, and I thought sleeping with someone meant just that: dozing off in their arms, and waking up with them. I'd believed that was the closest thing men and women could do, the glue that kept marriages together, and an act so important that doing it on the sly was a scandal.

How silly and naïve I had been! And yet I hadn't been entirely wrong. It did seem a big deal that Mum and Mark were going to be sharing a bed, when we'd never known them to before. Maybe it was going to be a test of whether they really liked each other. Or maybe it was a test for me and Ava, to see how we'd adjust.

The bellboy lifted Mum's and Mark's cases up onto the bed, and Mark tipped him with admirable smoothness, as if confident that he had exactly the right amount of money to give. The bellboy went out and Mum opened her case and Mark said, 'I can unpack if you don't feel up to it.'

'No, no, I'm fine,' she said, but she didn't quite look it.

'You should have a nap before dinner,' Mark said. He turned to Ava. 'How about we meet you on the balcony at six? We can have a drink and then go down for dinner. Look round the hotel if you want, but make sure you take Ellie. Stick together. We don't want her getting lost.'

'Of course I'll look after her,' Ava said. 'You don't need to tell me to. We'll see you at six.'

I followed her to our room next door, where she promptly bagged the best bed, the one nearest the French windows that opened onto the balcony. I let her get her way; it was rarely worth fighting Ava once she'd set her heart on something, unless you really, really wanted it. Then I left her lying there in the sunlight and went off to have a bath.

The bathroom was amazing. It was really clean, with no mould at all, and it was stocked with little bottles of shampoo and body cream and the fluffiest, whitest towels and dressing-gowns you could imagine. I filled the bath very full and had a long soak and lost track of time. When I finally emerged my skin was pink and my fingers and toes were wrinkly like a newborn baby's, and I felt all scented and fancy and like I could get used to this.

Ava was still lying on her back on her bed and looked as if she hadn't moved, but when I came closer I saw that she had her earphones in. She looked up at me and opened her eyes and smiled. I wished she could look like that all the time, as if she wasn't at all angry with anybody.

'The bathroom's very nice,' I said.

She frowned, sat up, took one earphone out, asked me to repeat myself. Then she said, 'So it should be. This little trip must be costing Mark the earth.'

'Shouldn't you start getting ready?'

'In a minute. You might be all keen to play happy families, but I'm not.'

She put the earphone back in and sank back down onto the bed.

'You know, if you're not careful Mark's really going to end up hating you,' I said, thinking that she either wouldn't hear me or would pretend she hadn't.

'He won't,' she said without opening her eyes.

'How can you be so sure?'

She sat up again and took out both earphones. She looked really irritated now. 'Because he can't afford to.'

'Why not?'

'Because they have news for us, dummy. Big news. Or little news, depending how you look at it. They're probably going to tell us tonight.'

'What are you talking about?'

'You think you're so smart. You figure it out.'

She put her phone and earphones down on the bedside table – however annoyed she got, she was always careful with her phone

– and stalked off to the bathroom. The door shut firmly behind her. Not a slam, but a warning. The lock clicked into place.

Why did I have no idea what she was talking about? Why did I never know anything… until it was too late?

I went over to the wardrobe to pick out an outfit for that evening's meal. It was going to be three courses in the hotel restaurant, which I'd admired in the brochure: it had rose-coloured walls and fancy lights, and round, tablecloth-covered tables. I was a bit apprehensive, but mostly I was excited. Why did Ava have to go and spoil things? And why did she always have to be so superior?

Big news or little news. It didn't sound like bad news, anyway.

Maybe it wasn't Mark who was going to end up hating her. Grown-ups didn't hate children, anyway, they were past that kind of thing. It was children who hated grown-ups. Or each other. And Ava was still young enough to count as a child, whatever airs she might give herself.

Maybe the person who was really going to end up hating Ava was me.

Chapter Ten

Ava

Even though I was pretty confident that I'd figured out what was going on, I was much less sure about when they were going to tell us. Left to herself Mum would probably have broken the news fairly quickly, but Mum with Mark was a different ball game. They'd have to agree. Mum wasn't running the show any more, and she wouldn't want to upset him, especially not now. Whatever he felt would be the best timing of the announcement, she'd probably go with.

In the end, they told us that first evening on the balcony.

Mum was waiting out there when we arrived. She was leaning against the balcony and looking out at the view, and she was wearing a blue dress I hadn't seen before: it was a loose but flattering cut and made her look slim, and I wondered whether I'd got it wrong. She really did look pretty good for a woman with two kids who worked all hours and spent them on her feet.

Then I saw the way Mark looked at her – really soppy, and really, really pleased with himself – and I decided I had it right after all.

They didn't launch straight into it. First of all Mark fussed around getting us drinks. Ellie had some lemonade from their mini-bar fridge, and I had some of the half-bottle of white wine Mark had ordered from room service. Dad never drank white if he could help it, but presumably Mark wasn't bothered by its slightly effeminate connotations. Or maybe he just didn't want any stains on the fresh clothes he'd put on.

Mark checked with Mum before pouring it for me and she agreed to it as if the risk of me following in Dad's footsteps and developing an appetite for the stuff was the least of her worries. Which was right, in my view. I liked the idea of pacing myself. A bit like Mark, actually. Dad would've polished off that half-bottle pretty much as soon as you could say swallow, whatever colour the wine was. But Mark still had plenty left for me.

Mum was drinking iced water. No surprise there. I glanced at Ellie to see if she was taking any of this in. She was frowning slightly as if she wasn't too sure about things, but it didn't look to me like she'd realised what was going on yet. Sooner or later she was in for a shock.

Well, I had tried to warn her. Maybe I should have told her what I thought, but how could I when I didn't know for sure?

'To us,' Mark said, proposing a toast, and we all clinked glasses. 'To the holidays.' Then: 'Girls, we have some news to tell both of you.'

OK. This was it. I braced myself. Mark put his arm round Mum and pulled her in close. I'd have been irritated if he had done that to me. Well, maybe not if I was in love with him. Mum didn't seem annoyed. She looked overwhelmed and hopeful. Like she might be about to cry the way people do when they win something big and it catches them by surprise.

'We're having a baby,' Mum said.

I wondered if they'd rehearsed it. The double act: Mark introducing the topic, Mum following up. There was a short, very intense silence, during which I was mainly conscious of Mark watching me as if I was the only one who really mattered, as if all this had somehow been done for my benefit. Then Ellie squealed and launched herself forward into Mum's arms, and Mark withdrew his arm from Mum's shoulders and carried on watching me.

Ellie buried her face in Mum's chest and Mum embraced her fondly, but as if there was something else going on that was likely to require her attention at any moment. Perhaps this was how it was going to be from now on. Maybe that was how we would lose her:

not tragically, not with any drama, but because she would always be distracted. The new baby would inevitably take over and we, who were old enough to more or less look after ourselves, would fade into the background.

Mark was *still* watching me. It was too much. It made me want to shout at him. Why did he have to be so intense about it? Did he want me to fall over myself to accept him, like *Oh please won't you be my daddy?* If that was what he expected he could forget it. I'd got by for years without a dad around, and I certainly didn't need a replacement.

Anyway, surely he'd stop caring now he was having a baby of his own.

Ellie withdrew and said, 'It is all right to hug you, isn't it, Mum?'

'Oh, yes,' Mum said, and stroked her hair – if she had tried that on me, I'd have told her to keep her hands to herself. But then, she would probably have known better than to try. 'Of course it is,' Mum went on. 'You can hug me as much as you like. You won't hurt the baby. It's safe.'

And then she looked up at me and her expression was proud and pleading all at once, and I knew she wanted me to hug her too and say that it was great news and congratulations to them both.

Which would have been a lie.

It *wasn't* great news. Apart from the mysterious fling or flirtation or whatever it was that had happened between them when they'd first met, Mum and Mark had only been together for about five minutes, and now they were going to be parents, which was running before you could walk with a little new human life added into the mix. Not the best idea.

And as for congratulations… who did they think they were trying to kid? They'd either forgotten to use contraception or had decided not to bother, which was exactly the kind of behaviour that people my age were always being warned against.

But anyway, I went over to her and put my arm stiffly around her shoulders, and the three of us stood there in a little huddle with Mark to one side… *still* watching me.

'Congratulations,' I said. 'When's it due?'

'Oh… some time in December.'

'A Christmas baby?' I asked.

'A bit before that.'

'Is it going to be a girl, or a boy?'

'What a lot of questions,' Mum said, and I knew I'd wounded her with my lack of enthusiasm. But really… did she expect me to fake something I didn't feel? I'd only just found out this baby was going to exist. Maybe when it had actually arrived I'd figure out how to feel fond of it, but for now it was just a tiny party crasher.

'It's a boy,' Ellie said straight away.

'We don't actually know,' Mum corrected her. 'We thought it was time to tell you two, but it's still early days and we need to keep it to ourselves for now. So don't go telling people at school or anything.'

'It's not exactly the kind of thing we talk about,' I pointed out.

Mum ignored me and carried on. 'That's why I've been feeling a bit off-colour lately, but hopefully all that will stop soon and I'll be a bit more back to normal.'

'No, you won't,' I said, withdrawing my arm. 'You're going to be pregnant, and then you're going to have a baby. That's a whole new kind of normal. So are we going to move? Because it doesn't seem like there's a whole lot of spare room in the flat. Unless you're going to keep Junior in a shoebox under the bed.'

Mum's reaction to this was one of pure, almost comic horror. *How can you be so cold?* But Mark stepped in before she could reproach me.

'There are a couple of options,' he said, 'which we want to discuss with both of you. We want you to feel that your views are being taken into account. That you're part of this whole thing. But maybe it's a bit early to get into all of that just now.'

I folded my arms. 'I don't think it is. I have exams to do. Important exams. I shouldn't even be here. I should be back home, revising. And then I'm going to sixth-form college. I need to know if this is going to affect all that.'

Mum had her arms round Ellie, as if soothing her, and was gazing across at the view of the sea. Now that Mark had intervened she appeared to have given up on the whole conversation, and was paying no attention to me at all.

'I have a future, too, you know,' I said.

'Believe me, the last thing anyone wants is for this to disrupt your education,' Mark said. 'That isn't going to happen, I promise you. All the changes are going to be for the better.'

I scowled at him. 'How can you say that when you can't even tell me where we're going to live?'

'Because I'm going to make sure it all works out for the best. For everyone.'

Suddenly Ellie piped up: 'Are you going to get married?'

That got Mum's attention. She didn't look at me, though. She looked at Mark, who was watching me again. His expression was almost pleading, as if he wanted to ask me for permission.

'Yes,' he said.

Ellie squealed. Literally. It was the most ridiculous sound of excitement I'd ever heard in my life.

She said, 'Can I be bridesmaid?'

'Of course you can,' Mum said. 'But it's not going to be a church wedding or anything like that. It's going to be very small and low-key.'

I could feel the fight starting to go out of me. There was nothing at all that I could begin to do about any of this. How I felt about it – and I wasn't sure how I felt about it – might make some difference to them, and even more difference to me. But it wouldn't *change* anything.

Mark was looking half hopeful, as if he thought I might suddenly start being nice to him. He didn't seem at all bothered about Ellie's response, but maybe that was because she'd made it so obvious she was thrilled.

I turned to Mum. 'Does Dad know about this?'

'Not yet,' Mum said. 'Nobody else does. We wanted you to be the first to know.'

'So your ex-wife is in the dark too, still,' I said to Mark. 'You only just got shot of her, didn't you? Whatever her name is. It's not like you ever mention her. It's like she never even existed.'

His eyes blazed and his mouth set in a hard line. Ooh, temper. I smirked at him to annoy him even more. He'd sent Dad reeling down the street dripping blood, wanting nothing more than to get away from us and seek out the haven of the nearest pub. He didn't deserve to have it all his own way.

I said, 'I take it she's not going to be invited?'

'Paula won't be coming to our wedding, no.'

'Are you sure she's not going to pop up when the vicar gets to "If anyone knows any just cause or legal impediment why these two should not be joined in holy matrimony, let him speak now or forever hold his peace?"'

Mark exhaled, attempted a smile. 'I think that was the longest sentence I've ever heard you say.'

'I'm doing *Jane Eyre* at GCSE, remember? The one where the guy has a first wife locked away in the attic?'

'Ava, stop it,' Ellie said. Then, to Mum: 'What kind of dress are you going to wear? Can I have something matching?'

And then the fight went out of me completely.

Ellie had a thing about weddings. She was obsessed, as only girls like us, girls from a broken home, could be. The ones who loved the idea of the big day in white were always the ones whose parents hated each other, in my experience; I was an exception.

When Ellie was little she'd drawn endless pictures of wedding dresses, each one more ornate than the last. They'd been great big tiered creations like something from the court of Marie Antoinette, with bows and frills and flowery embroidery, painstakingly coloured in around the white of the blank page. She'd asked for the same bedtime story night after night: it was about a little girl who got to be a bridesmaid and was naughty and spoiled her gloves, and was rescued at the last minute when somebody gave her a spare pair. *Sit still and look nice*, was the moral of the story.

I was always the one who had to read it to her, while Mum sorted out her appointments diary and checked her supplies and so on. Eventually I got so sick of it I said she couldn't have it any more, and made her choose something else.

'As long as you don't expect me to be a sodding bridesmaid,' I grumbled.

Mum hugged Ellie close again, as if she was embracing her all the more tightly because I was being so difficult, such a *teenager*. But why should I be anything else?

Mark exhaled. The battle was over before it had even begun: I'd capitulated. He turned to Mum and said, 'I think we should leave it there for now, don't you?'

She hesitated. Suddenly it struck me that she looked exhausted. It must have taken it out of her, all this. Figuring out how to tell us. Worrying about it. I felt bad for not having made it easier for her.

'There'll be plenty of other chances to talk about things,' Mark said. 'Everything else will keep. Let's finish our drinks and go down to dinner.'

She met his eyes, and that was when I realised for the first time how serious this was. She trusted him. In some way that I didn't fully understand, she'd given herself up to him. Was this love? Was this what love looked like? My mum, who had always been so independent, was willing to put her life in this man's hands.

'All right,' she said.

'Good. You look a little bit pale, and it's been a long day. I expect Junior needs feeding.'

I sipped my wine. *Junior!* Probably he was going to talk to Mum's tummy and all that rubbish. Or already did. Which was really just a way of being smug about having got her pregnant.

Where could they possibly have done it? They must have done it *somewhere*. They went on dates all the time, but it wasn't like he ever slept over. Mum had said he had a house in the countryside somewhere, near Oxford, but that was miles from London.

Probably he'd impregnated her on the back seat of the Jag. Yeah, right on those leather seats that Ellie and I had to sit on whenever he drove us around.

Welcome to the world, Junior. What a family. Still, there were only two years to go and I'd be eighteen and adult, and out of it. I could move to the other side of the world if I wanted, or at least to the other side of the country. I would be a free agent.

Maybe in a way this was a good thing: if Mum had a husband and a new baby, it would be that much easier for me to walk away.

And yet… when it came down to it, how could I leave her? Now she was on the verge of having a new life of her own, I was forced to recognise just how much of a wrench it would be to be parted from her.

Dinner that night was challenging, to say the least. It wasn't just the situation, it was the setting. All around us there were French people seriously eating, mesdames and messieurs and a few impeccably behaved children, and there were waiters with snowy-white shirts and spotless dark uniforms hurrying about with silver plates and bottles of red wine, as if they were all on a mission of extreme but secret importance.

The food looked beautiful, though. For my starter I had melon, which came with a pool of blood-red port in the middle, where the seeds had been scooped out. 'You'll get drunk,' Ellie said accusingly, and I scowled at her to make her shut up. Mark had already poured me another glass of wine to follow on from the one I'd had on the balcony, and Mum hadn't raised any objections.

Both of them were probably too preoccupied to keep count of how much I'd had. If ever there was an occasion to take the edge off by getting slightly tipsy, this was surely it.

I was half expecting Mum to get out her phone and start taking pictures the way she'd done when Mark took us out for the first time back home in England, but she didn't. Her Facebook page had been positively enigmatic over the last month or so. Since she'd realised she was pregnant, maybe? Well, sooner or later she'd have a big double announcement to make. *I'm getting married. I'm having a baby.* And everyone would say, *Congratulations! I thought you'd been quiet lately, and now I know why!*

After the melon I had *crevettes*, whole prawns in their shells, which I had no idea how to eat. Mark showed me, which he loved doing, obviously. *Teach me, Mark. Show me what to do.* Why was I being so mean to him, anyway? The wine seemed to make it easier to be nice. Everything was both more vivid and more unreal than usual, and nothing seemed to matter quite so much any more: the colours and textures had taken over.

Maybe this was what it was like for Dad; maybe this was exactly what he'd been seeking out all those times – this mix of a rush and being out of it.

The soft light of the electric chandeliers, the blue shade of Mum's dress, the pile of taken-apart prawns on my plate, with their insect-like folded legs and little jelly eyes and pink translucent shells... it was all an adventure, so much brighter and more glamorous than my life had been up to that point, and at the same time it seemed like a dream, as if it could all vanish in an instant.

Mark looked very pleased with himself, and more so as the evening went on. The proud father-to-be. Everything was going his way, wasn't it? Mum was looking at him adoringly, and Ellie was thrilled, and even I was being less objectionable than usual. The new softer, sweeter, slightly drunker, more daughterly me.

At the end of the meal Mum asked for a herbal tea and I had a decaffeinated coffee, which was probably not a very French choice – France so far was all about things being the strongest possible version of themselves, the reddest wine, the crustiest bread, the bluest sea and sky, nothing pale or weak or wishy-washy like the colours and flavours back home. But so what if the French waiter thought I was unsophisticated and bland and English? I didn't want anything that was going to wake me up. I was up for a big long sleep, and not having to think about anything for a bit.

My coffee came with a little round chocolate wrapped in green foil, and I gave it to Ellie, who hadn't ordered anything.

'You two get along pretty well, don't you?' Mark said.

'Well, I wouldn't go *that* far,' I said as Ellie peeled the foil off the chocolate and popped it in her mouth.

She ate it slowly and thoughtfully, then delivered her verdict: 'You're probably not the *worst* big sister it's possible to have.'

'It would help if we didn't share a room,' I said.

'Well, we should be able to do something about that,' Mark said. 'But really, I'd say you cope with it pretty well. I mean, it's not as if you're at each other's throats.'

'You sound like you expect siblings not to get on,' I said to Mark.

'Well, they don't always, do they? From what I can tell.' He glanced at Mum. 'Your mother's a case in point.'

'Amanda and I are just very different,' Mum said.

She'd fallen out with our aunt Amanda after Grandma's funeral, but didn't like to talk about it. Perhaps that was what prompted Ellie to pipe up and ask Mark, 'Do you have a brother or sister?'

'No. I don't have any relatives. Apart from my mother.'

Ellie's face took on that strange look she had sometimes, like someone gazing at weather that none of the rest of us could see. In the olden days they'd said that people who weren't quite right in the head were *touched*. That was how Ellie looked: touched.

She said, out of the blue, 'They hurt her.'

There was silence round the table. Mark stared first at Ellie, then at Mum, who raised her hands in a gesture of hopelessness. He cleared his throat. 'Ellie, nobody hurt my mother. Nobody would dare.'

I said, 'When are we going to meet her?'

'Soon, I hope,' Mark said. He attempted a smile; it came across as lukewarm. 'She's already heard a lot about you all.'

I said, 'Does she know you're getting married?'

'Not yet,' Mum told us. 'Like I said, we wanted to tell you girls first.'

The waiter arrived with the Armagnac Mark had ordered, a large dose of thick amber fluid in a large balloon-shaped glass. I could smell it from where I was sitting. A memory came to me of Dad holding a tumbler of the same stuff in one of the flats he'd lived in, at Christmas-time. He'd held it up so that I could see the thin streaks of clear fluid, like water but thicker, clinging to the sides of the glass.

They call them tears, he'd said. *The tears of the Armagnac.*

He'd said it admiringly, as you might if you were talking about someone or something you were in awe of. It was as if the Armagnac was a person, and a powerful one – one of those terrifying rulers from the olden days, fond of feasting and also of abruptly ordering executions, then regretting his actions when it was too late.

'I've never tasted Armagnac,' I said to Mark.

'You probably wouldn't like it. You're a bit too young for it,' he said.

'I suppose.'

He regarded me as if I'd asked for a favour and he wasn't sure whether or not to grant it. Then he reached across and picked out a sugar cube from the pot the waiter had brought with my coffee. He dunked it into the Armagnac and then held it out to me.

'The French called this *faire un canard*,' he said. 'Which means "to make a duck". I've no idea why.'

I took it and popped it in my mouth. It was like nothing else I'd ever tasted: so strong, so sweet, so... *wrong*.

Wrong or not, I sucked it and crunched it and swallowed it all down.

Part of me wanted to say, *What do you think you're doing? Don't you know I'm the daughter of an alcoholic? Hasn't it occurred to you that I might be the teensiest bit susceptible?*

But then, I hadn't even hesitated about taking it, and I knew as well as anybody where too many *canards* might lead. Perhaps it was a fitting tribute. *See, Dad, I'm not betraying you. This is my way of remembering.*

When we had finished Mum yawned and stretched and said, 'How lovely that we can just walk away and leave somebody else to do the tidying up, and go off to bed.'

'*I* don't want to go to bed,' I objected. 'It's much too early. You're forgetting the time difference.'

Mum checked her watch. 'It's not *that* early. Ellie would usually be asleep by now.'

'Yes, but Ellie's *eleven*. I don't normally go to bed at the same time as her, so why should I have to when we're on holiday? It's not like I'm going to wake her up when I go in. Unless she has a nightmare, she can snore her way through pretty much anything.'

Ellie frowned. 'That's mean.'

'Yeah, and it's also true. Look – there's a bar here, right? What if Ellie goes to bed, and the rest of us go for a drink? Just one drink. That wouldn't hurt, would it?'

A look passed between Mum and Mark – a look I couldn't quite read.

'OK,' Mum said. 'I'll take Ellie up to bed, and you can go to the bar with Mark and I'll come down and join you once Ellie's settled. You'd better have a mocktail, though, something non-alcoholic.'

I shrugged. I didn't want anyone thinking that I'd only wanted
to go to the bar so I could have another drink, as if the *canard* had
whetted my appetite, as if I was already on the slippery downward
slope to turning out like Dad. It wasn't true, anyway. I just wanted
to have some fun, for once. Was that such a crime? I was on holiday,
in France, and it wasn't as if my everyday life back home was full
of adventures and treats, so why shouldn't I make the most of it?

'A mocktail would be fine,' I said.

'All right, fine,' Mark said. 'We'll go to the bar, have a nightcap.'

The waiter arrived to start clearing our table, and Mum and
Mark exchanged unreadable glances again.

'Come on then, Ellie, let's get you to bed. It's been a long day,'
Mum said.

She leaned forward to kiss Mark – on the cheek, not the mouth
– a quick, darting kiss, accompanied by a tight squeeze of his arm.

'I won't be long,' she told him, getting to her feet. 'You can order
me a mocktail, too.'

Mark said he would, and Ellie reluctantly stood too and went off
with Mum. Just before they reached the exit she glanced back over
her shoulder at us; she looked resigned and resentful and fearful
all at the same time.

And then they were gone, and it was just me and Mark sitting
at a suddenly empty table.

It might have felt awkward if the wine and the *canard* hadn't
taken the edge off everything. As it was, I felt able to say something
close to what was on my mind.

'I hope we're going to manage to find something to say to each
other till Mum gets back.'

He looked startled. 'I should think we'll manage.'

We stood at exactly the same time and made our way out of the
restaurant together.

*

The bar was flashy and busy – lots of purple velvet plush, black lacquered furniture and mirrors. There was a piano player in a dinner suit playing a baby grand on a raised dais in one corner – soft, old-fashioned jazz, cheerful and melancholy at the same time. Everybody else looked right at home and elegant and expensive, like they spent their whole lives lounging round in places like this, sipping from frosted glasses and laughing idly at nothing in particular.

I couldn't see anywhere to sit. If I'd been on my own I would have walked right out again. But Mark spotted an empty booth near the piano and homed in on it. As I followed him I was aware of people lazily, appraisingly turning towards me. The piano player – some old man, or old-ish, anyway – raised his head and gave me an ironic smile as I went by.

Maybe this was what all bars were like – people eyeing each other up, checking out newcomers like kids at a recreation ground keeping tabs on who was coming in. Not even with any serious intention, more the way you would scroll past images on a screen, to keep yourself entertained and pass the time.

Or maybe this was just what *French* bars were like. I didn't have a lot to compare it to. I'd been to the Dog and Duck down the end of our road for a lemonade and salt and vinegar crisps, but that was about it.

We sat down and I studied the drinks menu and picked out mocktails for me and Mum. Then Mark went off to the bar to order them and I stretched and exhaled and tried to relax and look around a little.

The piano player came to the end of something and ran his hands over the keyboard with a little flourish. How great it would feel, to be able to do that – to be so confident, for your hands to work away as if you didn't even have to think about what you were doing. Then he looked up and caught my eye.

He wasn't as ancient as I'd thought at first. Maybe it was hard for him to gauge how old I was, too. It didn't seem as though he realised I was only sixteen and barely legal – though most of my peers had been busy flouting the laws around what you could and couldn't do at certain ages since they were at least fourteen.

I was the first to look away, but he'd made such an impression on me that even when I was just looking down at the table it was like I was still taking him in.

He had dark eyes and dark hair, turning silver at the temples, and he was playing that piano like he was doing the rest of us a favour, not like he was being paid to do it. I was pretty sure men like that didn't exist in England. An English piano player would have been pale and hungry-looking and harassed, as if he was waiting for someone to come over and ask him to play 'Chopsticks'.

My reflection in the mirror on the other side of the wall looked flushed and slightly dishevelled. But not bad, not bad at all. The lighting in the bar emphasised my cheekbones: if I tilted my head there were deep shadows underneath them. It brightened my hair and eyes, too – I looked blonder than usual, and bluer-eyed. It was like me with a filter on. A filter composed of the Grand Hotel and *crevettes* and Armagnac and being hundreds of miles south of home.

The piano player started his next tune. He caught my eye again and slowly, deliberately bowed his head, as if in tribute.

Mark reappeared with our drinks on a tray, and set them down on the table. I raised my glass to him and said, 'Here's to the new arrival.'

He looked delighted. 'Yes! To new beginnings.'

We clinked glasses. I said, 'Is that Armagnac again?'

'It is.'

'With the tears.'

'Yes, with the tears.'

The piano kept playing – light and fast, rising and falling, soft on the harmonies but with a strong touch on the melody. Mark swallowed a couple of mouthfuls of Armagnac and set down his glass, and I sipped my cocktail. He said, 'Is it good?'

'Yeah, it is. It's delicious. Thank you.'

He beamed. 'Good. You're welcome. What do you think of France so far?'

'Oh, it's amazing.' Was it really me, enthusing like that? With Mark? He looked as surprised as I was. 'The hotel's gorgeous. It's quite a treat.'

'That's what I thought,' he said. 'I wanted to take you all somewhere special.'

'That's nice of you, but you know what, you don't have to bribe me and Ellie into liking you. If you're good to Mum and the new baby and halfway decent to us, I should think we'll manage to accept you.'

'I hope so,' he said. 'It matters to me what you think. Probably more than you realise.'

'I do realise,' I said slowly. 'What I don't really understand is why.'

He pulled a face and pressed his lips together, as if he wanted to speak and couldn't let himself. It was uncomfortable to look at him. The music rose to a climax and ebbed away, and I turned away from Mark and caught sight of my reflection in the mirror again and saw him there beside me.

Two fair-haired, blue-eyed, not bad-looking people.

From the piano player's perspective… what would we look like?

That was when I saw it. And then I turned to Mark and said it.

'You're my father. Aren't you?'

He gazed at me. I couldn't hear the piano music any more. It was if no one else was there at all.

'You have no idea how hard this has been for me,' he said. 'I wanted to tell you before. I wasn't sure how you'd react.'

He let out a half-suppressed sob and put his head in his hands.

I couldn't move. I was incapable of reassuring or comforting him. It wasn't just the music and the people around us in the bar who had vanished. It was everything I thought I'd known, everything I'd believed about myself.

Because if Dad wasn't really my dad – if that had been a lie all along – what else might be untrue?

After what seemed like a long time Mark raised his head and looked at me again. His eyes were slightly wet, but he wasn't crying. Neither was I. Should we have cried, or hugged? I still couldn't move.

'I'm not meant to tell you,' he said. 'Your mother wanted us to sit down and talk about it all together. She'll be furious with me.'

'Well, you didn't tell me. I guessed.'

Why hadn't I realised before? Why hadn't I guessed the minute I met him? But then, it would never have occurred to me that Mum would lie to me for so long about something so important. Or that Dad would.

'Does Dad know?'

Mark winced. He opened his mouth as if he was about to protest, then thought better of it.

'Sean does know. Yes.'

'And he knew all along?'

'Yes. He knew all along.'

'So what happened? You were married when you met Mum… and then when she got pregnant, I guess you didn't want to know?'

'She didn't tell me,' Mark said. 'I didn't find out till much later.'

'You're not Ellie's dad, are you?'

'No.'

'Well, that explains a lot.'

He frowned. 'Explains what?'

'Why you're not really that interested in her.'

'That's not fair. I've made every effort with Ellie.'

'Hardly. You've made a token effort. And Mum's probably had to remind you to do that.'

Suddenly he looked more angry than wounded. 'You shouldn't speak to me like that.'

'You don't have any right to tell me what to do.'

'I'm your father.'

I shook my head. 'As far as I'm concerned, you're just someone who showed up out of the blue.'

A shadow fell across the table: Mum, back from saying goodnight to Ellie. She said, 'What's going on?'

I got to my feet. Miraculously, now Mum was here I was able to move again.

'I know,' I said. 'Mark's worried you'll be angry with him, so just for the record, he didn't tell me. I guessed.'

Mum looked from me to Mark and back to me again. She looked so horrified I almost felt sorry for her.

'Ava, I was just trying to do what I thought was best at the time,' she said. 'I never would have wanted to hurt you. You girls are the most important thing in the world to me. You know that.'

'Yeah? Well, you've got a funny way of showing it.'

And with that I got up and walked away from them both.

She did get up to follow me, but only once I was already nearly at the door. I turned the handle and let myself out, and found myself in the hotel corridor, suddenly completely alone.

Chapter Eleven

Jenny

When I got out of the bar I couldn't see her anywhere.

She couldn't possibly have gone far…

Why hadn't I been quicker off the mark?

Stop. Think. I had to get this right.

This was sensible Ava, with her sound instinct for self-preservation. Who'd never had a boyfriend, or smoked, or got drunk on cider and been sick, or got up to any of the other foolish things I had done myself when I was around her age.

Ava, who didn't take risks.

She'd had a shock. A terrible shock. But she was still the same girl.

I hurried off up the stairs to the corridor where our rooms were, and caught sight of her with her keycard in her hand just as she was about to let herself in.

'Ava! Thank goodness. I thought you might have taken off somewhere.'

She hadn't gone out to wander round the streets, or walk in the moonlight by the beach. She wasn't about to fall victim to muggers or worse. This was Ava, and she'd responded to the news that Mark was her father by leaving the bar and going off to bed. In spite of the furious coldness of the look she was giving me, I could have cried with relief.

'I don't want to talk,' she said warningly.

'We don't have to. You can come into our room for a bit, watch TV…'

If only I could spend a little time with her, I was sure I could make this right. I had to make it right. Mark would have to stay out of it, back down in the bar. He'd done enough damage for one night…

'He said you didn't tell him,' Ava said.

'Well, it wasn't quite like that… No. All right. I didn't.'

'I guess that's something,' Ava said. She was looking at me in disgust. 'Finally, you're telling me the truth. But right now, that's about as much as I can take.'

She reached forward and slid her keycard into the slot. The catch clicked and she opened the door. Inside it was dark and quiet; Ellie was sound asleep.

'Ava,' I said, and reached out and touched her arm.

She shook me off. 'Were you ever going to tell me? If Mark hadn't come back?'

'I don't know,' I said slowly.

'Liar. You wouldn't have done. It messes up the story, doesn't it? All those years I felt sorry for you. Now it turns out that you were the last person I should have felt sorry for.'

'Please, Ava, let me try to explain. Mark was married. He'd just gone back to his wife. He made it pretty clear he wasn't interested.'

Ava was looking at me with the full force of disgust that only an adolescent is capable of.

'I don't want to hear it,' she said, and retreated into the bedroom and shut the door.

I was left standing there in the corridor, at a complete loss.

Should I hammer on the door? Insist on talking to her? What good would that do? She'd just told me, in the clearest of terms, to get lost. It would have to wait until she was ready… if she ever was.

I retreated to the room I was sharing with Mark and sent her a message: *I'm next door if you change your mind.*

Then I messaged Mark: *I'm in our room. Ava's in hers. Very angry, doesn't want to talk.*

I was half hoping I'd hear a little tap on the door, or that she'd reply to my message, but my phone stayed blank and silent and when I heard footsteps approaching outside it turned out to be Mark.

He came over and sat next to me on the bed; I was lying back, propped up by pillows. He attempted a smile. 'We really screwed up, didn't we?'

Various horrible, hurtful things came to mind to say. *We screwed up? You mean you screwed up. We had an agreement. Now look what's happened. What were you thinking?*

But what was the point of blaming him?

'It's really me she's angry with,' I said.

He couldn't hide it; he was relieved.

'Maybe it's not such a bad thing that she knows,' he said. 'She'll probably feel better about it once she's slept on it, won't she? I suppose we'll just have to give her time.' He reached out and patted me on the knee. 'You should try and get some sleep. You look worn out. After all, Ava's not the only one of our children we have to worry about.'

He stood up and began to head towards the bathroom.

'Mark…'

He stopped in his tracks and turned back. He looked slightly apprehensive, like someone who has almost got away with something but not quite.

'If I'd told you I was pregnant at the time, would it have made any difference?'

'Jenny, please… is there any point in raking over all of this now?'

'But do you think it would have done?'

'How am I supposed to know? The fact is, you didn't.'

'That lets you off the hook nicely.'

'What did you say?'

'Oh, nothing. I'm sorry. I'm just worried about Ava.'

'You never know, once she's had a bit of time to digest it she might actually be pleased,' Mark said. 'After all, who'd want Sean as a father? It's really Ellie who's the one who's got the rough deal here.'

With that he went off, leaving me to try and decide whether it was reasonable for me to feel angry with him, or whether I was the one who was responsible for all of this and there was absolutely nobody else to share the blame.

That night I went over and over what I'd done, while Mark slept peacefully beside me. If I'd had a clear conscience I might have been able to sleep too. But I still couldn't see what I could have done any differently. How could what I'd done have been the wrong thing to do, when I hadn't really had a choice? But somehow, it *had* been wrong, and my only hope was that Ava would forgive me.

It wasn't particularly charitable of me. Or loving. But I couldn't help but suspect that Mark had been so willing to overlook my not having told him about Ava because he knew he wouldn't have been interested at the time. Even if he couldn't quite bring himself to admit it.

When Mark had come back into my life I'd let myself believe that this really could be a fairy tale, and all the years of effort were about to be rewarded by a princessy ending: the new husband, the new baby, the new home.

But now Ava knew what I'd taken such care to hide from everybody all these years. I'd failed her, and she knew it. And the only thing that could save me now was whether she could bring herself to forgive me.

I'd never forgotten Mark. All the time Ava was growing up, I'd thought about him often. From time to time Sean must have done, too, though we never spoke about him. After all, we had Ava to remind us.

Mark was there in her face, her mannerisms, her bones. I'd never realised before what a powerful thing genetic heritage is: I'd never seen that much of either of my parents in myself, and I didn't think I looked at all like my sister. But there was Ava: fair-haired, blue-eyed, neat-featured. Mark's role in making her had been impossible to forget.

Still, he'd been frozen in time for me as the man he'd been when I first met him. And then he'd come roaring back into my life as a man in his early forties who was champing at the bit to take on family life and all the contradictions and difficulties involved.

People talked a lot about how much women wanted babies, how they got broody at a certain age and had ticking biological clocks and all of that, even though it was patently obvious that plenty of them didn't, and most of the rest of the time, for most of us, suddenly discovering we were pregnant was pretty much the last thing we wanted.

Stitches, mastitis, caring for a young baby who kept you up all night and then going to work the next day… surely any woman who'd been through it would have at least some mixed feelings about the prospect of doing it all again?

Men had so much less skin in the game. It was so much easier for them to want kids. You wouldn't think it from the way the newspapers talked about these things, but men could get baby hunger just the same way women could, and in some ways, there was less to put them off.

Though sometimes, they came up against a partner who really didn't *want* to have children, who was prepared to stop using contraception and see what happened but who wasn't willing to explore the possibility of fertility treatment. Like Paula. Mark hadn't spoken about it in any detail – I could tell he felt he ought to make at least some effort to protect her privacy – but he'd told me enough for me to figure out what her attitude had been.

In a way, I could understand where she'd been coming from. They'd had a good life, from what I could make out: a flat in a decent part of London, dinner parties with other couples, lots of foreign holidays. She'd had a career doing something in publishing, Mark had said. Why would you want to swap all that calm and order for the chaos and unpredictability of having children? You couldn't blame her for having doubts. And if Mark had felt the same way, it would have been fine. But over time, he'd changed his mind. The hunger had got to him. And when it came down to it, she hadn't been willing to contemplate what might be needed to give him what he wanted.

You couldn't really blame her for that, either. All those hormone injections, the invasive procedures, handing your body over to the control of doctors... why would any woman begin to put herself through it unless she was longing for the baby she might have at the end of it? You couldn't do something like that half-heartedly, just because your partner was keen on the idea. You'd have to be passionate about it. Dedicated. Like a hero on a quest.

I hadn't been like that at all. I'd taken a risk and my body had presented me with a fait accompli... but even so, it hadn't been a given that I would go through with it.

It was just as well that Paula hadn't really wanted children. Imagine if she had... how much more reason she would have had to hate me. Not that it really mattered how she felt; she wasn't part of Mark's life, and she wouldn't be part of ours. They weren't in touch any more; they weren't the kind of exes who stayed friends. I'd asked Mark once, 'Did you break up because of the children thing? Because you really wanted them, and she didn't?' and he'd hesitated and said yes, that had been a big part of it, and it had been obvious he didn't want to talk about it any more and I'd changed the subject.

I knew he'd been as generous as possible when sorting out the financial settlement; he'd let her have the house, which was unusual these days even if a woman had children and was going to be the main carer, and especially if she didn't and had an income of her own. I hadn't asked him if he'd done that to try and make the whole thing less acrimonious. It was pretty obvious that was the case. It was just another example of that capacity he had to give big – bigger than most people. It didn't always work. It hadn't with Ava, with the present of the red books, though Ellie loved them. And it seemed not to have made a blind bit of difference with Paula.

Anyway, I was never going to meet her, so it didn't really matter what she thought. But I didn't like the thought of anyone having cause to hate me.

That night, when I finally got off to sleep, I dreamed about her.

I couldn't see her face. I don't know how I knew it was her, but it definitely was. It was dark in the dream and she was walking towards me, and I wanted to run but I couldn't. Then she said, 'You've made a big mistake,' and I realised she was coming for me and my baby and then I woke up.

It was still early and Mark was asleep; the room was beginning to get light but only just, and our room service breakfasts hadn't arrived yet. Later on I'd have to try again to talk to Ava, but for now I didn't make any move to get up. Instead I carried on lying in bed and remembered how I'd ended up deceiving her.

I'd called Mark three days after our time together. Just the one call – I'd been very restrained. I'd left a breezy, cheerful message, one I'd practised a hundred times.

'Just wondering how you are, if you fancied meeting up for a drink or coffee or whatever.'

He called me back the next day. A good sign. A great sign. Or so I thought, at first. Before the conversation went the way it did.

'Jenny, you have to understand that there is absolutely no way we can see each other again. I met up with my wife and we're back together, and we both really want to make it work. But, Jenny, she can never find out, do you understand? You must never, ever call me again.'

I didn't cry. I just felt numb. What else had I expected? Served me right for getting mixed up with a married man.

'OK,' I said, doing my best to sound blasé. 'I guess it was fun while it lasted.'

'It was.' He didn't even try to hide his relief. 'So I don't have to worry about my bunny rabbit?'

'I'm sorry?'

'Pet rabbit,' he said, slowly and patiently, as if I was stupid. 'Like in the film. *Fatal Attraction*. A married man has a one-night stand with someone and then he doesn't want to see her again, and she gets obsessed with him and breaks into the family home and boils his kid's pet rabbit in a pot.'

'How horrible. I'd never do that. But anyway, you don't have kids. Or a rabbit.'

'It's a joke. A figure of speech. Haven't you ever heard people talking about bunny-boilers? That's what they mean.'

He was still speaking unnecessarily slowly, and I was reminded of how clever he was, and how clever I wasn't.

'Well, I promise I will never do anything horrible to your rabbit. Or to anything else of yours.'

My voice sounded weird. Dry mouth. Nerves. Not because I was trying not to cry. It was only a one-night stand, for heaven's sake, and didn't everybody have those, at one time or another? It wasn't like an actual proper relationship that had bitten the dust. You couldn't even call it being dumped. It was nothing. Something that had stopped before it even got started.

'That's good to hear,' he said.

I expected him to ring off after that, but when it came to it, he hesitated. Even though he wanted nothing more than to get rid of me, he seemed to feel the weight of it: the saying of a final goodbye to someone who was once your lover, if only briefly.

'Take care of yourself, OK, Jenny? Good luck with everything. You're a great girl, and you deserve to be with someone who will love you properly.'

'So do you,' I said.

Was I imagining it, or had there been a slight catch in his voice when we exchanged our last goodbyes, just before he ended the call?

I replayed that conversation so many times in the days that followed. I knew it was silly of me to dwell on it. Bunny-boilerish, even. But I really didn't have any thoughts of vengeance. I was just sad about it. It felt so much as if there could have been something more… but there wasn't, and there never would be, and there was nothing for it but to accept that. Because the alternative was to turn into some kind of crazy, obsessed person, a stalker or worse, and what did that have to do with love?

It was just that I could suddenly understand how you might become that person. And I never would have done, before.

Then, a couple of weeks after the awful phone conversation, I finally told someone about it.

Not my mum – my calls home were always strictly cheerful and upbeat. Not my friend Karen – she'd got engaged and was moving to Manchester with her fiancé, and could talk about nothing but getting married. No: I told the unlikeliest person in the world, other than a complete stranger. The person I chose to confide in was my layabout housemate Sean, who worked in the pub across the road from the salon where I was a junior stylist, and who played the guitar loudly but not well.

Sean had dropped out of a degree at Kingston University to focus on his band, or so he said, though the band had since broken up. He loved music, but what he also loved was the excuse it gave him to sit up late, listening and talking and drinking and smoking, and generally carrying on like someone who had no particular need to get up in the morning.

He was also fond of board games, and he was generous with his whisky. One night I stayed up with him to finish a game of Monopoly. The rest of the house was quiet – everyone else had gone to bed – and it felt so cosy there, in our little rented sitting room with the strange wood cladding on the walls, that I'd just come out with it.

'Love is strange,' Sean said. 'Cupid's arrow is as good a way to describe it as anything. Once it hits you, it's likely to stick.'

'And it hurts,' I said.

He poured me some more whisky, and a bit later on he tried to kiss me and then stopped.

He said, 'Is it because you're still hung up on that other bloke?'

And I let him think it was. It was easier than telling him I wasn't interested.

'Well, if you change your mind, you know where I am,' Sean said, and I went up to bed feeling better than I had since Mark had said goodbye.

A week or so after that I found myself in the bathroom of our shared house, staring at a pregnancy test.

Tests, I should say, because there were two in the packet and I used them both, and they both said exactly the same thing. Which was the opposite of what I'd hoped they'd say. But there it was. In blue and white. Twice.

Pregnant.

No way I could have it.

There was a knocking at the bathroom door.

'Hey! Anybody alive in there?'

It was Sean.

'Just a minute,' I said, and stuffed the pregnancy tests back into the box along with the wrapping. I put the box under my jumper and squashed my arm against it to keep it in place, then let myself out.

He was standing outside in an old band T-shirt and boxer shorts, holding a threadbare towel, unshaven and probably hungover as usual. He said, 'You all right?'

'Yeah… not too bad.'

I edged away from him to make it plain I wasn't in the mood to talk, but he didn't take the hint. He said, 'Are you around later?'

'What, tonight? I don't know. Probably going to turn in early. I'm pretty tired.'

He pulled a face. 'Shame. I was kind of hoping there might be someone decent to talk to when I finish work tonight.' Then he frowned. 'Are you sure you're all right?'

'Of course, why wouldn't I be?'

And then the packet shot out from under my arm and landed on the dirty carpet at our feet.

I scooped it up almost instantly, but not before he'd had a good chance to figure out what it was. His eyes widened. He said, 'Jenny…'

I could have scuttled away. Instead I carried on standing there, and he said, 'So that's what's going on, is it?'

'Yeah. I… I just found out.'

We stood there looking at each other for a little longer. Sean said, 'That sucks.'

I half managed a smile. After all, many things sucked: being fired, the bank refusing to extend your overdraft, being rejected by someone you'd fallen for… Things sucking was part of life, part of the natural order of things. But it wasn't disastrous. Usually it meant you could figure out a way to pick yourself up, dust yourself down and carry on.

'Yeah. It does,' I agreed.

Then a door opened further along the corridor – one of our other housemates on the move. Sean retreated into the safety of the bathroom, and I bolted.

*

Later that afternoon I got up the courage to creep downstairs and find the house phone, which was on a long, curly extension cord, and take it back up to my room.

I'd practised what I was going to say over and over again. I had to do it. I had to get it out of the way before I went out of my mind.

But it wasn't him who answered the phone.

It was a woman.

Her.

All she said was, 'Hello?'

I garbled something about a wrong number and hung up. How obvious was that? If he was there, he'd know for certain that it was me.

Sure enough, about an hour later the phone rang. I didn't recognise the number, but picked up anyway. I had a feeling it would be him, and it was.

'You really, really can't do that again,' he said. 'Paula's vulnerable. Unstable. If she has any idea that something's going on, I have no idea what she might be capable of doing. She can be a very volatile character. Do you understand?'

There it was, my chance to tell him.

I hesitated.

Then I said, 'Yes.'

He breathed a deep sigh of relief. 'Good. I had to leave the house to ring you. I don't think she suspects anything, but I might not be able to get away with it another time. Now, was there something you wanted to tell me?'

'No. Not really. I shouldn't have called. I get that, now.'

'OK. Goodbye, Jenny.'

'Goodbye.'

And that was it. I wished I hadn't even made the attempt, that I'd left him alone as he had asked. He could hardly have been clearer: whatever happened to me in future, he really didn't want to know.

*

A little before nine the next morning, I knocked on the girls' door and said, 'Ellie, can you let me in?'

Just as I had expected, she did, ignoring the faint grumbling from Ava who was still in bed. She must have got dressed and ready for the beach in the dark; the curtains were still closed. She'd picked at one of the room service breakfasts sitting on trays on the desk; the other was untouched.

'I had to read my book in the bathroom. Ava won't get up,' Ellie said as I went over to pull back one of the curtains.

'Probably feeling the after-effects of the night before,' I said. 'No more Armagnac for you, young lady.'

Ava mumbled something and sat up and gave me a look that was unambiguously hostile. Her face was puffy from sleep – or perhaps from crying – and her hair was tousled. Usually she would have hated anyone to see her like this. Usually I wouldn't have insisted on intruding, but if there had ever been a time for not respecting her boundaries it was now.

'Ellie, if you've got your all your things ready, you can go next door and get Mark, and go down to the beach with him,' I said. 'I'll come down and find you in a bit.'

Ellie immediately looked apprehensive, but steeled herself to do as I had asked. 'OK. Make sure that you keep my rose.'

'Your rose?'

Each of the breakfast trays was adorned with a single rose in a small silver vase. Ellie's rose was missing; looking round, I saw that she'd put it in a glass of water on her bedside table.

'Nobody ever gave me a rose before,' Ellie said, and I was reminded – not that I needed any reminding – of how strange this must all have seemed to her, right from the point when Mark had that first bouquet delivered to the house.

'It won't last,' Ava said.

'I don't care. I'm going to keep it as long as I can,' Ellie said. She hesitated. 'You won't be long, will you?'

'I shouldn't think so.'

'See you later, then.' She glowered at Ava and shot me a look of faint but resigned desperation, picked up her beach bag and went out.

I touched the coffee-pot on Ava's tray. Still warm. 'Do you want any of this?'

'You should go,' Ava said.

I peeled the lid off the container of orange juice, poured it into a glass and brought it over to set down on her bedside table.

'I don't want to go until I've apologised,' I said.

I sat down on the bed next to hers. That familiar face, defiant still, wanting to lock me out. Wanting to and needing not to at the same time.

'I never meant to hurt you, Ava,' I said. 'You're my daughter. I love you. I would walk over hot coals for you. I'm sorry for making such a mess of everything.'

'You didn't make a mess of everything.' Her voice sounded slightly strangulated, and her eyes were suddenly awash with tears.

I shook my head. 'I should have told you the truth years ago. The only reason I didn't was that I was afraid of what you would say.'

The next minute she was crying and I had my arms around her. It was the first time I'd held her like that for years – the first time for years that she'd let me. She felt so small and delicate, as light-boned and fragile as a bird.

It took me right back to holding her as a newborn. That little bundle of restless life, the sleepy face contorting in sudden dismay and the tiny hands feeling for something to hold onto, and the shock of knowing it was down to me to protect her.

Chapter Twelve

Paula

I had to work very, very hard at not hating Mark after that conversation about IVF. I had to work very hard at not hating any woman with a bump, or a pushchair or a child walking along with her, holding her hand.

People had been asking when, or if, we were going to have babies for as long as we'd been married. Sometimes they were direct about it, sometimes they were more tactful, but they always seemed to want to know. Since we'd been trying for a baby the questions had stopped being merely embarrassing and intrusive. By this stage, they really hurt me.

There was the pregnant neighbour who said, 'It'll be your turn next…' and the proud new mum, a former colleague who came back into work to show off her baby, openly eyeing me up as I held her offspring, as if she was speculating about why I didn't yet have one of my own.

Thankfully, her baby started crying a minute later, and I was able to hand it back. But still, I was furious with her, and my feelings were hard to hide. We were all standing around her in an admiring circle, and everybody noticed. Nobody said anything, but I caught them looking at me askance.

Worst of all, there was my mother. I'd bitten her head off once or twice when she mentioned the subject directly. She probably thought she was doing a good job of avoiding it. But tact was not her strong point, and every now and then she'd remark on how some acquaintance or other barely had a life of her own now that she kept on getting called upon to babysit her grandchildren. Or she'd ask me how work was going, and then say something like: 'It must be so liberating, being able to forge ahead without being held back by worrying about childcare.'

I wasn't really forging ahead at all – I'd been in the same job for years; it was hard to summon up ambition, or the energy for a change of direction, when all I really wanted was to sail off on maternity leave. I was stuck. Impotent. Humiliated. Somehow I carried on going through the motions, getting up and going to work, being married. But I had no idea how much longer I was going to be able to bear it.

Then the miracle happened.

Four weeks after that wedding anniversary trip to the hotel in Oxford, I did a pregnancy test and there it was: the sign I'd been wishing for so hard it seemed impossible that I could be so lucky.

I did another test and there it was again. Unambiguously positive. No ifs or buts or maybes.

Finally, our baby was on the way.

Mark's initial reaction was one of pure shock. When it had sunk in, he was pleased as punch: 'Well then, my sperm obviously does work after all!' For a little while he was wildly overprotective: was I overdoing it, carrying on working? What was I thinking of, standing on a chair to change a lightbulb – what if I fell? Wasn't bagged salad potentially bad for the baby? OK, so I'd rinsed it, but was I sure I'd really washed it thoroughly, because if not there might still be some traces of contaminant? Then the novelty began to wear off. He stopped being quite so conscious of the host of threats I might inadvertently allow to damage our child, and, on the whole, went back to expecting me to take things in my stride.

Occasionally he'd ask if I'd read any of the parenting books he'd bought in the first rush of enthusiasm, and I'd make soothing noises about how there was still plenty of time and that seemed to satisfy him. A more persistent question was whether we could tell people yet. I knew he was longing to share the news. 'I think it'll seem more real, once it's out in the open,' he said once, as plaintively as if I was withholding a treat from him.

My instinct was to keep it to ourselves for as long as possible. Being secretive was a way of making the most out of my victory, of raising a middle finger to everyone who'd ever asked. I was certainly in no particular rush to tell my mother. But Mark was desperate to tell his, which was odd because out of all the people we knew, she was the only one who had never gone near the subject of babies. 'She'll be delighted, I promise you,' he said. 'I know you two haven't always seen eye to eye, but this is going to be a game-changer.' I wasn't so sure: even if she was thrilled to bits, I didn't think she'd show it, and I was already steeling myself for criticism of my parenting skills.

Still, we couldn't put off telling our families forever, and for both of us, our mothers were pretty much all the family we had. Once I was safely past the three-month mark we made a pact that I would visit Mum and get it over and done with, and then we'd go and see Mark's mother and break the news to her.

At the time Mum was living in a houseboat moored near Vauxhall with a boyfriend who was in his forties, a couple of decades her junior. He specialised in making sculptures of feet; there were usually a couple of works in progress lying around in the bow. He was out when I showed up, not that it made much difference because he always removed himself when I was present, either retreating to the cabin they used as their bedroom or going outside to attend to the various chores that came with living on the river.

It was a fine autumn day, but chilly, and we decided to stay below deck. Mum made us peppermint tea and we settled in a pair of slightly uncomfortable cane chairs in the big, curved-walled room that was the houseboat's main living space. It was dim, with diffuse light coming in through the row of portholes high on either side, and it was never quite still: the current was too gentle for the movement to feel like rocking, but there was a sense of instability, of slight but constant motion. It made me queasy. Visiting my mother was actually worse for me than morning sickness.

Mum was wearing long jade earrings and a vivid green dress, and had a yellow silk scarf tied round her curly red hair; she was the only person I knew who still used henna, and she smelled of it, very faintly – a sort of muddy undertone, overlaid by incense and patchouli. I tried to imagine her holding a baby in her arms. It was a lot easier to imagine her putting it down and getting on with something else.

She said, 'So have you got any holidays planned? I know how Mark loves to travel.'

'We haven't at the moment, actually.'

'Well, you must at least have a few ideas.'

'Not really. We've put all that on the back burner for the moment.'

'Oh. Well, don't leave it too long. You're in such a privileged position, having plenty of money and no ties. You really should make the most of it.'

'You mean, while we don't have any children,' I said. 'But you can keep on going on holiday once you have them, you know. Lots of people do.'

'I know people try, but it's just not the same, is it? You're so much freer to see the sights when it's just the two of you. Babies come with so much kit, and they do limit your options. Not that I ever went anywhere much with your father, before or after I had you – but at least I've had plenty of chances to make up for lost time.'

I was going to have to tell Dad about the baby too, sooner rather than later; maybe that evening, if I had the energy. Our phone conversations were invariably short, but were still oddly demanding; he wasn't much of a talker. Since he'd retired, he seemed happy to live the life of a recluse.

Poor Dad. In the end, he'd been faced with unavoidable evidence of Mum's infidelities – he had quite literally come home and found her with the milkman, a story she had made much of since. He had startled her by insisting on a divorce, and had fled to a small house in a pebbledashed terrace in south Wales, which he could comfortably afford with his share of the value of the family home and his salary as a signalman on the railways. He'd lived a quiet existence there ever since, and had never, to my knowledge, risked falling in love again.

'It may be that our options will be a bit more limited in the near future,' I said. 'Mark and I are having a baby. I'm due in the spring.'

'Oh! I did wonder.' She got to her feet and came over and draped her arms lightly around me, embraced me, then detached herself and withdrew to her seat. 'I thought you looked a little tired. Have you been very sick?'

'Not at all, actually.'

'It must be a boy. Girls make you terribly sick. I felt awful for the first three months when I was carrying you. Then I felt brilliant, and never looked back. How's Mark coping?'

'He's absolutely thrilled.'

She raised one eyebrow. She plucked them very carefully, and then went over them with a pencil the exact same colour as her hair. 'Really?'

'Yes, why wouldn't he be?'

She wrinkled her nose. 'Well, because Mark's Mark, isn't he? A place for everything, and everything in its place. Does his mother know yet?'

Mum and Ingrid did not see eye to eye. They had engaged in a spectacular battle of the hats at our wedding: Mum had sported a multicoloured turban adorned with feathers and painted beads, while Ingrid had gone for a brim so wide it had been impossible to stand anywhere near her. They'd had very little contact since. Ingrid always asked politely about Mum, but with an expression that suggested she wouldn't mind hearing that something unpleasant had happened to her. Mum was downright rude about Ingrid and only just managed to restrain herself if Mark was in earshot.

'No. We're going to tell her next.'

Mum looked pleased. 'I don't suppose she'll be very happy about being second. Don't be surprised if she tries to take over. Women are always funny about their sons. They never seem to be able to let them go. Of course some women are like that with their daughters, too. But I've always taken the attitude that the best way to motivate you to make the most of your life is for me to make the most of mine.'

I could have told her then and there that we'd already decided to sell our garden flat in Stoke Newington and buy a house in Oxford, or as near as we could afford, which would be much closer to Ingrid than it would be to her. But I decided not to. It would keep, and she might as well enjoy feeling that she'd beaten Ingrid for a little bit longer.

Oxford was where Mark and I had met, when I was working in my first job in publishing and Mark was in the first year of the PhD he'd never finished. It was where we'd fallen in love, where he'd proposed, and where we'd had our registry office wedding. And it was where our baby had been conceived. We'd always wanted to live there, and now that Mark was earning good money and was travelling all over the country for his job, it finally made sense as a base – as long as I didn't go back to my job in London after maternity leave. But I was ready to move on, anyway. I certainly wasn't going to gain anything by staying put.

For the next hour or so Mum talked about the chiropractor she'd been seeing and the next holiday she was going on with the sculptor boyfriend and the politics of the houseboat community, and I managed to avoid giving away any more about what Mark and I were planning. Then Mum accompanied me up to the gangplank and we said goodbye.

'Be careful, won't you? Watch your step,' she called out as I set off towards the riverbank, followed by some other warning I couldn't quite hear.

I turned and smiled and waved and said, 'Don't worry, I will.'

It was a relief to get back onto firm dry land. I waved again and set off towards the tube, and it wasn't until about half an hour later, when I was somewhere in a Northern Line tunnel, that I figured out what she'd said: *Don't let Ingrid bully you. Or Mark, either.*

It had always been obvious that Ingrid adored Mark, but she was more the intimidating kind of doting mother than the gushing kind. She tolerated me, but this was strictly conditional. If she ever thought I was letting Mark down, in however trivial a way, I found myself bathed in disapproval.

When we showed up on her doorstep for Sunday lunch the following weekend, her opening gambit was to embrace Mark, then hold him at arm's length and look him up and down before pronouncing judgement: 'You look pale. Isn't your wife feeding you properly?'

She released him and turned towards me; I kissed her drily on the cheek. In terms of personal style Ingrid was Mum's polar opposite, with her pearls and collars and pleats and knife-edge ironed-in creases. But she shared Mum's uncanny knack for highlighting my shortcomings.

'I don't think it's my job to feed him,' I said. 'He's perfectly capable of feeding himself.'

'You modern wives don't think it's your job to do anything, but you still expect your husbands to change the light bulbs and put the bins out,' Ingrid retorted.

She ushered us in and took our coats and offered us drinks, and Mark and I perched side by side on her overstuffed sofa and made small talk about the weather and the traffic, which she didn't seem to find any more interesting than we did – though she made less of an effort to pretend otherwise. After a while, with the air of one who is discharging an unpleasant duty, she set about changing the subject.

'Do you remember me telling you about the paintings I was asked for, Mark? The ones they want for that collection in London?

I've left them out in the spare room so you can have a look. I have to say, though, I'm not sure quite why you're interested. Or why anybody would be, come to that.'

'I suppose it seems poignant. Given that it's all that's left,' Mark said, putting down his empty sherry glass. I'd had sparkling water, but as I was driving back that wasn't much of a giveaway.

'You didn't mention any paintings to me,' I said to Mark as we followed Ingrid into the little spare room. He didn't answer, but gave me a look I recognised, the look that meant I should tread carefully.

'They're not paintings, really,' Ingrid said. 'More like daubs. Mind you, you could say the same thing about the local amateur art show, and *they're* meant to be in full possession of their faculties.'

There were two unframed paintings leaning against the pale pink walls of the otherwise bare little room. One was large and rectangular, and the other was small and square. They had both been done with oil paints on canvas. Otherwise, they were alike only in being wildly different to each other and to anything else you might have expected to see in Ingrid's flat.

The large painting was painstakingly detailed, and showed a landscape that was just about recognisable as the parkland surrounding us, with the wall that ran along the roadside and the wrought-iron, spike-topped gate that separated the end of the drive from the highway. It was all rendered in tiny circles in gaudy shades of brown and green; there was something peculiarly intense about it. It seemed to vibrate with energy, so much so that it was almost uncomfortable to look at.

The small square painting next to it was a complete contrast. It was little more than a series of outlines, done in a faded brick-red that looked like old blood; most of the canvas had been left blank. It showed a group of heads in profile, with bandaged eyes and toothless, open mouths.

'This is all I kept,' Ingrid said. 'The old shower room was full of them. I got rid of the rest. I actually couldn't face going through them all – they were rather depressing. I held on to these because they were on top of the first pile I came to.'

I said, 'So these were done by people who were patients here? When it was still a hospital?'

'Exactly,' Ingrid said. 'They would hardly have been done by the people who live here now. Mr Dobbs upstairs likes his colour-by-numbers, but on the whole we tend to prefer the tidier sorts of hobbies, like coin collecting and Sudoku and bridge.'

'I had no idea you'd kept any of this stuff,' Mark said.

'It was as a memento of my father, really. He was so keen on all of this. He thought it might help to diagnose them. Very forward-thinking for the time, though these days people like to write nasty things about what went on in places like this. It must have been terribly difficult. Especially for him. Well, you know…'

She faltered. I said, 'You mean because of your sister.'

Mark had told me very little about his aunt, who had spent most of her life being cared for in that very building, back when Ingrid's father had worked there. I was curious; Ingrid never usually spoke about her. Mark had only discovered that she existed after her death, when Ingrid rang up out of the blue and told him about the funeral. That had been during our brief rocky patch, when he'd moved out for a couple of weeks, though thankfully, Ingrid didn't know about that. It was just as well that she'd never found out about my long-ago crush on my work colleague; Mark might have just about forgiven me, but Ingrid would never have done.

'Exactly,' Ingrid said, pulling herself together. 'My father was very careful not to bring his work home with him. It was essential to have clear boundaries, under the circumstances. For him as well as the rest of us.'

Mark said, 'The landscape's easy to recognise. The one of the people looks like a nightmare.'

'Actually, it's quite factual,' Ingrid said. 'Crudely done, of course. But it's much older – late forties, if I'm remembering rightly. They used to take the patients' teeth out – there was a theory about it, something to do with gum disease making them worse. And they would have worn bandages like that after they'd had leucotomies.'

I said, 'Leucotomies?'

'An operation on the brain,' Ingrid said. 'You must have heard of it.'

'You mean… like a lobotomy?'

'Well, yes. It's a particular type of brain surgery.'

'Surgery? I thought it was pretty much a case of sticking an ice pick into someone's skull.'

Ingrid raised her eyebrows at me. 'They used to do it as a last resort, to relieve patients' symptoms when nothing else could be done for them. You must remember, they didn't have the medication then that they have now. It's what *she* had. My sister. Did Mark not tell you that?'

Mark said, 'Do we have to have this conversation? We're about to have lunch, after all.' And he stalked off back in the direction of the living room.

For a moment Ingrid faltered. Then her expression hardened and she turned her attention back to me.

'I suppose it's as well for you to know,' she said. 'Mark's very squeamish about it, as you can see. If you know, you'll be able to be sensitive about things like this if it ever comes up. Not that it's the kind of thing that would usually come up. But I don't know what passes for dinner-party chat these days.'

I said, 'How come they did that to her?'

'She'd always been backwards, but when she became a teenager she became much more wilful. If they didn't do something, she was going to end up getting herself into trouble – that was what my mother said to me about it later. My father signed the consent form. He thought it was the best hope she had. I never saw her afterwards, but my parents did. They weren't to know it would leave her so much worse. Manageable, which was an improvement in a way, but pretty much incapable. Or so my mother told me.'

I said, 'How old was she? When they did it?'

'She was eighteen. I was fourteen. I knew there was something wrong with her, of course. She used to get by in public. But only just.'

'Did you… miss her?'

Ingrid gave me a long hard stare.

'You have to understand, I adored my father. And for him to have a child who was like my sister… You have to remember what a stigma it was. He was a doctor. He'd devoted his whole life to caring for people like that.' She shook her head. 'It was brutal. I just felt so sorry for him.'

'But not… for her?'

The look Ingrid gave me then would have frozen a waterfall. It reminded me of the way Mark could be sometimes, but infinitely icier.

'You shouldn't judge what people did or how they felt in the past by today's standards,' she said. 'More to the point, you shouldn't judge me, or my parents. After all, the time may come when somebody has cause to judge *you*.'

And with that she ushered me out, pausing only to close the door firmly behind her before escorting me back to the living room.

After another sherry Mark seemed to forget all about his aunt and how she had come to live out her life in that very building, and remembered that he had an announcement to make.

'I have some good news,' he said. 'Very good news. We're having a baby.'

Ingrid almost dropped her sherry glass. Then she recovered herself and set it down.

'You mean… I'm going to be a grandmother? I never thought… I mean, I had the impression you were perfectly happy as you are…'

The transformation in her was astonishing to see. I'd never seen her look like that – hopeful and shaken at the same time, as if life had just presented her with a gift that was so wonderful, so off-the-scale generous, she couldn't quite believe her luck.

She got up and went over to Mark to embrace him, and then, to my astonishment, embraced me, too.

'Thank you,' she murmured in my ear. Then she withdrew and sat down again, still visibly stunned.

'I take it you might be willing to babysit every now and then,' Mark said.

'Of course. If only you weren't so far away…'

'We won't be, for much longer. We're planning to move out of London. We won't be right on your doorstep, but we'll certainly be a lot closer.'

'Well, that really couldn't be better. That is *perfect*.'

'It is,' he said, turning to me for affirmation. 'Isn't it?'

He reached for my hand and squeezed it, and I smiled and agreed with them both.

It didn't occur to me to be apprehensive. It seemed to me that Ingrid was right: everything was perfect. And when, a couple of months later, I was confronted with evidence that it might not be, I was so preoccupied by my pregnancy that I completely missed it.

Every family has a skeleton or two in the closet, and every marriage has ghosts. They're the might-have-beens, the also-rans, the ones who got away. Mostly they stay in the background, like the kind of phantoms you might be told about by a tour guide at a stately home. But sometimes – usually when you're least expecting it – bygones cease to be bygones, and the past comes roaring back to life.

That was what happened on the day of my twenty-week scan, although I didn't know it at the time.

Mark took the morning off work to accompany me to the hospital. There were times when I felt a cold shiver of doubt about how much he was really looking forward to having a baby; he'd been pretty lukewarm about the ante-natal classes we'd gone to, and although he'd dutifully put the cot together, he'd been more than happy to leave the business of choosing it to me, along with shopping for all the other things it seemed we'd need. But then, he loved talking about the future and what our family life might be like, and he was as just as keen on going through the baby name book as I was. It was a big change, that was all, and he was adjusting. We both were. And when it counted – when it really mattered, like today – he was there.

Probably he was just apprehensive. That was fair enough: so was I. And even if he was finding the whole thing a bit daunting, I had complete faith that he wanted to be the best dad it was possible to be.

We took a taxi to the hospital so we wouldn't have to worry about finding a space in the invariably crowded car park, and arrived with plenty of time to spare. There was a newsagent's in the little row of shops just inside the entrance, and Mark suggested going in to browse before heading to the waiting room.

'I thought you had work to be getting on with,' I said. Mark had brought his briefcase with him; he was dressed in a suit, so he could go straight on to the office afterwards.

'I do,' he said. 'But I wouldn't mind looking at the things I might read if I had time.'

Inside the newsagent's, Mark went to look at the display of books by the tills and I headed towards the rows of women's magazines. I'd become a walking collection of pregnancy clichés; my attention span was shot, and all I wanted was a soothing drip-feed of familiar themes – makeovers, problems overcome – that would distract me from the prospect of giving birth. In spite of the birth plan and the classes and so on, if I was honest I was dreading it.

I didn't actually hear what Mark said to her to start with.

I looked up to see him standing next to her. She was nothing special: a tired-looking woman who'd just finished paying at the checkout. She had a sulky little girl with her, and she didn't seem at all like the kind of person that Mark would know.

I heard what he said next, though. He was looking down at the little girl, and he said, 'So who's this?'

The woman nudged the girl to move aside so that other customers could make their way from the tills to the exit. She mumbled a name I didn't catch, and then the girl piped up: 'I hurt myself on the iron. Mummy unplugged it and left it on the worktop, and I climbed up to sit on the windowsill behind it and I touched it with my leg and it burned me.'

She pointed to the bandage around her knee; she was wearing school uniform under her coat, a red jumper with a sensible grey skirt and slightly drooping socks.

'I was very brave and didn't cry at all,' she went on. 'But Mummy said we should have it looked at, so we took Ellie to school and then we came here.'

Mark said, 'Ellie—?'

'My youngest,' the woman said.

'She's only four,' the little girl said disdainfully. 'It's just as well we didn't have to bring her, because I think she would have got very bored waiting and been naughty and played up.'

'We should get you back to school,' the woman said. I had moved so that I was standing by Mark, but she didn't acknowledge me at all, or even glance in my direction. 'Come on, Ava.'

And with that she took Ava by the hand and hurried out, with Ava protesting loudly that some sweets really would have made her knee feel better and maybe they could find a shop that was a bit cheaper on the way home.

Once they had gone I said to Mark, 'I hope that isn't a sign of things to come. That woman looked exhausted. Also, it didn't seem the smartest thing to do to leave a hot iron somewhere where the kid could get to it.'

'Sounded like one of those freak accidents to me,' Mark said. 'I wouldn't rush to judgement. She's probably doing her best.'

'Who was she, anyway? Not an old flame, I hope?'

I said it as a joke. I'd seen pictures of Mark's college girlfriends – long-haired, pretty, sporty girls, girls he would have enjoyed showing off. It never would have occurred to me that he might have history with a worn-out blonde with an inch of dark at the roots, who'd gone out in jogging bottoms and trainers but looked like she only ever ran anywhere if she was late.

'She's a hairdresser,' Mark said.

'Really? She didn't exactly look the part. Maybe she's on a career break.'

'Maybe.'

'If I let myself go like that, will you tell me, so I can do something about it?'

Mark didn't smile. Maybe I had been too mean. I hadn't intended to be harsh – but I really *didn't* want to end up like that. Looking so harassed, so overburdened – so much as if it was all down to me.

'Don't worry, I'll tell you,' he said, and I went back to browsing the magazines and forgot all about it.

Chapter Thirteen

Ellie

That first night in France I dropped off almost instantly, then surfaced to find Ava standing by her bed in her pyjamas and folding back the covers. I wanted to speak to her but couldn't rouse myself enough, and maybe it was half a dream anyway. Then I fell back asleep even more deeply than before.

When I came to again the bedroom was middle-of-the-night dark, and the long net curtains were stirring in the breeze from the sea; we'd left the French windows slightly open. Someone else was standing there, in the darkness, between my bed and Ava's, close enough to reach out and touch.

A girl. She was younger than me, perhaps five years old. I couldn't make out what she was wearing in the gloom; a nightie perhaps. She was rubbing her hands together as if she was cold, even though the room was warm, and she had her back turned to me and was humming a tune I didn't quite recognise. Maybe it was a theme tune to a children's programme I'd liked myself a few years ago, but had grown out of.

She was there and not-there. I couldn't move, so I had no way of finding out what would happen if I tried to make contact – if she'd just disappear, or if she'd turn round and start talking. And then she slipped away, or I slipped away, and sank back into my dreams.

Just before I woke up for real, when the bright daylight was already filtering round the edges of the hotel curtains, I found myself in the most vivid dream of all. I was flying over green countryside, which was spread out beneath me like a map, and then I was hovering over a house set in parkland, with a broad river snaking round the edge of the grounds. It was a big old house, red-brick, Victorian, not friendly-looking, with wings extending on either side, topped by spiky turrets and parapets. And then I was at the riverside, and it was very quiet but not entirely silent. I could hear birds and trees stirring in the breeze and the rushing of running water, and someone speaking, or maybe thinking out loud, in a faint but insistent voice: *This time it'll work. It has to. He'll bring them here and then we'll see.*

It sounded like an old lady, but it definitely wasn't Grandma. I would have loved to hear Grandma speak, but she never did: she was more a warm, comforting presence than an actual personality. This old lady was a presence all right, but she was neither warm nor comforting. She was proud and strong-willed, and she wanted something, wanted it badly, and nothing else would do. Even though her voice was hushed there was nothing frail about it.

I wanted to ask her, *What? What has to work out? What was the chance that went wrong?* But I couldn't speak, and nothing more was said.

I turned away from the house towards the river and saw a heron standing on a wall alongside it, patient as a statue, watching and waiting with its neck arched and its curved beak ready to strike. There was something ancient and reptilian about it: it was so still, so poised, and so sure of itself. It looked as if it could stay there forever without tiring or losing concentration, as if what mattered wasn't whether it made a catch or not, but only that it stayed ready to.

It turned towards me and regarded me steadily and levelly with its yellow eyes.

You'll see me again before this is over, it seemed to say.

The stillness of the moment broke like a bubble as it arched its wings and suddenly took flight, following the curve of the river out of view.

And then I came to in the room I was sharing with my sister in the Grand Hotel in France, and Ava was still sound asleep in the bed next to mine even though a maid had just come in with our breakfasts. There were two identical silver trays lined up next to each other on the desk, with croissants and juice and, for Ava, a little silver pot of coffee. Each tray was decorated with a single rose in a slim silver vase.

'Ava? Ava, it's time to wake up. Your coffee will go cold.'

She groaned something I couldn't make out, turned over and put one of her pillows over her head. Well, she was obviously going to be great company that day.

I decided against drawing the curtains – no point provoking an already irritable Ava – and took one of the trays back to my bed in the gloom. The strange dream was already fading, losing its power. Just a dream. No particular reason why I should be scared by it. It hadn't been that frightening, really. No blood, no corpses. Just that voice, and a sense of menace. And the bird, though that hadn't been scary either. Solemn, though. As if its message was one that mattered.

But there I was with the poshest breakfast in bed ever, and a rose! I thought of the bouquet Mark had got Mum back at the beginning of the year, the way the colour of it had made everything else in our flat seem pale and drab in comparison. He certainly was introducing us to the high life. Looking at Ava now, though, I couldn't help but wonder if she'd had a bit more of it than was good for her.

It turned out that Ava was determined to stay in bed for as long as possible, and wouldn't be persuaded otherwise. I wasn't surprised she had a headache: I'd seen the way she'd knocked back her wine the previous night. Just like Dad. Maybe I should have warned her not to overdo it, but I knew how much that would have annoyed her and it didn't seem like a great idea to get her back up on what was meant to be a celebratory night.

I retreated to the bathroom and read a bit more of *Wuthering Heights*, but when it was getting on for nine o'clock and there was still no sign of life from Ava I decided I'd have to take action. I prodded her as gently as I could and tried to persuade her to at least have her croissant, and she said I could have it if I was so worried about it. That was when I knew she really must be feeling bad and wasn't just making excuses because she still didn't like Mark that much and didn't feel like having to hang out with him all day. I wasn't sure why she wasn't keen on Mark – he seemed pretty much perfect to me – but there it was. It was like when you put two magnets together same pole to same pole and they try and push each other away; I couldn't help but feel that if events had lined up differently, they'd get along just fine.

They actually reminded me of each other. They were both soft-centre people – the kind that pretend to be cool and hard when at their cores, they're all mush. I was the opposite, and so was Mum: friendly and keen to please on the outside, invisible steel in the heart. People thought we were the easy-going ones, the weak ones, but actually, they underestimated us. Or so I liked to think.

After all, wasn't what I had – the flashes of perception, glimpses of half-understood things that later turned out to be true – a kind of strength?

And if it wasn't… then strength was definitely needed to cope with it.

All it took for Ava to lie in bed groaning was a bit of wine and Armagnac, and the news that Mum was getting married again and was expecting. How on earth would she cope with stuff coming in, if not from the other side, then at the very least from outside herself – little moments of knowledge from the blue?

I left Ava her croissant to have later, and put on my new swimming costume and sundress and the new straw sun-hat I'd had to choose really quickly because Ava had spent so long trying things on, and tucked my beach towel and other bits and pieces I might need in the raffia basket Mum had bought me on the very last day before we were due to fly out here.

Then Mum came in, all keen to talk to Ava – probably wanting to make sure that she was going to be all right with her getting married and having a baby and all that. Mum tended to think that talking could sort out that kind of thing. She sent me off to go down with Mark to the beach, and I found myself alone with my future stepdad for the first time since I'd invited him into our flat, the day he'd brought round the books.

We made our way towards the hotel's revolving doors together and out onto the sunlit road. Maybe he wasn't a morning person; he didn't seem particularly cheerful about having the chance to get to know me better. I supposed I was going to find out that kind of thing about him now that he was going to be a proper part of our lives, rather than a man with a fancy car who sometimes turned up to give us presents, or take us out for expensive treats.

As long as I made it perfectly clear to Dad that he'd always come first, surely it wouldn't be so very terrible to let this other person grow fond of me… would it?

Dad was Dad, but he was on and off and you never knew when he'd be back next. Mark at least seemed reliable, and that wasn't to be sniffed at. Going by the evidence, you had to wonder how much Dad had ever really wanted us. I let myself think this, though I knew I shouldn't, any more than you should pick at a scab to see what's underneath.

Even though it was still early, the beach was already crowded with bronzed sunbathers in brightly coloured swimwear and their happy, uncomplaining children. I suspected very few of them were English – or if any of them were English, they'd done a very good job of adapting. Mark and I were both paler than everybody else, but I felt I stuck out more than he did.

He had on a polo shirt and linen trousers and espadrilles and was carrying a canvas holdall with his beach stuff in it, and there was something quite Continental about him, what with the breathable fabrics and the casual air of sophistication and choosiness. There was nothing at all Continental about me, but maybe that was something to do with never having been overseas before. In fact, I'd never even left the south-east; the furthest I'd been was the beach at Brighton.

Mark managed to find a good spot, in spite of how busy it was, on a sandy incline a little way back from the sea. He took a big blue-and-white striped beach towel out of his bag and unrolled it and sat down on it, and I took my own beach towel out of my basket and did the same.

We both looked at the sea. It was glittering invitingly in the sunlight, and was bright blue all the way to the horizon. Mark said, 'I quite fancy a dip. How about you?'

'Me? Oh, no, I don't think so. I've never swum in the sea before. It might not be safe.'

'But you can swim, can't you? Jenny said you could both swim.'

'Well, yes, we can. I can swim better than Ava, actually. I've got more badges than her, and I did lifesaving and she didn't bother. But I'd still rather stay here.'

'Fair enough. You're on holiday, you should do what you want.'

'Are you really just going to go off and leave me here?'

'You'll be all right, won't you?'

'Well, I expect so,' I said with a shrug.

He looked at me through slightly narrowed eyes, as if having second thoughts, then suddenly got up and approached a woman who was sunbathing at a slight distance to us, reading in the shade of a parasol stuck in the sand as her child tottered round with a bucket and spade.

He said something I couldn't quite make out – we'd done a little bit of French at school, days of the week and so on, but nothing that really equipped you for dealing with this kind of situation. Then he gestured towards me and I distinctly heard him say *fille*. That was girl, and it was also daughter. Had he told this lady I was his *daughter*?

The lady smiled and nodded and Mark came back and sat down again.

'She said she'll keep an eye on you,' he explained.

'What did you say to her about me, exactly?'

'What do you mean?'

'I heard you say *fille*. That means "daughter", doesn't it?'

I couldn't decide whether I was angry or pleased about it. It was a bit of an insult to Dad, in a way. But I could see that it saved on explanations. And if Mark felt that way about us – if he was up for playing the part of being our dad – wasn't that a good thing?

He narrowed his eyes again. I got the impression he was finding me hard going, but trying not to show his exasperation. No wonder he wanted a swim.

'I said *belle-fille*,' he explained.

Beautiful girl? Why on earth would he describe me like that?

'It means "step-daughter",' he went on. 'I know it's jumping the gun a bit. But you will be, one day. Anyway, I'm going to have a quick dip, if that's all right. I won't be long, and I'll be able to see you from the sea.'

'Fine,' I said. 'I'm used to looking after myself, anyway.'

Oh well, Dad would probably have cleared off for a swim too, if he'd wanted.

Mark slipped off his espadrilles and I took in the sight of his bare feet with scientific interest. I wasn't really used to seeing men's feet. Mum's feet were wide and pale and soft, almost child-like. Ava's were annoyingly elegant and she was proud of them, though she wouldn't admit it. She spent ages painting her toenails, and she was always going around in little strappy sandals, as soon as the weather warmed up enough. But bare male feet were a rarity in my life.

Mark's were probably quite attractive, not that I had anything to compare them to. He had very high arches and very large big toes, and a sprinkling of freckles and no obvious sprouts of hair – a good thing, in my opinion.

Would Mum object to finding *his* toenail clippings in the bath? No – because Mark would never, ever leave them there. He'd always check, and rinse the bath as much as was necessary to remove every last trace of himself. In fact, he was probably the kind of person who would clean the bath *before* he used it.

Mark unbuttoned his shirt and took it off. His back was smooth and unblemished – no hair, no scars, no moles, no identifying marks. I tried to remember if I'd ever seen Dad with no top on. I didn't think I had.

Suddenly Dad seemed a very, very long way away, which he was, as far away as someone can be. I had no idea where he was. He could have been anywhere. And you can't get further away than that.

I tried to summon Dad up: perhaps I could get a picture of where he was, at least, or a flash of how he was feeling.

Nothing. The knowledge didn't seem to work like that, or do anything I might actually want it to do. Sometimes I wondered what on earth was the point of it, what it was *for*. It certainly didn't seem to be there to help *me*.

Mark stood up and unzipped his trousers and stepped out of them. He had his swimming trunks on underneath. I quickly looked away, over towards the expanse of the sea. It really wouldn't do to stare, especially if he noticed.

Presumably, when he was married to Mum and we were all living together, he'd go round in a dressing-gown at home like we all did? It would be less awkward and strange when we were all used to each other, anyway. Wouldn't it?

'Back in a bit,' he said, and went off across the sand to the sea.

Poor old Dad. He'd let Mark hit him… he'd slunk away as if he wasn't even entitled to be there.

I watched Mark launch himself into a fast front crawl and churn his way through the water. As I looked on the waves seemed to become stronger and greyer and darker, as if a storm had blown in from somewhere, as if this wasn't such an idyllic spot after all.

He hadn't even reminded me to put suncream on. What kind of parent was he going to make? He certainly had a lot to learn.

I got the suncream out of my basket and dotted it on my legs and arms, then rubbed it into my skin till the white smears disappeared. It was Ava who had shown me how to do that. It smelled good; it smelled of laziness, of the kind of days when the ice-cream van comes round and you make daisy-chains and stay up late because it's too hot to sleep.

When I looked up at the sea again, it was as blue and sparkling as a postcard or an illustration in a storybook.

I lay down on my back and rested my straw hat on my face and listened to the sound of the waves. The little kid whose mother was meant to be keeping an eye on me was chatting away to herself in French. Soothing, beachside sounds. Holiday sounds. I closed my eyes: the insides of my eyelids turned a warm orangey-brown, like the glowing embers of a fire, the way I imagined Grandma.

I couldn't feel her now, though. Maybe I wasn't calm enough. I didn't feel calm at all, and that wasn't good.

I had missed something. Something important. Something big, something to do with Mark. Something I didn't know yet. But did Mum? Did Ava? I could feel it, but I couldn't make out anything other than the scale and weight of it. It was a burden, a terrible pressure, and it was his – it was something he carried around everywhere, and that meant now it was ours, too.

Maybe he thought that he'd be able to escape it, or let go of it. Or at least forget it. But it didn't seem like the kind of thing that would get better just by being left alone. It seemed like it might get bigger the more he ignored it, until it had almost completely taken him over, until there was almost nothing else.

After he'd finished swimming he came back and sat down on his towel next to me to dry off in the sun, and then Mum appeared, waving at us from a distance across the beach and picking her way round the sunbathers to get to us.

She didn't look very happy. In fact, when she came closer, I could see that she'd been crying. I wondered what on earth Ava had said to her.

'No Ava, then,' Mark said as she sat down on his towel, in the space between us.

'No. I think she's all right, though. Or she will be.' She drew a deep breath. 'Ellie, there's something we have to tell you.'

Mark said, 'I thought you said we should all be together for this.'

Mum said, rather sharply, 'Ava doesn't want to be here.'

'Shouldn't we have discussed this?' Mark said.

I said, 'Discussed what?'

Mum said, 'We have to tell her, Mark. We can't just let it linger.'

And then she told me.

Ava *wasn't* my sister after all.

Or at least, she wasn't *totally* my sister. She was Mark's daughter. And I was Dad's.

It was a shock. Of course it was a shock. Quite apart from anything else… why hadn't I *known*? What was the point of sensing things, if I didn't get a heads-up on something as fundamental as this? And when Mark finally came on the scene… why hadn't I realised?

But it all made sense…

It made sense in the awful, jarring way that things do when they suddenly become true, and you realise why you've been smelling a rat all along, and the rat was the truth and you don't like it any better for having found it where you live.

Maybe it was just that I hadn't *wanted* to know. Perhaps I had picked it up, after all. I had definitely picked up *something*… something that Mark carried around with him.

Guilt?

Mum was very careful to make it clear that it wasn't Mark's fault, that he hadn't known, that he'd been married to someone else. But that didn't exactly reflect very well on either of them, did it?

Maybe it was just the kind of thing that happened when you were grown up. Like car accidents, or the little purple veins that Mum had on her thighs. These were things that you wouldn't choose to have. But sometimes, they were difficult to avoid.

After Mum had finished telling me I was quiet. I looked at the sea and the people in it and thought that maybe it didn't matter where any of us came from, or who we were biologically related to. Which was an odd thing to think, as odd as being dropped into somebody else's life. It made me feel artificially calm, as if I was at a distance from myself and from everybody else too.

And yet up until that moment I would have said that Mum and Ava were the most important people in the world, and that nothing could possibly matter more than family and who your family were.

Mum asked me if I had any questions. I said, 'Does Dad know? My dad, I mean.'

'He does,' Mum said. 'He always has.'

So he'd lied to me and Ava, too. But maybe he had felt he had to?

'He thought he was lucky to have her,' Mark said, and there was something in his voice I didn't like at all.

'We should go back to the hotel,' Mum said. 'I don't want to leave Ava alone for too long.'

'She hasn't exactly shown much sign of wanting to be with us,' Mark said.

'It doesn't matter what signs she shows,' Mum said.

I'd never heard them bicker like that before. They were beginning to sound like real parents.

I said, 'Is there time for me to have a paddle before we go back?'

'I thought you didn't want to go into the sea,' Mark objected.

'I didn't. But I changed my mind.'

Mum said, 'You won't be too long, will you?'

'I won't,' I said. Suddenly I just wanted to get away from the pair of them.

'Go on then,' Mum said, and I got up and went down to the water's edge.

When I turned round they were deep in conversation. Arguing? It was difficult to tell. Mum waved, though. At least she was still keeping an eye out for me. At least if I plunged into the water and started swimming towards the horizon, out of my depth, she'd probably notice.

I didn't, though. I paddled and looked at the light bouncing off the water and listened to the swish and rush of the waves and the wet rattle of the sand, and to my surprise I was all right. I was sad, too, the way you are when something has come to an end, whether it's because it's time to put away the Christmas decorations or because your favourite old dress doesn't fit you any more. I couldn't help but see all the time Ava and I had spent together – eating meals, walking to and from school, sleeping side by side – in a different way. It made me nostalgic. As if all that time was already over.

But still, I was weirdly comforted. There was a sort of golden glow to everything, as if the brightness all around wasn't just the sunshine of the south of France but was also a kind of light that you might be able to find anywhere if you looked for it.

What would my grandma have made of all this, of the choices Mum had made and the way she had deceived us? Would she have disapproved? It seemed quite possible. But anyway, she wouldn't have been angry with *us*. None of it was Ava's fault. Or mine. We were just caught up in the aftermath of what the grown-ups had done.

It made sense. Now that I knew what I was looking for, I could see it. It wasn't just the physical resemblance… it was all sorts of smaller, subtler things. Little mannerisms. Reserve. Neatness. That way both Mark and Ava had of looking at you if you asked a question. As if they had an answer ready but weren't sure you deserved to hear it.

Would she be even *more* distant with me, after this?

Ava had always annoyed me and I had always admired her. She was a giant, and always had been: an unpredictable giant, neither entirely friendly nor an ogre, but always a huge, towering presence, someone who might just as well take you for a ride on her shoulders as shut out the light. She set the standards to aspire to: she was the one I had to either follow or break away from. I could try to do better than her, I could try to be different, but either way, I always needed her. Without her, I didn't know myself.

Was that the real reason why Mark had been so keen to be part of our lives – to claim Ava? Once he knew about her, had it really all been about her – not about Mum at all?

It wasn't that he'd been horrible to me – he'd always been perfectly nice and kind. But from his point of view, I probably just came along as part of the package. It was like when you were house-hunting, and saw somewhere with a box room that might turn out to be useful but wasn't much of a draw in itself. I was an extra, but I didn't matter all that much either way.

But soon there was going to be a new baby. The baby that was more Ava's sibling than I was, even though I'd been around so much longer, and had shared a room with her, and put up with her for years. And the baby would barely even get to know Ava, because Ava was so big now and would probably have left home by the time the baby was a toddler.

That hurt. I wasn't sure if the hurt was made up of jealousy or sadness, or both. It felt a bit like hate. How could you hate a baby that hadn't even been born yet? But I did. It was easier than hating Ava or Mum or Mark or Dad. *My* dad. It wasn't fair, but that didn't make a lot of difference.

Then I pulled myself together and went back up onto the beach to join Mum and Mark, and Mum said we should head off and we left the beach and made our way back to Ava.

It was a beautiful walk, along a promenade and up a path past shuttered white houses with great boughs of brightly coloured flowers spilling over their walls, just like in the pictures of the town in the hotel brochure. I asked Mum what it was called and she said it was bougainvillea. It was all so pretty that it should have been impossible for us to be anything but happy.

The path rose steeply, and the sun was at our backs. In a minute we'd come out onto the busy main road that led to the hotel, and then we'd have to find Ava, and then we'd probably all have a rather awkward lunch together and begin the business of getting used to each other again.

It was then that I saw it, on the ground alongside us.

A fourth shadow. Not so long as mine. The shadow of a girl, a little girl, a girl who wasn't really there.

Mum was oblivious. She was looking at the sky, the flowers, the passing buildings – anywhere but at her feet. Mark didn't look as if he'd seen it, either. He had the focused, uncomfortable expression that I'd seen on kids' faces at sports days, when they were tired out but the end of the race was in sight and there was no question of giving up.

And then the shadow vanished, and there were just the three of us.

I decided not to mention it. I had a feeling that even if either – or both – of them could have explained what I'd seen, they would have pretended to have no idea. They'd have made out I was just being weird. And if they really didn't know, they'd start to have serious doubts about my grasp on reality.

*

Ava was by the hotel pool, lying under a sunshade in her bikini. She was wearing her sunglasses and she looked grown up and glamorous, like a film star in disguise who wouldn't bother about the kinds of things that worried ordinary people.

Mark went off to get drinks for us and Mum took the sun lounger on one side of Ava and I took the other.

Ava said to me, 'Did you swim?'

'I paddled.'

'Chicken,' Ava said. 'You had the chance to swim in a sea that's actually warm, and you didn't take it?'

'I didn't feel like it.'

'Yeah, right.'

'Ava,' Mum said, 'don't tease her. Have you been for a swim?'

'No, I've just been sunbathing.'

'Well then,' Mum said.

'I didn't realise it was compulsory,' Ava said.

I understood what she was trying to do – to show that we didn't have to talk about the dad stuff, and have some kind of big embarrassing heart-to-heart. We could just carry on as before, as if nothing really fundamental had changed.

But it had. I knew it had. Up close, I could see that her face was puffy where she'd been crying. I could feel the shock coming off her, and the woundedness.

She didn't feel safe any more – how could she? She didn't trust Mark, and she couldn't really trust Mum in the same way as before, however much she might want to. And we'd all learned not to trust Dad long ago. But she would never want to talk about it – or at least, not to me.

The very worst of it was I had absolutely no idea how to console her, or to help. I couldn't tell her what I'd seen. And I didn't feel safe either.

Chapter Fourteen

Ava

If we had been at home I could have retreated to our room and kicked Ellie out; I would have had my books and all my stuff around me, and I could have got on with my revision and forgotten all about my family, at least for some of the time.

As it was, though, it was hard to escape. We had the sunshine and the beach and the three-course meals every night and the drinks in the hotel bar, and at the same time we were all stuck with each other and there was nothing I could do but wait it out.

The morning after the night of revelations, when Mum had come in to talk to me and I'd completely embarrassed myself by crying, I'd asked her whose idea it had been to break the news this way. On holiday! I'd think twice before I ever went on holiday with them again. It was Mark, of course. Left to herself, Mum would have had more common sense. She would have understood that I needed space, that I couldn't be rushed into accepting him, let alone loving him. He must have steamrollered her into it, otherwise surely she would have at least tried to raise a few objections. But maybe she was just too preoccupied with the new baby to have any energy to spare.

She wasn't the greatest advertisement for pregnancy. Miracle of new life and all that, yes, but she did seem pretty tired and she wasn't exactly glowing. Maybe that was just a myth that had been put about to con women into keeping on having babies. Like telling kids that if they ate their carrots, they'd end up being able to see in the dark. Mum had told me that and I'd always eaten my carrots and the dark still looked like dark to me.

After that morning, we didn't really talk about it. We didn't really talk about anything, other than the kind of things you talk about on holiday; where we would go next, what we would do, what we would eat. I didn't want to talk. What more was there to say? It wasn't like anyone had asked for my opinion – just my blessing, after the event.

All that remained was for me to get my head round it. I was no longer the daughter of an unreliable alcoholic who had walked out on us when my little sister was a baby. I was now the daughter of a control freak who'd had a one-night stand with my mother when he was married to someone else, and who'd looked her up when he finally got divorced, then got her pregnant once again. They certainly had a good hit rate where conception was concerned. Maybe they'd just keep going, like one of those Victorian couples with a dozen kids: one for every year they were together, but with a sixteen-year-gap between me and Junior.

I carried on calling him Mark. I thought I'd probably start calling Dad Sean. If we ever saw him again. If Mark hadn't scared him off for good. How much did I really need a dad, anyway? I was sixteen years old, not far off adulthood. But all of a sudden I had two of them: the returning sperm donor and the distant drunk. Two dads too many. I wasn't sure that either of them really deserved to be called Dad, however much they would have liked it.

How could Mum and Sean have lied to me for so long, and so convincingly? It was a lesson well learned. I'd always remember it: it was almost impossible to know whether other people, even the ones closest to you, were telling the truth or not.

I didn't know what to say to Mark, and he didn't really know what to say to me: our every conversation was a misfire, an anti-climax. There was no way of reclaiming all the years we'd lost. Whatever we had would always buckle under the weight of what it wasn't, and could have been.

And yet there we were. Eating together. Walking to the beach together. Lying on the same stretch of sand. Swimming in the same sea.

When I actually saw him, it was hard to carry on hating him. He was just a man, after all. A man who'd done something he'd regretted, and had tried to put it behind him... and had finally decided to face it.

No wonder he'd been up for having another baby. This way he got both the hostile teenager and the chance to start over.

Thankfully, he seemed to understand how I felt. I realised he wasn't going to try and make me talk. He was putting up with me because I was testing him and if I was ever to begin to trust him, he'd have to earn it.

And there was a physical rapport between us that underlay everything else, that seemed unbroken: a kind of recognition. Even though we'd never had a chance to bond, even though the chances were we would never be close – not unless I had a complete personality transplant, and he did too – the tie was still there. I could see him in me, and even though I still wasn't sure how much I liked him, it was shocking how right it felt to have him around.

Over the last dinner of the holiday he laid out a few more details of their plans for us. Top of the list was moving. Well, I'd known that was coming. But Mark confirmed my worst fears: his big idea was for all of us to move out of London and into his house in the country.

'But what would I do there?' I protested. 'I've already applied to sixth form college. It's all decided.' I knew other people who were going – Molly, Jasmine, Toby Andrews, Brian Johnson. Not that I was bothered about Toby, but I'd kind of got used to having a boy with a long-suffering crush on me moping about the place.

'I know it's a big change for you,' Mark said. 'But there are lots of good sixth forms in Oxfordshire, too. I know you're going to be busy with your exams when we get back, but I'll get some information sent to you and you can look through it with your mum and we can go on some visits.'

Ellie was sitting there giving him her best hangdog glance, like, *Remember me?* Mark glanced at her and threw her a bone: 'We'll need to get a move on to secure decent school places for both of you.'

Ellie instantly perked up. 'Will I be able to go on some visits, too?'

'I should think so. We'll have to see what we can do, in the time available,' Mark said tightly.

'Will we go to the same school?' Ellie said with a slightly frightened look in my direction, as if even I would be better than nothing in a school that was otherwise filled with strangers.

'That will depend on what we can sort out and what's best for both of you. The whole thing's actually a little bit more critical for Ava,' Mark said. Ellie's face fell. 'I mean, in the sense that she's got important exams coming up,' he explained.

The waiter arrived to take our orders for dessert and coffee. As usual, Mark passed on pudding. Too proud of his washboard stomach. Mum abstained too, probably trying to avoid piling on the pounds before the wedding. Mark of the washboard stomach wouldn't want a bride who was fifty inches wide. He didn't order Armagnac with his coffee this time. As far as he was concerned, the need for Dutch courage seemed to have passed.

I had something with strawberries in to try to be healthy, but Ellie went for chocolate mousse, as she always did. It was served in a little glass pot, and she scraped it completely clean. Like always.

Seeing that gave me a pang of something – I don't know what. Like I'd been somewhere else, these last few days. Like I'd begun to miss her – my serious, intense, goofy little sister, who always ate her chocolate mousse right up.

I gave the complimentary chocolate that came with my coffee to Ellie without her asking, and she took it with a little smile that was almost teary.

She definitely must be finding all this overwhelming. But then, she was still pretty young, and she took things to heart. In spite of everything – the lack of money and Sean's unreliability and the moving around – Mum had somehow managed to provide us with stability. That had gone, now. Everything was shifting, and it wasn't so surprising for Ellie to be stressed out by that.

Suddenly Ellie came out with a question that she must have been mulling over for some time: 'So are you going to get married in church?'

Mum and Mark exchanged glances. 'Neither of us is particularly religious,' Mark said. 'We're planning a very small registry office ceremony, with dinner at a really good restaurant afterwards.'

Ellie's face fell again. None of this was panning out in line with her most dearly held dreams. 'So… how many people?'

Another exchange of glances. They might not have been together for long, but Mum and Mark definitely had the non-verbal communication thing down pat.

The upshot seemed to be that it was down to Mum to handle this one. 'We were thinking we'd keep it small,' she said. 'After all, the really important thing is to make it a special day for the four of us. *Five* of us.'

'*How* small?' Ellie wanted to know.

'Well, just family.'

'But we don't *have* any family,' I objected. 'You're not about to invite long-lost Aunt Amanda, are you?'

'No, but there's Mark's mother, who we're all going to meet really soon, hopefully. Mark's house is quite near her flat, so we'll almost be neighbours.'

Mum said this with a smile that was meant to broadcast how much she was looking forward to this meeting, but only succeeded in showing how nervous she was about it.

I said, 'So it's going to be us and Mark's mother… and that's it?'

'Yes, well, I'm afraid she's the only living relative that Mark and I can summon up between us. That we're still speaking to, I mean.'

I glanced at Ellie, expecting her to be tragically disappointed. But she was looking at something on the other side of the room. Then she screwed her eyes tight shut and opened them, and blinked a couple of times as if she'd got something in her eye and was trying to clear it out.

'Ellie,' I said, 'are you OK?'

'Oh… yeah. Yeah, I'm fine,' Ellie said.

I found myself wishing, not for the first time, that she wasn't quite so jumpy and highly-strung. If anything, she'd got worse since Mark had come on the scene. Most of the time she seemed to be either spaced out or apprehensive, as if she was anticipating some kind of disaster but didn't think there was anything she could do to head it off.

'The thing is, it's second time round for both of us,' Mum said. 'It seems like the best way to do it is to keep it really low-key.'

'But didn't you have a really tiny wedding when you got married to Dad?' I said. 'I thought it was you and him and Grandma and Aunt Amanda, and that was it.'

'Well, yes. And you were there, too, Ava. And you cried and Grandma had to take you out.'

'Yeah. You told me. But anyway, it's not like you had a massive celebration when you got married to Dad, I mean, Sean. This isn't a contrast. It's just more of the same.'

Mark said, 'Did Sean take you to one of the best restaurants in London afterwards?' I shook my head. 'You see? It is different.'

I said, 'But what about your friends? Like Karen, and all those other people you keep in touch with on Facebook. Wouldn't some of them like to come?'

Mark and Mum did the conferring-look thing again. It was Mark's turn to respond this time. He said, 'The thing is, Ava, I know that at your age friendships seem very important, but as you get older that may change. If you're busy with work and family life, you may not see your friends so often. And that's just a natural part of getting older. Then sometimes things happen. Significant life events that may have a bearing on some of your friendships. Like getting divorced, for example.'

'But none of Mum's friends care that she's divorced. I mean, they're her friends, not Dad's. I mean Sean's.' I stopped in my tracks. 'Oh, I see. You're talking about *your* friends. What happened? Did they all take your ex's side when you split up or something? I thought that kind of thing only happened in school.'

'Ava,' Mum said warningly.

'OK, I'm sorry. I didn't realise it would be such a sensitive subject. Just trying to find out why you don't want any guests at your wedding. Didn't realise that would be offensive.'

Mum had gone very pink. She looked at me as though she might cry. 'Please don't spoil things, Ava,' she said.

Ellie piped up, 'But I can still be a bridesmaid, can't I, Mum? You did say I could.'

'I'm sure you can,' Mum said.

'Well, don't look at me,' I told them. 'I don't want to be one.'

'You can be the *only* bridesmaid,' Mum said to Ellie.

'What are you going to wear, Mummy?' Ellie wanted to know. 'Will you have a proper wedding dress?'

'Ellie, you seem to have forgotten she's pregnant,' I said. 'That's the only reason they're getting married in the first place.'

Silence fell round the table. Mum slapped down her cup of herbal tea into its saucer hard enough to chip the china. I wasn't used to seeing her the way she looked at me. Really angry. Almost like she hated me.

Then Mark reached across and took her hand and held it, and carried on holding it, like the two of them were planning on starting a séance or something. The knot of their joined hands lay there on the table and it was both a reproach and a warning: *We are as one now. Do not presume to mess with us, or you will pay.*

'That's not actually true,' Mark said. 'I should never have stayed with my ex as long as I did. I should have left her years ago. Before you were born, Ava. I should have gone as soon as I met Jenny. I knew there was something special there. We just clicked. But I didn't trust my instincts. I thought I had to cut Jenny off, and do everything I could to make my marriage work.' He grimaced. 'I can't tell you how much I've regretted that. It was a huge mistake. But I'm trying to make up for it now.'

'So it was really just timing,' I said. 'If you'd met Mum before that other woman, you'd have been with her all along. Is that what you're saying?'

'It's very tempting to play at might-have-beens. I try not to. I'm just relieved and happy that we're together now.' He smiled at Mum. 'You're a wonderful mother, Jenny. A true natural. And this time I get to be there for you. I can't believe my luck.'

Ellie looked pleased by this, as if it had been enough to reassure her that he really did love Mum enough for all of this to work out. She said, 'So what about the honeymoon?'

'We haven't decided yet, but we thought we might go to Italy,' Mum said.

'Oh! Where in Italy? Would we go to Florence? And Rome? I'd love to see the Sistine Chapel.'

Another shared look between Mum and Mark – a pained one this time. I said, 'Ellie, they're not planning on taking us with them. They're going to go on their own.'

I'd never seen her so crushed. She seemed to fold up into herself as if she wanted to disappear. In the smallest possible voice she managed to say, 'Are you going to look after me, then, Ava?'

I was about to say yes, but Mum spoke over me: 'Actually, we were going to ask Mark's mother if she'd come and stay, and keep an eye on you both while we're away.'

'Stay where?'

'Well, at Mark's house.'

'Home,' Mark said. 'Your new home. One thing I haven't mentioned about my house is that I have three bedrooms. You'll be able to have your own rooms. It'll do us all for now, but we're going to have to start thinking about extending. Or moving.'

'Is it an old Victorian house?' Ellie asked.

We all stared at her. Mark said, 'What makes you say that?'

'I just wondered if it was one of those kinds of houses,' Ellie clarified. 'You know, the red-brick sort with pointy roofs and a big walled garden all around it.'

I said, 'What are you expecting, Wuthering Heights or something?'

Ellie pulled a face. 'I just wondered.'

'Well, I'm sorry to disappoint, but it isn't,' Mark said. 'It's a new-build with no history whatsoever.'

'Mark was very generous to his ex-wife when they divorced,' Mum said. 'He let her have the house they'd lived in.'

'Yes, well, we really don't need to go into that,' Mark said stiffly.

The waiter arrived to clear the table, and Mum asked if I wanted to do anything after dinner and I said I just wanted to pack and have an early night. 'I'll help Ellie pack, too.'

'I don't need help,' Ellie protested.

'You look like you should get an early night, too, Mum,' I said, ignoring Ellie. 'You look done in.'

She yawned and stretched. 'I am,' she said. 'Believe me, I am. I really had no idea it was going to be so hard third time round.'

Her face had already filled out a little, though I was only aware of that because I knew her so well. It wasn't at all obvious that she was pregnant, not yet anyway. Her new clothes were mainly loose and flowing, chosen to hide her shape rather than draw attention to it, and although she'd brought a swimming costume she hadn't actually gone any closer to the water than a quick paddle in the shallows: the selection of kaftans she'd brought with her had come in useful.

As we made our way out of the restaurant and up to our rooms I actually felt guilty, as if *I* was the one who was at fault. What they really needed was a daughter who was capable of being a bit more bohemian, who could shrug and say, *So what? So things got a bit confused. Big deal.* But they'd ended up with me, and I wasn't ready to let either of them off the hook just yet.

My sense of moral superiority did not last much longer. It didn't feel like a decision to do something bad, though. It felt like a fait accompli.

I went to bed at the same time as Ellie – later than usual for her, early for me. Then I couldn't sleep. I was plagued by a general sense of dread about everything. There were the exams, the visit to Mark's three-bedroom new-build house, the schools I might go to. The wedding, with nobody we knew there to wish us well. Mark's mother, who was going to be supervising us even though I was perfectly capable of looking after Ellie myself, and often had.

And then I'd be starting over. No more Molly, no more Jasmine, no more Brian looking fit from a distance. No more Toby.

No more of our flat. No more of nice old Peter Carman, the downstairs neighbour, tending his roses and inviting Mum down for sherry and opera. No more of the nurses upstairs, coming home at odd times after night shifts or nights out.

No more London.

OK, so we weren't in London proper but we were close enough for a bit of its dirty glamour to rub off. I didn't know much about the countryside apart from that there was plenty of empty space, there was nothing to do and people were nosy. Our neighbours were easy to get away from: all we had to do was make a short journey by bus or train to lose ourselves in crowds of people all minding their own business, none of whom knew or cared who we were. In the countryside it would be different. People might be curious about us. We'd probably have to make the effort to be nice to them.

London let us be. The countryside would kill us slowly and watch us die.

It wasn't right. It was all happening too fast and I had no say in any of it. If Mum was so desperate to reunite with my father and have another baby, couldn't she at least have had the decency to wait till I'd left home?

I tried to like the idea of a little baby arriving in our lives, but it really didn't come naturally. Shauna Perritt from the year above had got pregnant before GCSEs and had to leave the school; I'd seen her since a couple of times, walking round pushing a pram looking like she didn't know what had hit her. I'd peered into the pram and said polite things like you were meant to do, but all I was thinking was, *There is no way I am ever, ever letting that happen to me.*

The longer I lay in bed thinking about all of this, the less likely it seemed that I would ever get off to sleep. And there was Ellie right next to me, the supposedly neurotic and anxious one, sleeping like a… sleeping like a baby. Like babies didn't, usually. I remembered that much from when Ellie was little. Once Mum had given birth, we were in for a whole lot of screaming and crying.

Suddenly I couldn't bear it any more.

I must have been lying there for an hour or more: it took less than five minutes to get dressed and escape.

My clothes for the next day were the only things of mine in the wardrobe. I'd left out the cardigan and sundress I'd worn on the flight; everything else was packed.

I got dressed, slid my feet into my sandals, grabbed my purse and my phone and the hotel room keycard and let myself out. The door clicked shut quietly behind me. I was back in the brightly lit, lushly carpeted adult world, where you could please yourself and things were arranged so as to make it easy for you.

There was no one else around, no sound coming from the next room. Mum and Mark were probably both asleep. Anyway, it was a risk worth taking.

I marched along the corridor as if I knew exactly where I was going, and headed straight for the hotel bar.

It was quieter than before, but it had been Saturday night then and it was Monday now. An entirely different proposition. The people in there seemed mainly old, and were talking quietly or not at all. There was no music, and as I walked in no heads turned my way.

Maybe the barman wouldn't serve me. And what if they told Mum and Mark – *my parents* – that I'd been there?

But it couldn't be a crime just to go in. It wasn't even that late.

I'd just ask for a lemonade and drink it, and then go back to bed.

There was someone sitting at the bar already, a vaguely familiar someone with his big back turned towards me. Part of me flinched from the idea of going over there to stand next to a lone man, but I carried on regardless.

And then I recognised him. It was the piano player from our first night there. I recognised the barman, too; it was the waiter who'd served us dinner the first night.

I asked for a lemonade in my best French. I had just enough money to pay for it. And then – to be polite, to make conversation, because I was lonely – I said, in French, to the man sitting next to me, 'You're not playing the piano tonight?'

He inclined his head and looked me up and down.

'I don't do that every night. It's a hobby, really,' he said in English. 'I do it as a favour to the manager as much as anything else. Also, it's a very good piano.'

'You're English,' I said stupidly.

'So are you.'

That seemed to make what I was doing safer. In that environment, it was virtually like bumping into a neighbour. I settled onto the bar stool next to him, because why not? Who else was I going to talk to?

The barman tactfully withdrew to the other side of the bar and started discreetly polishing glasses. I said, 'So where are you from?'

'London, mostly. I have a flat there, but I move around. I have a job selling holiday apartments, here and in other places. You?'

'Oh… We live near London. For now. But my parents have decided to move.'

My parents. Not a phrase I'd ever had much use for. I didn't really talk about my family, with Molly or Jasmine or anybody else.

But at one time, if I had decided to open up a little, I might have said something like: *My parents are divorced, I don't see my dad very often…*

And now *my parents* meant something else, and so did *my dad.* It meant Mark taking over, basically. His sudden and enormous power over all our lives.

I carefully sipped my lemonade and set my glass down on the bar.

'I take it you don't get on,' the piano player said.

'I don't really know whether we get on or not,' I said. 'I've only known my dad for a couple of months.' There, I'd done it. I'd called Mark my dad, though not when he was there to hear. 'That scene in here a couple of nights ago? That was when he told me he was my father.'

So this was the point of hanging out in bars. Maybe this was why Sean liked it. You said things that mattered to you, things that you would have thought were impossible to say to anyone.

There was a long pause, so long that I thought maybe he hadn't taken in what I'd just told him. Eventually he said, 'So that's what's been going on. I thought he looked like he felt bad about something.'

'I guess he did.'

It was reassuring to picture the scene as he must have perceived it. It turned it into something that could be reviewed and picked over for little nuggets of insight or truth, the way you might analyse a set text in an English literature exam.

The barman broke off from drying glasses and took us in with an expression that was disconcerted and resigned and impressed all at once, a mixture of *is that really happening?* and *so that's the way the wind's blowing*.

I said, 'What did you think was going on?'

He shrugged. 'I didn't really try to figure it out. I just thought, *What a beautiful girl.*'

That was all it took: that little affirmation, that little compliment, as sweet and heady as Armagnac sucked off a sugar cube.

It was a rush I hadn't realised I'd been craving. He'd noticed me, and I wanted him to notice me more. More than that, I wanted him to like me. I *needed* him to like me. I was new to this, but I knew what it meant anyway, and I didn't care what I might need to do to make it happen.

By the time I went back upstairs I had his name and number in my phone. He was called Jake Hillerman: a name I could already imagine myself doodling, then destroying all evidence of. Ellie didn't stir as I let myself into our room, and as soon as I got into bed I fell into a deep and dreamless sleep.

A few weeks later, on the free day between my final Maths paper and my first History exam, I lied to my mother, caught the train into central London and met him at the Barbican.

I wore a dress that I'd taken with me in my schoolbag, and changed into in the ladies' at Waterloo station. I'd agonised about what to wear; I wanted to look sophisticated – I didn't want him to be put off by how young I was.

He hadn't asked my age, and I hadn't told him. I assumed he thought I was older than I was, and I didn't want to scare him off. I soon realised I needn't have worried. He complimented me on the way I looked, but it was obvious even to me that he wasn't really interested in my clothes.

We looked round a gallery, had lunch. I was scornful about the artworks and made him laugh, and we shared a bottle of wine. All the social muscles I'd always resisted using sprang into action and started working overtime. I was off: I was doing everything I could to hold his interest, to make him want me.

He told me I was a philistine. I said, 'You'll have to educate me, then,' and he looked at me thoughtfully and said, 'Well, I might.'

I asked him if he'd fallen in love with me. I meant it as a joke, but actually, I was wondering if he might, or if I would fall in love with him.

He said, 'I think I have. You're charming and funny and bright and beautiful. Why wouldn't I fall for you?'

A lie can sound just like the truth, especially if it is what you want to hear, and the biggest and most dangerous lies of all can be the ones you most want to believe. And so I accepted this compliment unquestioningly, as if it was a gift too good to say no to. And then I let him take me upstairs to his small, bare, plainly furnished apartment, and to his bed.

We spent an hour together before I needed to go and catch my train. And he did educate me, just as he had promised.

He showed me that you can take something precious from someone without them realising it's gone, and that the easiest way to do this is to persuade them to give it to you.

And he introduced me to the comfort of being close to someone, as close as it's possible to be. But as I found out on the train afterwards, however much you try to make the moment last, and however much you give up for it, sooner or later you'll find yourself travelling home alone.

Chapter Fifteen

Jenny

On the flight back from France I sat next to Mark with the girls behind us, as we'd done on the way out. Ellie and Ava were both quiet, and Ava looked tired. She let Ellie have the windowseat – uncharacteristically generous – and got out one of the textbooks she'd insisted on bringing so she could revise from it, but hadn't touched all holiday. They both spent the journey with their noses in their books, apparently oblivious to the clouds floating past the plane window and everything else.

Well, Ellie had always been capable of losing herself in whatever she was reading, and Ava was bound to be preoccupied. Her time out was over, and it was back to the reality of exams.

It was always a mistake, with girls that age – of any age – to jump to conclusions about what was bothering them.

If she seemed all right, it was probably as much of a sign as we could hope for that she was. She needed time and space to get used to Mark, and we had to respect that.

But I worried about her anyway. It was a dull, constant worry, like a niggling toothache that might yet explode into a crisis.

I was so lucky, so blessed. My mum would have been so happy if she could have known that she was a grandmother of three.

So why didn't I feel it?

Back in London it was raining – not heavily, just a persistent drizzle falling from a sunless grey sky. It was like leaving one dream for another, in which everything was familiar but too faint and faded to be real.

Mark put us in a taxi; he was going to travel separately to his house in Oxfordshire. I said to him, 'I wish we were going with you,' and he said, 'It won't be for long, Jenny. I'll call you tonight,' and closed the taxi door and waved us off.

We hadn't got far before Ava fell asleep. She was sitting next to me, and Ellie was facing us because she was the one who didn't mind travelling backwards. She could read in cars quite happily too, and had *Wuthering Heights* open on her knees.

As the traffic stopped and started Ava's head sagged and her shoulders slumped until she was leaning on me with her head nestled on my shoulder. She was warm and soft and heavy – a little too heavy, given that she was as tall as I was now, but I was very happy to be slightly squashed by her. It was so rare to be this close to her for any length of time. She smelled of Ava, sweet but not too sweet, the way she always had.

It was humbling to think that she'd once been as tiny as the baby I was carrying now. I was filled with a sudden rush of pity for Mark for having missed all the stages that had passed in between, for not having known Ava the toddler or the little girl or the younger adolescent who had smiled in such a way as to hide the braces on her teeth.

Pity... and guilt.

That whole childhood, all those years of scraped knees and friendship problems and crazes and times-tables, all the things she'd loved – snowdays, Easter eggs, ice pops stored in the freezer compartment for summer, sparklers on Bonfire Night. He'd missed it all.

I had been so sure that Mark had meant what he said when he told me he'd got back together with Paula, and I shouldn't contact him again. I had believed that he didn't want to know. That there was no point telling him about the baby, and it was down to me to decide what to do next.

But how could anyone ever be sure how anyone would react to anything? I hadn't persisted. I hadn't given him the chance. I'd fallen into Sean's arms because he was there and it was easy… and it had been comforting, and flattering. And also, if I was really honest, because all the pregnancy hormones had driven me wild with lust, and even though I'd never really found Sean attractive before, all of a sudden I'd found him irresistible. Besides, I hadn't been able to come up with any particularly convincing reasons why I *should* resist him. What did I have to lose? Or so I thought at the time.

After all, I'd already lost Mark, not that he'd ever really been mine in the first place. But I'd been left with vivid memories of our short time together – painfully vivid. Being with someone else seemed like the best way to force them to fade.

One day, when Sean and I had the house to ourselves, we made love and then took a bath together: the kind of thing young lovers do. He soaped me tenderly and dried me, and we got dressed and went to the pub – lemonade for me, a pint for him – and he said, in a sudden rush as if it had only just occurred to him, 'I think we ought to get married.'

And I was thrilled. Thrilled – but stunned.

'But, Sean—'

'You don't have to answer now. But I do mean it, and I have thought about it. I love you, and I want to take care of you. You and the baby.' He swigged a mouthful of beer, set his glass down. 'Just think about it, OK? No rush. Whenever you're ready, I'll be here. I won't change my mind.' He knocked back some more beer. He was clearly nervous. 'I'm not saying we should lie to anyone. But, you know… if we get married you can just let people think what they're going to think. It might make things easier for you.'

He was right. People did assume that he was the father of my baby, and we didn't bother explaining that he wasn't. And I could see that this made things easier for Sean, too.

Then, when I was beginning to show, our landlord started asking awkward questions and Sean found somewhere for us to move into together.

Our new home was a converted loft in a house that belonged to a regular at the pub Sean worked in. It was always either too hot or too cold, and given that it was up three flights of stairs, it was hopelessly impractical for a couple with a baby on the way. But I didn't care about any of that at the time. I was over the moon about it.

I'd been avoiding my mother, for obvious reasons, and she clearly suspected something was up, and had been sounding more and more worried when we spoke on the phone. But then I invited her to visit and introduced her to Sean and she seemed thoroughly relieved. As soon as he'd gone off for his shift at the pub, she said what a nice lad he was. And then I told her he was looking for another job, something that would pay more, and broke the news about the baby and she hugged me and cried and said she'd been wondering how long I was going to leave it before saying anything.

Turned out she'd had her suspicions for a while, though she hadn't been sure. She often had an uncanny way of knowing things she had no way of knowing... though, as I was to find out, that didn't mean she was always right. There was a lot she didn't see. And some of it, like Sean's drinking, was pretty obvious; even on that occasion, he'd got through a couple of cans before leaving for work. But she liked him, and that was all the approval I needed.

We put his name down on Ava's birth certificate – 'After all, it might as well be true,' Sean had said – and a few months later we tied the knot.

What a disaster that had turned out to be.

Well, not completely a disaster, because I had Ellie. But not easy, either.

I looked out of the window and listened to Ava's steady breathing and the occasional riffling sound of Ellie turning pages.

What had happened was as close as Mark and I would get to turning back the clock. And this time, we would get it right.

We had to.

For years, the girls had been all I had. I'd lost my parents. I'd lost my sister, though she was still alive. And Sean was Sean, lost from the start, though I hadn't realised it.

Now I had Mark and a new baby on the way. But I couldn't allow the price of that to be a more distant relationship with Ellie and Ava. There was absolutely no way in the world I was ever going to lose anybody who was close to me again.

My falling-out with Amanda had started with her accusing Sean of being drunk at Mum's wake, which he was, of course. I defended him anyway, and then she asked him to leave, which he did, and told me I was a bad mother for letting him carry on seeing the kids, and I told her to stay out of it and called her a snob and other things were said that shouldn't have been. Afterwards neither of us had made the effort to apologise, and the row had hardened into an estrangement and become fixed. An end point. Perhaps it had always been inevitable that without Mum to hold us together, we were bound to fall out. I just never would have imagined that it could happen so quickly, or so completely.

But even when I didn't see Amanda any more, even though we didn't call or send Christmas cards, I still thought about her.

Sometimes the people we haven't spoken to for years are the ones who made us who we are. More than anyone else, Amanda was the person who turned me into a hairdresser. And if I hadn't become a hairdresser, I never would have met Mark.

When she was a girl Amanda's hair was long and blonde, like Ava's but curlier. I always wanted to play with it, and she would never let me. She was much older than me, and she was always the kind of person who knows her own mind.

One of the quickest ways to annoy her was to shorten her name. She wanted to be serious, and she didn't see nicknames as affectionate. She saw them as evidence of disrespect. When she was little people had called her Mandy, but then she had insisted that everyone ought to use her full name. And everyone did, which tells you something about her strength of will and stubbornness.

Eventually Mum got me a Girl's World as an outlet for my hair obsession, and I loved it, but Amanda disapproved. She was fiercely serious, not at all into pop music or make-up or fashion or any of the things that I was interested in, and that I was supposedly too young for.

My dad died of a heart attack when I was seven and Amanda was fourteen. A few weeks later, before the funeral, I overheard Mum on the phone, talking to one of her friends. She was singing Amanda's praises. What a help she'd been, in the last few weeks. What a tower of strength. So grown up, so reliable, mature beyond her years. She really didn't know what she would have done without her.

She didn't mention me.

I hadn't really cried about Dad – it would have been like crying about a crater that had suddenly opened up in the house, or a black hole. You can't cry about something you can't understand, that you can't feel: and you can't feel or understand a void. His sudden and complete and overwhelming absence was too big and shocking for tears.

But I cried about the fact that my sister was so very helpful, and I was nothing at all.

When Mum came upstairs and comforted me and asked me if I was crying about Dad, I told her the truth. She was surprised, but she wasn't angry. She told me that it wasn't a good idea to listen into other people's conversations, that what you picked up was only ever part of the story. And then she held me tight, and told me that I did help her, all the time, and especially now that Dad had gone.

'You're my reason for getting up in the morning,' she told me. 'I know Amanda will get herself up and out of the house and off to school on time, but if I didn't tell you to get out of bed you never would, would you? You see, it's good for people to be needed. It keeps us going.'

And then, the morning before the funeral, she arranged for a hairdresser to come to the house and plait my hair with ribbons, and pin it up in a circle around my head.

I felt like I was wearing a crown. Somehow, it made it possible – necessary – to get through it. To be dignified. To manage. And pretty much every single adult who spoke to me at the funeral (often through tears, and sometimes it was hard to make out what they were saying) told me how much they liked my hair.

That was when I discovered what I wanted to be when I grew up.

Before then, I'd loved doing hair, but I'd assumed that when it came down to it, it was unlikely that I'd get a job that was so much fun, any more than people in real life were ballerinas or fairies or any of the other interesting things that they were in books. But afterwards, I was determined. I didn't want to do anything else.

Both Amanda and I wanted to leave small-town life behind. Almost inevitably, she did it first and better. By the time I met Mark she'd already bought a flat in a nice bit of London and been promoted to manage a team at the bank where she worked, as Mum was fond of telling just about everyone. Plus she was going out with a tax consultant who owned a horse and a house in Fulham. Mum was fond of telling everybody that, too.

By way of contrast, I was renting a room in a shared house in Chessington, on the outskirts. I wasn't seeing anybody. And after six months at the salon, I was already desperate to leave. There was a clear pecking order, and the only member of staff who was lower down than me was Sarah the Saturday girl, who did the sweeping up and shampooing and wasn't allowed to go near the scissors.

I was counting down the minutes to five o'clock and the end of the working day when Mark walked in.

All I had to do was finish off Mrs Brinsdown's blow-dry, which I'd timed perfectly. It was Saturday night and I was going out, and I had my new pink top on and so what if Anita, the manager, had commented snootily that it was a bit lower-cut than she usually liked to see in her salon? In a couple of years' time Anita would probably still be here, and I'd be a hairdresser to the stars, being flown around the world by private jet so I could attend to VIPs.

Then there he was, the best-looking man I'd ever seen in the flesh, standing by the desk with the till at the front of the salon.

He was everything just about right: nice height, nice eyes, good build. Good hair. Decent clothes, not obviously try-hard or flashy or fashion.

Chances were he had a girlfriend, probably a devastatingly attractive one. He was the kind of man Mum would have loved, and Amanda would have had to work hard not to be jealous of, and who I would never in a million years have a chance of bringing home.

Anita had nipped out to the kitchen to fix her client another cup of complimentary coffee – in other words, to have a fag break. It was down to me to talk to him.

I put down the hairdryer on the shelf in front of the mirror, excused myself to Mrs Brinsdown and approached him.

'Can I help you?'

'I hope so,' he said. 'I'm really sorry to turn up so late, but I've tried everywhere, and they've all said no. I just need a trim – you don't need to bother washing it or anything, I did that this morning. I know you're probably about to close, but what with one thing and another I just haven't managed to get this sorted.' He tugged at the lock of hair that was falling across his forehead into his eyes; it was a good two inches long. 'I've got a family funeral to go to tomorrow,' he added.

That did it. There was no way I could turn him away now. I, of all people, understood how comforting a trip to the hairdresser could be at a difficult time.

'I'll see what I can do,' I told him. 'What's your name?'

'Mark. Mark Walsh.'

'All right then, Mark, take a seat. I'm Jenny, and I'll be your stylist today. I'll be with you as soon as I can.'

He settled down in one of the cane chairs by the bay window and watched me as I picked up the hand mirror and showed Mrs Brinsdown the back of her new hairdo.

'Hm. I can't help wondering if it isn't a little bit long,' she said doubtfully as I put the mirror away. 'I do like my hair to *last*.'

'I think it looks great,' Mark said.

Mrs Brinsdown couldn't help but look pleased.

'Hm. Well. Perhaps you're right.'

Anita came back in and opened up one of her client's foils to check the colour. I went over to her and said, 'Anita, we've had a walk-in. All he wants is a dry trim. I can do it before I go.'

Anita looked at me, took in the new arrival, then looked at me again, even more suspiciously than usual.

'I don't pay overtime, you know,' she said.

'I know. It won't take me long.'

Anita pursed her lips. 'Well, don't rush it. If a job's worth doing it's worth doing well, and I don't need any complaints.'

'I won't complain,' Mark said. 'You'd be doing me the most enormous favour.'

He could even make Anita blush. And smile.

'Well, if you're happy with what we do for you today, I hope you'll come back,' Anita said. 'And do spread the word.'

'I'm sure I will,' Mark said.

Anita went off to the basins with her client and I ushered Mrs Brinsdown to the till. When she'd gone I took Mark's coat and hung it carefully in the cupboard. It had a slim, old-looking paperback sticking out of one of the pockets: *Madame Bovary*. He was reading a French novel: how sophisticated was that? He settled into the chair Mrs Brinsdown had just vacated, and I stood behind him and sprayed his hair with water and detangler and ran a comb through it.

It really was good hair – thick, fair, slightly wavy, a bit like Amanda's but not so curly. I leaned forwards and spoke to his reflection in the mirror. 'OK, Mark, so what can I do for you today? Just a bit off the length, is it?'

'Yes, that'll do nicely.'

'Would you like to grab a magazine? Or I could get your book?'

'No, no, that's fine. It's nice to have an excuse to sit round thinking of nothing in particular.'

I started combing and snipping. Anita and her client came back from the basins and Anita set about cutting too. They were soon absorbed in a boring conversation about north-facing conservatories.

'It's really very decent of you to make the time to do this,' Mark said. 'I hope I'm not going to make you late.'

'It's OK,' I said.

I thought of my friend Karen, who was probably already in the Green Man across the road from the salon, getting hot under the collar. She hated to be kept waiting, and she'd hinted that she had big news to tell me. Either she was engaged, or she had a promotion. I couldn't see how she would have saved enough for a house just yet, and there was no way she'd be getting started on having babies.

Oh well, she'd already met Sean, my housemate, who worked there behind the bar. If it was quiet, maybe he'd get chatting to her and take her mind off things.

I worked my way back towards Mark's crown. At first I'd been dazzled by his good looks, but now I could see he was pale and tired out. Not surprisingly, given that he'd recently had a bereavement. I wondered who it was who'd gone. But it wouldn't have done to ask.

He smiled at our reflections, and my heart skipped a beat. Suddenly my knees felt weak. Genuinely weak. I'd never experienced that before.

One trick of the trade I'd never had any trouble with was making conversation and using the scissors at the same time. But making conversation with a client who made me weak at the knees? Perhaps not such a good idea. Not if I wanted to send him on his way to that funeral looking his best.

I worked round his ears with the scissors – nice, neat ears, and clean, too.

'Have you got far to go tomorrow?' I asked.

It seemed like a fail-safe question. Asking about places and journeys was usually all right. Like, *Did you come far to get here?* The Queen used that one, apparently, and if it was good enough for the Queen, it was good enough for me.

Mark's expression in the mirror didn't change, but his posture stiffened a little. Well, there was nothing comfortable about going to a funeral.

'Not too far,' he said. 'A place you probably won't have heard of. The cemetery's in a village south of Kettlebridge, in Oxfordshire. It's near where I grew up.'

'Sounds like a nice part of the world.'

'Mm. It is. Beautiful countryside. Wouldn't mind going back some day.'

'I'm a small-town girl myself but I always wanted to live in London. This is as close as I've got.'

'I'd say you'd done pretty well. If that was your dream, you've come a lot closer to making it than most people.'

'I don't know about that,' I said. 'So near… and yet so far.'

I ran the trimmer round his hairline and brushed the little bits of hair away.

'There you are,' I said. 'You're done.'

I retrieved his coat for him and he shrugged it on. *Madame Bovary* was still safely lodged in his coat pocket. I said, 'You're a keen reader, then?'

He gave me a rather melancholy smile and tapped the paperback as if it was a shared secret.

'This,' he said, 'is research.'

'Research into what?'

'Oh, why women do the things they do,' he said. 'Cheat. Have affairs. Betray their spouses. You know the kind of thing.'

Something about the bitterness with which he said this made me anxious. It was my job, after all, to make sure he left feeling better than when he'd arrived. And he'd been so lovely, and it was obvious that he was going through a bad time, what with this funeral coming up and some woman having done the dirty on him, by the sound of it. Though why you would mess around when you had a man who looked like that was beyond me.

'Not all women are like that,' I said.

Our eyes met. He gave me a rueful smile. 'I'd like to think so,' he said.

He paid in cash, and walked out into the spring sunshine without looking back. The tip he left me was so generous I nearly ran out into the street to give it back to him.

I didn't expect to see him again. I thought it'd be a one-off, an anecdote: the good-looking guy who I gave a last-minute trim just before closing time, the day before he was due to go to a funeral.

When I walked into the Green Man, I was fully expecting to find Karen there waiting for me, annoyed because I was late but also pleased to see me, and eager to tell me whatever the latest developments were in her love life.

Sean was there, pulling a pint for someone. But there was no sign of Karen. Instead, sitting at the bar, was a recently familiar, freshly trimmed head gleaming in the muted light, the short back and sides I'd just worked on: Mark, reading his book again.

Maybe I should have let him be. But I didn't. Instead I went right on over and said, 'Hello again.'

He looked up and grinned. 'My hair saviour. Can I get you a drink?'

'Well…'

'Please, I insist. You might as well tell me what you like, or you'll have to take pot luck.'

'I'll have a gin and tonic, then. Thank you.'

'Gin and tonic, please,' Mark said to Sean.

Sean made a non-committal noise that could have meant anything from *Get lost* to *All right then*. As he moved to fetch a clean glass he gave me a filthy look.

He had no right to be jealous. I'd never given him the impression he was in with a chance. And the last thing I needed right now was him glowering at me from behind the bar.

'Mark, this is Sean, my housemate,' I said.

Mark looked at Sean without much interest. 'Oh, you share a house, do you?'

'Yes, there are five of us.'

'It gets pretty rowdy,' Sean said, looking daggers at Mark now. 'Usually lots of people around, playing music, that kind of thing. Especially on a Saturday night.'

I felt myself blushing. Sean was seriously trying to put Mark off coming back home with me… as if that was likely to happen! Really, he was being ridiculously possessive. Completely out of order.

'Sounds fun,' Mark said blandly.

'It passes the time,' Sean said with another cold look for me.

He gave me my drink and took Mark's money and gave him his change, giving off a vibe of poorly suppressed antagonism the whole time. I hoped the pub would get busy quickly so that he'd be run off his feet and wouldn't have time to glare at us. It wasn't exactly going to be easy to enjoy a nice relaxed chat with Sean radiating hostility the whole time.

But then, to my relief, Sean seemed to give up. He took himself off to the other end of the bar, flicked through one of the papers and started doing the crossword.

'Friendly chap,' Mark said under his breath.

'He's usually all right,' I said. 'I don't know what's got into him.' Though I had a pretty good idea what was up. I just hadn't realised Sean liked me quite so much.

Mark asked who I was meeting and I told him about Karen, and gradually I became less self-conscious. It felt so good being there, talking to him, it was as if we'd always been meant to meet.

When we'd both finished our drinks he said, 'How about another?'

'But you've got a funeral tomorrow,' I said. 'Shouldn't you be taking it gently? You know, having an early night?'

'It's only just gone six,' he pointed out.

'True.' My stomach rumbled. 'But I'm a lightweight. If I have another drink without eating anything I'll fall over on the way out of here.'

'Let's go get something to eat,' he said.

I said yes. Of course I said yes. I was hungry. And I felt sorry for him, and I fancied him rotten. Also, I was curious. Intrigued. I wanted to know more about him. About the funeral he was going to. The woman who'd betrayed him. He seemed so lovely, so perfect... why on earth would anyone do that to him? And what on earth could anybody else possibly have that he lacked? I wanted his story – all the things he might have told me if he'd learned to trust me, if I'd cut his hair not just the once but again and again, over months and years.

Karen would understand... wouldn't she? I decided to ask Sean to let her know where we'd gone... *if* she ever showed up.

He was still busy pretending to be engrossed in his crossword and looked up resentfully, as if I'd just interrupted something important.

'You remember my friend Karen, right?' I said. 'The blonde one who talks very fast, who's going out with the bald guy with no neck?'

He shrugged. 'Yeah, I remember.'

'If she turns up, will you tell her I've gone to the pizza place round the corner? She's welcome to join us.'

Sean raised his eyebrows. 'Yeah, right. Sure she is. Who is that guy you're with, anyway? Do you even know him?'

'I'm starting to,' I said.

As if it was any of his business! But then, he had a crush on me, so of course he didn't like seeing me with someone else. He couldn't help himself, any more than I could.

Mark took my hand as we left the pub together, and it felt quite natural. We found a phone box and he waited patiently outside while I got my little floral address book out of my bag and rang Karen.

One of her housemates answered and told me she'd had a big row with her boyfriend the day before and then he'd turned up that evening with flowers and wine and her favourite takeout, and they'd been in her room ever since. I left her a message and hurried off to join Mark.

'Turns out she's fine. She's with her boyfriend. Sorry about that – keeping you hanging round waiting,' I said.

He gave me a grin that told me I was more than worth it. 'Don't apologise. It was nice of you to be worried about her. Most people would just assume they'd been stood up. And you don't even look that annoyed. You must be very forgiving.'

I took his hand again. 'Let's just say I think it's turned out all right.'

We went to the pizza place, ate, shared a bottle of wine. He drank most of it, but I still had enough to get tipsy – I was a lightweight, as I'd told him. The conversation was easy. I entertained him with stories of my customers, and he allowed himself to be entertained. He didn't seem to be in the mood for talking about himself, and I didn't push him to. I figured he was after distraction, and I was only too happy to help.

Over coffee I said, 'Won't it make it worse, tomorrow, if you turn up with a hangover?'

'No, that's exactly what I want,' he told me. 'I want to be so hungover I can't think about anything else.'

'So… how are you getting there?'

'Oh, don't worry, I'm not driving. I'm going by train. I can't drive.' He sighed. 'I'm a useless person, Jenny. A failure. I did one year of a PhD and then I didn't get any more funding and I had to give it up, and now I work in a bookshop and I have no idea whatsoever what to do with the rest of my life.'

'I'm sure you're not useless at all.'

He looked at me seriously. 'You're very sweet, aren't you?'

I shrugged. 'I try to be.'

There was a pause during which he carried on looking at me and it became possible for me to ask the question that had been on my mind ever since he'd told me why he was so keen to have his hair cut that day.

'So… if you don't mind me asking, whose funeral is it? Was it someone close?'

His eyes went very cold. They were pale blue, the kind of blue that reminds you of the colour of the sea on a cloudy day, and that lends itself to turning icy.

'No, not close,' he said. 'It was my aunt. I actually didn't know her. It's really just a family obligation thing. My mother's on her own – my dad passed away a couple of years ago. So I'm going along as moral support.'

'That's good of you,' I said, then, with a sense of exposing something important about myself, 'My dad isn't around any more, either. He died of a heart attack when I was little.'

'Mine crashed his car into a tree. There were questions asked about it, but in the end the verdict at the inquest was accidental death,' Mark said.

'I'm so sorry.'

He was looking at me in that special, serious way again. Under the table, his legs pressed against mine on either side and squeezed them together. As if what he wanted wasn't sex, but someone to embrace, to hold on to.

'I'm sorry about your dad, too,' he said.

Then he asked for the bill and insisted on paying, and we went out onto the street and found that it was pouring with rain.

We joked about it ruining his haircut and he suggested taking shelter at the nearest possible place and I asked where that was and he said just round the corner... his flat, and would I like yet another coffee? Or maybe something stronger?

I said, 'What about tomorrow?'

'Oh, don't worry about that.'

He pulled me in towards him and kissed me, and then I really was completely lost.

Later on, when we were in each other's arms on his sofa with the lights down low and the album of the moment playing in the background, he said he had something to tell me.

'I'm married. But we're separated.'

'Did she have an affair?'

His face twisted up as if he'd just been physically hurt. Then he composed himself. 'She fell in love with someone else. A colleague.'

'Oh.'

I could have said thank you and goodbye, got up, straightened my clothing and gone home. But I didn't. I carried on lying there.

'So technically this is cheating,' I said.

'You could see it that way, I suppose.'

'Nobody could ever cheat on anybody unless someone helped them do it. I'm not really that kind of person.'

'I know you're not,' he said. 'I could tell that about you straight away. You're kind, and decent and honest, Jenny. And those are rare qualities, believe me.'

'If I was all the things you've just said, I'd go.'

'Don't go.' He pulled me towards him and held me tight. 'Don't leave me, Jenny.'

And I didn't, and by and by I let him lead me to the bedroom.

He had told me that the flat belonged to a friend who was away and had let him stay, that he had never been there with his wife. Paula. He said her name with a peculiar mix of softness and bitterness and protectiveness, as if he was letting me into something intimate, something he wouldn't normally have wanted people to see. Something he was ashamed of.

I'd heard that tone of voice, that mix of hatred and nostalgia, plenty of times when people talked about their exes. It was the sound of love gone wrong. It was that, more than anything, that convinced me it was over between them, and allowed me to put the thought of her out of my mind.

It didn't occur to me that what he was doing might be a kind of vengeance. It didn't feel that way. I'd had boyfriends before, but this was different. It was the first time sex really made sense. That was the night I understood it wasn't all about awkwardness and risk, and whether you looked all right and were any good at it, and whether his body was going to do what it was supposed to do and whether yours would too.

Mark showed me that it was about being with someone. Really being with them. And forgetting everything else.

Afterwards, when he said he thought the condom had split, I did a swift but vague calculation of the odds and said, 'Oh, never mind. I'm sure it'll be fine.'

'You sure? I wouldn't want you to be worrying about it,' he said.

'I'm not worried.'

He pulled a face to say that in that case, he wasn't worried either. 'Apparently it's a lot more difficult to get pregnant than people realise.'

'You seem to know an awful lot about it,' I said, with a smile to show that I was teasing him.

'What I *do* know,' he said seriously, 'is that right here, right now, I'm happy. With you.'

And then he took me in his arms again and kissed me. And there I was, drowsy and lucky and warm, all wrapped up in the cocoon of the moment as if neither us nor time would ever be going anywhere. And it really did feel as if nothing could go wrong.

Chapter Sixteen

Paula

Someone once said that those whom the gods want to drive nuts, they give what they want. I had wanted a baby more than I'd ever wanted anything in my life (including my husband, not that I was going to tell him that). But living with Daisy turned out to be very different to longing for her.

All the awful bits of motherhood (childbirth, lack of sleep) were so much worse than anyone let on, and the good bits (peaceful, milky cuddles, admiring the baby when she finally slept) were satisfying in their way, but took a lot more slogging to get to than I'd imagined.

I began to have a sneaky sympathy for my mother's concerted selfishness throughout my childhood. After all, she'd been through all this with me. No wonder she thought she deserved to enjoy herself.

My daughter finally arrived after a twenty-four-hour labour that ended with a caesarean section. The whole thing felt like being bombed from the inside, and then trying to make a new life in the rubble. For a long time I couldn't see beyond the next sleep, the next feed. I knew I couldn't really complain. After all, I'd asked for it. And who would I have complained to? Not Mark, who clearly wasn't entirely loving it either, but at least got to disappear off to work once in a while. Not my mother, who would just have said, 'I told you so.' And not my friends, who would have thought there was something wrong with me.

It was just nature's savage little practical joke, and I was on the receiving end. There was nobody to take it out on… and nobody to blame but myself.

I was completely cured of baby hunger – I couldn't even imagine being broody ever again. My figure, which I'd once been vain about, was wrecked: I was suddenly soft and saggy where I'd once been firm and supple, and it would have taken a much more rigorous campaign of exercise than I had time for to restore it. And then, as the broken nights took their toll, my looks began to go, too.

As for my libido… that had pretty much disappeared, or was it that Mark had stopped fancying me? It was hard to tell. We managed to have sex occasionally, but it wasn't what it had been, and since it was the one part of our life together that could be relied upon to smooth out everything else, I was aware that I ought to make a bit more of an effort. But somehow I couldn't summon up the energy.

It wasn't just that I wasn't wild with lust for Mark; I wasn't wild with lust for anybody. I couldn't even imagine having a crush. The feelings I'd had for Lewis, my long-ago colleague, seemed to belong to another life.

I was actually glad that brief infatuation had never been consummated, and had never moved beyond a little drunken handholding, for all the trouble it had caused. I'd never seen Lewis naked, or found out what he was like in bed, or whether he snored and hogged the duvet and was moody in the morning – in some ways, I'd never really got to know him at all. All I was left with was a vivid memory of his warm brown eyes and the knowledge that, for a little while, he had really, really liked me, and I had really liked him too – which wasn't nothing, given that even in my twenties, when I didn't look knackered and harassed all the time, I had never been the kind of woman men made a beeline for.

With Mark, I'd made most of the running – I'd pursued him, not obviously, of course, but strategically. With Lewis, there had been no strategy; it had just been something that happened. An accident. With hindsight, it was obvious that I shouldn't have told Mark about it. If I'd waited, it would have died a death of natural causes. Instead of which Mark had moved out for a couple of weeks, and I'd had to change jobs to persuade him there was really no risk of anything ever happening, and then had spent months, if not years, making it up to him. Right up until the point where we'd had Daisy.

And now I wasn't capable of making anything up to him any more.

At least I'd learned the useful lesson that you didn't have to tell your husband everything. It didn't even occur to me to try to talk to him about how gruelling I was finding motherhood. After all, it was pretty obvious, if only he chose to see it. And I really didn't want to have to listen to him telling me that he felt the same way about fatherhood. It just would have been too infuriating, given that I was the one who looked after Daisy most of the time. And there was absolutely no point in me explaining how much I resented him for sleeping peacefully while I struggled to settle her during the nights. He was the one who was working and earning, and I wasn't. I would just have to keep going, and wait for things to change.

Once or twice other women I met at coffee mornings or music classes, women who had older children as well as babies, recognised that I felt I wasn't doing a very good job of motherhood and kindly told me it would get easier. It did, in some ways. But in other ways – ways I had never anticipated – it got harder.

When Daisy was a year old I found a childminder and started to do a bit of proofreading a few days a week from home, and the guilty freedom I felt as I walked home after leaving her was offset by the sudden new challenge of having deadlines to meet, as well as the depressing reality of how little was left of my earnings after I'd paid for her care. It was also matched by guilt of another kind – guilt that I could barely begin to acknowledge, even to myself.

All parents are dreamers. Romantics. Fantasists. The flipside of the fear we feel for our children is hope. Who hasn't looked at their little one and wanted great things for them? Mark and I were no different. As months went by and Daisy became more settled, there were intervals of calm when we gazed at her in her cot and imagined lives for her – all kinds of lives. She could become a doctor, a ballerina, an explorer... a scientist, a poet, an entrepreneur. So many possibilities, all wide open. Or so it seemed.

Ingrid was the first person to suggest that for Daisy, those opportunities might not be open at all.

It started with a disastrous evening of babysitting, when Daisy cried solidly for hours and she had to call us and ask us to come home. Then I caught her looking suspiciously at me when I fed Daisy with a spoon rather than her feeding herself. There were questions about potty training, sleeping, whether Daisy was talking yet. Insinuations, or so I felt.

I complained to Mark about it. I wanted him to come down on our side, to say she was being ridiculous, but he didn't. Instead he had words with her and afterwards he was sombre-faced and refused to tell me what she'd said.

Suddenly, having my mother-in-law nearby stopped meaning free babysitting and started to mean trouble. I no longer left Daisy alone with her, and we began to see her less and less. I'd have been happy to stop seeing her entirely, but I knew Mark wouldn't be able to bring himself to cut off contact, no matter how insensitive she was, so resigned myself to occasional frosty visits.

'We just need to give Daisy time,' I said to Mark more than once. 'She'll catch up.'

But time, as it turned out, was not on our side.

Never underestimate the power of denial, as someone else once said. But some kinds of denial can't last forever. And on the day of the pre-school Christmas show, when Daisy was three years old, our time was finally up.

When we arrived, half an hour before the performance was due to start, there was already a queue lined up along the wooden porch that ran the length of the pre-school building, spilling out onto the shallow steps alongside the ramp. They were mainly mums, with a few dads and grandparents, all huddled in their anoraks and hats and scarves. Mark, who had taken the morning off work, was the only one there in a suit and overcoat.

He did not look best impressed. 'Looks like we should have got here even earlier,' he grumbled.

'We should still be able to get seats. I hadn't realised it was going to be quite so popular.'

Mark looked round at the Portakabin that housed the pre-school, and the outdoor play area with its old tyres to sit on and faded plastic ride-on toys. The fence that separated the pre-school play area from the neighbouring primary school playground was decorated with hangings crafted from old CDs that the children had covered with glitter and stick-on jewels. To my eyes, it looked cheerful and friendly. But it seemed that wasn't how it appeared to Mark.

'I do wonder if this is really the best we can do for her,' he said, not quite quietly enough for only me to hear. 'We need to help her get on, not hold her back. Especially now, while she's so little. The brain is just like a sponge at that age, soaking everything in. We need to make sure she's in the right environment.'

The dad who was ahead of us in the queue, who was scrawny but tough-looking and had the air of being up for a fight, turned round to give us a brief, baleful stare.

'For heaven's sake,' I hissed at Mark, 'if you're going to criticise the place, keep your voice down. Can't we talk about it later?'

Mark had the grace to look a little sheepish.

'It's just, you know… I want the best for her.'

'I know. Me too.'

And then, as if there was no point talking to me at all if we couldn't discuss what was really on his mind, he got out his phone and gave that all his attention instead.

One of the mums I sometimes chatted to joined the lengthening queue, spotted me and waved. I waved back and hoped she wouldn't see me with Mark engrossed by his phone and assume we had a terrible marriage. Anyway, it was just as well she was too far back in the queue for me to need to try to introduce her, because I couldn't remember her name. I thought of her as Lydia's mum, and probably she thought of me as Daisy's mum. This was how it was, for all of us: inside the school gates, we belonged to our children.

Mark put his phone away, turned to me and said, 'Have you got the tickets?'

I fished the two copies of the show programme that had been sent home in advance out of my handbag and held them out to him. He took one, opened it, briefly scanned it, and then folded it and stuffed it in his pocket without comment.

Out of sight. But not quite out of mind.

The programme was illustrated with a selection of Christmas-themed drawings by the children: wobbly six-pointed stars made of two triangles drawn over each other, stick people with wings, even a more or less recognisable angel. I hadn't asked Daisy whether any of the drawings were hers. Just like Mark, I had known at a glance that they weren't.

Daisy showed no interest in drawing at all. Either that… or she just couldn't do it. She did like to paint, though: she just didn't paint anything in particular. Every now and then her artwork came home in her bookbag. Everything looked like an abstract sunset: great washes and stripes and whorls of colour blurring into each other, but nothing you could identify as anything else.

You couldn't put abstract sunsets on a photocopied programme for a Christmas show. Shrunk down and reproduced in black and white, they'd just look like… like something that didn't make sense. A mistake. Something with no reason to be there.

But Daisy's birthday was in the spring and some of these kids were four already, and at that age, six months made a big difference…

Anyway, we knew her development was lagging behind, but we'd been given to understand that there was no immediate cause for concern. After all, she *was* developing – just not as quickly as might have been expected. I'd spoken to the health visitor about it at her two-year check; I'd chatted about it to Donna, the pre-school supervisor, after filling in all the background information forms and being struck all over again by how much she couldn't do. They'd both said *keep doing your best* and *wait and see*. Nobody, apart from Ingrid, had insisted that there was something to worry about.

But what if there was?

The queue suddenly began to move forward. 'Finally,' Mark said. 'Let's hope this is worth the wait.'

As I made my way up the steps behind him I felt a pang of foreboding. But that was ridiculous; there was nothing ominous about this. Precisely the opposite. What could be sweeter than a Christmas show put on by little children?

It was just a weird kind of nerves, that was all… it was another of those parental firsts. The children were so little, nobody would be expecting too much of them, and Daisy wouldn't be the only one who had never done anything in front of an audience before. This was just a bit of fun, a chance to show off to the grown-ups.

I showed our programmes to the pre-school assistant at the door – it was Amy, the plump, blonde, motherly woman who was Daisy's key worker.

Amy beamed at me. 'She's done ever so well,' she said. 'It's a lovely show.'

On top of the bookshelf to one side, I spotted something Amy had put there specifically for Daisy: a little pot of gluesticks. Daisy loved nothing better than to take one of them and roll them between her hands. She would do the same with almost any small object – straws or teaspoons were favourites, too.

Part of me felt that Amy should be trying to stop her doing this, and part of me felt Daisy needed to do it and would have found a way of doing it anyway. I hadn't mentioned it to Mark. I was pretty sure he would have objected, and it was easier just to accept it, the way we had both accepted that it would be a struggle to get Daisy off to sleep every evening, and that sometime in the early hours of the morning she would wake up and come into our bed and Mark would sigh and go off to the spare room.

Mark was aware of Daisy's twiddling habit, of course. He'd once tried to take something she was rolling around in her hands away from her, and she'd been absolutely inconsolable until he gave it back. Screaming, crying, lashing out, rolling round on the ground. You'd have thought somebody was trying to kill her, or at the very least abduct her. He'd never tried that again.

There were rows of the low chairs the children used set up for the parents to perch on, as if we were an audience of overgrown pre-schoolers. Mark had grabbed the last two seats at the front, facing the makeshift stage. I smiled at Amy and made my way over to settle next to him and wait for the show to begin.

An awful lot of early childhood – perhaps of education in general – is learning how to behave as part of a group. Basically, you have to learn to submit to doing what you're told, and to get through the boredom that usually follows.

This was not Daisy's forte, and it was immediately obvious that this had been taken into account when the staff were planning the Christmas performance and working out how to stage it.

A couple of big cardboard boxes had been reassembled and painted to create the curved prow of a ship. Most of the children were sitting in rows on the carpet; others were sitting on chairs inside the boat, visible from the chest upwards. Daisy was right in the point of the prow, wedged into place so she couldn't wander.

She and the other children were meant to be stars – they were all wearing navy-blue Fruit of the Loom T-shirts with star shapes in silver sewn onto them, and holding silver paper stars attached to silver-painted sticks, like wands. Daisy was rolling her star wand to and fro between her hands – not frantically, but slowly, thoughtfully, with a serious expression, as if she was a junior ballerina executing exercises at the barre.

I had sewn the star on Daisy's T-shirt late one night, after finally getting her off to sleep. I hadn't made a great job of it. I was never going to be the costume-making, cake-baking kind of mother. But I'd done my best... hadn't I?

Could I have done more?

Should I?

Mark called out to her: 'Daisy!' She ignored him. Next to her, a small child regarded her in bemusement.

'Billy! Billy, mate! Break a leg!'

It was the tough-looking dad who'd glowered at us in the queue: he'd also made his way to a seat in the front row, a couple of places along from us. A lively boy in brown who was sitting on the carpet waved frantically to him, and the man gave him a big thumbs up sign and an encouraging smile. Suddenly he didn't look quite so tough after all.

Next to the boy was my friend's daughter, Lydia, wearing blue and holding a baby doll, beaming and blushing as her mother looked on fondly from a seat somewhere behind me.

Billy and Lydia were Joseph and Mary, obviously. The children who had been entrusted with the responsibility of leading roles. Children who were not only conscious of their parents sitting in the audience, but were pleased and proud to have them there, and determined to impress them.

But Daisy seemed not to see us that way, as people she could please or disappoint, or exert any influence over – when she noticed us at all.

Mark fell to staring gloomily into space. I wanted to say something to him, to make him feel better, to jolly him out of it, to remind him that I was there too – anything, from *I don't think she saw you* to *she's probably feeling a bit overwhelmed* to *don't they look lovely?*

But I couldn't. I knew I wouldn't be able to comfort him.

And now it was showtime.

I had a slightly sick feeling in the pit of my stomach as Donna, the pre-school supervisor, stood in front of the stage and gave us the spiel about fire exits and not taking photographs until the end and not sharing them on social media, and reminded us that a video recording was being made and would be available for purchase.

Meanwhile Amy picked her way round the edge of the audience and slipped into the boat. The other children shuffled along, and she sat down next to Daisy in the prow.

Next to me, Mark was rigid with tension. Was it anxiety he was feeling? Or humiliation? Or shame? What was the name for this – this sense of falling forward into a dark pit, of not knowing what you were hurtling towards?

Donna withdrew to press a button on the CD player that had been set up on a table at the side of the stage. Music began to play: 'Twinkle, Twinkle Little Star', picked out on a piano.

The children got to their feet and sang, their high, thin, clear little voices mingling to create a kind of music that is purer and more hopeful than any other that humans are capable of: the choir of the very young. The sound of people who are finding their voices, whether sweet or warbling or robustly off-key: who haven't yet learned to think of themselves as able to sing or not, or to distinguish their own voices from the effect they create by mingling with everybody else.

A few of the mums were sniffling and dabbing their eyes with tissues. Further along the front row, Billy's dad sat with his head bowed, as if he was struggling manfully not to join in with the weeping.

But Mark was stony-faced, and Daisy wasn't singing.

With Amy's encouragement, she had got to her feet, a beat behind everybody else. Her mouth was open, but it was obvious that nothing was coming out of it.

She didn't know the words. She didn't know how to pretend to know the words. She didn't know how to sing. Of course she didn't. How can you sing if you've barely learned how to talk?

And yet she *did* sing... At home sometimes, in the garden, when she was as good as alone, sitting on the grass with flowers in her hands, twiddling them. She had a habit of picking the flowers, and I let her – they weren't precious prize flowers or anything like that, after all, and Mark wasn't really into gardening and would barely notice. And as she played, she'd sing – a song without words, a kind of gentle ululation that rose and fell and repeated itself without coming to any particular conclusion.

She had stopped rolling her star round between her hands, and was gazing questioningly beyond all of the parents at the ceiling, as if there might be something there that would make sense of all of this. But clearly no answers were forthcoming.

Then, with the resigned air of one who has been forced by unenviable circumstances to find her own solution, she turned her back on the lot of us and started twiddling her star again.

A small, barely suppressed titter of laughter ran around the room. I managed a smile myself – it seemed like the most suitable, the most sporting response. *Kids, eh? They're so new to all of this. She just hasn't got the hang of it yet.* I knew the laughter wasn't meant unkindly. It was the kind of thing you might see on an out-take compilation – *the funny little girl who thinks the best thing to do with an audience is not to face it!* But I hated it. I hated this whole thing, and all I wanted was for it to be over.

But it wasn't. It went on and on.

Amy induced Daisy to turn round and sit down again, and she did, and carried on twiddling, and the story began to unfold.

It was about the stars sailing through the night sky to deliver the Star of Bethlehem in time to light the way for the shepherds and the three kings to find the baby Jesus. When they had all made it through the final song – 'Little Donkey' – there was heartfelt applause, and the staff looked relieved and the children looked delighted and the parents looked pleased and proud.

All except us and Daisy.

Daisy had got through it, somehow, but every time she was expected to get up and sing she'd pulled off the same trick as for the first song – she had turned her back on everyone. People had actually stopped laughing about it. It was as if there was an unspoken agreement to turn a blind eye to it, the way you might to somebody muttering to themselves on the bus.

Donna stood up in front of everybody and gave a short thank you speech about the hard work and effort that had gone into the show, and said she was sure we would all want to congratulate our children and could take a few minutes to do so, but could we please stay seated and let our children come to us.

The other children rushed forwards and merged with the audience. All around us there were hugs, questions, backslapping and reassurances, and the noise levels in the Portakabin were instantly turned up from hushed to tumult. But Daisy didn't move.

Amy tapped her on the shoulder and said something in her ear and pointed in the direction of the route out of the boat, the way the other children had gone. Finally Daisy understood: she was free. As if she'd just been released from prison, she got up and shot forwards.

As she went she knocked over the mast of the boat, which was a big silver star attached to a cardboard pole. It toppled onto some mother's head and Amy sprang forward to check the woman was all right. Daisy fled past us and made her way to the exit.

The door to the cloakroom was slightly ajar and Daisy sped on through, with me following her as fast as I could.

'Daisy! Daisy, wait for Mummy. Daisy, stop!'

Thankfully, the main exit was still closed and secured. She hadn't tried to get out anyway; she'd made her way to her peg. Each of the children had one, with a laminated name label written in a clear, cursive adult script and decorated with an animal. Daisy's was a smiling crocodile. Not a word I'd ever heard her attempt to say.

Apart from us, the cloakroom was empty and quiet. There were coats hanging all around, and lunchboxes lined up on the shelves above the pegs, and a faint smell of wet wellington boots. All as usual. All as it should be.

Daisy had a picture of Thomas the Tank Engine on her lunchbox; most of the other girls had ones with Disney princesses on, but Daisy had shown marginally more interest in Thomas and friends than any other characters. You were meant to worry about kids watching too much TV, but Daisy barely seemed to see the point of it. Thomas was pretty much the only thing she liked, and even then there were just a few scenes that caught her interest, and they didn't hold it for long.

Her red coat was still hanging up, just as I'd left it when I'd dropped her off an hour earlier. Daisy was standing next to it with her star in her hand, looking lost. No, not lost. Shellshocked, as if she was standing in the middle of a scene of apocalypse.

'Daisy.'

I went closer. She turned round and seemed to recognise me. I went closer still and she reached out with the hand that wasn't holding her star and slipped it under my jumper at the waist, feeling for my tummy.

That was what she did at night, when she was trying to sleep. She'd started doing it soon after I stopped breastfeeding her. It seemed to comfort her.

'You did good, Daisy,' I told her. 'You did just fine.'

And for once, I felt sure that she understood what I was saying.

Then Mark came out and saw us, and froze, and I stepped away and Daisy's cool little hand slipped away from my warm skin.

Mark said, 'What on earth are you doing? It looks bizarre. What are people going to think?'

I shrugged. 'They won't care. Everybody's just thinking about their own children. They're not bothered about ours.'

'Oh, come on. Everybody was noticing everything in there.'

Daisy raised her free hand to her wand and began to twirl it, rolling it steadily and watching the star as it turned.

Mark came closer and said, 'That was one of the worst experiences of my life.'

'Mark…'

'It was awful. Humiliating. I don't think I could bear to sit through anything like that ever again.'

We stared at each other.

'She did her best,' I said.

'She turned her back to the audience, Paula. She doesn't have a clue. It was embarrassing.'

'She's right here, Mark.'

'Yes, and obviously she doesn't have a clue what I'm saying. Do you remember how furious you were with my mother for saying there was something wrong? I think you owe her an apology.'

And with that he turned, struggled briefly with the catch securing the door, let himself out and was gone.

'Daisy,' I said. 'We have to go back inside. They need to check that all the children are going home with the right people.'

I prised one of her hands off the wand and tried to lead her back in, but she was a dead weight pulling back and sinking her little nails hard into the palm of my hand, and shrieking as if I was trying to abduct her.

'Daisy!' I flung her off and shook out my hand: there were little crescent-shaped welts in my skin. 'You don't do that – ever!'

I was suddenly so furious I could have slapped her. She was furious, too: her little face was a snarl of rage.

At that moment Amy came in. I should have been embarrassed to be found shouting at a child who was completely out of control. Instead I felt like I'd been rescued. I had no idea what I might have done next if someone hadn't intervened.

Amy spoke calmly over the uproar: 'If you'd like to take Daisy straight home, Mrs Walsh, Donna says that's fine.'

She might not have been able to hear me say thank you, but my gratitude must have been obvious. I grabbed Daisy's coat and lunchbox and propelled her towards the door. She charged off down the ramp, and I had to chase after her again to catch up with her before she got to the gate that led out of the pre-school play area.

People were meant to shut it, but it had been left wide open. Probably by Mark, who had just spoken to us both with something close to hatred, and hadn't been able to get away fast enough.

And suddenly it wasn't Daisy I wasn't angry with any more. It was him. Him and his mother, and their coldness and judgement and contempt. I was so angry it was like being lit up with a kind of power I hadn't known I had. A power that was stronger than humiliation, stronger than fear, stronger than the desire to fit in and win approval: that drew its strength from other people's indifference or hostility, and had absolutely no idea when to stop.

Chapter Seventeen

Ellie

One of the most dangerous things about being a kid is that grown-ups tend not to listen to you unless it suits them. Also, they're usually so set on their way of doing things that there isn't a whole lot of point in even trying to suggest that there might be trouble ahead. And so you end up tagging along with them, and then you feel bad twice over: not only because whatever ideas they had about the future they were heading towards have turned out to be mistaken, but because you didn't manage to warn them. And maybe you didn't even try.

I wasn't at all keen on going to meet Mark's mother. When I tried to imagine it, all I could make out was a kind of darkness all around her. But a visit had been planned, and it was obvious that Mum wanted me to go and to make a good impression, and I couldn't bring myself to disappoint her. She was so full of hope, so keen on the new life she could see ahead of her, and she wanted us to put our best feet forward – she wanted us to reflect well on her: the two girls she'd raised more or less single-handedly, the brainy beauty and the daydreamer who always had her nose in a book.

Besides, Mark's mother, Ingrid, was Ava's grandmother. It stood to reason that Mum would want them to meet. I'd only ever known the one grandma, Mum's mum, the one Ava and I shared. OK, so I had the privilege of still being able to sense her, sometimes – that benign golden presence, so kindly, so safe – but there was something to be said for a grandmother who was actually in the land of the living.

But Mum also seemed a bit apprehensive about meeting Ingrid. She hadn't actually said so outright, but given what Mark was like, with his well-paid job and fancy car and ability to be generous, my guess was that Ingrid was well-off, and Mum was worried that she'd look down on us.

Maybe she was afraid that Ingrid would think she was some kind of gold-digger, offering up babies in exchange for bouquets of red roses and fine dining and four-star hotels. Not to mention the in-your-face engagement ring Mark had given her. When Ava had seen it, her first words had been, 'You'd better watch it, you could take your eye out with that.' And now I thought about that whenever I saw the diamond catch the light.

Could you take an eye out with a diamond? Probably. You could do all sorts of terrible things, and I was beginning to realise that pretty much anything awful you could think of, someone else would have thought of first. And then gone and done it. There was really very little about the real world that made it a good alternative to books, where at least all the horrible things were just invented, and there was a fighting chance that the villains would go down in the end.

But whatever Mum thought was really neither here nor there. I knew there was something close to Ingrid that was bad, something hidden away so that all you could see was the stain it had left. But at the same time, I had no idea what it was.

My instinct was to stay as far away as possible. But I couldn't figure out a way of avoiding the visit. If I faked sick, Mum would just put it off, and if I refused to go it would just cause a drama until I gave in. Whatever was there to find, I would have to face it. And so, even though I was more scared than I had ever been in my life before, I decided to go.

Mum drove us there from London, which felt like something that wouldn't happen very often in future; whenever we got into a car with Mark, he seemed to end up taking the wheel. But he'd been away somewhere for work and was going to meet us at Ingrid's place, so it was down to Mum to get us there.

Actually, the whole trip felt like the end of an era, which was weird because it wasn't, not yet. There were still several weeks to go before the wedding, so it wasn't as if we were leaving anyone or anything behind. Still, the mood in the car wasn't one of anticipation: it was resigned and a bit melancholy and very quiet. An autumn kind of mood, even though it was a glorious summer day.

Mum was too preoccupied to chat. She was busy concentrating on the satnav, which had a nasty habit of taking you down strange turnings if you let it, and didn't pay proper attention to what was actually in front of you. Ava was sitting in the front next to her, and didn't say much either. She'd been like that ever since we got back from France. In the past at least she'd always had something to say for herself, even if it was usually annoying. This new Ava gave nothing away at all.

Luckily, the countryside we were driving through was beautiful, and that helped to make up for everything that wasn't quite so great. Everywhere you looked there was a view you could have painted in watercolours and hung up on the wall. I couldn't believe that I'd lived so long in places that were jumbles of houses and people and hadn't known all this was here. It was bizarre that there were such huge areas of land that were just fields or trees, with nobody around at all.

We followed a winding road through dense woods alongside a deep valley, then came to a town split on either side of the river Thames, which we crossed by a hump-backed bridge with the county sign displayed to one side: OXFORDSHIRE.

This was Henley, which was all pretty church towers and old, sash-windowed houses. It looked like one of the illustrations in the book of fairy tales I'd had when I was younger, of the magical town at the bottom of a lake. Everybody who belonged there carried on their business as usual, but outsiders couldn't visit without drowning. That was the countryside for you: pretty, but not necessarily welcoming.

The town thinned out and we drove along a broad tree-lined avenue and then we were back in woodland, miles and miles of it. Eventually we descended a steep hill and passed a few low, stragglylooking cottages and a sign for Fairmarsh, and Mum said, 'Nearly there.' She turned off the main road and drove along a lane with a high hedge on one side and farmland on the other, and then we turned off at the sign for Fairmarsh Place and followed a narrow road through prettily landscaped grounds, shaded by a mixture of grand old trees.

'Made it,' Mum said as we pulled up in a parking space in front of a huge and rather intimidating red-brick Victorian building.

I recognised it immediately, even though I'd never been there in the flesh before.

I'd seen it in that dream I'd had that first night in France. It was built in an E-shape, with wings to either side and a grand, porticoed entrance. It looked like the kind of house that might have featured in one of the old classic novels that Mark had given us. A fitting home for a vengeful, ancient bride, or a locked-up wife. Or ghosts.

'It's huge,' I said.

'It's all broken up into flats, silly,' Ava said. 'Mum, didn't you say it used to be a loony bin?'

'Don't call it that,' Mum said. 'It's a former mental hospital. You should watch what you say, because Mark's dad used to work here, and so did his grandfather – Ingrid's father. Ingrid's father ran the place for years, and Mark's dad was one of his assistants, which was how Ingrid met him.'

'Mark's dad died in a car crash, right?' Ava said. 'Under slightly suspicious circumstances.'

'Not that suspicious. There was an inquest, and the coroner said it was an accident. His car hit a tree. But anyway, it was obviously very upsetting, so best not to mention it. His state of mind hadn't been brilliant beforehand, not surprisingly – after all, I should think it's a very stressful line of work. So there were some lingering doubts, for Mark at least, which the coroner's verdict didn't really resolve. Also, just so you know, Ingrid had a sister – Mark's aunt – who had problems, and spent years actually as a patient at the hospital before she was moved out when it closed. Mark only found out about her after she'd died, which was back before you were born, Ava. Probably best not to mention her, either.'

Ava sighed. 'There seems to be a lot we can't talk about,' she said.

I looked up at the big red-brick building and tried to imagine what it would be like to be inside it and not to be allowed out. It looked pretty spooky, though maybe that was just because I knew what it had once been used for. Or maybe it was because the windows were so very tall and narrow, as if to discourage the inmates from thoughts of escape.

In life as in the dream, it was forbidding. A place where old secrets might be shut away, to be remembered only rarely and without tenderness.

I said, 'Did Mark grow up here?'

'Oh, no. No, he never came near the place. There might have been a time when staff and their families lived in, but I don't think Ingrid grew up here either.'

At that moment the face of an old woman loomed up in the car window on Mum's side, accompanied by a sharp rapping, and all of us nearly jumped out of our skins.

Mum wound down the window. 'Yes?'

The old woman looked at us without smiling. She had a pearl necklace on, and carefully applied pink lipstick, and nicely coiffed silver hair. She was well-groomed and not at all friendly: Miss Havisham after a makeover.

'You can't park here,' she said. 'There are visitor spaces over in the corner, by the bay trees.' She pointed to the far side of the car park, next to a line of tall, neatly clipped shrubs in silver pots. Then, with a slight frown: 'You aren't *Jenny*, are you?'

She pronounced it as if to be *Jenny* was almost certainly not a good thing – as if a Jenny might be prone to wind, or to falling asleep on public transport with her mouth open and a trickle of dribble running down her chin.

Mum was looking at her in the same way she looked at our landlady during inspections – hopeful, anxious, very slightly resentful. No, not like that – more wary. The way I'd seen her once when we bumped into a client of hers in a supermarket near my school, and she'd been terrifically polite and afterwards I'd found out that the woman had complained about a cut and colour and made Mum do it all over again for nothing.

Mum said, 'Are you Ingrid?'

Ingrid nodded. She peered past Mum to Ava, and said, 'So you're Ava. I've heard a lot about you.'

'This is Ellie, my youngest,' Mum said loyally, gesturing towards the backseat. 'I mean – my youngest for now.'

Youngest for now?

Of course, Ava would always be the oldest. That was one thing that would never change.

I attempted a winning smile. Ingrid was unwinnable, though, at least as far as I was concerned. She looked at me even harder, then turned back to Mum.

'Mark's running late – there's some trouble or other on the roads, an accident and a tailback, people being careless as usual. So we'll be able to have a nice girls' chat and get to know each other without him around. When you've moved the car, press the buzzer and I'll let you in. Flat 3 is on the ground floor, directly off the main entrance hall and opposite where you come in. You can't miss it.'

With that she walked off and disappeared into the house.

The three of us sat and looked at each other. Then Mum pulled herself together and said, 'I'm sure she'll thaw. Buckle up.'

Ava and I put our seatbelts on again, and Mum moved to the part of the car park Ingrid had pointed out. Then we made our way into the building, crossed the chequerboard floor of the big entrance hall and were admitted to Ingrid's flat.

Inside, it had a hushed, slightly cramped feeling. The front door opened onto a small lobby that gave way to a narrow corridor. Ingrid waved us through to a big living room that had thick green carpet and lots of dark, heavy antique-looking furniture, and long French windows that opened onto a terrace and gave a view of the lawn.

It smelled of polish and lavender pot-pourri, and was immaculately spick and span, even though Ingrid had plenty of the kind of ornaments that were magnets for dust: china candle holders, statuettes, and a ticking, golden carriage clock. There were photos too, in ornate gilt frames: a younger, rather handsome Mark on his graduation day, a younger Ingrid with the younger Mark having a picnic by a river somewhere, Mark – presumably – as a little blonde boy holding tadpoles in a jar, Mark looking tanned and happy in a boat on a lake that didn't look at all English. That photo looked as if someone had been cut out of the other half of it. Mark's first wife, presumably; there were no pictures of her anywhere.

Tucked in a corner, behind a very tall, very green pot plant, I spotted a picture of a bald man with glasses and a thin smile: Mark's dad, presumably. He very definitely didn't have pride of place. But there was a space reserved on the mantelpiece for a black-and-white photograph of a couple who I guessed were Ingrid's parents. The man looked old and fierce and like he wasn't used to anybody disagreeing with him. A bit like Ingrid, in fact. The woman looked like the sort of landlady Mum would have complained about, who'd bill you for stuff you didn't even know existed when you moved out. They were next to a picture of Mark in a suit looking nervous and serious and as if there was absolutely no way he was going to run the risk of letting anybody down.

'Do take a seat,' Ingrid said, looking us over with a touch of regret, as if we might have brought dirt in with us that would mess up the upholstery but there was nothing she could do about that now.

She wafted a hand in the direction of the round table on the far side of the room; it was already laid, and there were dishes in the centre covered with tea-towels. 'We'll sit down to lunch when Mark gets here. It's rather a picnicky sort of meal, I'm afraid. Cooking for several people is too much for me these days. I'm lucky in that I enjoy very good health, but I do know my limits.'

We sat down as directed. Ava perched next to me on the over-stuffed sofa and Mum settled on a manly-looking leather armchair with wings, the kind of seat you could imagine someone snoozing in by the fireside in an old red-curtained library. Ingrid went off to the kitchen to get us drinks, and once she was out of the room we all relaxed a little.

Mum yawned and stretched, and said she was going to have to make a definite effort not to drop off. I could see her point, though I didn't feel at all sleepy myself: it was rather stuffy in Ingrid's flat, and the French windows were shut tight.

Ava looked up at the old picture of the couple on the mantelpiece, the one I'd assumed was of Ingrid's parents. She said, 'They look like a barrel of laughs, don't they?'

'Ava, please,' Mum said.

Ingrid came back in, carrying a tray which she set down on the coffee table in front of the sofa. 'Please, don't let me interrupt. What are you talking about?'

'Oh, nothing,' Mum said airily.

'Then I look forward to joining the conversation,' Ingrid said, and passed me my ginger-beer.

When I was a bit younger I'd read pretty much every Enid Blyton in the library, and ginger-beer was the kind of thing children in Enid Blyton liked, which was why I had opted to try it. It turned out to be strange and rather disappointing, and I decided I wouldn't have it again. Ava didn't have anything. She was good at saying no in circumstances under which it might have been polite to say yes. Mum had water (Ingrid frowned at her request for decaffeinated tea) and Ingrid had a very small sherry, which she sipped rather devoutly, as if all this was as strange and difficult for her as it was for us. Perhaps it was.

Ingrid had taken the most ladylike chair, all padded and pale blue velvet with little matching buttons, the sort of thing you'd expect to find in a boudoir. She was sitting very upright with her legs crossed at the ankles; she had pretty good legs, the kind you don't expect an old lady to have, and she was wearing black patent high heels with buckles on them. Witch's shoes, basically.

I tried to catch Ava's eye – it would have been nice to exchange conspiratorial glances, as if to say, *This is something else, isn't it?* But she ignored me. Instead she got her phone out of her pocket and said, 'Have you got wi-fi?'

The look Ingrid gave her would have frozen a firestorm. She said, 'Are you in the habit of using your device when visiting long-lost relations?'

Ava blushed – not something I could remember ever seeing before. Then she looked sullen. 'I just wanted to check my emails,' she muttered. 'Anyway, you're the only long-lost relation I have.'

Ingrid glanced at Mum. 'But there's an aunt somewhere, isn't there? Mark told me you have a sister, Jenny.'

Mum was instantly on the defensive. She hated talking about my aunt Amanda. 'We're not in touch any more.'

'No. I heard. Well, these things happen.' Ingrid permitted her a small smile that was almost as unnerving as her scowl, and turned back to Ava. 'Were you expecting an email from someone in particular?'

'No,' Ava growled, and put the phone back in her pocket.

'Oh. There isn't anyone special, then? You're sixteen, aren't you? And quite attractive. I wouldn't have thought it would be too difficult for you to find yourself a boyfriend.'

Ava went an even brighter red than before. 'I don't need a boyfriend.'

'Probably just as well you're unattached, since you're just about to move house. Young love so rarely survives physical distance. At that age, people seem to need constant reminding of just what it is they're supposed to be so hot under the collar about. Anyway, Mark tells me you're clever, and boys can be terribly distracting. All it takes is for one man who isn't a complete toad to compliment you on your brain and not your looks, and then…' She shrugged. 'Infatuation is almost entirely incompatible with studying for examinations. Believe me, I know. I was thought to be quite clever myself, at one time. And then I met my late husband.' She waved a hand rather dismissively in the direction of the picture of the bald man behind the pot plant. 'There was a time when I was besotted with him. Every woman should know that kind of passion at least once in her life. Even if it doesn't last. Anyway, I take it you've got all of that out of your system, Jenny, being at a quite different stage in life, and having been married once already?'

Now it was Mum's turn to blush. 'I'm very much in love with your son,' she said.

'Mm-hm,' Ingrid said, as if Mum might be or might not be, but it really wasn't for her to judge. She sipped a little more sherry and set her glass down on the occasional table next to her. 'I'm sure you're aware that Mark and I are very close. It's inevitable, really, with a widowed mother and an only child. And he is a good son. You'll find him an excellent husband. And father. He's at a stage in life now where he really wants it and is very much ready for it. You'll understand, I'm sure, Jenny, that I was rather concerned about him committing himself to another relationship so soon after a very painful divorce. You'll be familiar with the strength of the protective instinct. I really would do anything for him. I would lay down my life for him.'

'Of course,' Mum murmured, looking distinctively unnerved.

'But I must say, now that I'm familiar with all of the circumstances, I'm absolutely delighted that everything has worked out so well,' Ingrid said, and treated us all to a magnanimous smile. 'I can't tell you how pleased I am to suddenly find myself a grandmother several times over. My neighbours here are going through quite the adjustment, given that they all had to go round feeling sorry for me not so long ago. And as for Mark's unfortunate ex-wife...'

Unfortunate ex-wife sounded a little like *my late husband*, gone but very much not forgotten. Ingrid gave a small, expressive shrug. 'Well. She really has got her just desserts.'

Ava said, 'How come? You mean because she hasn't got Mark any more?'

Ingrid frowned. 'Really, Ava. Do you have to call him that? He's your father. I know that he wasn't able to dandle you on his knee and all of that, but given how things have turned out, is it really so impossible for you to call him Dad?'

Ava looked faintly sick. 'I think I'm just a bit old for that,' she muttered.

'Nonsense. Your father is always your father and always will be, and now you actually know who he is, it's the least you can do to acknowledge him.' Ingrid turned back to Mum. 'That really is a splendid engagement ring, by the way. I believe you were involved in choosing it?'

'Yes, we chose it together.'

'Lovely. How very modern. I did offer him mine, once I knew he had proposed, but he declined. I think he felt it might be a bit old-fashioned for you. But I'll leave it to you in my will, anyway. Then you can have it reset or do with it as you wish.'

'That's very kind of you,' Mum said stiffly.

'Oh, you're very welcome. It's all been rather a rush, hasn't it? But then, you're wise not to hang about. You look well on it, I must say. Some women really do carry better than others, don't they? How old are you, if you don't mind me asking? Thirty-six? Thirty-seven? Mm. Well, yes. I can see why you might have felt it was time to get cracking. I presume you've heard about Paula's trials and tribulations in that area.' She mentioned Paula with a mix of satisfaction and wary disgust, as if Mark's first wife was a criminal who was now safely locked up. 'Given how things have turned out, that woman's life is ruined. Deservedly so, in my view.'

Mum looked bemused. Ava said, 'You mean, ruined because she's not blessed with Dad's presence any more?'

Ingrid raised her eyebrows. They were very well shaped; perhaps she had them professionally done, something Mum had experimented with once or twice but without great success, having come back either too bushy or too hairless to look like her normal self. Ingrid's eyebrows made her look like a gracious lady. That was exactly what I wanted mine to look like when I was grown up.

'It's not a subject to be flippant about,' she said.

'Why not?' Ava demanded. 'What happened to her?'

Ingrid looked round at all three of us. There was an unexpectedly wicked glint in her eyes, as if Ava had just given her a dare and she was minded to surprise us all by rising to the challenge.

Was this going to be it? The thing I had been afraid of, the thing I was scared to face?

Suddenly Ingrid was hard to take in. It was too much – this strange place, the mood of it, as if there was disaster ahead and darkness behind, and this was a point at which you could glimpse it all, but not make sense of it—

And then I saw her, clear as day, as if she was standing there.

Just a little girl, perhaps six or seven years old, with fine fair hair cut in a bob with a fringe that was in need of a trim, dressed in school uniform: polo shirt, skirt, little white socks, Velcro-fastening shoes. She was holding a pencil with a yellow teddy-bear eraser on one end, and as I watched she slowly rolled it to and fro between her hands, but she wasn't watching what she was doing. She was looking at me.

She was studying me without either surprise or suspicion, as wide-eyed and innocent as a baby. Her mouth was slightly open and there was something completely otherworldly about her. I knew at once she wasn't dangerous or malevolent. If anything, she gave off a kind of unselfconscious sweetness, as if it wouldn't even occur to her to do harm, or that she could do anybody harm if she wanted to, or that anyone else might want to harm her.

'Paula's child is severely disabled,' Ingrid told us. She sounded like a judge passing sentence in a TV movie, all fake seriousness and self-importance, as if what she was saying was some kind of necessary service to society. 'Retarded. In my young day, they would have called her a moron.'

The little girl vanished as if she had never been. The room suddenly darkened and was as stifling as if all the air had been sucked out of it.

And then I was really frightened. Not by the little girl I'd just seen, and had glimpsed on several occasions before. No: what scared me was what I'd heard in Ingrid's voice. That condemnation. Revulsion. Hatred, even. *That* was the abyss, and it was infinite and it was everywhere and all around me.

Then the pain started.

It was as if I'd been stabbed through the eyes. As if someone had positioned a spike by each one and hammered it through the thin bone of the sockets to my brain. But even as the pain took hold I was conscious that it was only an echo of what someone else had felt.

I thought I was going to be sick, right there on Ingrid's expensive carpet. I managed to say something to excuse myself and stumbled out and somehow made my way to Ingrid's bathroom.

The pain was now almost unbearable. It was like having had someone scrape around inside my brain, as if my skull was the shell of an egg someone had pierced and stirred with a straw. But it wasn't just the pain that hurt. All the words I could have used to beg for help had been taken from me, and the power to remember them had been put out like a light.

Chapter Eighteen

Ava

Ingrid was totally loving this. She had a look on her face that was almost exactly like the expression I'd seen on Marsha Gale when she let off the fire extinguisher in the physics lab one dull day at school: the sort of glee that people feel when they're being destructive.

Mum had gone very pale. She said, 'Mark never said anything about Paula having a child.'

'I know, dear. I'm sorry, I know it must come as a shock. I know he has wanted to tell you many times. It's an extremely painful subject, as I'm sure you'll appreciate.'

Mum said, 'But… how old is this child?'

'She would be six now, I believe,' Ingrid said. 'I haven't seen her since she was a baby. But I hear about her from time to time. As you know, Paula's still living in the house she shared with Mark. I know people who know people in the town. And the child is quite… conspicuous.'

'Then Paula would have had her when she was still married to Mark,' Mum said. 'Are you telling me this is Mark's child?'

'Probably,' Ingrid said calmly. 'Not that we know for sure. She was unfaithful to him. Did you know that?' She paused, took in Mum's uncomfortable expression and went on. 'It's good that he told you. He didn't say anything to me until after the marriage was over. And then she was the one who wanted him to leave. She has made it absolutely impossible for him to have any contact with the child. Of course he's heartbroken about it. But it's difficult enough to build a relationship with a child like that if you're around them all the time. If you're only permitted to see them occasionally, and the other parent is hostile…' She pulled a face and drew her finger across her throat. 'But in a way, from your point of view, it's just as well, isn't it? I don't suppose being a stepmother is easy at the best of times, and I suspect you wouldn't want a child with behavioural problems anywhere near your new baby.'

'Does she… have behavioural problems?' Mum had instinctively moved her hands to her tummy, as if to protect the baby there.

'Oh, yes. Quite severe, I believe. Can I get you some more water, dear? Or I've some nice Bath biscuits, if you'd like something to nibble on? You look like you've just seen a ghost.'

'I'm all right, thank you. I'm just… it's a lot to take in. And I'm not sure now is the best time…'

'The girls both needed to know,' Ingrid said. 'I don't believe in beating around the bush. It's hardly more shocking than the news they've already had to absorb, is it?'

Mum swallowed. 'I have to speak to Mark about all this. Privately.'

'Talk to him if you must, but tread carefully, won't you? None of this need have any bearing on his life with you. It's just a mistake he made. A big one. A detour.' She looked at Mum, then at me. 'You're his fresh start. You're the route he should have taken all along.'

'But this is his child,' Mum said. She looked as if she was about to cry. 'How can he let her go like that?'

'This is exactly why he didn't tell you. He was afraid you wouldn't understand. He tells me you're a good mother. The best he can imagine. It's bound to be difficult for you to understand how vengeful and selfish someone like Paula can be.' Ingrid sighed. 'If there's anything that all my years on this planet have taught me, it's that sometimes you have to accept that things can't be fixed. Mark has a child he can't be a father to. I have a grandchild I can't be a grandmother to. But it will be different with your children.'

'I'm sure it's convenient to cut your losses,' I muttered.

'Ava! That is a dreadful thing to say. You'd better apologise,' Mum told me.

'No need,' Ingrid said smoothly. 'I realise it's a shock. You have to understand that Mark has done his very best to ensure this child is financially provided for. He gave Paula the house, just like that. And he pays child support. He gets absolutely nothing in return. By all accounts, Paula does her best by the child – you see, I do like to stay informed, and I have my methods. But she was not a good wife. And she was a very possessive and manipulative daughter-in-law. She did her best to cut me out of Mark's life. Which I'm sure you would never do.'

'Of course not,' Mum said faintly.

'I must say I'm very glad to have had this opportunity to clear the air. I was beginning to wonder when it was going to be possible. In practice all of this is neither here nor there. They're in Kettlebridge, a good ten miles away, and there's really no reason why your paths should ever cross. But it's as well to be aware, isn't it? I thought it would be much better for you to know, to help you to avoid any awkwardness.'

'This little girl,' Mum said. 'What's she called?'

'Daisy,' Ingrid said, wrinkling her nose slightly. 'Paula's choice, naturally. They have both kept Mark's surname, which was another reason why I felt you should know. Walsh is not that common a name. And Paula can be rather attention-seeking. I saw a picture of them in the local newspaper just the other day, at some fundraising event at school. Why she would want to put a child like that in the spotlight I have no idea, but there we are. It's a perverse kind of vanity, maybe. She must want people to feel sympathetic towards her. And maybe they do, if they don't know the whole story.'

I got to my feet. 'I'm going to check on Ellie,' I said. 'She's been gone forever.'

Neither of them said anything as I went out. Mum looked faintly guilty, as if it had just occurred to her that she ought to have checked on Ellie herself. I could see life as a mother of three was going to be a challenge for her.

It was a relief to be away from the two of them, and to get out into the little entrance hall. Not half as much a relief as it would be to get out of there entirely, though, and to have the visit to Mark's mother's house out of the way and to be in the car going back home.

And then I'd be free to think of Jake and no one else.

Jake! Jake… I'd tell Jake about all of this, over dinner maybe, or in bed together, in that special after-sex time when it suddenly became possible to say anything. And he'd listen and stroke my hair and hold me close, and say that I shouldn't worry, they were just an assortment of random people I shared genetic material with, but I didn't need to feel tied to them, or defined by them, or as if I owed them anything at all. And then he'd tell me I was much too beautiful to worry about anything, and then he'd kiss me and then…

I knocked on the bathroom door and said, 'You all right?'

'Yeah. I'll be out in a sec,' Ellie said.

'You OK? It was all pretty heavy in there, right?'

'Yeah.'

'Look, try not to worry too much. It's really nothing to do with us. I think Ingrid just thought we ought to know. But we're never actually going to meet these people. They've got their lives and we've got ours. We can pretty much forget about them, to be honest.'

'I guess.'

'Ready to go back in?'

'I suppose so.'

She opened the bathroom door. She looked paler than I'd ever seen her. Her eyes were huge, as if she'd been witnessing things that were too awful to share.

'Are you OK? You look terrible.'

'I'll be fine,' Ellie said, without conviction. 'I had a headache. I thought I was going to be sick.' She put her hand to her head as if not quite sure what she was going to find there. 'It's beginning to go now.'

'Do you want to tell Mum we should leave?' I said, half hopefully.

'No. We should stay. Maybe it doesn't matter that it's too late to help. Someone has to remember what happened here.'

'Ellie, what on earth are you talking about?'

Ellie shrugged. The colour was beginning to come back to her cheeks. 'It was something bad. Some kind of torture.'

'Ellie, this was a hospital.'

'It was definitely right here,' Ellie insisted. 'Can you seriously not feel it? Not a thing?'

'Not really. I mean… the place is definitely a bit creepy. But that could just be Ingrid.'

'I don't think it is only to do with her. There's something else. Something that isn't in the past. But it's difficult to make sense of it when people have been keeping things to themselves.'

'There can't be any more to come out. Mark has a kid Mum didn't even know about. That's enough for one day, surely? Even in this family.'

Ellie looked me in the eyes. She gave a little shiver and shook her head. 'You're a liar too,' she said, and went back to the living room.

Was she talking about Jake? But how could she possibly know? I wanted to challenge her, but instead I followed her into the living room just in time to see her stop in her tracks.

There was a local newspaper open on the coffee table, with a great big colour photograph splashed across it.

Paula and Daisy. It had to be.

The picture showed a knackered-looking woman in jeans and a T-shirt crouching down next to a dazed little girl in a stripy dress, who was staring at a set of light-up rings on her fingers. They were in a school playground; there was a stall just behind them, and blue and yellow pennants had been strung up along the edge of the awning overhead.

Both Mum and Ingrid were staring at the picture. Ingrid looked as if she wouldn't mind if Paula and Daisy were wiped off the face of the earth. But Mum's expression was one of recognition.

She pointed at Paula and said, 'I've met her.'

Ingrid folded the newspaper and put it away in the storage space underneath the glass top of the coffee table. 'Are you sure, dear? It doesn't seem very likely.'

She turned to me and Ellie. 'You might not remember, Ellie. But you will, Ava. It was the day you burned yourself on the iron, and we took Ellie into school and then took you up to A&E. We bumped into Mark afterwards, in the newsagent's in the hospital. I hadn't seen him for years… since I'd had you. Just one of those chance encounters. But he saw you, and you… made an impression on him. That was what prompted him to look me up, later on. When he was free.'

'I remember the burn,' I said. 'I had a scar, for a bit. It's completely gone now. I wanted to get some sweets afterwards, and I pestered you and eventually you let me. I don't remember her, though.'

'She's not especially memorable, really,' Ingrid said.

'I never did find out why they were there,' Mum said. 'Mark didn't want to say.'

'I think that's enough dwelling on the past, don't you?' Ingrid said. She got up from her knees, settled back into her chair and took a sip of sherry. 'Do sit down, girls. If Mark isn't here in another five minutes, we had better start our lunch without him.'

Ellie and I took up our places on the sofa again. Mum had fallen to studying the engagement ring on her finger, turning it fractionally this way and that to catch the light.

She looked worn out. Resigned. Maybe she'd manage some kind of confrontation with Mark – *Why didn't you tell me? You should have told me* – but really, it was too late. She'd already thrown in her lot with him, and she was in too deep to walk away.

Ingrid said, 'I'm sorry, you'll find me very direct, but in my view it's much better for us all to know where we stand. Now we've got all that out of the way, I don't want any of you to give Paula and her daughter another thought. I wonder if you wouldn't mind holding off mentioning all this to Mark, for now? He's bound to be stressed after the awful time he's had getting here, and there's no point spoiling his lunch. It's not as if I get to see him all that often. He does his best, of course, and he's very good about phoning. But he's so busy all the time.'

'I suppose I could talk to him about it later,' Mum said.

'I do think that might be best. Just let him know I've filled you in. It'll be an enormous relief to him. I know he's been very worried about it. Whether you would find out, what you would think, when and how to tell you and so on. Not that he really had any reason to worry. After all, it's not as if he's done anything wrong.'

Suddenly Ellie piped up in a thin little voice: 'Did they used to do operations here?'

It seemed like an inoffensive thing to want to know, except somehow anything Ellie asked had an edge to it. Ingrid responded by staring accusingly at Mum, as if she must have let something inappropriate out of the bag for Ellie to think of asking such a thing.

'I have to say, I don't think this is a very suitable subject for conversation,' she said. 'But yes, on occasion, they did. If you want the grisly details, I suggest you ask your mother later.'

Ellie folded her arms and went quiet. I said, 'Does Paula know that Mark is getting married again?'

I couldn't imagine that Paula would exactly be happy for us when she found out, however unfaithful she'd been to Mark. After all, it would surely be a kick in the teeth for her ex-husband to marry again so quickly after their divorce, no matter how unsatisfactory the marriage had been… Especially if his bride-to-be was someone he'd slept with when he was still married to Paula. And then had a child with.

Perhaps Paula didn't know about that? After all, Mark hadn't told us about Daisy. Maybe he hadn't told Paula about me.

But if Paula *did* know…

Well, she wouldn't exactly be planning to send the happy couple something nice for a wedding present, would she? She wouldn't be wanting to send them anything nice at all.

Ingrid raised her glass of sherry to her lips, finished it, and slowly and thoughtfully set it down.

'I suppose you have a point. Paula ought to know,' she said.

'Perhaps Mark should handle it,' Mum suggested.

'Please, Jenny, don't concern yourself,' Ingrid said sharply. 'I don't want Mark to be concerned, either. You've got much more important things to think about. Like your wedding. I'm so pleased that you're going to get all that sorted sooner rather than later and I quite agree that under the circumstances, a simple registry office ceremony is all that's required, but still, there are things to think about, aren't there? Not to mention setting up home together, and finding new schools for the children and all of that. And you'll need to wind up your hairdressing business.'

'I might pick it up again once I've had the baby,' Mum said. 'When we're settled in the new house, and I've begun to get to know people.'

'Oh, I don't suppose that'll be necessary,' Ingrid said. 'You'll be able to concentrate on being a mother. I'm sure that's what you've always wanted, isn't it?' She got to her feet. 'Now, how about some lunch? I've got some smoked salmon. I thought it might be a nice treat. And we do have rather a lot to celebrate. I do hope you can eat it, Jenny? I lose track of what they say pregnant women can have these days.'

'I think it's all right,' Mum said, not looking particularly sure.

'Good. Then let's eat.'

We moved over to the table. Ingrid whisked away the covering cloths and went off to the kitchen to get the smoked salmon out of the fridge. She was the kind of person who had butter in a proper butter dish, with a proper butter knife, and crystal glasses and napkins in antique silver napkin rings.

Ellie and Mum and I sat there in silence, as if we had no idea what to begin to say to each other. Mum was staring into space, and Ellie might as well not have been there at all. It was as if she'd decided that the only way to get through lunch was to fade into non-existence.

And that was when I realised how close the three of us had been, once… all those years when I'd thought our lives were really awful, when we were moving from one rented flat to another and Sean was being useless and there was never any money and one thing would break after another – the telly, the kettle, the soles of Ellie's shoes. A seemingly endless sequence of little disasters that required the spending of money we didn't have.

And yet we hadn't been broken. We'd been unbreakable. A perfect equilateral triangle, each one of us balanced out by the other two.

And now?

We'd splintered. An impartial observer who'd been parachuted in to sit at that table would have concluded that we were almost entirely disconnected from each other. And I could only see that it was going to get worse.

Mum had her fiancé, her new baby… Ingrid to keep happy… her other half's other child to try not to think about. All that was going to take up energy and time, and there would be next to nothing left for us.

And I had my big plans for the future: university, a career, money. Plus I had Jake to see me through everything that was wrong with now. Meanwhile, Ellie seemed to have withdrawn into some remote attic of her imagination. She'd always had a tendency to get overwrought, but this strange, fraught little scene appeared to have done for her completely.

Still, I wasn't responsible for her, was I? There was a limit to what I could do. I wasn't the one making decisions about her future. I was her sister, the one she was still sharing a room with. Not her mother.

Ingrid came back in with the smoked salmon on a tray, along with some quiche and a pot of pâté. Mum and I tucked in. Ellie picked at things and forgot to put her napkin on her lap; I had to kick her under the table to remind her. Ingrid asked Mum about the wedding, and Mum told her about the restaurant that had been booked for afterwards and the dress she'd chosen and so on. Then they got onto the subject of the honeymoon and Ingrid said she'd be very happy to keep an eye on me and Ellie, and I protested that we didn't need a babysitter and then Mark arrived.

The impact on Ingrid was immediate. It was quite a transformation; she smiled and looked adoring, and everything about her was softer and more vulnerable than before. That was when it hit me: she really did live for her son. His happiness, his success, were everything to her. And we were part of that, and Paula and her little girl most definitely weren't.

But Mark wasn't really paying attention to Ingrid. He went over to Mum to kiss her on the cheek, and she was stiff and awkward with him, the way she was with Sean. It wasn't quite as bad; she wouldn't have let Sean kiss her. She preferred to keep Sean at arm's length, if not further. But she was being cooler than I'd ever seen her be with Mark before.

Ellie and I exchanged glances, and I gave a tiny shrug, too small for anyone else to notice. What could we do about it, anyway? This was their business.

Ingrid went into the kitchen to fetch Mark a glass of non-alcoholic beer. The rest of us settled at the table. Mark said to Mum, 'Is everything all right?'

She stared at him. 'When were you going to tell me?'

'Tell you what?'

I had never seen anyone look so nakedly guilty. If criminals looked like that when questioned about their wrongdoing, there would be no need for forensic science.

Mum's eyes were wet with tears. 'She said you have a child you never see.'

They gazed at each other. Ellie and I might as well not have been in the room.

'I do,' Mark said. 'But it's not my fault.'

'Whatever happened, I had a right to know about it before I agreed to marry you.'

'But, Jenny, under the circumstances… would it have made any difference?'

'That was for me to decide! I am not dependent on you. I'm here because I choose to be, not because I need to be. I coped on my own with two children and believe me, if I have to, I'll cope on my own with three!'

'Jenny, please.'

'I don't understand why you didn't say anything. You knew everything about me. So why keep something like that to yourself?'

'Why do you think? Because I was ashamed!'

Mark hid his face in his hands. His shoulders were shaking and I realised he was crying. I'd never seen a man cry before.

Ingrid came in with Mark's drink and set it carefully down on the occasional table next to him.

'It's all right,' she said to Mark, and rested a hand on his shoulder. Gradually he quietened. 'Jenny isn't like Paula. I knew that the minute I set eyes on her. She's angry now, but she'll see reason and she'll be willing to listen. She won't punish you. Thank goodness, I think she'll be capable of forgiveness.'

Mark straightened up and faced Mum again.

'I'm so sorry, Jenny,' he said, and looked at her like a kicked puppy pleading for affection.

'That's the way,' Ingrid said, sitting down again. 'By and by you should have a little bit to eat, Mark. You'll feel better.'

Mum said, 'I think the girls and I should go.' She glared at Mark. 'We can talk about all this another time. When I've had a chance to digest it.'

She didn't get out of her chair, though. She looked exhausted. The fight seemed to have gone out of her the minute Mark started crying.

'Don't go,' Mark said. 'Please. I know it was unforgivable of me. It was just… it was all so wonderful. At first I didn't want to put you off. And then I didn't want to wreck it.' He glanced at his mother – a wary look, as if he was scared to be angry with her. 'I just never found the right time. But I had no idea my mother was going to spring this on us today.'

'It's not her fault,' Mum said.

She had begun to soften. It was obvious. That was the thing about her; she never stayed angry for long. I'd seen it with Sean, again and again. I'd even seen her do it with me and Ellie. If someone confessed and apologised, she always, always gave them the benefit of the doubt.

'I've made summer pudding,' Ingrid said. 'You can't all go without at least trying it.'

I think Ingrid knew we wouldn't go, in the end. And we didn't.

Ellie looked very pale, and only managed a bite or two of the summer pudding, which neither of us had ever tried before. It was a strange creation – a dome of wet purple bread, soaked with juice and filled with glistening blackberries and blueberries. When Ingrid brought it in, Ellie looked as queasy as if she was being offered brains or tripe.

If she'd actually been sick, that might have got us out of there. But she wasn't. She sat in silence as Ingrid served up and asked Mark about his work trip and his journey, and Mark gave a long, boring answer that I didn't pay any attention to.

Ellie picked at her pudding and the rest of us tucked in, and the conversation shifted into small talk: roadworks and potholes and taxi firms, and the ongoing problems over spaces in the car park by Ingrid's flat. It might have been almost comical if the atmosphere in the room hadn't stayed deadly serious.

After a while Ellie and I helped Ingrid clear the table and she brought out a pot of coffee and a little silver dish of peppermints.

Did other families do this – sit round pretending everything was normal when it wasn't? Perhaps they did. Perhaps this was an essential skill for family life… along with knowing what secrets you could get away with keeping, and when you were going to have to come clean about others.

So Mark was a dad already. It wasn't really that surprising – he was kind of old. There was a pretty high probability that anyone Mum had started dating would have a kid. If not more than one.

I sometimes talked to Toby Andrews at school about stuff like that. Maybe because he had a crush on me, he seemed to think I was a good person to talk to, even though, in the normal way of things, I really wasn't. Toby had three step-brothers, shared a room with one of them and hated them all. Step-sibling relationships, as far as I could tell, were like other sibling relationships, but with even less in common. Light relief from the parent or parents, sometimes, and the forced bonding of enduring the same domestic set-up. But also, frequently seriously annoying.

At least I'd had plenty of time to get used to Ellie. Even if, as it turned out, we only shared one parent and not two…

Last thing I needed was yet another kid around. The baby was quite enough to be going on with. Was it callous of me, being unbothered about this other one being out of the picture? It just seemed to make things easier. Because if she was how Ingrid had described her, what on earth would we say to her if we did meet her? It wouldn't just be awkward. It would be completely impossible.

Ingrid and Mark and I had coffee, which made me feel as if I was more one of them than I was like Mum or Ellie. Well, I was, wasn't I? I didn't go out of my way to be nice to people, and I quite liked expensive things and sometimes other people thought I was a bit up myself. Yeah, I was a Walsh all over. My father's daughter, learning how to live a double life. There I was with my big secret, my hot affair with an older man, my thoroughly lost innocence, and nobody had any idea.

It seemed that it was a whole lot easier to live with a secret than to be exposed. There must be people all over who understood that. Adulterers, bigamists, people who knew where the bodies were buried but fancied a quiet life.

I was a liar. So how could I condemn Mark for being one too?

After coffee we all said thank you and goodbye to Ingrid in the entrance hall to her flat and went out to the car park, where Mum's old banger was parked next to Mark's Jag. Mark said to Mum, 'Do you still want to call in at the house?'

She glanced down at her engagement ring, then up at him. 'I do,' she said. 'Isn't it ridiculous, to have got this far without me ever having seen where you live?'

'I guess we have form when it comes to doing things in an unconventional order,' he said.

'You're not wrong there,' she said. 'You'd better lead the way. Don't go too fast. Or too slow. Let's aim for nice and steady, OK?'

'OK.'

Ellie and I got into Mum's car and she followed Mark out of the landscaped grounds and onto the main road.

Ellie said, 'Is that it?'

Mum didn't respond, and Ellie repeated herself. Mum said, 'Is what it?'

'About the girl. Mark's little girl. The one he doesn't see, and didn't tell you about. You aren't even angry with him?'

'You sound as if you want me to be,' Mum said.

'Well, are you?'

'I can't talk about it when I'm driving.'

'Then you're just going to let him off the hook?'

'Look, good people sometimes end up in bad situations, OK? And he's a good man. His mother might be a little difficult… She really shouldn't have come out with all that stuff in front of you. But she has, and now I know and I need to digest it and talk to him about it. But there's no reason why it should have any effect on you, so can we please drop the subject? At least for now?'

I turned round and pulled a face at Ellie. She shrugged. 'OK. I was just trying to clear the air.'

'*I* don't think it's that big a deal,' I said to Mum. Then I said to Ellie, 'How's your headache?'

'Headache? What headache? You didn't say anything about a headache,' Mum said.

Ellie frowned at me to signal that she didn't want Mum fussing about it. 'It's gone now. I just didn't feel too good when we were at Ingrid's. What kind of operation was it they used to do there? You know, the one Ingrid didn't want to talk about?'

Mum started telling us about an aunt of Mark's who'd had a lobotomy there in the fifties, and then Ellie wanted more details about what kind of operation it was and how it worked and Mum ended up telling her to look it up. I tuned out. The idea of people sticking sharp objects into other people's brains didn't really sit well with smoked salmon and summer pudding, and Mum was having to drive a bit faster than usual to keep up with Mark, which wasn't great round the bends.

Once she'd got the grim medical information she wanted, Ellie went very quiet and fell to looking out at the view and periodically rubbing her temples, as if in sympathy for Mark's mutilated aunt. We drove the rest of the way in silence. It wasn't far – not far enough, in my opinion. I could have done with Ingrid being a bit further away.

Then Mum pulled up behind Mark's car in a cul-de-sac of identical-looking detached houses, brand new but built in creamy stone so as to look traditional, and all crammed in with about a foot between them.

There were no pavements – I guessed that was so the developers could fit in as many properties as possible. Each house had a pocket handkerchief of immaculate lawn in front of it; Mark's was adorned with a weedy sapling in a central bed. It was fantastically impersonal.

Talk about a clean slate – this was perfect: it was just the place for a family that had plenty of reasons not to look back.

Inside, the house was a bit tight in terms of proportions but nice – very clean, freshly painted, with new-smelling carpets. It would get cramped pretty fast once we were all living there and the baby had arrived, but Mum and Mark were already talking about remodelling the place and building an extension. As long as I finally had a room of my own and could close the door on them all, it would be all right.

The room I wanted was the second biggest, after the master bedroom, and was at the back of the house, overlooking the tiny garden. I could imagine myself in there, with my stuff… not that I had much of it: GCSE textbooks, clothes, a bit of make-up, and that was about it. Not like Ellie, who kept everything – old friendship bracelets, books, toys, and whatever random junk was left over from playground crazes of several summers ago.

What a relief it would be, not to have her clutter all around. Just me and my space and plenty of it. I'd be able to sit round messaging Jake without worrying that Ellie was going to forget the knock-and-wait rule and suddenly burst in on me.

Maybe I'd even be able to get Jake in here, one day. It wouldn't really feel like doing it at home – more like being in a hotel, with a bit of added risk.

I went out and knocked on the door of the little room that was going to be Ellie's. There was no answer, so I went in. She was standing with her back to the door, looking out of the window onto the small square of garden and the other houses of the estate.

'You didn't wait for me to invite you in,' she said. 'If I did that to you, you'd have a fit.'

'Well, I'm here now,' I said, and came to stand next to her by the window. 'What do you make of it?'

'Do you mean the room, or the house, or the place? Or the whole thing?'

'Any of it. All of it.'

Ellie paused. There was a weird, tight energy around her, the kind of energy people give off before they start a fight.

'I think it's doomed,' she said.

I started laughing before I realised she wasn't joking. She said, 'Laugh all you like. If you weren't so wrapped up in yourself, maybe you'd feel it too. And your father is not a good man, whatever Mum wants to believe. He told us something that wasn't true and we believed him. That means we shouldn't trust him. And he didn't love that little girl. You could tell. I don't think he wanted her at all.'

And she turned away and hurried out to the landing, and began to scamper down the stairs.

'Yeah, well your dad isn't all that either,' I muttered, and started after her.

We found Mum and Mark in the kitchen, playing kiss-and-make-up – they jumped a foot apart the minute we came in.

Mum ran a hand through her hair. She was flushed but happy and I could see that whatever he'd said to her, she'd decided that he was the wronged party and she was going to feel sorry for him and forgive him. Well, what did I care? It was really nothing to do with me. Or not much, anyway.

Ellie glowered at both of them and I suddenly got a glimpse of the kind of teenager she might become. Happy days ahead – though I'd be well out of it by then. I just had to get through the next few years… I figured that once we'd moved, I could probably come up with a couple of reasons to get the train back to London, and talk Mum into letting me go on my own. After all, she was going to be pretty distracted once the baby came. That way Jake and I would be able to carry on seeing each other.

I fiddled round on my phone while Ellie sulkily read her book and Mum and Mark looked round the garden. Then Mum kissed Mark goodbye and they both told each other they wished we could stay, and she drove us back to London.

Mum asked us what we thought of the house and we both said we liked it, and that was that. After a while Ellie fell asleep in the back and I told Mum I didn't think the thing about the kid was that big a deal and I was sure Ellie would come round to the same way of thinking once the shock of it had worn off, and Mum seemed reassured and I decided it was all going to be fine.

But that night Ellie woke me up – not the way she sometimes did, by crying out at a nightmare. Instead I surfaced to hear her quietly sobbing.

I switched the bedside lamp on and scooted across to her bed, and she sat up and I held her tight. She was cool and clammy to the touch and shivering slightly, as if she'd caught a chill.

'It was only a dream,' I said, but she shook her head.

Her body felt as light and insubstantial as a bird's, as if she was hollow. I could make out the bumps of her backbone through her nightie; she didn't have any spare flesh on her. She was all nervous energy, like a weathervane spinning round in a storm.

She said, 'Didn't you feel it? When we were in the car coming home. It was like a dark shadow.'

I tried to remember what the drive had been like. Some spooky woods. The countryside, which was fairly creepy in itself. So much easier to hide secrets in a big landscape with hardly anybody around. Then we'd got onto the motorway and joined the familiar London traffic, and finally we'd got back into the flat and I'd barred Ellie from our room so I could message Jake.

'I don't know what you're talking about,' I said. 'I mean, sure, it was a weird day and Ingrid isn't exactly cosy. But the car journey was fine. It was just a bit dull.'

'You *must* have felt it,' she said. 'It was so strong.' And then she started crying again. I held her close and she said, 'Someone's going to die.'

Her face was against my chest and her voice was muffled, and I wasn't sure I'd heard her right. I said, 'It's all going to be fine, Ellie. You must be coming down with something. I'm going to get Mum.'

But she shook her head. 'No. It won't make any difference. Let her rest.'

She pulled away from me and I thought I'd offended her, but then she gazed up at me and her peaky little face – all hollows and shadows in the light of the bedside lamp – was so full of affection, and so sincere, that I was completely unnerved.

She looked exactly the way she might have done if she thought *I* was the one who was about to kick the bucket. Or as if she wanted me to remember what she was about to tell me, whatever happened.

'I do love you, Ava, you know,' she said. And then she just couldn't resist adding, 'Even if you are a bit mean sometimes.'

'And I love you too,' I told her.

It felt really strange to say it. I wasn't sure when I ever had. But it struck me as true, too.

She said, 'You think you're a horrible person, and you don't trust anyone who actually likes you. But you're not that bad. You're really not bad at all.'

With that she turned away from me and snuggled down under her bedcovers and closed her eyes. I turned the light out and got back into my bed, and soon afterwards I heard the soft, gentle breathing that meant she was asleep.

That sound had been part of my life for so long, it was hard to believe that the time was not all that far off when I would leave home, and night after night would go by without me hearing it. I would have thought that was something to look forward to. But now it came to it, I could see how much I'd miss her.

Chapter Nineteen

Paula

It was probably just as well that Mark was out at work when the special needs teacher from the local authority called round for a home visit. Given the way things had been going since the Christmas show, I wasn't at all sure he could have been trusted to be polite to her.

I'd tried to talk to him… I'd tried to be civil. The rage I'd felt after the show was still there, but I prided myself on keeping it under wraps. It hadn't made any difference. Mark had gone into lockdown, and was refusing to discuss Daisy at all until the professionals had told us exactly what was wrong.

Given the waiting list we were likely to find ahead of us, that wasn't going to happen any time soon, but that was Mark all over. He liked to kid himself he was in control… but actually, he just had a habit of avoiding anything that reminded him he wasn't.

I made sure the house was spotless before the teacher arrived; at least that made me feel that I'd done as much as I could to prepare. I couldn't help but feel that everything about Daisy was now under the microscope, including me and Mark, our relationship, our parenting, and the home we had provided for her.

Mary Greengage turned out to be a pleasant, grey-haired woman with a calm, authoritative manner, dressed in the kind of clothes that teachers wear to appear smart but approachable – cardigan, floral blouse, skirt, sensible shoes. I showed her a couple of Daisy's favourite toys – most of them lit up, or made sounds that drove

Mark crazy – and she watched Daisy play and made a few notes, and then I offered her a cup of tea and she said yes.

It was soon after four, and already dark outside. Daisy was in the dining room, rolling out playdough worms on the table, and Mary stood next to me in the galley kitchen in front of the blind-covered window as we waited for the kettle to boil.

I said, 'Did you meet Amy? At pre-school?'

'I did have a chat with her, yes.'

'I don't know if she would have told you this, but Daisy loves playing with gluesticks. I don't mean with glue on them – clean ones. She likes to twiddle them round between her hands. Amy keeps a little tub of them on a shelf by the door specially for Daisy, so she always knows where to find them.'

'Mm,' Mary said non-committally.

The kettle boiled and clicked off. I poured the water onto teabags in two mugs and was hit by a sudden and intense spasm of doubt.

I said, 'Do you have any idea why Daisy does it?'

'Does what?'

'Twiddling things, or twirling them between her hands. She's always done it. I mean, she's done it for as long as she's had the physical ability to do it. She used to sit in the middle of the living-room carpet surrounded by toys, playing with an old sock – flipping it up and down as if that was the most interesting thing in the world.'

Mary cleared her throat.

'It could be what is sometimes described as repetitive behaviour,' she said.

'Repetitive behaviour? What does *that* mean?'

Suddenly she was as stiff and expressionless as a piece of paper, and I knew straight away that it *did* mean something, something big, and that Mary Greengage was worried about how I might react to it.

'It could suggest a diagnosis of autism spectrum disorder,' she said.

I very carefully poured a little bit of milk into both our mugs, fished out the teabags and dropped them in the pot with all the other used teabags and put on the lid.

I wanted to say, *It can't be.* But I couldn't. Because what did I know? Nothing. Nothing at all.

I said, 'So how do we find out for sure?'

'It's not a quick process, I'm afraid. After this visit I'll send a copy of my report to your family doctor and recommend further investigation. Your doctor will need to write a referral. Then you'll get an outpatient appointment from the community paediatrics team at the hospital in Oxford. Depending on how that goes, you might be offered a full assessment. That's when you could potentially be given a diagnosis.'

I don't know how it happened. My mug somehow slipped from my fingers. Before I knew it I was looking down at a puddle of tea and bits of broken china on the floor.

Then I was apologising and soaking up the spill with kitchen paper and Daisy had emerged from the living room to find out what all the commotion was about. She was twiddling something furiously between her hands – a wooden spoon she'd decorated with stuck-on hair and eyes at pre-school to make a kind of puppet, though she'd never actually played with it as such. Then she stopped twiddling and reached for my stomach, as she sometimes did for reassurance, and I found myself glaring at Mary as if she might be about to criticise me as Mark had. Because if this was a way I could give Daisy the comfort she needed, why on earth would I listen to anyone who might tell me to make her stop?

When Mark came home that evening I tried to tell him about the visit.

He said, 'Look, I can't talk about this now. I need to email a couple of clients. Will you call me when dinner's ready?'

And with that he withdrew to his little office at the end of the kitchen, and shut the door.

After dinner Daisy settled down in the living room with the keyboard that played 'Greensleeves', and Mark grimaced and said, 'So much for a nice relaxing evening.'

'At least she's happy,' I said, putting the pot on the hob for coffee.

Mark sighed. He'd just cleared the table, which was something he always helped with, though he would never fill or empty the dishwasher, or wash up; those were my jobs.

'I quite fancied watching some telly, but I won't be able to hear a thing,' he said. 'Guess I'll have to wait till you've got her in the bath. Or watch it on my laptop in the office.'

I decided to ignore this. 'Mark… is now an all right time to talk to you for a minute?'

He was instantly wary. 'Talk to me? What about?'

'I wanted to tell you about the visit we had today,' I said. 'The teacher who came round, she said…' My heart was racing. I wasn't sure I'd be able to get the words out. 'All the twiddling Daisy does, you know, the way she rolls things around between her hands – apparently that could actually mean something.'

Mark's eyes narrowed.

'It could suggest a diagnosis of autism spectrum disorder.'

'*Autism*? I thought that meant you were either a genius or lying in a corner banging your head on the floor. That doesn't sound like Daisy at all.'

'It's a spectrum, Mark. That means there's a range of behaviour. After the teacher had gone I looked it up online. There's lots of stuff you can read about it. I'll send you some links.'

'But this isn't definite, is it? You said it *could suggest* that's what she's got. It might not be that. It might be something completely different. Maybe it's nothing at all.'

'From what I've read up so far, it seems to fit…'

'Oh, so you're diagnosing her now, are you? I wouldn't have thought you'd be so quick to write off our daughter.'

'I'm not writing her off. I just looked it up.'

'Yeah, well, everyone's an armchair doctor now, aren't they? All you need to do is type in a couple of symptoms and bingo, you've got a syndrome. You know it drives real doctors crazy, don't you?'

'I know you're worried,' I said, 'but you don't need to take it out on me.'

'Oh, spare me the entry-level psychotherapy. This is bullshit, Paula. All of it. They haven't got a clue what's wrong with her and neither have you.'

'The teacher's going to write up an official report. I'll give you a copy when I get it.'

'Can't wait,' he said, rolling his eyes. 'Will you bring me in a coffee when it's ready?'

With that he stomped off to his office.

I carried on standing in the kitchen, listening to 'Greensleeves', trying to take deep breaths, willing myself not to go in there and pour the coffee over his head.

How could he be so insufferable? So arrogant? Even if he didn't care for me any more... how could he be like this about his child?

After a while I went upstairs to run Daisy's bath. I could hear someone talking, and at first I thought it was Mark watching TV in his office. Then I realised it was him, on the phone to someone.

He came to bed late, and I didn't get the chance to ask him who he'd been talking to till the following morning, when he was about to leave for work.

'I rang my mother,' he said. 'Do you have a problem with that?'

He slammed the front door on the way out. It was actually a relief to be alone with Daisy.

*

The report came home in Daisy's bookbag a couple of days later, in a sealed brown envelope. After I'd read it, I set it aside to present to Mark after dinner. But when I gave it to him he yawned, protested, said how tired he was, and wondered if he really had to read it just then, since he had a lot of work to do that evening.

'You can read it whenever suits you, but I would have thought you'd want to read it sooner rather than later.'

He pulled a face as if I was being unreasonable. 'Yes, well, some of us actually have to earn some money round here.'

'Oh, come on. I work too.'

'You work part-time, and it's hardly demanding, is it? A bit of putting in full stops and taking out commas, a couple of days a week. You only started doing it so you could pay to leave Daisy with a childminder. Maybe if you'd focused on her, we wouldn't be where we are now.'

'Don't you dare blame me.'

'You're the one who spends the most time with her.'

'Yes, and it wouldn't hurt you to take a bit more of an interest. I see other dads out with their kids all the time, in the park or whatever. You never do anything with her.'

'That's because it's so bloody impossible!'

Daisy stopped pressing the button on the keyboard that played 'Greensleeves' and let out a long, high-pitched shriek.

'You shouldn't have raised your voice,' I hissed at Mark as I rushed to reassure her. 'She's very sensitive to noise.'

A few minutes later I heard the front door slam.

I couldn't believe it. How dare he? And where the hell had he gone?

He didn't come back till much later, by which time I was more anxious than angry. I'd managed to get Daisy off to sleep and was in bed myself, waiting up for him, wondering whether I should start calling people to track down where he was, and trying and failing to read.

'I'm sorry,' he said as he came into the bedroom. 'I just had to get out. If I didn't I was going to kill somebody.'

'Oh. And that's meant to make me feel better?'

'No,' he said, taking his dressing-gown off the hook. 'It's meant to be the truth.'

'Where have you been, anyway? I was worried.'

'I went to the pub.'

'Oh. That must have been nice. I'm sure some of us would love to go off to the pub once in a while.'

'Well, if you hadn't totally alienated my mother you might have a willing babysitter. But as it is, I don't think anybody else would be up for dealing with Daisy, so you're a bit stuck, aren't you?'

And with that he went off to take a shower.

He'd started with an apology. Why hadn't I tried to be nicer to him? But then, with his next breath he'd been talking about murder. It wasn't much of a way to make peace.

I looked round at the bedroom: the framed photographs of our wedding and of us with Daisy trying to look happy, the designer dressing table Mark had picked out for me that I'd never used, and the mementoes of past foreign holidays: the vase from Turkey, the wood carving from New Zealand, the Italian glass candlesticks. So much stuff, so carefully curated: a life built out of perfect little things.

If this was how it was going to be between us… how on earth could we stay together?

Suddenly I could foresee a future in which everything around us would vanish, and Daisy and I would have to face the rest of the world alone. It felt like being poised to step off the edge of a cliff.

A few days later, while Mark was at work, I stole into his office to look for the report.

He had clearly not read it. It wasn't that he hadn't got round to it; he had decided to bury it. It was at the bottom of a small, orderly pile that included a brochure from the nearby gardening centre, his annual pension statement and a guide to the best PCs and laptops on the market.

That night he was back late; Daisy was already in the bath by the time he pulled up in the drive. It had occurred to me that he was putting in extra hours just to get out of spending time at home. I wasn't sure whether it was me or Daisy he was keener to avoid... or both of us.

I called down to tell him there was a pasta bake in the oven, and got Daisy out of the bath and cleared up the water she'd splashed everywhere. By the time we came down he'd finished eating and had nearly polished off a big glass of wine.

'Do you want some? There's plenty left,' he said.

I poured myself some wine and sat down opposite him. This was how we'd done it in the old days, wasn't it? Sharing a bottle of wine on a Friday night, a bit of conversation, a box set, sex... no interruptions? Well, we ought to be all right for a bit – Daisy had gone straight to her keyboard, and its tinny electronic version of 'Greensleeves' was playing yet again.

'I see my daughter couldn't keep herself from rushing in to say goodnight to Daddy,' Mark said.

It took an effort to suppress the urge to chuck my glass of wine over his too-handsome, self-pitying face.

'You could always go and say goodnight to her yourself if you're so keen.'

'Oh, come on,' Mark said. 'You must hate it too. Don't you? Don't pretend you don't.'

'I don't hate Daisy, if that's what you mean.'

'I mean her being the way she is. With this thing that there's no cure for.'

'Hang on a minute. Last I knew, you weren't even willing to talk about this until she'd had the diagnosis.'

'Yes, well, I still had a little bit of hope then. I wasn't ready to admit how completely screwed she is. She's never going to be able to lead a normal life, Paula. Never.' He downed the rest of his glass of wine. 'You know what I was thinking the other day? How nice it would be to book a summer holiday. I've been working hard, I deserve a break. But then I started thinking, where on earth can we go? With her? The truth is, we can't go anywhere. We're screwed, too.'

'That is not true.'

Mark refilled his glass. 'It is, and you know it.'

'Is this what you've got out of talking to your mother? I should have guessed that she'd just make everything worse.'

'Don't talk about her like that. She's just a realist. You might choose to see this whole thing through rose-tinted spectacles, but I'm not going to.'

'You can't just give up.'

'I'm not giving up. There's nothing *to* give up.'

'Mark, if only you'd read that report, there was some advice for us, some ideas for things to try...'

'Don't nag me, OK? None of that's going to cure her, is it? There isn't a cure.'

'Well, no. But there are still things we can do that might help.'

'Really? Like what?'

My mind had gone blank. 'Well, one of them was to play turn-taking games... like catch...'

He rolled his eyes. 'I've tried that. She can't do it,' he said. 'So is this your thing now? The self-sacrificing special needs mum, bravely soldiering on? Bit of a new look for you, playing the virtue card.'

'If that's you getting at me for having a crush on someone else about a decade ago, then you're even more pathetic than I thought.'

'Oh, I'm pathetic now, am I? Then why are you still married to me?' He pointed in the direction of the living room, where Daisy had turned up the volume the keyboard to maximum volume. 'If you're being so honest now, why don't you just admit it's because of *that*? You're the one who wanted her. It wasn't *my* idea.'

'That is unforgivable!'

'Then don't forgive me. I'm past caring.'

He scooped up his wine glass and strode off in the direction of the office, and I heard the slam of the door even over the blaring of Daisy's toy.

The next day I steeled myself to call my mum. She was full of her own news, so the first part of the conversation was fine. She had broken up with the boyfriend who owned the houseboat and was sub-letting a tiny bedsit above a sex shop in Soho, and had just started a long-distance relationship with an Australian sheep farmer she'd met online. She was already making plans to fly out to meet him in the flesh.

Eventually I brought myself to tell her what Mary Greengage had said.

'Oh, for heaven's sake,' she exclaimed. 'What is this mania with sticking labels on children? Look, are you worried about her?'

'Well… yes.'

'Well, try not to be, is my advice. I mean, is she happy? That's all that really matters, isn't it? Not whether she's got the five times table down pat.'

Daisy hadn't yet learned to count to ten and didn't have much language beyond yes, no, a series of useful nouns and the ability to echo back what other people had said, but I decided not to point this out.

'She isn't always happy,' I said. 'Sometimes she gets really stressed out, and has these awful meltdowns where she's just beside herself.'

'Oh, you used to have tantrums too. I'm sure she'll grow out of it. And they put them under a lot of pressure at a very young age these days, don't they? I mean, once upon a time, she'd still have been at home, and you wouldn't have had anybody poking round paying you visits. She's not even five yet. Look, Paula, forgive me for being blunt, but are you sure you don't just want to be let off the hook? Because, you know, if you manage to do this, if you succeed in having Daisy labelled in this way… doesn't that mean nobody will ever expect anything more of her, or of you?'

'Screw you, Mum,' I said, perfectly calmly, and hung up.

I was astonished by what I'd said to her, and I knew she wouldn't be quick to forgive me – she was likely to be sniffy for months, especially if I didn't go out of my way to apologise. But when I reflected on it, I was rather pleased with myself. I just didn't have the energy to spare for letting her get to me.

Somewhere along the line, I'd begun to develop tunnel vision. Daisy and I were in the tunnel, and everybody else was on the outside, and unless what they were saying was helpful to us, I rejected it or ignored it.

I knew Mark hated the way I'd frozen him out. But it was necessary. By this stage, the only way I could protect myself and Daisy was by refusing to take what he'd said on board. He looked as if he felt very hard done by almost all the time. But as far as I was concerned, if he wanted to feel close to me again, he'd have to learn to offload his fear and anger elsewhere, and he'd shown no sign of being willing to do that. He seemed to think it was my job to deal with his feelings, in much the same way that I was meant to shop and cook and clean and weed the garden.

I'd hardened. It didn't seem like such a bad thing. It seemed necessary. After all, someone had to care for Daisy, and I couldn't leave much of that to her father… or either of her grandmothers.

It was time to face facts; I might not be up to much, I might not be the best and most dedicated parent out there, but when it came to Daisy there was no one who could be her mum as well as well as I could, however flawed or inadequate I might be.

Finally, in May, Mark came with me to a meeting about Daisy for the first time. It was the session at which we were to discover whether or not she had been given an official diagnosis.

The diagnosis meeting came at the end of a full multidisciplinary assessment at the hospital in Oxford, a series of appointments spread across five days. Daisy didn't join us; one of the hospital playworkers was looking after her in the nursery across the corridor, which was reserved purely for the use of children going through the assessment process. The meeting took place in a small, bare, tiled room furnished with a circle of chairs. Mark and I sat next to each other, each of us with a sheaf of papers on our knees, waiting to hear what the professionals sitting around the room had to say about Daisy.

The paediatric consultant led the meeting. She ran through the summaries of the various reports and gave her conclusion: a diagnosis of autism spectrum disorder, just as Mary Greengage had suggested months before.

Despite the long wait, it felt weirdly like an anti-climax. Mark and I were given the opportunity to give our views. Mark cleared his throat, and said, 'Do you have any idea what caused it?'

The consultant shook her head. 'No. It's very common to want to look for a reason, to try to find someone or something to blame. But this is not anyone's fault.'

I looked at Mark, but he wouldn't meet my eyes.

The consultant turned to me. 'Mrs Walsh? Any questions?'

I shook my head and said it was what I had been expecting.

The consultant said she'd ring us in a couple of weeks to see how we were getting on and would see us again in her clinic for a check-up in a year's time. Daisy had been referred for speech and language therapy, and someone would be in touch about that. And we could go on the waiting list for a parenting course, but it might be a while before we were offered a place.

Then she passed us both a handful of leaflets and a list of support groups. Mark murmured a polite thank you and put the information away in his briefcase, along with his copies of the reports about Daisy. I could tell by the expression on his face that he was never going to look at any of it.

I stuffed all my paperwork into the bag I'd brought with Daisy's emergency snacks, change of clothes and favourite toy of the moment, a bear with a button on its tummy that lit up and played soothing lullabies when you pressed it. I supposed I'd have to file everything. Get organised. As if I was at work and Daisy was a project, with targets and milestones and measurable progress, and an archive of important records.

And that was it. The meeting was over. We had our diagnosis, and we were free to take Daisy home.

It was a bit like the moment when she'd been discharged from hospital as a newborn: now it was up to us. The monumental responsibility of figuring out what to do for the best, of looking after her, caring for her, loving her, stretched ahead for years and years, and was ours and ours alone.

It was a beautiful sunny day. Blue skies, big white clouds. The world didn't even look that different. Just a little bit, in a way it was hard to put your finger on.

Mark drove, and we didn't talk. Daisy slept in the back. By the time we made it to Kettlebridge the school run traffic had died down and the rush hour hadn't yet got going. It was quiet, and our road, which was bordered by a small patch of woodland on one side, looked idyllic. The backdrop for a perfect childhood. Safe, friendly, neighbourly, with a little bit of nature to look at: wildness on a manageable scale.

Mark parked on the driveway and we went inside, and everything was just as we'd left it that morning.

I made tea and sat in the sitting room to drink it, and Mark went off to his office to catch up on emails and Daisy lay down on the sofa and fell asleep in the sunlight. She always seemed to be tired out after spending time in the hospital. I sympathised; I was exhausted, too.

Nothing had changed, really, had it? She was the same little girl, after all.

I thought about ringing Mum to tell her, but decided against it. It would keep. And she'd been funny with me lately, ever since I'd been rude to her on the phone. Problem was, if she said the wrong thing, I couldn't guarantee that I wouldn't be rude to her again.

Instead I sat and drank my tea and gazed at the sunlight on the wall and allowed myself to think of nothing. I left all the reports on the side; I couldn't even summon up the energy to file them. It was as if I'd been emptied out of everything that had once made me who I was.

I was vaguely conscious of Mark moving round upstairs, of a few thuds as if he was moving something heavy, and of the bedroom floorboards creaking as he paced about. What on earth was he doing? Spring cleaning? Building a bonfire in readiness to torch the place? Sitting next to him in the diagnosis meeting, I'd almost been sorry for him. He'd looked so forlorn. But I knew that he felt absolutely no sympathy for me.

He blamed me. Still. Even though he must have realised it wasn't rational, or fair. And I couldn't accept the blame. It would have killed me. So where could we go from there?

After what seemed like a long time he came heavily downstairs into the hallway, and I hurried out to catch him before he could slip out of the front door.

He had a suitcase with him. Not the overnight case. The big one.

I said, 'What do you think you're doing?'

He said, 'I'm going to stay with my mother for a couple of days.'

'You mean, after everything that happened today, you're going to run away?'

'Nothing happened today. Nothing that hadn't already happened a long time ago. We both knew what they were going to say.'

'So why are you going now?'

'Because I can't do this any more.'

'What do you mean, you can't do this?'

'I want a family, Paula. A normal family life, like everybody else has. And this isn't it, and it never will be. Daisy's never going to graduate, or get a job, and as for getting married and having children... Forget it. She's probably never even going to be able to leave home. I should be able to look forward to walking my daughter down the aisle one day. Instead I think about the future and it fills me with despair.'

'Is that really your idea of what being a parent is all about? Getting to be father of the bride?'

'Do you know what, Paula? It is, actually. It's not the only thing, but it's part of it. And it would be for any man.'

'That's ridiculous! It's like saying her whole value is dependent on whether she has her big day in white.'

'That's not what I mean and you know it. Look, you can have the house and everything that's in it. You're welcome to it. Just as long as I never have to see either of you again.'

'You're just saying that to hurt me. You might feel that about me, but I don't believe you really feel that about Daisy.'

'Oh, but I do. I don't feel anything for her. I never did. And it seems to me that the feeling's mutual. Half the time, she barely seems to know I exist. So what difference will it make to her if I'm gone? She'd be more upset if someone took a hammer to that wretched keyboard. And don't kid yourself I haven't thought about it.'

'You wouldn't.'

'But I would, Paula. To be honest with you, if I stay in this house any longer I don't know what I might take a hammer to.'

We stared at each other. I said, 'Are you threatening me?'

'No, Paula. I'm leaving you. Both of you. Because otherwise, you're going to drive me mad. And you can't stop me.'

'You're a bastard.'

'You're a bitch. But that didn't make us compatible, did it?'

I moved closer to him. He was taller than me by several inches, and stronger. I wanted to hurt him but I knew I wouldn't be able to do it with my hands. He had to look at me with fear in his eyes. The least he could do was to show me that respect.

'You don't get to talk like that about my daughter,' I said. 'One of these days I'm going to come for you. And when I do, you're going to regret this for the rest of your life.'

He pulled a mocking face. 'Are you trying to threaten me? Right now, that is an infinitely less terrifying prospect than staying here with the two of you.'

And with that he picked up his case and sauntered out, closing the front door behind him.

I listened to the car start, reverse out of the driveway, turn in the road and roar away.

And then I heard something else: the beginning of 'Greensleeves'.

I went into the living room. Daisy had got down off the sofa and was sitting on the floor. She looked up at me uncomprehendingly, but with a kind of startled hopefulness, as if I might be about to make sense of a few things for her.

'Just you and me for supper tonight, Daisy,' I said. 'Daddy's gone.'

I had no idea whether she had understood or not. She pressed the keyboard and 'Greensleeves' started again.

I sat down on the sofa and stared at her for a long time. She didn't seem to mind. Then I pulled myself together and went into the kitchen and set about the business of figuring out what we were going to eat.

For once, looking after Daisy didn't seem like a chore. It seemed like a lifeline, and I knew I was going to need it. I'd use it again and again and again, and eventually the day would come when what Mark had said wouldn't hurt me any more.

After Mark had been gone for a month I wrote to Ingrid saying that she was welcome to remain part of Daisy's life, regardless of Mark's decision not to have any contact.

There was no reply.

I didn't hear from her until two years later, by which time the divorce was done and dusted and I had come to think of myself and Daisy as belonging to a family of two. Mum had recently emigrated to live on her Australian boyfriend's sheep ranch and I missed her more than I would have expected, though we talked about as often as we ever had. She retained her ability to offer up opinions I really didn't want to hear, even when chatting via FaceTime from a distance of more than ten thousand miles.

By then, I'd learned to cope with being the only adult in the house. I was lonely, but you can get used to loneliness and I wasn't isolated. The mum friends I'd made in the town hadn't shunned me, and I gave as much time as I could spare to supporting Daisy's school. We'd raised funds for a sensory room for children with special needs – a little haven with fairy lights and a bubble lamp where they could go to relax. Daisy and I had even been pictured in the local newspaper, and I'd wondered what Mark would have said if he could have seen us. Then I had remembered the scorn with which he'd rejected us when he was leaving, and was inspired to hate him all over again.

Naturally, my hatred for Mark was something I kept to myself. I wouldn't have admitted to anybody how often I thought about him, or how vengeful I felt. I didn't have a lot of time to spare for thinking about Ingrid, but I wasn't exactly fond of her either. The sight of her small, neat, crabby handwriting staring up at me from the doormat was all it took to reawaken my old resentment.

Daisy and I had just walked back from school. I scooped up the post, put the bills aside for later and took Ingrid's letter with me as I followed Daisy from the kitchen to the living room. She settled on her favourite spot on the sofa and started playing with an app on her iPad that made sparkling noises as she scribbled on the screen with her finger. With the sound of a magic wand playing over and over again in the background, I opened Ingrid's letter.

It was set out the old-fashioned way I'd learned at school decades ago, with Ingrid's address at the top on the right-hand side.

Dear Paula.

Dear! I was surprised that she had brought herself to write that. Maybe she'd crossed her fingers.

Mark has asked me to get in touch to let you know some news that I'm afraid may come as a shock to you. We felt that you ought to know and not to find out by chance.

Around the time of my sister's funeral, during the very difficult time when you and Mark were living separately, Mark had a brief relationship with a young woman called Jenny.

Jenny? Who the hell was *Jenny*?

A brief relationship? Did she mean a one-night stand?

Had it been revenge – payback for my poor little long-ago crush, that I'd never so much as followed through on?

I'd felt so guilty. I'd tried so hard to make it up to him. And yet he'd had a fling with someone else and had never even come close to confessing. He had slept so peacefully next to me night after night all those years… He'd shared meals with me, lived under the same roof, without ever letting it slip.

How could I not have suspected? How could he have kept it from me so completely?

He is the father of her daughter, Ava, who is now sixteen.

Ava.

Sixteen.

This girl – Mark's *daughter* – had been there all along. For most of our marriage.

And where had he been? With me. At dinner parties. On holiday. Putting on his suit and going off to work. Living a comfortable, affluent, childfree existence – right up until I had Daisy, at which point it had all begun to fall apart.

Too much noise. Too much mess. Too much chaos.

And then it had become apparent that Daisy wasn't developing in the same way as other children her age, and he had bolted. We had been in trouble, and he'd gone off and left us for dead.

'Bastard,' I said out loud.

When Jenny discovered she was pregnant, she decided not to tell Mark, as she knew he had gone back to you.

Jenny the martyr, the mother of Mark's other daughter, selflessly backing off so he could save his marriage to me. How very thoughtful. How marvellously, idiotically kind. Of course, we were doomed in the long run anyway, but she wasn't to know that, was she?

She received an offer of marriage from a longstanding admirer while she was expecting, and accepted it.

But seriously – this Jenny was something else. What kind of woman would do that? Marry someone while she was pregnant with somebody else's kid? And what kind of man would make the offer?

Maybe Jenny wasn't a martyr. Maybe she was Machiavelli.

Either way, she must have had something going for her. I couldn't imagine having attracted any offers of marriage when I was pregnant. Even Mark had pretty much stopped fancying me. He'd ended up looking at me as if I was a potentially unreliable co-worker rather than an object of lust – except for the times when I was really hormonal and bad-tempered, when he'd regarded me with alarm.

Well, I wasn't at all sorry now that I'd frightened him once in a while. Served him right. I only wished I'd frightened him a whole lot more. The lying, cheating…

My hands tightened on the letter. It was an effort to relax them enough to keep the paper from creasing.

Jenny went on to have another daughter with her husband: Ellie, now eleven years old. Jenny's marriage broke up when Ellie was a baby and ended in divorce.

Jenny wasn't all that perfect, then. She was divorced, too. I shouldn't have taken any satisfaction from this, but I was meanly pleased by it.

Following his divorce from you, Mark made contact with Jenny and they quickly became close. They are engaged to be married in the summer, and she is due to give birth to their second child shortly before Christmas.

There is no need to respond to this letter in any way. I'm sure you will appreciate that Mark is preoccupied with his new family, and I am getting in touch only to pass on information that might be relevant to you, given how surprisingly small the world can be. You might be interested to know that they plan to settle in Fairmarsh.

I hope you are able to find it in your heart to wish them all well.

Yours sincerely, Ingrid.

How many drafts of this letter would Ingrid have written, lining up the bombshell news ready to drop? But then, she'd probably loved it. Best fun she'd had in ages.

It had been two years. Two years of silence, and she hadn't so much as mentioned Daisy, let alone asked after her.

I dropped the letter and slammed my fist into the palm of my hand.

'*Bitch!*'

Daisy immediately let out a roar, scooped up one of her collection of diecast cars from the floor and hit the screen of the iPad with it. I dived forwards to stop her from hitting it again and was immediately plunged back into parental firefighting mode, and a present in which my former mother-in-law had no place, and nor did my ex-husband and his other family.

Chapter Twenty

Jenny

The sonographer ran the scanner over my big greased-up belly and said, 'It's definitely a boy.'

And there he was on the screen. His bones were like white shadows, hazy but easy to make out: the curve of the spine, the limbs, the skull. He looked like a fossil that had come to life.

He moved abruptly in response to the scanner, and my belly bulged and then subsided.

'He's got quite a kick,' I said. I didn't need to turn to Mark to know that he'd be grinning from ear to ear.

The baby kept moving. He was definitely going to be the splashiest swimmer in the pool when he was older. I imagined myself taking him into the water, encouraging him, gently letting him go so he could find out that he could float on his own. I hadn't had much time for any of that with either of the girls.

The scan showed that he was a healthy weight, and developing normally. It didn't pick up any abnormalities. I hadn't really expected or prepared myself for bad news, but both Mark and I had been apprehensive, and afterwards we went to a posh restaurant for lunch to celebrate.

Mark looked at me with so much love I couldn't quite believe it was all for me; even back in the days when he'd been fond of me, Sean had never looked at me like that. He raised a glass of sparkling water to me and said, 'One of these days, we'll have champagne to celebrate all this.'

We were as giggly and wrapped up in each other as newlyweds, which was exactly what we were; we'd tied the knot a few weeks before, in a quiet registry office ceremony attended by Ingrid and the girls. I'd found a work email address for my sister and had written to her to let her know about the wedding, but I hadn't invited her and I hadn't heard back. I'd been a little hurt by her silence, but not enough to spoil anything; after all, there was so much to be happy about.

In the end, we'd decided to go for a short honeymoon that would give us both a chance to relax, and had rejected the idea of an Italian sightseeing trip in favour of a weekend in a cabin by a Croatian lake. It was the longest time we'd ever spent alone together. Then we'd gone home together to the girls in Fairmarsh.

Moving out of our London flat hadn't been much of a wrench, though I'd been sorry to leave Peter behind – he was the kindest neighbour I'd ever had. But the girls had their own rooms at last... and it was such a good feeling not to have to worry about the three-monthly inspections any more, or feel that we could be turfed out at short notice if the landlady decided to sell up or move someone else in.

I'd stopped working after the move. Mark was concerned about whether exposure to the chemicals in hair dye might be bad for the baby; I wasn't too worried about that – since the official advice was that it probably wouldn't be – but I didn't really have the energy to relaunch my business in a new area. We'd agreed that I might start it up again when the baby was older, but I didn't feel any particular sense of urgency. For the first time in my adult life, I didn't have to worry about bringing money in. It was pretty much like having won the lottery.

But I must have been anxious, even though I didn't really acknowledge it to myself. Summer gave way to autumn and the girls started their new schools, and as Christmas and my due date drew closer, I began to have strange recurring dreams.

They were about insects. Tides of them. Little bugs, not malevolent, but too numerous to be disregarded. Not dangerous in themselves. But still a threat, if only because there were so many.

Perhaps I just didn't trust things to keep on going well. I was suspicious of good fortune, and I didn't expect happiness to last. Rightly, as it turned out.

The birth was very quick, much quicker than with Ava or Ellie. I went into labour at eight in the evening, after my waters broke – good timing, since it meant Ingrid was still awake when we phoned her to come over and mind the girls. Our son was born five hours later, and then Mark was sent home and it was just me and the baby on the postnatal ward. We both slept a little and then, to my great relief, we were discharged the next morning.

Even after such a short time in hospital, going home felt like an escape. There was the world again, all its goings-on moving past the car windows – the cafés, the parks, the shops, all full of stars and angels and fake snow because it was nearly Christmas.

That evening Mark gave me dinner and waited on me hand and foot. The girls were thrilled. Even Ava. Lit up with the gorgeousness of it, the delight of a new baby in the house. I sat by the Christmas tree in the rocking chair I'd bought because I thought it would be comfortable for nursing, and Ava said, 'So did you decide what you're going to call him yet?'

There had been a lot of contenders. Mark and I had been through the baby name book several times, and then we had bought another one and gone through that, too. I looked across at Mark, who was sitting on the sofa watching us as if we were a miracle he didn't deserve.

'Your call,' he said.

'He definitely seems like a Felix to me,' I said, looking down at the bit of the baby's face I could see, which was squashed against my breast. 'It means happy, doesn't it? He seems like a jolly little chap.'

'How can you tell?' Ava asked, not entirely sceptically.

'Oh… just a feeling. I don't mean he's never going to cry. We already know he's got a pretty good pair of lungs on him.'

After I'd fed him the girls carefully held him in turn, and then I put him down in the cot and had a deep, uninterrupted sleep in the king-sized bed next to him. I had the bed to myself, as Mark had retreated to the sofa to give us all the best chance of a rest. And that was the peaceful end of Felix's first day.

But in the bright light of the following morning, he didn't look right.

His skin was tinged yellow. Jaundice. We took him back into hospital. I wasn't particularly worried; Ava'd had jaundice, too, as a newborn, and it had passed within a day or so. The staff weren't all that worried either, until a paediatric consultant saw the results of Felix's blood test. She said there was a marker that suggested he had an infection, and he wouldn't be able to go home again until they'd figured out why.

Felix and I were given a room to ourselves on the fifth floor, the level of the maternity wing reserved for sick babies and their mothers.

I didn't panic. Actually, I felt like a fraud. I was sure that before long the mystery would be solved and the jaundice would clear, and we'd be home again and preparing for Felix's first Christmas.

They treated the jaundice. Correction: I treated the jaundice. Me and the sun. Felix needed milk and plenty of it. They weighed his nappies to check he was taking in enough of it, and he was. Mark went home to relieve his mother and make sure the girls were all right, and Felix and I were alone together.

It was a beautiful day. The sun coming into our room was very bright, and Felix lay in the sunshine after his feed and snoozed. He looked so peaceful, and his skin was turning pink, losing that sickly hint of yellow. I pored over him when I should have been sleeping myself. He looked a bit like Ava and a bit like Mark, and also, a bit like me. But most of all he looked like his own perfect, new-minted self.

I was sure he'd be well enough to be discharged soon. But they did another blood test and the infection was still there.

He had a cannula inserted into his tiny hand, and a line pumping antibiotics into him, and it persisted.

People came and went, checking his temperature, administering his dosage. Mark visited with Ellie and Ava, bringing grapes and flowers. We had a short stretch of uninterrupted time together, the five of us: a birthday party, of sorts, around my hospital bed. The girls held Felix again. I could tell they were all worried, and trying more or less successfully not to show it.

In a way, it was a relief when they had gone again, and I could just concentrate on Felix.

His second night of life went by in the hospital cot, with a succession of people slipping in and out of the room in the darkness to monitor him. The next morning someone decided a urine sample was needed. Well, that was a joke. I ended up sitting round with one of the midwives, watching Felix lying in his cot with his nappy off, waiting for him to wee, then missing the moment when he did. In the end one of the midwives came up with the idea of putting cotton wool inside his nappy and using a pipette to get the sample out of it. I congratulated her as if we'd cracked it. As if everything else would be easy now the problem of how to carry out the necessary test had been solved.

Soon Felix would be in the clear, and we would be free to go home.

But within the hour the test became unnecessary, and we were overtaken by events.

A paediatrician came to carry out a full body inspection, and saw what nobody else had: the cause of the infection. A twisted testicle, red and slightly swollen. When the blood supply to part of the body is cut off, it dies. And the body of a living person cannot accommodate a part of the body that is already dead.

We had got through the birth together, both of us. We had made it home. I had thought we were safe. But we weren't safe. Felix had emerged from my body to begin his life, and his life was confusion and disaster. Something had happened to him – maybe in the womb, or maybe during the birth – something exceptionally rare. Rare but real. We had been struck by lightning. Of all of the places misfortune could have chosen to come to earth, it had picked us.

There was a rapid escalation. A more senior paediatrician came in. His face was anxious, his voice gentle. He spoke of scans, of the possible need for surgery. I burst into tears and he looked more anxious still.

I had always prided myself on being able to stay calm in an emergency. But I was beyond being calm now. My milk had just come in, and I was still bleeding. My whole body felt as if it was awash with sadness, and there was nothing I could do to stop what was happening and make it better.

I rang Mark at home; it was first Monday of the Christmas holidays, and he was there with the girls. I cried again on the phone to him. He came as quickly as he could, leaving the girls behind, and arriving just in time to meet the new, very senior doctor who had come to review our case.

There was a frisson of respect from the staff in the room as the specialist delivered his verdict. Felix would need an operation, as soon as possible – that very day. The only way to tackle the infection was at source. The part of Felix that had died had to be removed.

We asked questions, but they didn't make any difference to the answer. The operation had to happen, the sooner the better, and if it didn't, Felix wouldn't get well.

Then the specialist told us that Felix was to have nil by mouth until after the operation, and left us.

Felix was to have general anaesthetic, and I couldn't feed him, and my breasts were bursting with milk. I wanted to feed him so much. I had never wanted anything more. And yet I couldn't, because if I did, he might die.

And he wanted my milk – he cried for it. His crying was terrible. I gave him to Mark to hold because I couldn't bear it – I couldn't keep our baby in my arms and hear him and see his distress when it was so completely within my power to satisfy him and soothe him, and so essential for me to refuse him. We gave him our clean fingers to suck, we tried a dummy, but none of that was any good at all. It would satisfy him for a moment, and then he would realise it wasn't what he wanted and begin to wail again.

Eventually he wore himself out, and slept.

A midwife showed up with a breast pump for me, and I milked myself and that was a relief, but only a physical one. It was nothing to what I would have felt if I could have fed my baby again.

He was still asleep when they came to take him away, and wheel him down to the special care baby unit where he would be prepped for surgery. We were to stay behind until we were called down to join him, and then we would be able to go with him as far as the operating theatre.

We talked about what had happened and what might happen next. Mark wanted to lay out the possibilities, to understand them, to take charge of them, as if being able to list all the eventualities would make them bearable, as if it was possible to prepare for whatever lay ahead. As if this was a challenge he couldn't afford to fail. I let the details wash over me. I looked at the fear in Mark's face, I heard the strain in his voice, and I was grateful that he was there with me, that I wasn't completely alone.

And then a midwife came in and told us Felix was ready, and we went down to the special care baby unit to see him.

So many little sick babies in incubators. So many worried parents. And our baby in the middle of them, still asleep, lying in his hospital cot with its wheeled base and transparent rim with the drip running into his hand.

Mark stood by and watched me, and I sat by Felix and touched his little hand. He was awake now but drowsy, and I sang to him – very quietly, almost under my breath, just loud enough for him to hear. I sang him the same lullabies that I'd once sung to Ava and Ellie: 'Hush, Little Baby', 'Lavender's Blue', 'Greensleeves'. I couldn't let him lie there in silence. I wanted to sing to him as if this was just any sleep, the ordinary kind, the kind we all wake up from.

And then the time came and they were ready for him.

It seemed a long walk to the operating theatre. They offered me a wheelchair but I said no: I was still sore from the birth, but I was determined to manage, to do this for Felix on my own two feet. After all, I wasn't the one who was ill.

Felix was pushed along on his cot by the hospital porter, and Mark and I followed. The cot squeaked, and one of the doors of the cabinet under the mattress didn't quite shut properly and kept banging. Mark told me later how much that sound bothered him. It was the small, persistent sound of something overlooked, something that either couldn't or wouldn't be fixed.

The corridor narrowed and twisted and turned, and there were fewer people around as we progressed. Eventually it was just us. We turned a corner and there, attached to the wall in front of us, was a whiteboard with a list written on it: times, names of patients, operations. All of the others were crossed off, apart from Felix, who was the very last and had been squeezed in where there was barely space.

The porter turned to us with the regretful face of someone who is about to deliver bad news for which he is not personally responsible, and explained that out of me and Mark, only one of us could go further. He was sorry. But those were the rules.

Mark didn't hesitate.

'You go,' he said. 'I'll wait.'

I had never been as grateful to him as I was at that moment. To make that decision so calmly and quickly, without complaining, to make it easy for me to go on... Whatever might lie ahead, and whatever he might have done or not done in the past, I knew right then that he would always have my back.

There was no time to lose. I said a hurried goodbye to Mark and followed the porter and the cot with Felix on it through the silver double doors into the small, windowless room reserved for patients to be prepared for surgery.

It was like the airlock of a spaceship, a space between the known and the unknown. On the other side of the double doors was the rest of the hospital, and Mark, waiting. And the other door led to the operating theatre, where I would not be able to follow. This was as far as I could go.

The anaesthetist was already there, waiting. The porter went out, and the anaesthetist invited me to sit and showed me the consent form that had been prepared for me to sign.

He was a little younger than me, brainy-looking, wide-eyed and sincere in his surgical scrubs, and he spoke gently and slowly as he set about explaining the possible risks and side-effects of the procedure Felix was about to undergo. I could feel him willing me not to panic or give in to hysteria, to take in what he was saying as calmly as he was saying it, and then to sign the form so they could go ahead and do what was necessary to save Felix's life.

It wasn't reassurance he was offering, though. It was anything but reassuring. What he was doing was making clear that there was a choice, and I had to make it. And the choice was between risk and death, and there were no alternatives.

Felix was still awake, but only just. There was a mobile hanging on the wall opposite him, projecting colours on the wall behind it: something soothing for children to watch before slipping into unconsciousness.

I said, 'I don't care what the risks are. If this is his only chance, I'll sign.'

And I did. Then I reached out to touch Felix's tiny hand and his eyes flickered open and closed again. The anaesthetist put a mask over his face and I felt Felix reeling away from me, sinking into darkness.

I took one last look at him: his soft cheeks, the fluff of downy hair on the top of his head, his miraculous eyelashes. I said, 'Goodbye, my love.' And then I had to leave. I turned away from him and went the opposite way to the way he would be going, through the double doors back to the corridor.

Mark was still standing in the corridor exactly where I'd left him. There was nowhere to sit, and no one else around.

He looked frozen, not from cold but from time, as if ages had gone by while he was standing there and had transformed him, the way old wood turns eventually into something like stone. But for me the time had passed as if it was an instant: being with Felix, having to say goodbye. I had no idea at all how long I had actually been gone.

We made our way to the waiting room where we would stay until the operation was over. We got lost once or twice; the hospital was beginning to seem like a maze that we would never get out of.

The waiting room was bright and new, with a coffee machine and a vending machine that sold ready meals, and a microwave. There was a tired-looking woman sitting there by herself, eating warmed-up curry out of a plastic container. I assumed she must have a sick child too; she looked like she'd spent more time hanging round in waiting rooms lately than we had. She was giving off a definite vibe of not wanting to talk, so Mark and I sat quietly together and let her be.

It seemed strange to think of eating. Irrelevant. As if it was an old custom that should have fallen out of favour. I supposed I'd be hungry again eventually, but it was hard to imagine it.

Mark went off to the maternity wing to get the things I'd left up there – I'd assumed we would be going back, and hadn't realised that Felix would be transferred to a post-surgical ward for children. There wasn't much to collect: the bag Mark had brought for me when he'd visited, and a few bits and pieces that I'd left scattered around the room – a pack of nappies, wipes, and the little newborn babygros, yellow and white and blue, that I'd been rinsing out in the basin by hand. We hadn't bought many clothes that size, because he was bound to grow so quickly.

Back home I had drawers full of things for him to wear when he was bigger. Nought to three months, three to six, six to nine. Soft leather shoes, the sort babies wear before they can walk. A couple of sleeping bags in different weights and sizes, a snowsuit that he wouldn't fit into until next winter but that I'd spotted in the sale and hadn't been able to resist. Tucked in a corner, next to the snowsuit, was the Christmas stocking I'd got ready for him, filled with little gifts already wrapped in paper decorated with snowmen and sleighs. Rattles. Chewy toys. A cuddly monkey with a cute face. And there was his present, a mobile for his cot with stars and clouds and birds.

The woman who'd been eating curry got up and went out. I was completely alone, for the first time in what felt like a very long time. I sat and leafed through a magazine and tried not to think. The celebrities with their stories seemed to belong to a previous era, as if the magazine was an ancient artefact that I'd discovered.

Mark came back with the bag and we phoned Ingrid and the girls. Mark did most of the talking and once again I was grateful to him. I didn't want to cry, and I didn't want to frighten anybody. I didn't want to make anything worse. Maybe I secretly believed that if I was very good, if I behaved myself and didn't make a fuss, everything would turn out all right.

The evening wore on. It was long since dark by then, and the only sound was the faint hum of the strip lighting. We were still the only people there, and it was like being in a tunnel but without being able to move on or free ourselves. Or perhaps it was more like being trapped in a cave and waiting for rescuers to come and find you.

I remembered how it had felt one time when I was little and Mum had been late to pick me up from school. All the other children had gone; there was nobody else around, nobody but me. The playground seemed huger than ever. I had found a little heart-shaped chip of stone set in the pebbledash walls and stood there tracing it with my finger, hoping for her, willing her to arrive. And then she had appeared, hurrying towards me, all worry and haste and love. And I had been so grateful and so relieved, and the world had righted itself and carried on.

The next person to come into the waiting room was a doctor, and he wasn't carrying Felix in his arms.

I looked at his face and knew at once what was about to tell us. It was obvious from the pain he felt, and also the sense of duty. He didn't want to. But he had to tell us.

It was bad news. The worst.

The world as I knew it had ended, and it would never be right again.

The doctor explained what had happened and we had no choice but to take it in.

Felix had died on the operating table. His little heart had stopped and he had slipped away from us and from the world, and we would never see him alive again.

My heart stopped too, but its machinery carried on. I was still there, able to see Mark next to me and the doctor opposite us, and my hands moving and clasping each other, as if to pray, before breaking apart and coming to rest on my knees.

I trembled and tears came out of my eyes but offered no relief. Next to me Mark argued and blustered and shook, wanting it to be someone's fault, needing someone to blame. I put my hand on his arm and quieted him, and then he cried too. We were tiny in the face of what had happened, two small figures sitting side by side on the waiting room sofa on the edge of the whirling storm that had taken our son away.

Nobody had made a mistake. Nobody got anything wrong. It shouldn't have happened, but it had: lightning struck twice. One fluke had followed another, and our baby was gone.

We were taken to a room with a hospital bed and a crib and a padded bench to sit on. Then the doctor brought Felix out to us, swaddled in a little white blanket. The doctor's face was filled with regret as he passed our baby back into my arms and I sobbed and held him close.

Somewhere, in a parallel world, a Felix who had survived latched on to my breast and drank my milk till he was satisfied, and slept. And in that world, Mark and I were shaken by the storm that had come so close to taking him, and were grateful to be alive and together.

But we were trapped in a time and place in which Felix was lost.

In this world he was still and cool and the colour had gone from his delicate skin. He was there and it was him, but was no longer quite himself. That little jolly spark had vanished. Not into thin air but into thick air, air that seemed as solid as a wall between me and him. Air that I somehow went on breathing, but he could not.

I knew how sad the doctor and the surgeon and the midwives were. A sorrow like that reaches out like ripples on a pool. It spreads and widens. People struggle with it. Everybody does. New life should be the opposite of death. But sometimes it comes so close as to be interchangeable. The membrane between life and death dissolves, and you feel yourself falling and sinking, and hear the darkness lapping at the margins. And then you know that the world is as fragile as a breath, a pulse. No one is safe, no one, however beloved. Forgetting that may be comforting, but it doesn't make it untrue.

Mark held Felix too. We said goodbye. And then they took him away. They would take care of him for a little longer, before releasing him to us for good.

When he had gone Mark sobbed in a way I'd never seen any man cry before. Or any woman. As if someone had reached into him and pulled his heart out, and he was completely broken.

I hesitated, but only for a moment. Then I put my arms around him and soothed him and rocked him like a child, and something began to come back to me, very faintly at first and then more strongly: the sense that I still had a use in this world. That I could and would carry on, because Mark was not the only person who needed me.

We decided to tell Ingrid and the girls over the phone. It felt late – it felt like a time after history, when the sun had gone – but it was still early enough for them still to be up. We didn't want them to hear the car arrive and rush down expecting me to bring Felix in, and then realise my arms were empty.

Mark talked to Ingrid. I tried not to listen to what he said; I felt as if I was intruding. Then I spoke to Ava and Ellie in turn. They were both stunned. At a loss for words.

I said to both of them, 'We're coming home. We'll be back soon.' What I meant was, *Hold on. Be there for me, and I'll be there for you.* Then I said goodbye and ended the call, and Mark looked at me and said, 'We have to go.'

'I know. It's just… I feel bad about leaving him here all on his own.'

He put his arms around me. 'I know.'

Before we left, I used the hospital breast pump one of the nurses had found me to empty myself out. I asked the nurse if she would be able to give the milk to another mother who needed it, who couldn't feed her baby. I knew the hospital had a milk bank, and it seemed so wrong for it to go to waste. But she said regretfully that she couldn't take it. There were procedures, and tests to be done, and the milk bank was reliant on mothers who could commit to donating over a period of time.

At the end of the day, what I could produce wasn't enough. I tipped what was in the bottle down the sink.

We went out to the car with the bag and drove home. All the way, I was conscious of the empty car seat in the back. I supposed that sometime later that evening I would go to bed next to the cot Mark had so carefully assembled, which Felix would never sleep in again.

Ingrid was dressed in day clothes, but the girls were in their night things. They were all as pale as ghosts. I hugged the girls, and that was a comfort: they were so warm, so effortlessly alive, and both so big it was hard to believe I'd ever carried either of them inside me.

Then I tried to embrace Ingrid. I put my arms around her, but even though she let me I could sense her resistance to being touched. She seemed dry and rigid as an old bone.

She said to Mark, 'Perhaps in time you'll have another,' and he just looked at her and I never heard her say that again.

Mark drove Ingrid back to her flat; she wanted to sleep in her own bed, she said. The girls turned in, and I got into my pyjamas and, on impulse, took one of Felix's little babygros out of the bag and got under the covers and curled up with it in my arms. It still smelled very faintly of him.

But then I heard a small, semi-suppressed, unhappy sound. Someone crying. Ellie, in her room.

I got up, leaving the babygro on the pillow, and went in to her and held her till she was quiet. Then she withdrew and said, 'I knew something bad was going to happen. What's the point of knowing if you can't stop it?'

'You couldn't have known, Ellie,' I said. 'Nobody could have done.'

She shook her head. 'I did know, but I didn't know enough. I don't want to know anything any more.'

I tucked her up and tried to find soothing things to say, and turned off the light and left her.

Back in the master bedroom I curled up alone in bed and listened to the quiet and to the small sound of my own breathing. My body felt heavy and numb all over; I knew I was on the edge of sleep, but I couldn't quite let go and drift off.

Mark came in as quietly as possible, so as not to wake me. He lay down next to me, and I stirred and shifted closer to him so that we were spooning. He put his arms around me and the memory came back to me of when we'd met at the beginning of the year, that long, leisurely lunch that had then turned into a walk followed by a drink and, finally, a reluctant parting and a promise to meet again.

I'd cancelled a customer for him. I never did that. At least, not if I could help it.

But I couldn't help it. Once Mark had got back in touch, I'd been able to think of next to nothing else.

I'd read his Facebook message over and over:

I walked past the hairdresser's where you used to work the other day, but they couldn't tell me where to find you. I hope you don't mind me resorting to this. I just wanted to say that I hope you're well – really well – and that if you ever wanted to, I'd love to meet.

And then we had met, and he'd told me that he and Paula had divorced.

'Clean break,' he said. 'She wants me out of her life.'

'Maybe in a way it's just as well you didn't have kids,' I said.

And he let out a big sigh. 'So how are *your* kids? They must have changed a lot since I saw them last.'

I showed him a picture of Ellie, and then one of Ava. My finger was trembling as I touched the screen of my phone. He must have noticed. But I think he already knew the answer, and that was what gave him the courage to ask if Ava was his.

I didn't even hesitate. 'Yes,' I said. 'She is.'

I'd imagined that conversation so many times beforehand, wondering if I'd find the courage to tell him, dreading what he might say.

Thankfully, he wasn't angry. Not a bit of it. He took the phone and expanded the photograph so her face filled the screen, and gazed at her for a long time. He was awestruck. Then something else kicked in: pride. He passed the phone back to me and asked me to tell him about her.

And I did. I told him about Ava for hours. And when we met again, I told him even more. I talked about Ellie, too. Not quite so much. But he was interested in that, too. He understood that my children were part of me and I was part of them, and he wanted to look after all of us.

And now he was lying in bed next to me with Felix's empty cot beside us.

I remembered what it had been like to hold Ellie and Ava after losing Felix, and I thought of my own sister and how silly and strange it was that we didn't speak any more, or even exchange Christmas cards.

I knew that if I asked her to come to the funeral, she would. Like a shot.

I would have to. I had to give her the chance to do the right thing. I had to give myself the chance. There would be so much sadness, so much grief. I would need her to share it.

Mark and I fell asleep together. I didn't wake again until it was light, and I came to and for the first, miraculous second of the day, I didn't know that Felix had died.

Chapter Twenty-One

Paula

Something had got into Daisy. She'd always been slow to learn, but sweet – or so I told myself. But suddenly I found that a little bit harder to believe. She was changing, and in some ways, not for the better.

There was no reason that I could understand for it. Maybe school was harder for her now that she and her peers had less time to play and more lessons? The rest of them were crazily far ahead – reading and writing and signing their names and making clay models of Tudor houses; they were a bunch of prodigies, as far as I was concerned, and it was both phenomenally impressive and depressing to see what they could do. I had learned, over the years since Daisy's diagnosis, to try not to compare her to them. But I didn't always succeed.

She was my baseline. Other kids freaked me out – how quickly they learned, the things they could do, the kind of conversations they had with adults and with each other. They were virtually adults themselves. And Daisy just wasn't. She was much more like a toddler. As to whether she'd ever catch up... I had my doubts.

I had no idea whether she was aware of being treated differently to the others – of having her own personal teaching assistant and workstation, a chair and desk in the classroom that was set up just for her. On the whole, she was magnanimously accepting of all the extra help she benefited from. I didn't let myself think about how she would feel about it if and when she became more self-aware, or the questions and answers that would follow. I tried to be ruthless with my thoughts: I had discovered it was all too easy to sink into a self-obliterating cycle of despair if I started worrying about the future. The future would have to take care of itself, anyway. I had quite enough to be getting on with in the present… especially as, when Daisy got really upset, she had started taking it out on me.

Around the time of the diagnosis, I'd been able to tell anybody who asked me that Daisy wasn't aggressive. I saw that as a blessing; it meant she wasn't liable to hurt other children or the staff at school, and it eased her way to being accepted, even liked. She didn't lash out, even when she was really worked up and upset. If she was going to take out her anxiety on anyone, it was herself. She had a habit of biting her hands when she was anxious, and the autumn she moved up to primary school, the skin on her hands got so rough where she'd sunk her teeth into it that it reminded me of elephant hide.

But then *she's not aggressive* stopped being true.

Daisy still had an unblemished record at school where that aspect of her behaviour was concerned; she'd never attacked another child, or her teaching assistant, or a teacher. But she would sometimes attack *me*, and the ferocity on her face at such times left me in no doubt that she really did intend to do me harm. The moment always passed, eventually – it was a violent squall that would ride itself out in the end. But while it was happening it was a crisis, and there was nothing I could do apart from trying to limit the damage, whether to me, the house, or herself. When the mood was on her, she was a vicious little dynamo; it was surprisingly difficult to contain her, given how small she still was.

The one thing that always made it worse was to get angry with her. I had to wait until she was calm again to try to speak to her, to describe what had happened, to tell her why it was wrong. Even then it was hard to know if any of what I said was going in… but it certainly wouldn't have done if I had tried to talk to her while she was still in the throes of the storm. You couldn't do that with a child who was raging. You couldn't do it while you were raging yourself, either.

Because when we were in the middle of it, it was difficult – sometimes almost impossible – to contain my own fury.

It's peculiarly enraging to have your small child launch herself at you, hellbent on clawing your face or yanking clumps of your hair out or ripping your favourite top that, as bad luck would have it, you just happened to have risked putting on that day. After all, it wasn't as if I had all that many nice clothes – on the whole, after Daisy had been diagnosed and Mark had left me, I hadn't bothered much with all of that. And it wasn't as if I had masses of hair to start with, and my face, which was mostly grey with fatigue and puffy from comfort eating, really didn't need the bonus downer of being adorned with scratches. Luckily I was still working from home, copy-editing and proofreading, so it didn't matter how rough I looked from a professional, income-making point of view. And it wasn't as if I was likely to go out on any hot dates any time soon.

The last thing I needed was some man complicating my life, and anyway, who'd want to take on a woman whose autistic daughter refused to be put to bed by anybody else, and still woke up every night and came in to her to share her bed?

I was resigned: my sex life was over. I had nothing to offer anyone, anyway. I had no reserves to draw on; everything was in play.

There was just no way it could be worth it. There were things I needed – sleep, food, money, the house not to fall down around my ears – and things I could very well do without, and sex and romance was definitely in the 'maybe in the next life' category. Daisy was challenging me to the max; some days, I felt stretched by her to the point where I'd never be able to go back to being someone who could live a normal life.

Looking after Daisy was so exhausting, and so demanding, that I didn't spare much thought for Mark. But when I did, I loathed him. My feelings hadn't faded at all. I still longed to prove myself to him somehow… to show him his daughter in a way that would make him sit up and take notice and be sorry. But at the same time, it seemed very unlikely that I would ever be able to. It was just a fantasy. Chances were I would never see him again.

But then I heard something about him that made me think again about my daydreams of making him repent.

It didn't cure me entirely. I was still angry. After all, I couldn't be angry with Daisy, and all that emotion had to go somewhere. But still, it forced me to set my feelings aside. The desire for justice for my daughter remained, but it was dormant. Even I, with all my capacity for rage, couldn't long for vengeance on someone who had suffered so much, and who'd gone through a loss that I shied away from imagining.

On the day I found out about Felix Daisy had just blown up at me outside the supermarket in Kettlebridge.

Sometimes I could get away with popping into the shop with her, and sometimes I really couldn't, and it was impossible to predict with any reliability whether it was going to be a good day to make the attempt or not. I did as much of my shopping online as possible, but sometimes things ran out, and on that particular day I'd had to pay a cheque into the bank – also potentially tricky, though the self-service machine was a lifesaver – and then I'd tried for the supermarket as well. It was stupidly busy – the next day was Christmas Eve – and Daisy kicked off even before we got inside. The only way to calm her down was to give up, take her back to the car and get out of there.

Back home, I got Daisy settled with her iPad and dabbed anti-septic cream onto the scratches on my neck. My heart rate had just about returned to normal when the doorbell rang. I stomped off to answer it, prepared to be exasperated, and had to quickly adjust and put on my nice-person face when I saw who it was at the door.

It was my friend Elspeth, whose daughter Lydia had been at pre-school with Daisy and had ended up in the same class as her at primary school. The girls weren't exactly friends – Daisy didn't have any friends – but it was as close as Daisy got. Lydia tolerated Daisy, though she also seemed puzzled by her, and spoke to her slowly and patiently, as if she was a much younger child.

Back in the pre-school days, I had once turned up to collect Daisy to find her curled up on the carpet, sound asleep, while a group of little girls played tea-parties with plastic cups around her. One of them had covered her with a dolls' blanket; Amy had told me that it was Lydia. Elspeth was kind too: she invited us round for playdates even though Lydia couldn't really play with Daisy, and had obviously been warned not to expect to.

Elspeth was also helpful in practical ways. She had grown up in Kettlebridge and had lots of family there, and if I ever needed a mechanic, a plumber, a carpenter or an electrician, Elspeth knew someone who knew someone who could help. She knew as much about what went on in the town as anybody, especially as she had a part-time job booking out the civic buildings for weddings and other occasions.

She took in the scratches on my neck and said, 'Is it a bad time?'

It had been such an awful morning, I'd completely forgotten. She'd messaged me earlier to ask if I had a heater she could borrow, as her boiler had broken down.

'No, you're fine, it just slipped my mind. I'll go and get it. Come on in.'

'If that's OK. I won't stay long,' Elspeth said, and stepped in.

I went into Mark's old study to get the heater. I hadn't got round to redecorating, and it still looked pretty much the same as it had done when he'd used it as a bolthole from family life, though it was a bit more untidy. It was chilly, too; it had a tiny radiator that didn't really work, and was the one room in the house that never seemed to get warm.

It sounded like Daisy was still absorbed by the iPad; I could hear the commentary on a YouTube video she'd watched over and over again, which showed various washing machines in action. It was extraordinary what people made videos of, but if it kept Daisy happy for a bit I wasn't complaining. I might even be able to have a bit of a chat with Elspeth, who somehow had a knack for making me feel a bit more normal. As if I was as content as a proper mother should be, rather than spinning between stress and bitterness.

I grabbed the heater and went back to the hall to hand it over. 'Such a pain when the central heating goes,' I said. 'Always seems to happen just before Christmas. Hope you're not too frozen.'

'Oh, we're all right. Should be fixed tomorrow, with any luck. I can bring this back then, if that's all right?'

'No rush. Only if it's convenient for you. Do you have people coming round?' I would have been amazed if she didn't, given how much family she had living nearby.

'Yeah, but it won't do me any harm to pop out for half an hour, to be honest. Probably keep me sane. You?'

'My mother's moved to Australia so she can cohabit with her sheep-shearing boyfriend, so no.'

'Really? Wow. Is that… is that a good move, do you think?'

'Oh, she's over the moon about it. Almost insultingly so, given that she's living on the other side of the world from us. But hey, who can blame her? She's gone to find the sun. Even if it only lasts the winter, at least she'll have had that.'

My scratches were stinging, and I instinctively felt for them and then stopped, so as not to bring attention to them. 'Sorry if I seem a bit cranky,' I said. 'Daisy hasn't had a very good morning. She's a bit on edge. She's not coping very well with Christmas. It's too much change.'

'I guess we all feel like that sometimes.'

Elspeth was looking at me sympathetically, but also as if she was speculating about something, as if I wasn't quite behaving the way she might have anticipated. She hesitated, and I half expected her to say she should go, but instead she carried on standing there with the heater in her arms. Her cheeks, which were an enviably healthy pink, became a little redder, as if she was contemplating saying something profoundly uncomfortable.

'Paula… I hope you won't mind me asking this, and I know it's a really sensitive subject… but have you heard anything from your ex?'

'Mark? No, I don't think he's about to come down the chimney any time soon. Why?'

Elspeth grimaced. 'Ah. I thought you might not know.'

'Know what?'

'Do you remember what we talked about in the café that time? About the baby?'

'What, about the baby? You mean when I shocked everybody with a torrent of foul, abusive language? Yeah, I remember.'

A few months before, I'd been with Elspeth when I vented my fury over Ingrid's letter, and the whole of Lily's Tea Room had heard me. We'd gone there at Elspeth's suggestion after school drop-off, and we'd got chatting about our families and it had turned out that Roger, Elspeth's husband, was responsible for maintenance for the building where Ingrid lived, and had endured a couple of run-ins with her.

It was obvious from the way Elspeth told me this that Roger found Ingrid a complete pain to deal with, and that was what encouraged me to come out with the whole story. I'd told Elspeth that Ingrid had been one of the first people to spot that Daisy had problems, and had reacted as if it was a terrible tragedy, which was what Mark seemed to think too. And then she had always taken Mark's side, no matter how appallingly he'd behaved, even when he'd washed his hands of us.

Finally, I'd told Elspeth how Mark had gone back to the woman who had been waiting in the wings all along, and who'd already, unknown to me, already had a child by him… and was now married to him and having another baby, as Ingrid had so helpfully told me.

Elspeth had reacted to all of this with a mixture of shock and indignation and concern, and it was a comfort to feel that someone was on my side, for once.

But this was different. She looked serious and apprehensive, and I wasn't at all sure I was ready to hear what she was about to tell me.

She said, 'I'm sorry, Paula. It's sad news. The baby passed away. It was a boy, and he only lived for a few days. He had a birth defect, and he had to have an operation and didn't make it through. Roger heard about it because of Ingrid. Apparently afterwards she smashed up some stuff in her flat, and he had to repair the plaster.'

'Oh, no.'

What else was there to say? How was I supposed to react? All the blood seemed to have drained out of me. Was it really possible for me to feel sorry for Mark, after everything that had happened? And what about this other woman – this Jenny – who'd slept with him when he was still my husband and had his child, and then had gone off and married someone else?

But I did. I felt dreadful for both of them. And for the girls, too. Jenny's daughters, the one who was Mark's and the one who wasn't.

'I'm sorry,' Elspeth said again. 'I thought you ought to know.'

'I'm glad you told me. Thank you.' My mouth had gone dry.

'Call me, if you ever want to talk about it. Or anything,' Elspeth said, and reached out to squeeze my arm.

Suddenly Daisy cried out, and I said, 'I have to check on her.'

'I'll let myself out,' Elspeth said.

'OK. Thanks. I'll be in touch.'

I hurried into the living room and realised at once what was bothering Daisy: the washing-machine video had stopped because the iPad had run out of charge. I got the extension cord and plugged it in, and it came back to life. Daisy calmed down and the house was quiet, apart from the sound of somebody's unbalanced load in their washing machine, and it was such a profound relief to have been able to soothe her that I could have cried.

She was in her favourite place, her sweet spot, kneeling on the sofa with the iPad in front of her, propped up against one of the arms. I leaned against her and put my arms around her. She didn't resist or protest: she seemed quite happy to be embraced. I'd read that some autistic children couldn't stand this kind of contact, but as long as Daisy wasn't feeling agitated or upset, she seemed quite willing to accept it. She was tolerating me, maybe even indulging me, although she had no intention of being distracted from the washing machines on the screen in front of her.

I breathed in her smell. Melon-scented shampoo, strawberry soap. Her skin was so soft, so perfect. It was so good to see her content like this after the outburst in front of the supermarket… which must have had a cause, one that was terrible to her, but not one that she could communicate to me.

Not yet. But one day she might be able to.

She'd learned so much already, in her short life. Maybe not as much as others, or maybe not the same kinds of things as others, who hadn't learned the same kinds of things as her – who else could twiddle a teaspoon as efficiently and regularly as Daisy? But the more she could explain to me, the more sense we would be able to make of each other.

How frustrating must it be, to not be able to say what was wrong or what would be right, to be dependent on the guesswork of a mostly clueless adult?

But there was always hope. I would learn, and she would learn, too. Yes, I was afraid of what might happen when she was bigger and stronger. But who knew what the future might hold? Maybe she would learn to control herself, not to go on the attack when things took a turn she didn't like.

The brain was plastic – that was one thing I had learned: that was the word that neuroscientists used. Which conjured up images of carrier bags and dolls' heads, but didn't mean that at all. It meant it could change: rewire itself, make new connections. Not just in childhood, but at any age.

'We should do something,' I said. 'To say how sorry we are. We could send them a sympathy card, at least. From you and me. I could hold you up and you could put it in the postbox for me.'

Daisy didn't respond. She didn't seem to be listening. But she didn't pull away, either.

And suddenly I thought that if I could have this – this closeness, this comfort – this was more than enough. It was everything.

'I love you,' I murmured. 'I'll always love you, Daisy. I'm lucky to have you. And I'll always take care of you.'

And then, to my complete astonishment, she swivelled round, and in one swift movement, clasped both of her hands around my neck and hugged me back.

Chapter Twenty-Two

Ellie

Ten years later

In the months before Ava's wedding I'd been trying to straighten myself out. No more drinking. No more smoking weed. No more hooking up with boys on the night bus. I was renting a spare room off Peter Carman, our old neighbour, and that made it easier. Peter liked an orderly life, and had made it quite clear he wasn't about to tolerate a wayward lodger throwing up in his flowerbed, however willing he was to give me a chance to get back on my feet.

And it was a chance. I knew that. It was a place to live in London that I couldn't possibly have afforded otherwise. I had a part-time job in a vegan café, I'd enrolled on a couple of A levels at the local community college and I had the illusion of independence. I was a twenty-one-year-old school dropout, trying to give myself and adult life another chance. Mum was relieved and I was hopeful, and probably Mark didn't really care what I was doing as long as Mum wasn't upset about it. I knew I wasn't really standing on my own two feet, but at least I wasn't lying in the gutter.

But then it started coming back.

I'd managed to get myself hooked on smoking and had quit, after a couple of failed attempts, soon after I moved in with Peter. And then my sense of smell had come back and I'd realised that it had gone without me even realising I'd lost it: I could smell burning, or bacon frying, or lavender, like memories come back to life.

In a way this was the same. There were signs that I was able to notice, that would have been there whether I was receptive to them or not.

At first it was just little things, and they could have been coincidences. Before the café owner rang to offer me a job, I could feel the good fortune in the air, like snow poised to fall on Christmas Eve. And when I smoked my last cigarette I knew it really was the last. The next day I got through a whole dinner with Dad without taking one of his, which proved it.

There were no words, and there were no sightings of anything or anyone. It was like the ghost of what it had been, an old habit vaguely remembered. And that was fine by me.

And then it was better than fine, because during Ava's wedding ceremony something glorious happened.

After Felix died, when I'd closed my mind to the things I sometimes glimpsed or sensed, it had been like shutting up a room in a house and leaving it in darkness. Except it had been me who had found myself in the dark. The knowledge I'd been given had been partial and unclear, like a light flicking on and off, and I had decided I would be better off without it: that I'd be spared the guilt that went with knowing only a little, and not being able to change anything. But then I had realised that giving up on the confusion meant giving up on the light as well. I couldn't summon up the golden warmth that reminded me of my grandmother any more. It had gone along with everything else.

At Ava's wedding that changed.

I was sitting in the pew reserved for family at the front of the church, between Mum's rather grumpy sister, my aunt Amanda, and Dad, who looked really nervous and uncomfortable and was furiously tapping his foot. Desperate for a drink, basically. You might have thought he'd take this in his stride – that after all these years, it wouldn't be such a big deal to see Mark walk Ava down the aisle, instead of him, and give her away. But that obviously wasn't the case.

We all managed to exchange a few pleasantries about the journeys we'd had to get there and how beautiful the church was and what a lovely day it was for a wedding, and then fell into a slightly dazed silence which could have been prompted by awe or awkwardness, or a combination of the two.

Would Grandma have forgiven Mum for letting Ava grow up thinking my dad was her father? I could see now why Mum had done it. Mark had been married to someone else. And Dad had really loved Mum, in his way. And us. Still did. It was just that he had a problem that made it difficult, almost impossible, for him to love us in a way that allowed us to trust him, and he'd never been able to fix it.

You might say he hadn't loved us enough to fix it. But you could also say that we'd never loved him enough to try to help him.

Should we have tried to help him?

Might it still be possible?

It was never too late. While there was life, there was always still hope. The capacity to change. Right up to the very end.

And maybe even after.

At least Dad seemed to have calmed down a little. He'd stopped tapping his foot, and was looking around at the church like a very reluctant tourist who'd resigned himself to being shut in here for the duration.

His expression suggested he would rather have been anywhere but here. But then, he'd made it. That was something. He was only staying for the ceremony; he had given some complicated excuse as to why he couldn't hang round for the reception afterwards, involving a flight that could on no account be changed. We'd all secretly been a little bit relieved. Ava had said that she'd already witnessed one punch-up between Mark and Dad and could do without another, especially on her wedding day, and Mum had protested that neither of them would dream of doing such a thing and none of us had really believed her.

Anyway, soon enough Dad would be off on his latest urgent escape mission from his broken-down family.

Broken down, but still motoring. Yes, there was plenty of mileage in us yet.

And I was going to enjoy this. Ava's big day.

Any wedding is always a triumph of love over the odds. Who'd have thought that Ava, my ambitious, beautiful sister, with her fancy London flat and her nice car and her job in banking, would have ended up getting hitched to… Toby Andrews, the one-time spotty no-hoper who'd had a thing about her at school? Not that Toby had spots any more, and he seemed very nice and obviously Ava liked him. And he wasn't like either Mark or Dad… which was probably just as well. He was a chef, which was also good because Ava was a rubbish cook, so at least they'd have something decent to eat once in a while. Plus he was devoted to her, and that was the main thing.

The organ was grinding away, not solemn but definitely serious. There was plenty to look at, from the congregation – who'd have thought that Ava, never the chummiest of people, would have had upwards of a hundred guests at her wedding? – to the fine vaulted architecture and the bunches of white roses decorating the pews and the altar.

That was when I sensed it. Her. The old magic that had made me feel so cherished when I was small, and that came and went like unseasonal warm weather, or like sunshine between passing clouds.

It was as comforting as a hug: it was that real. Like having a pair of arms wrapped round me to reassure me that all would be well, and that I was loved.

That time I heard her, too.

Tell your mother not to worry. She just has to do the right thing for now.

And then it faded, leaving me comforted and unsettled at the same time.

Hearing things? My long-dead grandmother, speaking to me, right here in church on my sister's wedding day?

I couldn't tell anybody about this, especially not Mum. She'd think I was completely out of my mind.

When the ceremony was over I said goodbye to Dad and made my way with the other guests to the medieval hall where the reception was being held, and found my place next to Mark at the top table.

I would have rather sat next to Peter, to be honest; it would have helped me fend off the temptation to start drinking, and make sure I behaved myself. But this was how Ava had chosen to do things, and it was her big day.

There was no point remembering that I'd always been the one who was desperate to get married, while Ava had poured scorn on the idea. That was life, I had begun to realise: life was what happened in the space between what you wanted and what you got.

And then Mark stood up to give his speech and tapped the glass, and they appeared at the back of the hall.

I didn't recognise them, but knew I ought to. There was a tired-looking woman in jeans with a teenage girl who was dressed head to toe in varying shades of pink. They were holding hands. The teenage girl looked as if she had absolutely no idea what she was doing there but was willing to go with the flow for now. And the woman was as cold and calm and unwavering as an assassin.

Mark looked as if he'd seen a ghost. A real ghost.

The glass he was holding slipped from his fingers and smashed. He pressed his hand to his heart, then to his head. And then he collapsed onto the floor like a puppet whose strings have just been dropped, and the whole hall went silent.

Chapter Twenty-Three

Ava

'Dad!'

I'd never called him that before. And there he was, down on the ground at my wedding reception, groaning and clutching his head in agony.

Everyone and everything else faded into the background: the blue-tinged sunlight drifting through the big old windows, the scent of the roses, my white silk dress. The hum of conversation in the room gave way to a hush that was broken by urgent voices, but I didn't hear what they were saying. I was down on my knees beside him, pleading.

He looked as if he was dying. As if here and now was the setting Fate had chosen for his time to be up, on the worn wooden floorboards where monks had walked long ago.

Mum was down beside him, supporting him, loosening his tie. I managed to say, 'We need an ambulance.'

She said, 'Toby's calling for one. Mark… Can you hear me?'

Dad looked up at her. He was focusing. That was good, surely? 'Head hurts,' he mumbled.

His gaze drifted away from her towards Toby, who was still talking to the ambulance despatcher, and Ellie, who was standing by and looking down at us in horror. Then he turned towards the intruders, the woman and the girl who had come in just before he collapsed, and who were now standing by Toby and Ellie, close enough to touch.

What the hell were they doing here?

The woman had marched in so decisively, as if she was in exactly the right place; the girl less so. She looked as if she didn't have a clue what she was doing there. And why had the woman been holding her by the hand as they walked along?

It was Paula. Paula and Daisy. It had to be. They even looked familiar. I'd only ever seen them the once that I could remember, in the newspaper photograph that Ingrid had shown us years ago. But that was enough.

The other mother and the other daughter. The phantom family, the one that all of us preferred not to think about. The one that had been living quietly in this town all this time. From our point of view, as good as dead.

Dad managed an approximation of a smile.

When he spoke, his voice was strong and clear and there was no missing what he said.

'Here you all are. Is it judgement day?'

Chapter Twenty-Four

Jenny

The ambulance picked up speed as it made its way through Kettlebridge. How long would it take us? Twenty minutes? Half an hour? At least they'd let me come with him. I was sitting close enough to reach out and touch him; he was upright on the folding stretcher, belted into place, his face contorted with pain.

'My turn,' he managed to say.

My turn. Of course, he'd seen me screaming my head off when I gave birth to Felix all those years ago – I'd never been one for delivering babies in dignified silence.

'Maybe you shouldn't try to talk,' I said, looking up for guidance from the paramedic who was standing over us.

'Talking's fine,' he said. 'If he gets to the hospital conscious and able to speak for himself, that'll be a good sign.'

Mark said, 'Jenny... I have to tell you something. Something I did wrong.'

This was going to be about Paula. I was sure of it. I was here with him, and for all either of us knew he was dying... and he was going to waste his last breath on *her*? On the woman who'd cheated on him and made his life a misery, taken a house from him, refused to let him see their child... assuming it *was* his child? I knew he believed it was. But surely, given her track record, there was room for doubt?

I'd recognised her, but only just. She'd looked very different to the sleek, expensively dressed, professional woman I'd seen with Mark at the hospital that time. She'd had her hair hacked short, and she obviously didn't bother with colouring it – there had been plenty of silver on show. In her faded T-shirt and jeans, she'd looked like someone who had just wandered in off the street – which was pretty much what she was.

If I'd passed her in the street, I probably wouldn't even have noticed her.

Unless she had been with Daisy. It had to be said – Daisy stood out. It wasn't just the all-pink outfit. It was the way they held hands, as if they still did that all the time, without even thinking about it.

I hadn't held Ellie's hand for years and years. Let alone Ava's. I'd forgotten what it felt like to do that. To lead your child by the hand.

It wasn't Daisy's fault. She had obviously just gone along with whatever her mother had told her to get her there.

Maybe Paula had been waiting for this moment for years... the chance to wreck something for us. Well, she'd certainly succeeded.

I said, 'The only person who's done something wrong is Paula.'

Mark closed his eyes and I thought for a moment that was it, that he'd gone. I'd never seen anything like the way he looked then. So close to death. So agonised, and so hopeless.

Then he rallied and opened his eyes again and said, 'I lied to you. It wasn't Paula who stopped me seeing Daisy. It was me. I didn't want to. I couldn't cope. I said she could have the house as long as they both left me alone.'

'Mark, it was years ago. Whatever happened, Paula had no right to do what she just did. It was an awful shock for you. We just have to concentrate on getting you better.'

'Jenny... She didn't go off with someone else. I lied about that too. I told you that, and I told my mother that. But it wasn't true. She liked him. But she never cheated on me.'

I wanted to say something reassuring... but I couldn't find the words. All that time I'd believed that Paula had treated him terribly, that she'd betrayed him, that she was an awful person...

And Mark had just let me carry on thinking the worst of her.

The girl – Daisy – had looked shocked when Mark collapsed, as if witnessing the breaking of a taboo. As if she didn't fully understand what was happening, but had at least recognised that it was unusual for a man to writhe around on the floor like that.

I had yelled at Paula to go and take her daughter with her.

And then they had gone.

He said, 'She wrote to you. After Felix died. A condolence card. I made sure you never got it. She sent one to my mother, too.'

And then he closed his eyes and moaned in pain.

The ambulance began to climb. We'd reached the hill north of Kettlebridge; any minute now we'd descend, and merge onto the fast road to Oxford.

I leaned forwards and said, 'Did Ingrid get her card?'

He could barely part his lips to speak, but I just about made out the words: 'Burned it.'

'Don't leave me,' I told him. 'I need you to survive. Otherwise how can I be angry with you?'

He didn't manage to reply, but his lips curved in an approximation of a smile.

The ambulance sped down the slip road. Such a long way still to go. But I of all people knew that hospitals were not only places where you went to be fixed. That even the most skilful doctors couldn't always keep you alive.

And it all came back to me: Felix in my arms. Not being able to feed him. The weight of the milk in my breasts. And afterwards, having no choice but to pour it away.

Much, much later, Ava and Ellie and I waited together to find out if Mark could be saved.

Back in Kettlebridge, the evening do was going on without us: music and dancing, hubbub, slices of the cake that Toby would have had to cut all by himself. Meanwhile Mark was unconscious on the operating table while surgeons carried out the delicate procedure that would seal off the broken blood vessel in his brain and allow him to recover.

Ava was sitting next to me, still in her wedding dress, flicking listlessly through an old magazine. She had her hair loosely up, with little strands escaping, and a delicate seed-pearl tiara; she'd gone Hollywood glamour for her dress, all swishy silk skirts and close-fitting bodice. Even in that overheated, strip-lighted waiting room, with its atmosphere of anxiety and powerlessness, she was the loveliest bride I'd ever seen.

Not for the first time, I was filled with astonishment that she was actually anything to do with me. She looked as if she might have arrived in the world already adult, without bothering with all the indignities of childhood. But I knew better. I'd taken her round to people's houses in a carrycot, and given her toys to play with while I set about cutting their hair. When she was a toddler, I'd shared a double bed with her; when she was a little older, I'd made time to read books to her and had been startled by how quickly she'd learned how to read them for herself.

That was Ava all over. She always wanted to be as independent as possible. If there was one thing Sean, as her stand-in father, had taught her, it was that: the importance of not relying on other people. Which made it all the more surprising that she'd found someone she wanted to get married to. Though Toby adored her, and was a choice that made sense.

It had been Ava's suggestion that Toby should go back to Kettlebridge and call in on the evening do. After all, Mark's operation would take at least three hours, and there was nothing Toby could do for him by being here.

They'd left Peter, our old neighbour, in charge of things when they departed for the hospital, along with my sister and Brian, the rather good-looking best man. I couldn't imagine that the atmosphere would have recovered from Paula's uninvited appearance and its aftermath, but Ava and Toby seemed to want people to enjoy themselves as much as possible under the circumstances. Karen, my old friend who had come down from Manchester, had volunteered to help too, and my sister had, of course, been in her element. Glad to be needed. I had been profoundly grateful to her, not for the first time. She'd been such a rock after Felix died… She'd come straight away to see me, and had ended up staying a week: making phone calls and sending emails, cooking, cleaning, stepping up or fading into the background as needed.

As if by unspoken agreement, we'd never actually talked about how we'd fallen out at Mum's funeral, or how stubborn we'd both been during the years of our estrangement. Amanda seemed to be happy to pick up where we'd left off, and that suited me, too, especially as, after all this time, I could hardly remember exactly what had been said or who'd been wrong, and anyway, it didn't seem to matter any more.

Ellie was sitting on my other side, at a slight distance, a gawky, skinny-limbed girl in a red dress that was a little too short for a wedding, and clumpy, deliberately unladylike sandals. She'd taken the newlyweds to the hospital in the second-hand Mini Sean had got for her as a guilty twenty-first birthday present – it had fallen to her to drive, as the only member of the immediate family who was stone cold sober. Since we'd settled in the waiting room she'd opted to cut herself off by listening to music, and had that mute, closed-off expression young people get when they really don't want to talk to anybody about anything.

If somebody had asked me the day before whether she was close to Mark, I'd have said no. I might even have said – flippantly, bitterly – that she'd barely notice whether he lived or died. But I was under no such illusion now. They might not be close – in fact, they were poles apart – but that didn't mean she didn't care.

It was no time, really, to criticise him… but he hadn't helped matters by being so inflexible when she went through her phase of going off the rails. He'd set boundaries for her with a rigidity that was driven more by his need to be in control than by wanting to see her take better care of herself. And she'd known it, and had provoked him and pushed him at every opportunity. Still, things had improved, and over recent months they had moved towards a sort of wary truce.

Thank goodness for Peter, who'd taken Ellie in and was keeping an eye on her. Mark wasn't crazy about the arrangement, but he hadn't been in much of a position to object. Ellie's earlier attempts to live away from home had been short-lived – awful places, worse boyfriends – and her behaviour when she was with us had been so chaotic that at one point he'd wanted to throw her out.

It was as if she'd made a conscious decision to be the exact opposite of the thoughtful, bookish, otherworldly child she had once been – as if she wanted to do everything she could to put distance between herself and us, and disappear into a cycle of parties and hangovers and insecure relationships.

Mark had been angry with her, and sometimes I had been too, but it had been hard to stay angry when I knew the way she was carrying on was to do with Felix – was a delayed reaction to the shock of his loss, and to the sadness in the house afterwards. It was a kind of grief, a self-punishing way of proving to herself and us that she was still alive.

After Felix passed away, I never wanted to have another child – Mark might have been willing to consider it, but he knew how I felt and we had decided against it. I'd carried on functioning as a wife and mother – keeping house, providing comfort – but part of my heart had been burnt out, left cauterised and lifeless. It was like that line about courage being similar to a bank account: you write a certain number of cheques and one day it's all gone. I wasn't sure how much love I had left, and having another child struck me as a risk I couldn't afford to take.

Then Ellie had started to take risks with herself, and I had discovered that the old fierce protective instinct was still there, and as powerful as ever. I hadn't been able to save Felix; I wasn't about to lose Ellie. I'd had to learn to be careful, though… to nudge her towards wanting to sort herself out, rather than laying down the law or trying to fix things for her.

It wasn't quite the same for Mark. He cared about Ellie, and he felt responsible for her, and he was fond of her and tried to treat her fairly. But the strength of feeling just wasn't there. It wasn't his fault; there was no point expecting or wanting more. He couldn't help what he didn't feel, and the only living person who he was really devoted to was me.

At least Ellie and Mark had made peace, more or less. But what if this was it? What if there were no more chances?

What if Mark's operation didn't work, or there were complications and that was the end, right there in the operating theatre… just as it had been for Felix?

But I couldn't think about that. If there was one thing that I'd learned, it was that you might as well hold on to hope for as long as possible. Possibilities were precious. That was what life was – all those different pathways ahead. Death cut them off. And despair was a small, premature death – the sense that the pathways were already closed off, even when they were still there.

That was how I'd felt, after Felix: as if the end for him was an end for me as well. Which it had been. But enough of me had survived for me to be here today, still believing that Mark could come through this.

At least I wasn't alone. I'd tried to persuade Ellie and Ava to go back to the wedding with Toby, but both of them had insisted on staying with me until the operation was over and we knew how it had gone. And actually, I was grateful.

Ava put her magazine aside. It had a bride on the cover. Not half as pretty as she was, though.

'I would have thought that was the last thing you'd want to read,' I said to her.

'Yeah,' she said, and pulled a face. 'Paula must be delighted.'

'Somehow I doubt that,' I said.

'Oh, come on. She's probably been planning something like that for years.'

'I think it might have been an impulse thing. I mean, obviously she must have thought about it. And somehow she must have found out about the wedding, and maybe it struck her as a bit of a provocation...'

'It was the perfect venue,' Ava said, with that strange mix of pride and defensiveness that some brides seem to go in for – as if they were artists, and it would be unreasonable to expect them to compromise their vision. Not that I'd ever been like that, but then, I'd never tried to organise a big white wedding.

'I know, but it was pretty much on Paula's doorstep.'

'I can't believe you're taking her side on this. If you were worried about it, why didn't you say something earlier?'

'I didn't like to,' I admitted. 'I guess I thought it would be all right. I mean, I never would have dreamed that she'd just show up like that.'

Ava didn't look particularly mollified. She smoothed her skirts and examined her immaculately manicured hands. Next to her diamond engagement ring, her gold wedding band gleamed: new, unscratched, and until now, unworn.

Of course she'd wanted everything to be perfect. I'd never known that my cynical, secretive daughter was such a romantic... until she had accepted Toby's proposal.

'I can't help it if she happens to live nearby,' she said. 'I mean, how was I to know she and her daughter would have stayed in the house she got off Dad? She could have sold it up and moved somewhere else years ago.'

'Daisy is your dad's daughter, too,' I reminded her. 'Your half-sister.'

'Yeah, well, Ellie's all the sister I need, thank you very much. Quite enough to be going on with.'

Ellie removed her earphones. 'Leave me out of it.'

'How can I?' Ava said. 'You're here, aren't you? Even if you have been trying to make out you're not listening.'

'Yeah, but that doesn't mean I can't see Paula's point of view,' Ellie said.

'Oh, come on. Where's your loyalty?' Ava turned back to me. 'If Paula's held a grudge against you all these years, that's her problem.'

'Well... to be fair to her, it must have come as a shock to find out her husband had a child with someone else. Ex-husband. We probably shouldn't have left it to Ingrid to break the news. Not to speak ill of the dead, but she wasn't the most sensitive of people.'

'So you had a fling with Dad when his marriage was on the rocks. Big deal. It's not like it was a big, long secret affair. It was a one-off with unexpected consequences.'

'Well, that's one way to look at it.'

Ava was studying me with an unusual degree of interest, as if she was trying to get the measure of me. It was as if she was trying to think about all this objectively for the first time – trying on an onlooker's perspective for size, rather than being part of it.

'I don't think you ever would have carried on seeing Dad behind Paula's back,' she said. 'Not for any length of time, anyway.'

'I don't know if I'm quite as nice and good as you seem to think,' I told her. 'I never really challenged Mark about not seeing Daisy. It was easier to let sleeping dogs lie. But looking at it objectively... he let her down. And so did I. Don't you think she was entitled to more?'

Ava's blue eyes suddenly looked very dark.

'But it was Paula who made it impossible for Mark to see her,' she said.

I hesitated. It was on the tip of my tongue to tell her. But she'd only just called him her dad. Did she really need to know?

And what if he didn't make it through?

But then, he had wanted to tell me the truth because he thought he might not get another chance. He must have thought it mattered. In the end, he'd chosen to stop lying.

I said, 'Ava, that wasn't true. It was your dad who rejected Daisy. He couldn't cope with her. He didn't want to know. I don't think Paula is at all the kind of person we've been led to believe she is. Your dad just told me that she actually wrote to me, after Felix died. She sent a condolence card. But I never got it. He thought it might upset me.' Or so I had to assume. Unless he had wanted me to carry on thinking of Paula as heartless. 'He made sure I never saw it.'

Ava kept on staring at me but it was as if she wasn't seeing me at all; it was as if she'd gone somewhere else. Then she said, 'Now or never.'

'Something like that. Yes.'

Ava got abruptly to her feet, as if she'd suddenly decided on something.

'I'm going to go look for a cup of coffee,' she said. 'Can I get you anything?'

'You're not allowed hot drinks in here,' Ellie said. 'Haven't you read the signs?'

'Well then, I'll have a coffee somewhere outside. There's a café somewhere, isn't there?'

'It'll be shut,' I told her. 'But I think there's a vending machine somewhere.'

'Then I'll find it. Do you want anything?'

I shook my head, and Ellie said, 'I'll pass. Don't spill coffee on your dress.'

'Yeah, well, hardly matters now. After all, I'm not going to be wearing it again, am I? Might as well wreck it.'

Ava swished out. Ellie said, 'Maybe Paula just wanted to show Mark his daughter. Maybe she wanted to show all of us.'

'I suppose,' I said.

She wasn't looking at me, but into space, the way she had sometimes done when she was little, as if she was trying to remember something, or say something that was on the tip of her tongue. Then she said, 'At the risk of sounding absolutely crazy, I have a message for you.'

'A message?'

'Yeah. But you have to promise me not to freak out about it. I'm trying not to freak out myself. I mean, I don't usually get any words. Or I haven't before. It always used to just be a feeling. Anyway, I don't think it's anything to be scared of.'

'Ellie, what are you talking about? Have you taken something?'

Ellie raised her eyebrows. 'Don't you even want to know who it was?'

Weirdly, though, I already did, even before she said it. It was my mum.

And then she gave me the message – *Don't worry, just do the right thing now* – and I knew exactly what I had to do, whether the man I loved survived or not.

Before I could ask her anything Ava came back into the waiting room empty-handed and sat down next to me again.

Ellie said, 'Nice cup of coffee?'

Ava frowned. 'What?'

'You didn't have any. Did you?' Ellie was calm as a detective pointing out an elementary mistake.

'Oh. Oh yeah. Mm. I couldn't find the machine.'

Ellie raised her eyebrows. 'Helps if you look. Did you speak to him, then? Or did you just send him a message?'

Ava scowled. 'What are you talking about?'

Ellie sighed. 'The man you were thinking about. Whoever he was. It's OK, I won't judge. Not given my track record. Though at least I've cleaned up my act. I'm guessing you have too, now, Ava.' She looked Ava up and down, from her seed-pearl tiara to her white silk, silver-buckled shoes. 'Now that you're a respectable married woman,' she concluded.

Ava blushed. A vivid, dead-giveaway, tomato red. A guilty red. Not at all the sort of blush you would expect to see on the face of a bride.

'I still don't know what you're talking about,' she said.

'Toby's a good guy,' Ellie said. 'He deserves to have all your love. Not the bits that are left over because you're still stuck in a holding pattern with somebody else.'

'Ellie,' I said, 'I don't know where this is coming from, but Ava clearly doesn't want to hear it right now.'

Ellie shrugged. 'OK. Fine. Whatever.'

'It's all right, Mum,' Ava said. 'She hasn't upset me. It's just… it's a long story.' She stared at Ellie. 'How did you know?'

I said, 'What did she know?'

'Oh… there's this old boyfriend, someone I never told either of you about,' Ava said. 'Someone I met on holiday years ago. We… stayed in touch. I just told him not to contact me again.'

'Good,' Ellie said. 'I take it you're not going to tell Toby.'

'None of your business,' Ava said fiercely.

'Fair enough. I don't want to pry. Anyway, I think you've done the right thing. Just try and be good from here on in, OK?'

Without waiting for an answer, Ellie put her earphones back in.

Ava glanced at me and shook her head. 'I hope we're not going to have to get used to this,' she said, and reached for the bridal magazine again.

About half an hour later Toby turned up with slices of wedding cake in a box, and while we were eating it the doctor came in to say that Mark's operation had been a success, he had come round from the anaesthetic and was in a stable condition in intensive care.

Ellie was as relieved and thankful as the rest of us. But I thought she wasn't surprised.

Chapter Twenty-Five

Mark

Two months later

Here I am, a survivor. Patched up. People don't always get what they deserve. And believe me, sometimes that can work in your favour.

The thing that happened to me – the sound of something popping like a cork shooting out of a bottle, then the explosion of blood in the brain, the blurring vision, the agonising pain – it could happen again. But then again, it might not. I have been lucky. Or so they tell me. And on reflection, I have to acknowledge that this is true. Just to be here is enough. And as for the people who are missing, well… I know I'll get my chance to join them one day.

I made a mess of things, didn't I? And then I made it worse by trying to tidy it up. I thought that if I could keep them separate – the different parts of my life, the two wives, the children – I'd be able to manage. The failures of the old life wouldn't bleed into the new one. But in the end they did. And now I understand that they never were separate, really, and I've stopped trying to manage. It's all I can do to try to manage myself, let alone trying to draw lines between the lives of other people. It's out in the open now, all of it. They will just have to fend for themselves.

My recovery has been fast, almost miraculously so, I'm told. You see? Lucky again. I got my mobility back within a month or so, though it's still not what it was. I've given up driving, and have to walk with a stick. As for words, what I mean in my head and what comes out of my mouth are two different things. Luckily I have a patient wife. More patient than I deserve.

And, as it turns out, I also have an ex-wife who is prepared to be forgiving. Again, infinitely more so than I deserve. No wonder that when she found out that Ava was getting married in a church that was a ten-minute walk from our old house, it was an outrage too far. I'd behaved for years as if I could cut her and Daisy out of my life, just like that. She showed me that I couldn't.

And so here we are, in a cemetery in a village south of Kettlebridge, a quiet, grassy place in a sheltered spot not far from the river. Jenny and I are both carrying flowers. And all of us are on our way to where Felix is.

We've walked from the pub in the village – a stretch for me, but just about manageable. I'm the slowest, the one at the rear; Jenny is hanging back to stay at my side, while Ellie and Ava lead the way. It's a glorious summer day – blue skies, warm but not sweltering, and the air smells of cut grass and flowers. I am doing my best to take it all in, to take it slowly and not get frustrated because I can't move the way I used to.

At least lunch went well, better than the first time I met Daisy, when Jenny invited her and Paula to the house and Daisy insisted, in that blunt way of hers, that I couldn't be her father because she didn't have one. We have agreed to describe me as an old friend of her mother's, and that seems to make sense to her, for now. Just now, in the pub, she sat quite happily with us all through the main course – she had a ham sandwich, and left the salad – and then Paula took her out into the pub garden, which she seemed to like.

I sense that it's a relief for Daisy to be outside, away from the slightly strained conversation about Ava and Toby's honeymoon and Toby's new restaurant job and the pace of my recovery and what Ellie is planning to do next. Fair enough: it's a relief to me, too. We have at least that much in common.

Am I learning to love her? Am I capable of it? Is it possible to love someone you have wronged so badly, and carry so much guilt about? It is hard for me to be comfortable with her. If I have learned anything, it is that comfort is not something I have a right to expect.

But I try to bear in mind something Jenny has said to me, once or twice: *Don't worry, just do the right thing now.*

Who knows how long I have left? Now may be all I have. I am doing my best to live up to it.

It has been remarkable to see how efficiently and completely Jenny has taken up the reins of the household. To think that I imagined, all those years ago, that I was saving her from a life of poverty and struggle, her and Ava, the child I'd once cast aside without knowing, without even hearing Jenny out: the child who had become the biggest prize I could think of.

It was vanity, really. I could only see my children as reflections on me, to be held close or rejected depending on whether I thought they showed me in a good light or a bad one. Looking at them now, I am struck all over again by what a fool I was. And yet each one of them still reminds me a little bit of me… even though they are so very different, both from me and from each other.

There they are, together for now, though soon enough there will be goodbyes all round and they'll go their separate ways. Even this little mission, this walk to the grave, brings out the individual in each of them. Ava is leading the way, brisk and purposeful in crisp linen; she is walking along with Paula but they aren't finding a whole lot to say to each other, and Paula is distracted anyway by keeping an eye on Daisy, who seems calm and cooperative but maybe can't entirely be trusted not to slip away and get lost as a younger child might. Or maybe it's just that Paula has got in the habit of being vigilant and can't let it go even now that Daisy is older and less at odds with her surroundings.

I let Paula down; I let both of them down, and that's the bitter, unpalatable truth, and for as much extra time as I've been granted, I'll have to live with it. It fills me with guilty admiration to see Paula now, and recognise how she has changed without me. She's like someone who has passed through fire, who has survived but come back altered. She sometimes seems frail – strained, tired, worn down – and maybe she is, but at the same time she has become indomitable.

The transformation in Daisy is remarkable. Nothing short of a miracle. The small child I remember, the unpredictable, infuriating, occasionally terrifying little changeling who ruled our home with her dogged and implacable strangeness, has become a gentle girl whose approach to the world is one of both intrigue and bemusement. She smiles; she listens; she even talks a little. Her eyes still slide away from you, but not always; sometimes, just briefly, she takes me in like a kindly scientist peering at something through a microscope. I take that as a sign of trust. It's clear she bears me no ill will. She tolerates me. Accepts me. She might even miss me when I'm gone.

I had thought her indifferent, unreachable; now it is clear that she is not in a world of her own, but is in the same one that is around all of us, which, by and large, she seems to find much more absorbing than the people in it. And I think maybe I can see why. It's not that she doesn't care for the people, although she finds them sometimes confusing. It's just that the sky and the trees and the grass are so much more astonishing.

She is still conspicuously different – a tall, thin girl dressed in pink, her favourite colour, with one white sock drooping. She seems younger than she is. Perhaps even when she is old, she'll still have this child-like quality. But I can see now that there's something beautiful about it. I have never really appreciated what innocence is. But Daisy has it, and it gives her both vulnerability and freedom.

Daisy doesn't need to earn other people's congratulations to make me proud of her. She's herself and she is here, and that is everything. She herself has shown me what I didn't want to accept when she was younger: that she is perfect, just as she is.

On Daisy's other side, slightly ahead of her, is Ellie in an old tie-dye T-shirt and denim shorts and tatty sneakers. She dresses like a rebel, but she still has the nervous focus of the conscientious pupil she used to be before adolescence hit. She looks as if she is expecting something to happen. Good or bad? She seems too apprehensive for it to be clear either way.

At least things are better for her now. More settled. Jenny is certainly less worried about her. The time she gets most anxious about those girls is when Sean reappears in their lives, which he did a week or so ago, freshly returned from his trip to Spain – no idea what he was doing there, running away from himself as usual, I imagine – to take them and Toby out to dinner.

But that seems to have gone off all right. Maybe having Toby there made a difference. Or maybe Sean has just become a bit less important. Less needed. It's not like when they were little, when him being there or not made a huge difference to their lives. They're older now, and Ava's independent, and Ellie almost is. Whatever they feel about Sean – love, or something like it, though he doesn't deserve it any more than I do, in my opinion – they don't really need him any more.

And they don't need me. Not now. And when they did, I wasn't there.

I know they care for me, I know that one day they'll grieve for me, but I can already see them moving beyond me, into lives that I am hopeful about in a way that is new to me: the kind of hope you feel for things that you know you won't see.

Jenny and I pause by my mother's grave. I find myself thinking about her often... her determination, her ruthlessness. She only wanted the best for me. But if I'm honest, I was as terrified of her as everybody else was. It always felt as if she was at war with the world, and I was essential to her winning. I didn't allow myself to see that trying to please her meant letting everybody else down, including myself.

And anyway, I could never have given her what she really wanted. Nobody could. She might not have ever been willing to admit it, but I am sure that what she longed for was to have her sister back, whole and unscathed.

And here is Constance, my aunt, in the space next to my mother, where we laid her to rest the day after I'd met Jenny. I'd only just made it in time, and had been suffering from a raging hangover. That was the only time I'd ever seen my mother cry, and as she dabbed at her face with a handkerchief a single thought had presented itself to me: *There is no way I can tell her that my marriage is over.*

I leave flowers for both of them. White roses. My mother was particular about flowers, but she always regarded roses as an acceptable offering. And as for Constance… who knows? Maybe she once liked roses, too.

Jenny reached out and takes my hand, and we walk on.

Now I can see Felix's headstone. He was cremated (such a small body, so few ashes), then interred. That was what Jenny wanted. To have him somewhere she could visit, a peaceful place not too far from home, in the company of the other dead. She hated the thought of decay but wanted to lay him in the earth, as if to sleep. Wanted a grave to take care of. And she does: she has brought flowers to lay down, baby's breath and lavender and love-in-a-mist, and she'll be back in a day or two to clear them away and to check for weeds.

The headstone is small and simple. It gives Felix's name and the date of his birth and his death. It says, 'Dearly beloved.' And he is. The length of his life, those three short days, is no measure of it. There's no scale to measure how deeply we feel his absence, how much we miss him, and how much we love him still.

Ellie has stopped in her tracks. I pause to see what she is looking at, half expecting not to be able to see it; there's something uncanny about her these days, always has been, in fact, but I used to think it was just that she had an overactive imagination and now I am not so sure.

'Oh, look,' Jenny says. 'Isn't it beautiful? For a moment I thought it was a statue.'

There is a heron on the low outer wall of the cemetery, just by the corner where we are headed. We all stop to gaze at it, even Daisy. We can see it in profile – its fierce beak, the white bulk of its folded wings, its slender legs. I can see why Jenny thought it was carved: it's so still and poised. It really doesn't look alive.

It is looking out across the grass that stretches from the cemetery boundary towards the banks of a stream – one of the many streams that flow through Kettlebridge and the surrounding villages, and end up in the Thames. It is standing guard. Its concentration is extraordinary. Superhuman. It's like an encounter with a mythic beast, a gryphon or a phoenix or a hippogriff, something ancient and possibly only imagined, recorded in ancient texts. It looks as if it could stay there forever, or be gone in the blink of an eye.

And then it bends its neck and opens its wings and launches itself into flight, and swoops away in the direction of the stream.

Ellie turns to see it go and I catch the look of awe on her face. Awe and gratitude, as if something she's been hoping and waiting for has come to pass. It doesn't even strike me as odd, because I feel the same.

I open my mouth to say something, and the word I'm reaching for is heron. But these days, none of me can be relied on to do what I want it to. What comes out is my son's name, and it sounds as light and sweet as a blessing.

A Letter from Ali

Thank you for choosing to read *His Secret Family*. If you want to keep up to date with my latest releases, just sign up at the following link. I can promise that your email address will never be shared and you can unsubscribe at any time.

www.bookouture.com/ali-mercer

If anything's going to make you respect women, it's being brought up by a mum who is on her own. I vividly remember sitting at our kitchen table as a teenager, doing battle with some impossible algebra homework while my mum struggled to tile the splashback behind the sink. Neither of us really knew what we were doing, but in the end she managed and so did I. Turned out it wasn't quite so impossible after all.

I did most of my growing up in an all-female family. My parents split up when I was little and my dad lived overseas, so I didn't see him all that often. That experience fed into me writing about an all-female family of three in *His Secret Family*: Jenny and her two daughters, Ava and Ellie. I was also interested in exploring what happens when a family begins to change – when patterns that have become established are broken up, and there are suddenly more questions than answers.

When I'm shaping a story I always ask myself, 'What if?' What if the mum in the family-of-three suddenly got involved with a new man? How would the girls feel about the arrival of an apparent outsider in their close little world, which might not always have been financially secure, but which had at least given them a measure of emotional stability? What would happen when the new man clashes with their dad – who isn't a regular presence in their lives, but still matters to them both? What if none of the adults in the story are quite who they seem to be… and what if the decisions they made in the past are about to catch up with them?

Jenny, Ava and Ellie make up one of the all-female family units in this novel; Paula and Daisy are the other. The clash between them gave me the framework for the story. Mark's wives, Jenny and Paula, each have a child that the other doesn't know about, at least for a time. Mark, who is hung up on the idea of perfection and can't bear to face up to his own guilt and shame, tries and fails to keep the existence of both children a secret.

Ellie acts as a kind of bridge between the two parts of the story; she senses some of what has happened and what may be about to happen, but not clearly. Later on, she is so distraught about having been powerless to affect events that she rejects her powers of intuition entirely. It's another kind of denial of something you can't control, though what Ellie pushes away is an aspect of herself.

Paula and Mark's experience of having a child who is different to her peers, and who is subsequently diagnosed as autistic, was inspired in part by my own family experience. My son was diagnosed at a similar age to Daisy in the novel. If you like, you can find out a bit more about that from the blog on my website, alimercerwriter.com.

The scene in the novel where Paula and Mark watch Daisy in a Christmas show was prompted by years of watching my son in school assemblies and performances. Just like Daisy, when he was very little he coped with having an audience by turning his back on it. That's all changed now he's in secondary school, though – he loves drama and is eager to take part. He's been brilliantly supported all the way through that journey by staff who have been absolutely committed to finding ways to include him, and it's been great for his confidence as well as for his understanding of how other people behave and why they do what they do. Drama is magic, and can draw people together like nothing else.

Amy, who is Daisy's key worker at pre-school, has the key qualities of kindness and acceptance that I've come across again and again in people who work in education – qualities that both of Daisy's parents, in their different ways, have to find in themselves. Children and adults who are different or who are experiencing difficulties are not always met with acceptance, however, and sometimes kindness is in short supply. The history of the treatment of people with learning disabilities or mental health problems is tainted by cruelty and prejudice, and this is all too often still the case today.

In *His Secret Family*, Ingrid's prejudice and her own family history prompt her to reject Daisy as soon as she recognises that she is not like other children, and as a result Daisy becomes yet another loss in her life. Decades before, Ingrid's sister Constance was given a lobotomy and was left incapacitated. Any potential Constance and Ingrid might have had to have a relationship as adults was destroyed, and Ingrid has been left wanting and missing something she doesn't know how to find.

By way of contrast, Ellie and Ava have grown up together and the bond between them endures – though that doesn't mean they always get along. And eventually they have the chance to get to know Daisy, too. Any family is made up of all its members, and I was glad to be able to conclude *His Secret Family* with a reunion that was also a homage to the lost.

Thank you so much for reading *His Secret Family*. I hope it has touched you and surprised you, and drawn you in.

If you enjoyed reading my book, I would be so grateful if you could write a review. I'd love to know how you felt about the characters and to hear what you thought about the issues raised in the novel. Also, it's really helpful for other readers when they're looking for something new.

Do get in touch – I'm often on Twitter or Instagram and you can also contact me through my Facebook page.

All good wishes to you and yours,
Ali Mercer

AliMercerwriter

@alisonlmercer

alimercerwriter

alimercerwriter.com

Acknowledgements

Thank you to Judith Murdoch, my agent, and Kathryn Taussig, my editor. I'm very grateful to the team at Bookouture – so creative, so friendly, and so committed to great storytelling. Thanks to Kim Nash and Noelle Holten, publicity managers extraordinaire and now novelists too. And thank you to Jon Appleton and Celine Kelly for your inspired work on my books.

I owe a thank you to several people who read early drafts of this novel, including Neel Mukherjee and Patricia Duncker, who I met after Patrick Gale invited me to North Cornwall Book Festival (which is brilliant, so do go if you ever get the chance). Also, thank you to Nanu and Luli Segal and Helen Rumbelow.

Every writer needs people around them who help them to keep going through the tough bits, and I've been very lucky on that front. Heartfelt thanks go out to all my family and friends. Thank you to David Mercer. Thanks to Gary, Katie, Emma, Sam and Laurence. Mr P, Izzy, Tom – you know I couldn't do it without you. And finally, thanks to my mum, to whom this novel is dedicated.

CPSIA information can be obtained
at www.ICGtesting.com
Printed in the USA
LVHW111919101219
640062LV00004B/644/P

9 781838 881047